THE STRETCH

Also by Stephen Leather

PAY OFF

THE FIREMAN

HUNGRY GHOST

THE CHINAMAN

THE VETS

THE LONG SHOT

THE BIRTHDAY GIRL

THE DOUBLE TAP

THE SOLITARY MAN

THE TUNNEL RATS

THE BOMBMAKER

THE STRETCH

Stephen Leather

Hodder & Stoughton

First published in Great Britain in 2000
by Hodder and Stoughton
A division of Hodder Headline

10 9 8 7 6 5 4 3 2 1

All characters in this publication are fictitious
and any resemblance to real persons, living or dead,
is purely coincidental.

British Library Cataloguing in Publication Data
Leather, Stephen
The stretch
1. Suspense fiction
I. Title
823.9′14 [F]

Hardcover ISBN 0 340 77032 5
Trade paperback ISBN 0 340 79324 4

Typeset by Hewer Text Ltd, Edinburgh
Printed and bound in Great Britain by
Mackays of Chatham PLC, Chatham, Kent

Hodder and Stoughton
A division of Hodder Headline
338 Euston Road
London NW1 3BH

For Judy

PROLOGUE

The gun went off, catching Preston Snow by surprise, and he felt as if he'd been punched hard in the stomach. There was no burning sensation, and surprisingly little pain, just a dull ache and a spreading coldness. His eyes widened as he stared at the face of the man who'd shot him. Unfeeling blue eyes stared back at him.

Snow clutched a hand to his stomach and staggered backwards, blood pulsing from between his fingers. There seemed to be a lot of blood, but still he was hardly aware of any pain.

The man with the gun watched dispassionately, the gun now at his side. His face was totally blank as if he had absolutely no interest in whether Snow lived or died.

Snow felt the strength drain from his legs. He stumbled over a coffee table and fell on his side, barely conscious of where he was. The coldness was spreading from his stomach, up across his chest, a coldness that seemed to be drawing all the strength from his limbs. He tried to speak but no words would come and it was an effort to breathe. He managed to get up on his hands and knees and crawled towards the stairs.

The man who'd pulled the trigger stood in the middle of the room, watching Snow with a look of bored disinterest.

Snow scrambled up the stairs, frantically trying to get away from the man. He had a gun upstairs, somewhere. It was in one of the drawers in the bedroom. If he could get to it, if he could defend himself, then maybe, just maybe, he'd stand a chance.

His tracksuit top was drenched in blood and it flopped around as he crawled. He heard footsteps behind him but he didn't look back. He felt himself drifting in and out of consciousness and shook his head fiercely, trying to clear his thoughts. 'Stay focused, man,' he muttered to himself. 'Stay fucking focused.'

He looked down at his stomach as he crawled and saw blood dripping down on to the threadbare stair carpet. He tried to stem the bleeding but as he pressed his hand against his stomach a bolt of pain shot through his midriff. He grunted. It felt as if a hot knife had been twisted inside his stomach.

'For fuck's sake, Snow, will you stay still!' shouted the man with the gun.

Snow took a quick look over his shoulder. The man was standing at the bottom of the stairs, gesticulating with his gun.

Snow reached the upstairs landing and pushed himself upright. He staggered towards the bedroom, putting his free hand against the wall to maintain his balance, smearing it with blood.

The man followed him up the stairs. He took his time, with a lengthy pause between each step. It was the precision that Snow found terrifying. The man was taking it slowly, knowing that he had all the time in the world: no one would come to Snow's aid. If anyone had heard the gunshot, they wouldn't want to get involved. It wasn't the sort of area where people telephoned three nines.

Snow collapsed in front of the dressing table and pulled out one of the drawers. No gun. He cursed. Where'd he put it? Where the hell had he put it? He tried to concentrate, tried to remember where he'd last seen the weapon. He pulled open a second drawer and rifled through socks and underwear, cursing his stupidity for not having the gun out in the open. No gun. He tore the drawer out of the cupboard and tipped the contents on to the floor and searched frantically. It wasn't there.

There were footsteps behind him and Snow twisted around. The man stood in the doorway, the gun at his side, a confident smile on his face. Snow's head swam and he slumped backwards, sliding down against the dressing table, his head banging against one of the open drawers.

Snow's eyes fluttered shut. He could feel consciousness slipping away. The pain was going, replaced by a warm glow. He sighed and his hand slipped away from his stomach, drenched in blood.

The man walked over and looked down at Snow. He prodded Snow's leg with his foot, but Snow didn't react. Snow's chin was down on his chest and a bloody froth dribbled from between his lips. Blood pooled on the floor around his waist, a thick treacly redness that seemed to sit on the surface of the carpet, refusing to sink into the pile.

'You dead, Snow?' he sneered. 'Don't tell me you're dead already.'

He raised his foot and stamped down on Snow's hand, crushing his bloody fingers. Snow's eyes opened wide and he screamed in pain. The man grinned triumphantly and levelled the gun at Snow's face.

They filed into the jury box one by one, and Sam Greene could tell by the way they avoided looking at her that the news was bad. Her heart sank.

'It'll be okay, Mum,' said her son Jamie, giving her hand a small squeeze.

Sam shook her head. 'No, Jamie,' she whispered. 'It's not going to be okay.'

Sam's husband looked across at her from the dock. 'Chin up, love,' he mouthed. Terry looked tired. There were dark patches under his eyes and when he smiled Sam could see the worry lines etched into his forehead. She was sure there was a touch more grey at his temples but he still looked good for fifty-two though; broad-shouldered and flat-stomached with the confident good looks that turned the heads of women half his age.

Sam fingered the small crucifix that was hanging around her neck on a thin gold chain. And hadn't that always been Terry's problem, she thought. Too handsome for his own good.

Sam tried to smile back at Terry but she could feel tears welling up in her eyes and she blinked them back. It wasn't fair. Her husband's fate lay in the hands of twelve men and women who knew nothing about him, and yet they and they alone had the power to put him behind bars for the rest of his life.

Sam watched them as they took their seats. Eight women and four men. That was in their favour, Terry's solicitor had said, because Terry was a good-looking guy and women were less likely to convict a man that they fancied. Three of the jury were black, and even Laurence Patterson had to admit that that wasn't such good news, because the man Terry had been accused of shooting was black. 'When all's said and done they do stick together, Samantha, but let's look on the bright side, shall we?' he'd said, and he'd patted her gently on the shoulder the way you'd console someone at a funeral. That's what it felt like, Sam realised. It felt like a funeral. Everyone dressed in their Sunday best, faces sombre, avoiding eye contact, all gathered together to say a final farewell to Terry Greene.

A tear ran down Sam's cheek and she brushed it away with the back of her hand, determined that no one would see her cry. She knew there'd be photographers outside and they'd like nothing more than a picture of her with tears running down her face. She'd been in court every day, and without fail the tabloids had carried photographs of her arriving or leaving, always mentioning the fact that she was forty-eight years old and that she used to be a singer and dancer. 'Faded Sixties singer' one of the *Daily Mail*'s more acid female feature writers had called her, and Sam had silently seethed at the unfairness of that. Her career had barely started to get off the ground before she'd met and married Terry, and as for 'faded', that was just malicious. She was the mother of three grown-up children and under more pressure than she'd ever been in her whole life, how was she supposed to look? Radiant?

Considering the pressure she was under, Sam figured that she looked damn good. At least one of the prosecution lawyers kept looking at her with more than a professional interest, smiling each time he caught her eye. Every morning she took take extra care to get her make-up just right, enough to cover up the effects of not-enough sleep, but not so much that she'd look as if she was trying too hard. And she'd been to the hairdresser to get her hair colour topped up just before the case started. Again, nothing too obvious, but she needed a little help to keep its original dark blonde sheen.

Patterson twisted around in his seat and gave her a confident smile. She acknowledged him with a nod but couldn't bring herself to smile back at him.

'Will your foreman please stand,' said the clerk of the court.

A middle-aged man got to his feet and self-consciously rubbed the bridge of his nose.

Sam took a deep breath, steeling herself for the worst. Jamie squeezed her hand again and she squeezed back.

'Have you reached a verdict upon which you have all agreed?'

'We have. Yes.'

'On the charge of murder, do you find the defendant Terrence William Greene guilty or not guilty?'

The foreman rubbed his nose again, then cleared his throat. He was a small, nondescript man in a cheap suit and Sam figured that this was his one moment of glory in a life filled with mediocrity, and that he was determined to make the most of it. 'Guilty,' he said, stretching the word out as if relishing the sound of it.

Sam cursed under her breath.

Someone cheered behind her and Sam turned around. Two detectives were grinning and slapping their boss on the back. Detective Chief Inspector Frank Welch, the man responsible for putting her husband in the dock. Welch grinned at Sam and she turned away quickly, not wanting to give him the satisfaction of seeing how upset she was.

The judge nodded at Terry's barrister. 'Mr Orvice, is there anything you wish to say on behalf of the defendant?'

The barrister looked across at Terry, who shook his head. 'No, your honour.'

The judge fixed Terry with a look of contempt. 'Terrence Greene, stand up.'

Terry got to his feet and adjusted his tie, and straightened his shoulders. He was wearing a dark blue suit, one of his many Armanis, a crisp white shirt and a tie that Sam didn't recognise. He looked the judge in the eye, his chin raised defiantly.

'Before I pass sentence, I have a few words to say about the conduct of one of the witnesses in this case,' said the judge. He turned to look at Sam, and she fought the urge to look away. She felt her cheeks redden but she continued to stare at him, concentrating on his thin, humourless lips.

'Despite the weight of forensic evidence against the defendant, his wife Samantha Greene has insisted that she was with him on the night of the murder. I disbelieve her account of events, as did the jury, and I regard her claims as at best misguided and at worst a deliberate attempt to pervert the course of justice.'

'You should hang the lying bitch!' A young black man with shoulder-length dreadlocks had got to his feet and was screaming at the judge. A pretty black girl tried to persuade him to sit down. 'She knows he killed my brother! She should be in the fucking dock with him!'

Two uniformed policemen hustled him out of the court. The black girl followed, imploring them to let him go. Luke Snow and his sister Nancy. Brother and sister of the man Terry was accused of killing. A middle-aged black couple shook their heads tearfully but stayed where they were, not wanting to leave until they'd heard the sentence. Preston Snow's parents.

As the courtroom doors banged shut, the judge once again fixed Sam with his baleful stare. 'I hope the police will take a close look at the evidence given by Mrs Greene, with a view to considering a charge of perjury. The love of a wife for a husband is no excuse for lying to a court of law.'

Sam stared back at the judge, knowing that there was nothing she could say or do. Her mouth had gone dry and it hurt when she swallowed. It seemed like an eternity before the judge turned away from her and looked back at Terry.

'Terrence William Greene, you have been found guilty of

the murder of Preston Snow. A savage, brutal murder for which you have shown no remorse. The sentence of the court is life imprisonment. Take him down.'

Two burly custody officers moved either side of Terry. Terry blew a kiss at Sam, winked, then walked down the stairs leading from the dock to the holding cells below the courtroom.

'Are you going home, Mum?' asked Jamie.

Sam nodded and got to her feet. 'You coming?'

Jamie looked at his watch. 'I've got to get back to Exeter. Exams tomorrow.'

'How about a coffee first before you go?'

Jamie looked suddenly concerned. 'Are you okay?'

Sam screwed up her face. 'I feel a bit numb, really. I don't think it's hit me yet.'

Jamie nodded. 'I know what you mean. I sort of expected the worst, but life? I can't imagine Dad behind bars for life, can you? Not Dad.'

'We'll get through it, Jamie. So will he.' She gave him a hug. 'Thanks for coming.'

'I wasn't sure if Dad would've wanted me here.'

'Of course he did. Don't be silly.'

Jamie nodded towards the doors. 'I'll walk you out.'

'You will not!' said Sam quickly. 'The last thing I want is for you to be photographed with me. You've gotten off lightly so far, the last thing we want is for your face to be splashed across the papers with mine. Lawyer-in-the-making in court for drug baron's murder trial. Just what you need to kick-start your career.'

'I'm not ashamed of Dad,' he said.

'I know you're not. And neither am I. But let's not make things more difficult than they already are, shall we? You sneak out, they'll be too busy looking for me. I'll see you at the coffee bar we went to last time, yeah?'

'Okay, Mum.' Jamie kissed her on the cheek and headed out of the courtroom.

Sam stood where she was to give him time to leave the building. She desperately wanted a cigarette but smoking was forbidden inside the court building.

Patterson appeared at her elbow holding a stack of files. 'Samantha, I'm gutted. But it's not over.'

'Swings and roundabouts, Laurence.'

'We'll appeal, of course,' said Patterson.

'Whatever.'

Patterson placed a hand on her elbow. 'Can you call in at Richard's office this afternoon? It's at Terry's request.' Richard Asher was Terry's accountant, and Sam didn't feel ready to start talking money.

'Can't it wait?'

Behind her she heard raucous laughter, then a Geordie voice. 'Great job, Frank.' It was Doug Simpson, a detective inspector, the man who'd come around to Sam's house with a search warrant and who'd spent the best part of four hours looking in every nook and cranny with half a dozen uniformed policemen. Simpson was patting Welch on the back. 'The look on his face when the judge said life. Like he expected to be let off with a slap on the wrist.'

Welch said nothing, but he grinned triumphantly.

The Crown Prosecution Service's barrister walked by and gave Welch a thumbs-up. 'Thanks, Frank. Wish all my cases were as open and shut as that.'

Welch's grin widened as he walked past Sam, and Patterson steered her away into a corner. 'It's important, Samantha. I wouldn't ask otherwise.'

'Okay. Fine. Whatever. I'll be there.' She looked around the wood-panelled entrance hall. 'Is there a back way out, Laurence?'

'I'm afraid not. Not for members of the public.'

'What about for wives of convicted murderers?'

Patterson smiled thinly and shook his head.

Sam took a deep breath and walked towards the double doors that led out to the street. She heard the click-click-click of cameras and the buzz of questions before she even pushed the doors open. The Press were huddled around Welch and Simpson, whose faces were white in the glare of television camera lights.

Sam kept her head down but it was useless, they were waiting for her, and like hounds on a fresh scent they bore down on her, throwing questions from all sides. How did she feel, what were her plans, how had her husband taken the sentence, had she lied?

Sam tried to push through them. 'Please, I've nothing to say,' she shouted. 'Nothing.'

Two figures barred her way. A man and a woman. Sam raised her head and looked at them. It was Mr and Mrs Snow, the victim's parents, dressed as if they'd just come from church. They were both in their late fifties, he in a dark tweed suit and highly polished brogues, she in a blue flowery print dress and a dark blue coat, with a matching blue hat with a wide band into which had been tucked three silk daisies.

Sam tried to get by them, but Mrs Snow moved to block her way. 'How could you?' she hissed at Sam. 'You gave your word before God and you lied. How could you do that?'

Sam shook her head. Mrs Snow raised a gloved hand and Sam stared at her unflinchingly, waiting for the blow. The older woman lowered her hand and burst into tears. Her husband put an arm around her shoulders. His eyes were dull and flat, as if he wasn't even aware of Sam or the near-constant barrage of flashes as the photographers clicked away.

Sam pushed around them.

The questions continued. Did she know why her husband had killed Preston Snow, had her husband asked her to lie for him, where was she the night Snow was shot? Sam tried to blot out the shouts, tried to imagine they weren't there. A television camera appeared at her side and a bleached blonde with too much make-up thrust a bulbous microphone in her face. Sam pushed the microphone away. 'Don't you understand – no comment!' she shouted.

She reached her car, a black convertible Saab. It was penned in by two almost-new saloons and Sam knew instinctively that the Press had done it, cutting off her avenue of escape. She whirled around. 'Can someone please move this car!' she yelled, but she could barely hear her own voice above the noise of the Press pack.

A battered old Land Rover roared up, smoke belching from its exhaust. 'Mum! Get in!' It was Jamie. He threw open the door and Sam climbed in gratefully.

'Jamie, you're a life-saver,' she gasped.

Jamie grinned and accelerated. As he roared away from the still-shouting journalists, a bottle smacked into the windscreen, cracking it down one side. Through the side window Sam saw Luke Snow screaming and shaking his fist.

Jamie slammed on the brakes. 'Bastard!'

'Leave it, Jamie,' said Sam.

'Look what he's done.'

'Forget it.'

Jamie looked as if he was going to argue, but Sam patted him on the leg. 'Come on, I'll buy you a coffee. And a new windscreen.'

Jamie accelerated away, still cursing.

She rubbed the back of his neck as he drove. 'You should go and see him, soon as you can.'

'I will. Laura wasn't there.'

'Yeah. Probably too upsetting for her. You know what your sister's like. It's Trish I feel really sorry for. They're bound to give her a hard time at school.'

Jamie drove them to a coffee bar and they sat in the window sipping cappuccinos in silence.

'Why did you lie for him, Mum?' Jamie asked eventually. 'After everything he did to you.'

'We're neither of us kids, Jamie. Anyway, who says I lied?'

'The judge for one. Come on, the forensic alone was enough to convict him. Plus they had an eye witness. I don't know why you bothered.'

Jamie had a smear of frothy milk across his upper lip. Sam reached over and wiped it away with her thumb.

'What are you going to do, Mum?'

'Been asking myself the very same question.'

* * *

A cheer went up as Frank Welch walked into the CID office flanked by Detective Inspector Doug Simpson and Detective Sergeant Fred Clarke. Welch raised a hand in acknowledgment. There were two cases of lager on a side table, along with half a dozen bottles of red wine, stacks of paper cups and a few packets of crisps. Clarke headed straight for the lager.

'Drink, Frank?' asked Simpson.

'Get me an orange juice and lemonade, Doug. I'm going to have a word with the governor.'

Welch went down the corridor and was waved through to Superintendent Simon Edwards' office by his secretary. 'He's been waiting for you, Chief Inspector,' she said.

Edwards was buried in paperwork, but he stood up and shook Welch's hand as soon as he walked in. 'Great work, Frank. First class. Pass on my congratulations to the team. I took the liberty of arranging a small libation.'

'Much appreciated, sir.'

'Not every day we see a villain like Terry Greene sent down.'

'No, sir.'

Edwards sat down and picked up his fountain pen. When Welch didn't move towards the door, Edwards put his pen down again. 'Something on your mind, Frank?'

'Greene's wife. Samantha. She lied through her teeth. The judge gave her a tongue lashing, but I'd like to send the file on to the DPP.'

Edwards winced. 'I'm not convinced that's in anyone's best interests, Frank. You're not married, are you?'

It was a rhetorical question. Edwards was well aware that

Welch had never been married. Welch answered anyway. 'No, sir.'

'Wives stand by their husbands. That's what they do, bless 'em. For better or worse.'

Welch put his hands on the superintendent's desk and leaned towards him, but he could see from the look on his boss's face that he resented the territorial encroachment, so he stood up again and folded his arms. 'The judge said he thought there was a case of perjury to answer, that's all I'm saying. She lied in court.'

'But it didn't do any good, did it, Frank? Greene still went down. Let sleeping dogs lie. Okay?'

Welch said nothing. He wanted to argue the point, but he had worked with Edwards long enough to know that there was no point. Once the superintendent had made his mind up, it was like a steel trap. Nothing would budge him, and he'd regard even reasoned argument as a challenge to his authority. Welch nodded slowly. 'Okay, sir.'

'Good man,' said Edwards, and returned to his paperwork.

Back in the main CID room, Simpson held out a paper cup to Welch. 'There you go, boss.'

Welch took it but didn't drink.

'What's up?' asked Simpson.

'Difference of opinion with the governor,' said Welch. 'He thinks Sam Greene's a sleeping dog. I think she's a lying bitch.'

* * *

Terry Greene took off his jacket and handed it to the bored prison officer. 'Don't suppose you've got a hanger,' he said.

The prison officer looked at the label and sneered. 'Jacket. Dark blue. Armani.' He had a nasal Birmingham accent. He was a big man with a pot belly that hung in front of him like a late pregnancy. He screwed up the jacket and thrust it into a polythene bag.

Terry undid his belt and slipped off his trousers. A second

prison officer wrote the details down on a clipboard. 'Trousers. Dark blue,' said the prison officer, another large man, but well muscled as if he worked out. Like his colleague he had short-cropped hair and a neatly trimmed moustache.

A third officer walked over. A small man with a tight, pinched mouth and small eyes. He picked up the clipboard and looked at the form. 'The famous Terrence Greene,' he said. 'We are honoured.' He grinned. 'Armani, huh? Pity it's going to be out of fashion by the time you get out, Greene.' He handed the clipboard back to the admitting officer. 'I'm Chief Prison Officer Riggs. This is my wing.'

'You must be very proud,' said Terry. He took off his wristwatch and held it out to the first prison officer.

Riggs reached over and took it. He weighed it in his hand. 'Rolex Oyster. Gold.'

Terry took a pile of prison-issue clothes off the table. 'Perhaps you'd be good enough to show me to my room.'

Riggs smiled at Terry. 'You're a very funny man, Greene.' He dropped the watch on to the tiled floor and stamped on it. He kept his eyes on Terry as he bent down and picked it up. 'Rolex Oyster. Gold. Broken.' He tossed the watch into the polythene bag. 'Sign for your things and then these nice gentlemen can take you to your cell. You've missed lunch, and I'm sorry but room service isn't working today.' He paused for effect, holding his hand up as if silencing a child. 'No, wait a minute . . . I'm not sorry. In fact, I couldn't give a shit if you didn't eat for a week.'

Riggs laughed softly to himself as he walked away, his prison boots squeaking on the tiled floor.

* * *

Richard Asher's office was a little like the man, thought Sam: brash with hard edges and questionable taste. The furniture was all chrome and glass, the paintings on the wall merely squares of canvas with what looked like sprays of blood across them. As she walked in, Asher was wearing a telephone headset and pacing up and down in front of a floor-to-ceiling window that looked out over the City. He flashed her a quick smile and carried on muttering into his headset mike, something about moving money between the Cayman Islands and Gibraltar and how the taxman wouldn't get a sniff of it.

Laurence Patterson was sitting on the edge of Asher's white maple desk. He motioned towards a long black leather sofa on sweeping chrome legs. Sam sat down, crossed her legs and lit a cigarette.

The two men were both in their late twenties, tall and thin with the build of squash players, and they both virtually crackled with nervous energy. She'd only met Asher once, shortly after Terry had been arrested. He was half-Indian with a dark olive complexion and jet-black hair that was forever falling across his eyes. He smiled a lot and Sam never really trusted him. Patterson wasn't as good looking, with a long, narrow face and a rash of old acne scars across his forehead, but he seemed to Sam to be the more trustworthy of the two. Patterson always looked her in the eye, even when he was giving her bad news, but Asher seemed to avoid eye contact whenever he could, as if he were hiding a guilty secret. She tapped her cigarette on a crystal ashtray and smiled at the thought that appearances could be deceptive. A year ago and she'd never have believed that her husband would be behind bars, serving a life sentence for murder.

'Funny old world,' she said to herself.

'Sorry, Samantha?' said Patterson.

'Just thinking out loud, Laurence,' said Sam with a smile.

Asher took off his headset and strode over to Sam, his long legs moving as gracefully as a giraffe's. 'Samantha, thanks for coming.'

'Didn't sound to me like I had much of a choice, Richard.'

Asher air-kissed her, studiously avoiding any physical contact. Sam could smell his cologne, heady and sweet with a hint of sandalwood. 'I am so sorry about today,' he said, not looking at her, but concentrating on a spot on the wall behind her.

'You and me both,' said Sam.

'You'll be appealing, yeah?'

'Soon as we can. Is that what this is about?'

'Partly,' said Asher.

Asher and Patterson exchanged a quick look and something unspoken passed between them. Sam frowned and waited. Asher loped over to his desk and sprawled in his chair.

Patterson went to stand by the window. 'However the appeal goes, it's going to be expensive, you realise that?'

'I didn't think for one minute that you'd be doing it *pro bono*, Laurence.'

Asher sighed. 'Snag is, Terry's a bit stretched.'

Patterson nodded. 'He tucked away enough to pay for his defence up to today's case, but we're gonna need more if we're to appeal.'

Sam leaned forward. 'If? Now it's if?'

Patterson looked pained. 'When. If. It all comes down to the readies, Samantha. And the way things stand at the moment, Terry couldn't appeal a parking ticket.'

Sam sat stunned, not knowing what to say.

'It's what you might call a cashflow problem,' said Asher smoothly. 'Hopefully temporary, but you'd better hear it from the horse's whatsit.'

'What?' said Sam.

Asher didn't reply. Instead he picked up a remote control and pointed it at a large flat-screen television mounted on one wall. It flickered into life and he pointed the remote at a video recorder.

Terry appeared on the screen, smoking a small cigar. He was wearing the same suit he'd had on in court, but no tie. He smiled at the camera and waved the cigar. 'Hiya, love. Sorry about the cloak and dagger, but you'll only be seeing this if things have taken a turn for the worse.'

Sam looked at Asher and Patterson. Both men were watching the screen. She took a long pull on her cigarette.

Terry was smiling apologetically. 'What can I say? It's going to be rough for you, but at least you're not sitting in a cell stinking of stale piss and cabbage. Look, love, I'm going to need your help, big time. I'm sorry to drop this on you, but there's no one else who can do what needs to be done. I can't say too much in case this gets into the wrong hands, but Richard and Laurence will fill you in. You can trust them, okay? Oh yeah, look up Andy McKinley. He was my driver, he'll be useful. He's working for George Kay. And give my love to the kids. Tell them a visit would be nice.'

Asher pressed the remote and the screen went blank.

'That's it?' said Sam. Terry's short speech had posed more questions than it had answered.

'It's by way of a reference,' said Asher.

'So that you'll know that what we're telling you has Terry's blessing,' added Patterson.

'And what are you telling me?' asked Sam.

Asher took a deep breath as if steeling himself to break bad news. 'Terry's been a bit busy recently. Since you and he separated eighteen months ago . . .'

'Fifteen,' interrupted Sam. 'We separated fifteen months ago.'

'Fifteen. Okay.' He took another deep breath. 'Anyway, a lot's happened over the past fifteen months.'

'You're telling me.' She blew smoke at the ceiling. 'How bad is it, Richard?'

'Snapshot, it's not too bad. Pretty much balances out. But without injections of outside capital . . .' He left the sentence unfinished. He looked across at Patterson and nodded.

Patterson walked over to Sam and gave her a cardboard file. 'It's like a juggler keeping four balls in the air,' said Patterson. 'As soon he stops moving . . .' He shrugged and looked at her glumly.

Sam stared at the two men in turn. They had the guilty

looks of schoolboys called up in front of the headmistress, expecting a caning. 'So you're telling me that if Terry drops his balls, I'm out on the street?'

'Not exactly out on the street,' said Asher, picking up a glass paperweight and toying with it, 'but I think it's only fair to warn you that the mortgage on your house is actually paid from an account linked to one of Terry's property companies. And if that were to go into receivership . . .'

Sam opened the file. It contained several sheets of papers and computer print-outs. There were statements from a number of bank accounts, only two of which she recognised. And there were profit and loss statements from Terry's business enterprises. His nightclubs. His model agency. His courier service. His stake in the local football club. The timeshare development in Spain. And there was a list of the family's outgoings. The mortgage on the house. Car payments. Jamie's university fees. The payments to Terry's mother's nursing home. Sam shook her head. There were too many numbers to cope with. 'So we're broke, is that it?'

Asher looked pained. 'Of course not, Samantha. But you realise that without Terry earning, there's not going to be any cash coming in.'

'I don't understand this. Terry's always been a big spender, but he's been putting money away, too. Stocks. Shares. He's even got Tessas and Isas and all that stuff.'

Asher shook his head. 'Terry's borrowed against virtually all his assets. Effectively, they belong to the banks.'

'Why would he do that?'

'The property whatsit in Spain. Terry told you about it?'

'He mentioned it. It's with Micky Fox, yeah?'

Asher nodded. 'Micky Fox and a few other like-minded individuals. It's been a big drain, cashflow wise. They had to buy the land, grease a few Spanish palms, pay the architects and the builders . . .'

'I get the picture, Richard.'

'Money's been poured into the development. Millions.

And I have to say, Samantha, it was against my best advice. I did tell Terry that this was a longterm investment and that he should only use money he didn't have tied up elsewhere. It was his idea to leverage against his portfolio.'

Sam tossed the file on to a chrome and glass coffee table. 'Can't we sell out now? Pay back the banks. Then sell the shares.'

'They're timeshares, Samantha. No one's going to pay for them until the building work's finished. The days of punters buying off-plan in Spain are long gone. Too many horror stories.'

'Okay, so we sell off some of the other businesses. The model agency's got to be making money, right? And there's his stake in the football club. That's got to be worth something.'

'Neither is showing much in the way of profits, and, realistically, they're not going to, not in the near future.' He pulled another pained face. 'Frankly, Samantha, the model agency and the football club weren't much more than hobbies for Terry. He wasn't over-concerned whether they made money or not.'

Sam flicked ash and crossed her legs. 'Terrific,' she said. 'What about the courier company? That's got to be a real business, right? And he told me he'd invested in a couple of West London taxi firms.'

Asher and Patterson exchanged a quick look. Sam was becoming fed up with their little looks, as if they were working to a script, telling her only what they wanted her to know. They were manipulating her, and Sam hated being manipulated. 'What?' she said sharply. 'What's going on?'

'Terry does have extensive business interests, Samantha,' said Asher, 'but many were acquired for their cashflows rather than profits.'

Sam frowned. 'You're not making sense, Richard. Just spit it out, why don't you?'

Asher took a deep breath. 'In a word, Samantha. Money laundering.'

Patterson walked over to the window as if trying to distance himself from the conversation.

Sam smiled tightly. 'That's two words, Richard.' She took a long pull on her cigarette and blew smoke up at the ceiling.

Asher smiled back but his eyes were ice cold. It was the smile of a predator, and Sam realised for the first time that Asher didn't really like her. 'Terry uses the cash-rich companies to clean his profits from his less than legal operations,' said Asher. 'On their own, profits are minimal.'

'This is getting better and better,' said Sam bitterly.

Asher rubbed the paperweight between the palms of his hands. 'Terry does have a solution,' he said. 'He put together two . . . business deals . . . shortly before he was arrested.'

Sam raised an eyebrow. 'Business deals?'

'Terry has arranged for a consignment of cannabis resin to be imported from Spain. He's already paid for it, there's just the delivery to be organised.'

For a moment Sam thought that she'd misheard. She put up a hand as if warding him off and shook her head in disbelief. 'What? What are you saying?'

'Terry has paid for four tons of cannabis resin. It's arriving in three days.'

'Cannabis? Drugs? A drugs deal?'

'Terry has also invested in a currency deal in Spain. The notes are going to have to be brought back to the UK in the very near future.'

'Currency? You mean counterfeit notes? A drugs deal and counterfeit money?'

Asher stared up at the ceiling. Patterson was looking out of the window, his hands clasped behind his back.

'Terry expects me to do his dirty work?'

'He's handed over all aspects of his business to you, legitimate and otherwise,' said Asher. 'You will have control over all of his companies, signing rights for his bank accounts. All we need you to do is to sign a few forms.'

Sam twisted her cigarette into the crystal ashtray. 'You're taking the piss.' She stood up. She could feel her whole body trembling and she fought to stay calm. 'You're as bad as he is. Both of you.'

She stormed out and slammed the door behind her.

Patterson turned away from the window and gave Asher a pained smile. 'Told you she wouldn't like it.'

'Like it or lump it, she'll come around. She doesn't have a choice.'

* * *

Laura Nichols sat on the sofa, her legs drawn up underneath her. The television was on, the sound muted. She had just watched the third news report of the day covering her father's sentence. Little had been added since the story was first broadcast that afternoon. West London businessman Terry Greene, sentenced to life for the murder of small-time drug dealer Preston Snow. A major Customs investigation naming him as a suspected drugs importer. Pictures of Sam being pursued from the court by the Press pack, escaping into Jamie's Land Rover, and a screaming Luke Snow throwing a bottle at the vehicle as it drove away. A photograph of her father, smiling and looking younger than his fifty-two years, his black hair swept slightly back, his eyes sparkling as if he'd just seen something amusing. Then a photograph of her mother, taken more than twenty-five years earlier, a publicity shot from a Christmas variety show, singing on a stage flanked by long-legged dancers.

The front door opened and then slammed shut and Laura winced. Jonathon Nichols walked into the sitting room and threw his briefcase on to a winged chair. 'Have you any idea what sort of day I've had?' he hissed. He went over to a table laden with bottles and poured himself a whisky. He drained the glass in one gulp, and refilled it before turning to glare at her. 'There I am, trying to put together one of the biggest fucking deals of my career, and what happens? The fucking *Evening Standard* has me in its City gossip page.' He took a rolled-up copy of the paper from the pocket of his suit and hurled it across the room at her. It flew apart in the air in a shower of pages.

Laura curled herself up into a tighter ball, keeping herself as small as possible, not wanting to provoke him.

'Son-in-law of a convicted murderer, making a killing from dot com deal,' he said. Whisky spilled out of the glass and on to the carpet. 'How do you think that makes me look, huh? They're laughing at me behind my back. Taking the piss. Because of your fucking father.'

'I'm sorry,' whispered Laura, hugging a cushion to her chest.

'Sorry. You're sorry? How does you being sorry help me, huh?'

Laura turned her face away. She knew there was nothing that she could say that would placate him. She'd just have to wait until his anger had run its course.

'Don't fucking ignore me,' said Nichols, striding across the room towards her.

'I'm not ignoring you,' she said, her voice trembling.

'So look at me.'

Laura looked up at him tearfully.

'And stop fucking crying. What have you got to cry about, huh? Your job's not on the line. No one's taking the piss out of you.'

'My father's in prison!' shouted Laura.

'And whose fucking fault is that!' Nichols yelled back.

'It's not mine!'

Nichols threw his drink over her. The whisky stung her eyes but she refused to wipe it away. She let it run down her face and over her shirt. Her lower lip trembled and she bit down on it, hard enough to taste blood.

'Are you happy now?' yelled her husband. 'See what you made me do? See what you've reduced me to?'

Laura got up and tried to get past him, but he grabbed her by the hair and twisted it savagely.

'You always do this, you always push me too damn far. It's not enough that I have to go through hell in the office, you have to make my life a misery at home as well.'

Laura couldn't contain the tears any longer and her body was wracked with deep, mournful sobs. Nichols pushed her to the ground and drew back his foot to kick her. Laura gasped in anticipation of the blow, and Nichols grinned at her, cruelly. 'Now you're sorry, aren't you? Now you're fucking sorry.'

He turned on his heel and walked out of the room, leaving Laura curled up on the floor in a foetal ball, the taste of whisky and blood in her mouth.

* * *

Sam tapped on Trisha's bedroom door. 'Trisha?' There was no answer. Her daughter had gone straight up to her room as soon as she'd got back from school and had stayed there. Sam had heard her television go on and off a couple of times, and then she'd played CDs for a couple of hours. 'Trish, do you want any supper?'

'No, thanks.'

Trisha's voice was flat and emotionless, as if it had been generated by computer. Sam knew it was her daughter's own special way of punishing her. And she also knew that the only way of dealing with it was to ride it out, to pretend that it didn't worry her. 'Are you sure? I'm going to do pasta.'

'I had something after school.'

'Okay. Good night, then.'

'Good night.'

Sam hesitated. Part of her wanted to push open the door and to confront her daughter, to try to talk through whatever it was that was upsetting her, but Sam knew there was no point, Trisha would simply retreat further into her shell. Besides, Sam already knew what the matter was – her father was serving a life sentence for murder, and there wasn't anything she could say that was going to change that.

She went downstairs and lit a cigarette. She'd lied about making pasta. She wasn't in the least bit hungry, and the way she felt, she'd probably never eat again. It was starting to go dark outside, and swallows were making their final swoops of the evening, wheeling and diving for insects and calling to each other.

Sam inhaled smoke deep into her lungs as she wondered how Terry was feeling. He'd been on remand for two months, but remand was one thing, the first night of a life sentence was something else. How would he be able to cope with that, with the days and nights stretching out ahead of him? He'd be an old man by the time he got out. Ten years older than Sam's own father when he'd passed away, and he'd pretty much died of old age, a combination of liver failure, kidney trouble and several strokes. He hadn't smoked, barely drank, and lived a relatively stress-free life. It was just old age that killed him. Sam shivered at the thought of what lay ahead of her. Of everyone. But at least she was free to make choices, to live her life as she wanted, and not kept behind bars being told what to do every minute of every day.

The telephone rang and she jumped at the unexpected noise. She picked up the receiver from its holder by the fridge. 'Hello?' She wasn't expecting anyone, and it was well past the time when prisoners were allowed to use the communal phones.

'I know where you live, you fucking bitch!'

Sam's jaw dropped. 'What?'

'I said I know where you fucking live, you bitch, and you're dead meat. You're a lying whore and you're gonna get what's coming to you.' Sam put the phone down and took another long pull on the cigarette.

'Sticks and stones,' she muttered to herself.

Upstairs, Trisha opened her bedroom door. 'Was that for me?' she called down.

Sam went into the hall. 'No, love, it was for me.' Trisha's door slammed shut. 'It was definitely for me,' Sam said to herself as she went back into the kitchen.

* * *

Terry lay on his back staring up at the bunk above his head. It was occupied by a twenty-two-stone Liverpudlian called Charlie Hoyle who was doing seven years for GBH. Hoyle had got into an argument with two Everton fans in a pub car park. He'd won the fight by giving one of the men a bear hug that had broken three ribs, and fallen down on top of the other one, bursting the man's spleen. The judge who'd sent Hoyle down had what passed for a sense of humour and had referred to Hoyle's body as 'an offensive weapon, in more than one way'. Even Hoyle had been chuckling as he was led away from the dock. He was a nice enough guy, but Terry was already finding it a nuisance to flatten himself against the wall every time Hoyle wanted to move around the cell.

The springs above him groaned and Hoyle's face appeared over the side of the bunk. 'You all right, Tel?'

'I'm fine, Charlie. Cheers.'

'You want any wacky backy?'

'Not right now, thanks.'

'Anything else you want, you just ask.'

'Thanks, Charlie. I will.'

Hoyle heaved himself back on to his bunk and was soon snoring loudly. Terry grinned. His hands were interlinked behind his head on top of the wafer-thin pillow he'd been given, and both blankets were threadbare and stained. He figured Riggs was doing as much as he could to make him as uncomfortable as possible, but Terry could take whatever was thrown at him. If everything went to plan, he wouldn't be behind bars for long.

* * *

Frank Welch dropped a stack of newspapers on his desk and sat down. He unwrapped his croissant and broke off a piece and chewed as he read through the *Daily Mail*. He'd given the chief reporter an exclusive off-the-record briefing on the Greene case, and the journalist had done him proud.

There was a photograph of Sam on one of the inside pages, looking directly at the camera, her chin slightly up. There was an air of defiance about her, as if she knew that she'd be staring out of the pages of a newspaper and didn't care. She was wearing a pale green suit with a thin gold chain and a crucifix around her neck. Welch smiled at the crucifix. It had been a nice touch, that. She'd worn it every day in court, even though she'd never worn the same outfit twice. Whatever she wore, she always made sure that the collar was open so that the jury could see the crucifix and just a hint of cleavage. The skirts were always cut just above the knee, showing off her shapely legs. Her heels were high enough to keep the male members of the jury interested, but not high enough to offend the women. It had been a delicate balancing act, but Sam Greene had pulled it off.

She'd been a professional singer in her early twenties, and flirted with acting, and Welch had seen her give the performance of her life in court. Supportive glances across to her husband in the dock. The occasional dab of a handkerchief. Steely glares at the main prosecution witness. Slightly flirtatious smiles at the male jury members if the judge wasn't looking. And every day the walk to and from the court, head up, shoulders back, looking defiantly at the clicking cameras. It had been an outstanding performance, but Terry Greene had still gone down for life and that was all that mattered to Welch.

The *Mail* had also used a picture of Greene's family home, a modern five-bedroom detached house on the outskirts of Chiswick, complete with heated swimming pool and three-car garage. It was the sort of house that Welch could never hope of coming close to owning. The most Welch could afford was a two-bedroom flat in Maida Vale and the way that London property prices were surging there was little chance of him ever climbing higher up the property ladder. There was no swimming pool in Welch's immediate future. Or three-car garage. Welch smiled to himself. But at least he wouldn't be spending the rest of his life in prison so maybe there was some justice in the world after all.

Doug Simpson pulled the *Telegraph* from the pile and flicked through the pages. 'Page four, boss,' he said.

'Uh-oh,' said Detective Constable Colin Duggan, scratching his fleshy neck. 'You're not going to like this, boss.'

Welch looked up from the front page of the *Mail*.

Duggan threw over a copy of the *Mirror*. 'They spelt your name wrong.'

'They did what?' Welch grabbed the paper and read through the story.

'Welsh, like the sheep-shaggers.'

'For God's sake, how could they fuck up my name?'

Simpson laughed but stopped abruptly when he saw that Welch was serious.

'I don't know what you're laughing at, Simpson. You're not even mentioned.' Welch tossed the newspaper on to his desk, but it knocked over his coffee and the hot brown liquid went everywhere. Welch cursed and mopped it up with the *Mail*. 'Fuck you, Terry Greene,' he muttered.

He dropped the wet newspapers into his wastebin, then stood up and bellowed at the dozen or so detectives in the CID room. 'Right, everyone listen to this, please. Just because we've put Terry Greene away doesn't mean we've put a stop to his organisation. Someone's going to take over from him, so let's find out who, shall we? You know who his associates are, so let's put them under the microscope, rattle a few cages, call in a few favours. Let's keep up the pressure.'

Heads nodded, but Welch sensed a distinct lack of enthusiasm. 'Unless you've got anything better to do with your time? And maybe you should all remember that I'll be signing expense sheets today.'

Detectives started picking up phones and pecking away on computer keyboards, trying to give the semblance of productivity. Welch grinned and went back to his papers. At least the *Mail* had spelled his name right.

★ ★ ★

Sam found David Jackson on the touchline, shouting at twenty tracksuited footballers who were running around the pitch, breath feathering from their mouths in the cold morning air.

'Can see you've had your Weetabix, Jacko,' said Sam as she came up behind him. 'I thought it was the manager's job to do the shouting, and the chairman just pocketed the readies.'

Jacko was genuinely surprised to see her and kissed her warmly on both cheeks. 'Samantha, love. Great to see you.' His smile vanished and his face was suddenly serious. 'I'm so sorry about Terry, love. Damn shame.'

'Thanks, Jacko.'

'Anything I can do, Samantha. Anything. Just ask.'

'That's sort of why I'm here,' said Sam. 'Can you spare me a few minutes?'

'Sure. Just let me get the boys started.' Jacko cupped his hands around his mouth and yelled across the pitch to the footballers. 'Three more laps, and if your arsehole of a coach hasn't turned up by then, get a warm-up game started.'

Jacko thrust his hands into his overcoat and walked with Sam towards the tunnel that led into the belly of the stadium.

'The thing is, Jacko, Terry's got financial problems.'

'Who hasn't?'

'No, real problems. I've spent this morning wading through bills, and the bank manager's been on the phone already asking about the mortgage payments. Like sharks smelling blood.'

'I thought Terry was well set up.'

'Yeah,' said Sam ruefully. 'You and me both. His stake in the club's got to be worth something, hasn't it?'

Jacko sucked air through his teeth. 'We're not up there with the big boys, Samantha. The money stays with them, there's no bloody trickle-down economics here.'

'You're pulling in the crowds though, Jacko.' She could hear the desperation in her voice and hated herself for it.

'It's not about bums on seats any more. It's about TV. And who's going to pay to tune in to see us when they can watch Man U? Look, you're not the only one with a bank manager on her back – we owe our banks well over a million and a half.' He shrugged his broad shoulders inside the overcoat. 'I'm sorry, love, that's not what you wanted to hear, is it?'

Sam sighed. 'Not really. Terry's accountant already warned me that Terry's assets weren't up to much, but I guess I needed to hear it for myself.'

'You'll probably have more luck offloading his nightclubs, that's what I'd be trying. Or his modelling business. What's the geezer's name that Terry was pally with? Locke?'

'Yeah. Warwick Locke. I'm seeing him this afternoon, after I've visited Terry, but he didn't sound too hopeful on the phone.'

Jacko stopped and put his shovel-like hands on her shoulders. He looked at her sympathetically. 'I'll ask around, Samantha, see if I can find someone to take the stake off your hands. But don't hold your breath, girl.' He cuffed her gently under the chin. 'You'll be okay. Terry and you, you're fighters.'

Sam forced a smile and wished that she felt half as confident as Jacko sounded.

* * *

Sam's high heels clicked purposefully on the tiled floor as she walked across the visiting room. Terry was sitting at a corner table, a red vest over his prison-issue denims, his hands clasped in front of him on the Formica table.

Sam didn't give him a chance to get to his feet. 'You selfish, self-centred, arrogant bastard. You screwed up your own life, what the fuck makes you think you've got the right to screw up mine?'

Terry smiled up at her. 'Fine, thanks. The food's a bit ropey, but what can you do?'

Sam shook her head. 'This isn't funny, Terry. You fucked me over big time. Do you want me inside with you, is that it?'

Terry couldn't help chuckling at the thought of sharing a cell with his wife, but he stopped when he saw how upset she was. He stood up and put a hand on her arm. 'I'm sorry, love. Honest.'

A burly prison officer walked by. 'Sit down, Greene,' he barked. Terry did as he was told, and Sam sat down opposite him.

'You walked out of my life, Terry,' she said, keeping her voice low. The tables in the visiting room were so close to each other that it was hard not to hear neighbouring conversations. A young woman with a toddler was crying and her husband was trying to console her; another prisoner was accusing his wife of always being out of the house when he phoned; an elderly prisoner was asking about his racing pigeons. 'You've no right to do this to me. You should have told me first. Talked to me.'

Terry sat back in his orange plastic chair and fixed her with his pale blue eyes. He started counting on his fingers. 'First of all, I didn't walk out. You threw me out. Second of all, I didn't think it'd go this far. Jury should never have convicted me. No motive, no weapon, and a slag for a witness. Case shouldn't have even gone to court. Wouldn't have either if it hadn't been for Raquel. That bastard Welch has had it in for me for years.' Terry put his hands back on the table and leaned forward. 'Sam, love, if I'd thought for one minute that I was going to go down, I'd have got this better sorted.'

Sam's eyes narrowed. 'Fallback position, is that what I am? Fuck you, Terry Greene. Fuck you and the horse you rode in on.'

Terry smiled and raised his eyebrows archly. 'Do you kiss our kids with that mouth?'

Sam stood up quickly and heads jerked in her direction but she was too angry to care. 'You can't joke your way out of this one,' she shouted, pointing an accusing finger at his face. 'I'm not doing it. I'm not doing any of it. You can rot in here for all I care.'

Sam gave him one final glare, then turned her back on him and walked out.

Terry watched her go, nodding slowly to himself. He heard a soft chuckling sound to his right and he turned to see Chief Prison Officer Riggs revelling in his discomfort.

'Bit of marital discord, Greene?' said Riggs. 'Never mind, you'll be able to sort it out when you get home – in thirty years or so.'

* * *

'How's the fish, Sam?' Warwick Locke looked across the table and smiled like a BMW salesman.

'It's fine, Warwick. I guess I'm just not hungry.' She sipped her white wine. The restaurant had been Locke's idea, an expensive seafood restaurant in Kensington, not far away from his office. It was full of television executives and wannabe celebrities and the waiting staff all had Australian or South African accents and introduced themselves by name before reeling off the specials. Sam had sole and it was overcooked. The vegetables were almost raw and the wine wasn't as well chilled as it should have been.

Locke ordered oysters followed by lobster, and he ate everything with his fingers, occasionally licking them with relish. His big red napkin was tucked into his shirt, his jacket on the back of his chair. He kept turning to look at a blonde waitress with large breasts every time she came close to their table.

'So what do you think, Warwick?' asked Sam, lighting a cigarette.

Locke raised a greasy lobster claw. 'Delicious. Want some?'

Sam narrowed her eyes. She was sure Locke knew what she meant, and if he was trying to be funny he was failing miserably. 'About Terry's stake in the business?'

'His fifty per cent is worth about five grand. Top whack.' He sucked noisily at the broken end of the claw.

'Five grand?' said Sam incredulously. 'How many girls have you got on the books?

Locke waved the lobster claw in the air like a conductor warming up an orchestra. 'Just because they're on the books doesn't mean that they're working, Samantha. And fifteen per cent of a catalogue shoot doesn't amount to much.'

The big-breasted blonde waitress came over to their table and leaned towards Sam. 'I'm sorry, madam, but this is a no-smoking restaurant.'

Sam smiled thinly, took a last drag on the cigarette, and then stubbed it out on her barely touched fish. The waitress leaned over to take the plate away, giving Locke an opportunity to look down the front of her chest. She caught him looking and he grinned at her, unabashed, wiping grease off his chin with the back of his hand.

Sam looked at Locke with contempt. 'You know, Warwick, I'd hate to think that the agency's only function was to provide a supply of nineteen-year-old blondes for you and Terry.'

Locke's eyes hardened. 'That's unkind, Sam. Unkind and uncalled for.'

Sam didn't say anything. She drained her glass of wine and stood up. 'Thanks for dinner, Warwick. If five grand's the best you can do, I'll have to take it. Send me a cheque, yeah?'

Locke pretended to look hurt, but he was a bad actor. 'Sam, come on. Have a dessert. A coffee. Something.' He waved his claw over the table.

'I've lost my appetite,' she said, and lit another cigarette as she walked towards the exit.

* * *

Sam drove to a filling station, still fuming at Locke's patronising attitude. It was only the second time that she'd met the man, and she realised that Terry had probably wanted to keep him away from her. She regretted telling him to send her the cheque for the five grand – it would have made more sense to have Richard Asher go over the books first.

She filled the Saab with four star then gave the Indian cashier her Visa card. He ran it through the card reader, then frowned. He tried again, then handed it back to her. 'Sorry,' he said, 'it's not accepting it.'

Sam groaned as she remembered that one of the bills she'd opened that morning had been from Visa, pointing out that she had already exceeded her credit limit on the card. She handed him her gold American Express card and said a silent prayer as he ran it through the reader. It spewed out a receipt and Sam signed it. The Amex card was paid for by direct debit from one of Terry's accounts, but she had no way of knowing how long that state of affairs would last. Most of the accounts she'd seen in Asher's office had been in the red or heading that way.

She was half a mile from home when she heard the blip of a siren behind her. She looked in the mirror and saw blue flashing lights.

There were two policemen in the patrol car and neither of them was much older than Jamie. One of them said that she seemed to be driving erratically, and the other held out a breathalyser. Sam shook her head and told them that she hadn't been drinking.

'I can smell alcohol on your breath,' said the one with the breathalyser.

'I had two glasses of wine. Two glasses.'

'So you have been drinking,' he said.

'I'm not blowing into that. I had two glasses of wine. And I wasn't driving erratically. You know that I wasn't.'

The policeman put the breathalyser away. 'In view of your refusal, you'll have to come to the station with us, I'm afraid, Mrs Greene.'

Sam sneered at him. 'You know who I am, then?'

The officer's face hardened and she knew that she was right.

'So it wasn't a random stop, was it?' She held out her hand. 'All right, I'll blow into your little machine if it makes you happy.'

He shook his head. 'You've already refused,' he said. He nodded at the car. 'In the back, please, my colleague will secure your vehicle.'

'I know policemen are looking younger, I didn't think they were stupider as well.'

'If you want to be handcuffed, that can be arranged.'

They drove Sam to the police station in silence and showed her to an interview room. There was a table and four chairs, and a tape deck with two slots for cassettes on a shelf under a window made of glass blocks. Sam sat down and lit a cigarette. It had burned halfway down before the door opened again. It was Frank Welch.

'I might have known,' said Sam.

'The doctor's on his way,' said Welch, closing the door and standing with his back to it.

'I don't have to piss in a bottle to know that I've not been drinking,' said Sam, scornfully.

'Two glasses of wine, you told the woodentops.'

'What do you want, Raquel?'

'The last person to call me Raquel was your nearest and dearest, and look what happened to him.'

'Everyone calls you Raquel, it's just that most people do it behind your back.'

Welch's cheeks flared red and he opened his mouth to reply, but then he made a conscious attempt to calm himself down. He smiled ingratiatingly. 'Let's not get off on the wrong foot, Sam. Let's at least try to be civil to each other.'

Welch pulled a chair away from the table and sat down, carefully adjusting the creases of his dark grey suit. Sam watched his face, waiting to see what it was that he wanted. Welch had a bloodhound's face, jowls that hung around his chin and sad, almost watery eyes. His hair was receding but he was growing it long at the back as if to compensate for the shortcomings up front. He licked his lower lip with the tip of his tongue and fiddled with his tie as he looked Sam up and down.

'You were always too good for Terry, Sam,' he said, his voice a soft whisper. 'You've got class. Lots of class. You know how to dress, how to behave. Terry didn't even know which knife and fork to use before he met you.'

Sam looked around for an ashtray. There wasn't one so she flicked ash on to the floor.

Welch's voice hardened. 'I want to know who's running things while Terry's away. I know he was setting something up.'

'Grow up, will you?' said Sam savagely. 'Terry and I separated more than a year ago. And even when we were together, he never told me what he was up to.'

Welch licked his lower lip again. 'I always know when you're lying, Sam. I knew you were lying in court and I know you're lying now.'

Sam didn't say anything. She blew smoke in two tight

plumes through her nostrils and tapped more ash on to the floor.

'You don't owe Terry anything, Sam. He's a criminal. A murderer. He didn't give you and his kids a second thought when he pulled that trigger.'

Sam crossed her legs and saw Welch stiffen at the sound of her stockings rasping against each other. 'This isn't about Terry, is it? Not really. It's about you and me.'

'What do you mean?'

'Come on, Frank. I turned you down four years ago when you first tried to stitch Terry up, and ever since you've had a hard-on like a baseball bat every time you get near me.'

Welch's draw dropped. 'What? I never . . . that wasn't what . . . you can't . . .' Welch spluttered, unable to form a coherent sentence.

Sam smiled with satisfaction, knowing that she'd hit a nerve. She dropped her cigarette on to the floor and ground it out with her heel. She walked around and sat on the edge of the table, her breasts just about level with Welch's oyster-like eyes.

'You think life'll mean life?' she asked quietly.

'I reckon,' he said smugly. He licked his lip again and spittle glistened under the overhead fluorescent lights.

'Long time, life.'

There was a silence lasting several seconds in which Welch tried hard not to look at Sam's breasts. She leaned forward a little to give him the merest glimpse of cleavage.

'You got a girlfriend, Frank? Anyone steady?'

Welch cleared his throat. 'I get by.'

Sam leaned forward a bit more. She could see small beads of sweat on his upper lip.

'Couldn't really say yes, could I, what with Terry being in the picture and all. Even when we'd split up, he was still a jealous sod. Would've broken your legs. Mine too.'

'I'm not scared of Terry.'

'I am.'

'No need. Not now.'

'Iron bars do not a prison make?' She smiled. 'Maybe.' She lowered her voice to a husky whisper. 'Do we have to do this here, Frank?'

'What do you mean?'

'Couldn't we do it at my place? Tomorrow night. Maybe open a bottle of wine or something.'

'I don't drink.' He almost choked on the last word and he had to clear his throat.

Sam smiled and put her head on one side. 'You're missing the point.'

Welch swallowed and rubbed his mouth with the back of his hand. 'What time?'

Sam shrugged. 'About nine. Might even cook something. You like pasta, yeah?'

Welch nodded eagerly.

Sam's smile vanished and her upper lip curled back into a snarl. 'You sad fuck! You can always tell when I'm lying, can you? There's about as much chance of you ever getting inside my pants as there is of you getting rid of your halitosis.'

Welch rocked back in his chair, stunned by her outburst. Sam shook her head contemptuously.

Before Welch could say anything, the door opened. It was the police doctor, holding two specimen bottles. Welch stood up and hurried out of the room. 'Make sure she fills both of them,' he snarled as he brushed past the doctor.

Sam smiled sweetly at the doctor and held out her hand for the bottles. 'Shall I do it here or can someone escort me to the ladies?' she said. 'I've taken the piss out of Raquel, least I can do is make a donation myself.'

* * *

Trisha came tottering downstairs on high heels and grabbed her backpack from under the telephone table in the hall.

She'd tied her long blonde hair back in a ponytail and her school tie was loose around her neck.

Sam came out of the kitchen holding a plate of toast. 'Hey, breakfast.'

'Not hungry, Mum. I'll get something at school.'

Sam held out the plate and raised an eyebrow.

'Mother, I'm not going to clog up my arteries with cholesterol.'

'It's Flora. High in polyunsaturates. Whatever they are.'

'Are you sure?'

'On your mother's life.'

Trisha took a slice and sniffed it suspiciously. 'Smells like butter,' she muttered.

'A miracle of modern science. Are you going to school like that?'

Trisha frowned. 'What's wrong?'

'You look like you've just fallen out of bed. And you're wearing too much make-up.'

'Mum, everyone wears make-up these days. Even some of the boys.'

Sam couldn't help smiling. Trisha had her mother's high cheekbones and fiery eyes and looked older than her fifteen years. Sam had been the same at Trisha's age. Even in her mid-teens she'd been able to pass herself of as a twenty-something and had never had a problem getting into night-clubs and pubs. However, even Sam would never have thought of wearing pink glossy lipstick and eyeliner to school.

'And the earrings are okay?'

'So long as they don't dangle. That's the rule.' Trisha could see from the look on her mother's face that she didn't believe her. 'It's true, Mum,' she protested.

'How is it, school?' asked Sam, brushing a stray lock of Trisha's hair over her ear.

'School's school.'

'Did they give you any grief over Dad?'

Trisha scowled. 'No more than usual.' She looked at her chunky fluorescent-green wristwatch. 'I've got to go.'

'What time are you getting home tonight?'

'Why?'

'Because I've got to go out.'

'Again? You didn't get back until almost eleven last night.'

'Business. I'm trying to tidy up your father's affairs.'

'Bit late for that, isn't it?'

'His financial affairs.'

'Speaking of which . . .' Trisha held out a hand. 'Can I have a tenner?'

'I gave you twenty last week,' said Sam.

'Exactly. Last week.'

'What do you need it for?'

Trisha sighed theatrically. 'Tampons . . . actually.'

'That's what you said last week.'

Trisha groaned. 'Fine. Okay. Whatever.'

Sam picked up her purse off the hall table and gave Trisha a twenty-pound note.

'Thanks, Mum,' said Trisha and kissed Sam on the cheek. 'Any chance of a lift?'

'Do you see a chauffeur's cap on my head?'

'Kidnappers and child molesters use the bus. You might never see me again.'

Sam opened the front door. 'Chance'd be a fine thing.'

Trisha stuck her tongue out playfully, then tottered out of the door.

'And those heels are too high,' Sam called after her. Trisha waved without looking back.

Sam closed the door and picked up the mail. There were several brown envelopes that were obviously bills. A letter from the Inland Revenue addressed to Terry. A letter from American Express that Sam hoped was junk mail and not a demand for payment. A padded envelope with her name on it, written in capital letters. Sam carried them through to the kitchen. She used a breadknife to slit open the padded envelope and put her hand inside. She screamed as she touched something cold and damp and she jerked her hand out.

She turned the envelope over and shook it. A bloody chicken's head dropped out and slapped on to the draining board. Sam put a hand over her mouth and stared at it in horror.

* * *

There were two dozen men lining up for breakfast, holding plastic trays and chatting as they waited for their turn. Terry grabbed a tray and walked to the head of the queue where a prison cook was slapping greasy bacon and blackened sausages on to a plate.

A short man with pockmarked skin reached out for the plate, but Terry leaned across him and took it. The man protested, but fell silent when he saw that it was Terry. He nodded and Terry gave him a tight smile.

'How about another sausage, yeah?' Terry asked the cook.

The cook nodded and used plastic tongs to hand Terry a sausage, then spooned a dollop of baked beans on to Terry's plate.

'Oi, there's a fucking queue here!' shouted a prisoner halfway down the line.

Terry turned to look at him. He was a black guy in his twenties and he was looking around for support from the prisoners next to him. Most avoided meeting his gaze. One of the men leaned forward and whispered something in his ear. The man's body language changed immediately: he seemed to sag at the waist and he swallowed nervously. He gave Terry a half wave, then looked at the floor. Terry continued to stare at the man for several seconds before turning away.

He reached over and picked up three slices of toast. The rule was one slice of toast per prisoner, but none of the cooks said anything. Terry picked up a mug of tea and headed back to his cell. Several of the prisoners in the queue nodded and wished him a good morning. The two prison officers who were standing on the landing looking down had watched Terry push into the queue but it was clear they weren't going to intervene.

Terry wasn't particularly hungry, and he certainly hadn't wanted the extra burnt sausage. It was all about establishing his place in the pecking order, demonstrating to the prison population that Terry Greene wasn't to be messed with.

* * *

There were three bouncers at the entrance to the club, big men in dark coats with their hands clasped in front of their groins like bit players in a low-budget gangster movie. Behind them a thick purple rope ran between brass poles, the barrier through which customers had to pass to get inside Lapland.

Sam walked to the head of the line. It had been more than two years since she'd last visited the club, and that had been with Terry. It wasn't her favourite place, but George Kay had said that he was too busy to get away and that if she wanted to see him it would have to be there.

One of the bouncers moved to bar Sam's way, but another put a hand on his shoulder and nodded. He removed the rope and waved for Sam to go through. 'Mrs Greene,' he said, in a throaty Glaswegian accent. 'Long time no see.'

Sam frowned at the man. He was well over six feet tall, in his early thirties and with close-cropped receding hair and a strong jaw.

'Andy McKinley, Mrs Greene, I used to drive your husband.'

'Andy. I'm sorry.'

'That's all right, Mrs Greene. You were only in the Lexus one time and you probably only saw the back of my head.'

'It's not that, Andy, it's just that I didn't expect to see you on the door.'

'Needs as needs must, Mrs Greene. I'll show you through.'

Sam followed McKinley down a dimly lit corridor and into the club. Three busty girls, two blondes and a brunette, were dancing around silver poles on a stage while dozens of other equally well-endowed girls moved among the predominantly male clientele, accepting drinks and performing one-on-one lapdances. There were lots of bottles of champagne in ice buckets and men in suits shoving ten-pound notes in the garters of the dancing girls. It was, thought Sam, a hell of a way to earn a living.

'Busy night, Andy,' she said, as McKinley led her through the tables to George Kay's office.

'It always is, Mrs Greene,' said McKinley. He knocked on a door and opened it. 'Mr Kay. Mrs Greene to see you.'

McKinley stepped to the side to let Sam go in, then gently closed the door behind her.

George Kay was sprawled in a leather executive chair, his feet up on a cluttered desk reading a copy of *Exchange and Mart*. 'Sam, darling, lovely surprise.' He swung his feet off the desk and waddled over to greet her, planting a wet kiss on each cheek.

'I did say I was coming, George.'

'Of course you did, darling, of course you did.'

He waved her over to an overstuffed sofa opposite a large window through which they could see what was going on in the club. McKinley had moved away a rowdy group of men in shirtsleeves who were giving one of the dancers a hard time. McKinley quietened them with a few words and they dropped back into their seats as meek as mice.

Sam sat down and George went back behind his desk. He gestured at a chipped mug by a computer terminal. 'Coffee, Sam?' Sam shook her head. 'Something stronger, then? Shall I get a bottle of bubbly sent in?'

'No, thanks, George. I'm driving and I've already had to piss in a bottle once this week.'

Kay's brow furrowed. He ran a hand through his greying

goatee beard. He was at least ten stone overweight and was sweating despite a large air-conditioning unit on the wall behind his desk.

'How long's McKinley been working for you?' asked Sam.

'Since they arrested Terry, pretty much.' Kay looked uncomfortable, as if he might have said the wrong thing. 'Least I could do, you know? Help the lad out.'

Sam nodded and took a pack of cigarettes out of her handbag. 'Don't mind if I smoke, do you, George?'

Kay looked even more uncomfortable. He picked up an inhaler and showed it to her. 'Rather you didn't, if you don't mind. Asthma. Since I was a kid. Smoke shuts my bronchioles down.'

'Can't have that, can we?' said Sam, putting the cigarettes away. She tapped her fingernails on her handbag. 'The thing is, George – Terry has asked me to run things for him while he's away.'

Kay stiffened. He pointed a finger at her. 'Now just a fucking minute . . .'

'It's all right,' interrupted Sam. 'I'm not doing it. Don't worry. But I've got money problems. Cashflow.'

He shrugged. 'You and me both.'

Sam gestured at the window. 'Place is packed.'

'Overheads, Sam.'

Kay opened one of his desk drawers and took out a cheque book. 'If it's a loan you want, I'm more than happy to help out.'

'It's serious money, George.'

Kay dropped the cheque book back into the drawer. 'Terry's never been short of a bob or two.'

'Yeah, well, times have changed. Look, Terry owns half the clubs, right? This place, the one in Clerkenwell, the one south of the river. Can't you buy him out?'

'It's not a good time, Sam. I can barely keep the wolf from the door myself.'

'Come on, George, you're not pleading poverty, are you?'

Kay took his inhaler and sucked on it, then patted his barrel-like chest. 'It's not a question of poverty, Sam, but I'm over-extended with the banks. And it'd need a big chunk of change to buy Terry out.'

'What about getting someone else to buy his stake?'

Kay pulled a face. 'That's possible, but I wouldn't want to get into bed with just anyone.' He smiled at the double entendre. 'If you know what I mean. I wouldn't want the wrong sort of people in here. There's the licence to think of.'

Sam stood up. 'That's it, then. I guess there isn't anything else to be said, is there?'

'Come on, Sam, there's no need to rush. Let's have a drink. Catch up on old times.'

'We don't have any old times, George,' said Sam.

Sam lit a cigarette as she walked towards the exit. She was sure George Kay was deliberately being unhelpful. If the clubs were making money, he'd have no problem getting a loan from the banks, no matter how extended he was. He probably assumed that with Terry behind bars, he'd be able to keep the lion's share of the profits. Sam trusted Kay about as far as she could throw him.

Andy McKinley unclipped the rope to let her out and slipped a business card into her hand. 'You need anything, Mrs Greene, anything at all, you call, hear?'

'Thanks, Andy,' said Sam, gratefully. McKinley was the first friendly face she'd seen in a while.

She got into her Saab and drove home, checking her rear-view mirror regularly, convinced that the police would pull her in again. The fact that she was driving away from a nightclub would give them all the excuse they needed to breathalyse her again.

* * *

The curtains at Trisha's window were moving as Sam got out of the Saab and let herself into the house but the light in her room was off. Sam went upstairs and knocked on her door. 'Trish? You awake?'

There was no answer.

'Good night, love. Sleep well.'

Sam went downstairs and opened a bottle of chilled Chardonnay. She poured herself a glass and lit the flame-effect gas fire in the sitting room. She sat on the floor, her back against the sofa, and stared at the flames as if hoping to find the answer to her problems there. The phone rang, startling her, and she spilled wine down the front of her dress. She picked up the receiver as she dabbed a tissue against the wet patch. 'Yes?'

'You are fucking dead meat. You hear me? Dead fucking meat. I know where you live and I'm gonna fucking cut you. I'm gonna fucking take a knife to you, do you—'

Sam banged the receiver down. She didn't recognise the voice but guessed that it was one of Preston Snow's relatives, probably the brother, the one that had thrown the bottle at Jamie's car. Under normal circumstances she'd go to the police, but she doubted that they'd bother to do anything, and there was no way that she was prepared to give Raquel the satisfaction of asking for his help.

She took another sip of her wine. The bills that had arrived that morning were spread out on the coffee table in front of her and she ran her fingers over them. There was an electricity bill and a reminder that she had to pay for her television licence, and statements for two of her credit cards. In all she owed a little over three thousand pounds, just on that day's bills alone. There were others on the way, she knew. She had had no idea of how short of money Terry was, she'd just blithely assumed that money would keep flowing into the bank accounts as it always had done in the past.

The phone rang again. Sam snatched at it. 'Why don't you just fuck off and leave me alone, you sick bastard!' she snarled.

There was a short silence on the line. 'Gosh, Mum, I love you, too.' It was Jamie.

'God, Jamie, I'm sorry.'

'What's wrong, Mum?'

'Nothing. I've just had a bad day, that's all.'

'Has someone been bothering you?'

'A few phone calls, that's all.'

'About the trial?'

'What else?'

'Do you want me to come home?'

'Jamie, I'm a big girl. And you know as well as I do, people who make threats rarely carry them out.'

'He's threatening you? For God's sake, Mum . . . go to the police.'

'Yeah, wouldn't they just love that? I can handle it, Jamie. How did the exams go?'

'No sweat. Look, I don't want to bother you with everything else you've got on your plate, but the admin office has been on at me about my tuition fees. Do you know if Dad sent a cheque before . . .'

He tailed off. Before he was arrested, he was going to say.

'I don't know, Jamie. I'll find out.'

'Do you mind? It's a bit embarrassing, that's all.'

'I'll talk to his accountant tomorrow. Have you written to your dad?'

'Yeah. Sent him a letter yesterday. Thought about sending him a cake with a file in it, but I guess the screws don't have a sense of humour, do they?'

'What sort of language is that for a future solicitor to be using? Screws indeed.'

'Solicitor? I should cocoa. Barrister's where the money is, Mum. You won't catch me working in a solicitor's office when I've graduated. Say hi to Trisha, will you? And Laura, when you see her. I've tried calling but I keep getting her machine.'

They said goodbye and Sam replaced the receiver. She looked at the phone for several seconds, then took off the receiver and put it on the table. She figured she deserved a quiet evening.

* * *

Oakwood House looked more like a stately home than a nursing centre, a large Georgian house in almost a hundred acres of woodland and gardens with a sweeping gravel drive and a fountain in front of the main entrance. The hallway was a grand affair with ornate furniture and a massive chandelier hanging over a wide oak staircase. Despite the luxurious fittings and the vases of fresh flowers, their was an underlying smell of urine and disinfectant and Sam wrinkled her nose. Sam smiled at the receptionist and walked along the west wing to Grace's room. Several doors were open along the length of the corridor and expectant faces looked up as Sam walked by, faces that fell as soon as they realised that she wasn't there to visit them.

Grace was sitting in a large winged chair looking out of her window, an untouched cup of tea next to her on a small side table. 'Hello, Grace. It's me.' Sam closed the door and pulled up a chair next to her mother-in-law. 'How've you been, then, Grace?'

Grace said nothing. A small trickle of saliva was running from the side of Grace's lip and Sam took a handkerchief from her handbag and dabbed her chin.

'Well, I don't know about you, but I've had one hell of a few days. Your darling boy is behind bars, he's left me with barely a penny to my name, and now he wants me to mastermind a multi-million-pound drugs deal to pay for his appeal.' There was no reaction from Grace. She was fiddling with her wedding ring as she stared out over the lawn. 'So how was your week, Grace?'

The door to the room opened. It was a young nurse with a starched white uniform and a BUPA smile. 'Would you like a cup of tea, Mrs Greene?'

'No, I'm fine, thanks.'

'Mrs Hancock asks if you'd pop into her office before you leave.'

'I'll do that.'

Grace turned to Sam as the door closed. There was a faraway look in her eyes as if her mind elsewhere. 'Who are you?' she asked.

'I'm Sam, Grace. Your daughter-in-law.'

'Laura?'

'No, Grace. Laura's your granddaughter. I'm Sam. Laura's mother.'

'Such a lovely girl, Laura.' She smiled serenely and went back to looking through the window.

'Yes, Grace. She is.'

Sam sat with her mother-in-law for the best part of an hour, and as always the conversation was one-sided, with Grace's comments confined to asking who Sam was and why they hadn't brought her a cup of tea, even though Sam kept pointing out the cup by her side.

Mrs Hancock was waiting for Sam in her office. She was in her fifties with grey permed hair and a pair of gold-rimmed pince-nez spectacles perched on the end of her nose. The first time Sam had met her she'd thought that she had the look of a spinster who'd rejected her one chance of love early on in life and spent the last thirty years hating all men, but there was a picture of her with a good-looking man and three teenage children on the desk and a ring on her wedding finger.

Sam was all too well aware of how deceptive appearances could be. Grace Greene looked as elegant and intelligent as she had ten years earlier, but she was an empty shell.

'There's been no decline this past month, Mrs Greene, but no improvement either,' said Mrs Hancock. It was almost word for word what the administrator said every time she met Sam. 'Alzheimer's is a terrible illness. All we can do is to make her as comfortable as possible. She's in no pain. Sometimes she even appears to be happy, in her way.'

'Happy? Yeah, I remember happy,' said Sam ruefully.

Mrs Hancock frowned and Sam forced herself to smile. 'So, is that why you wanted a word? To update me on my mother-in-law's lack of progress?'

'Actually, no.' Mrs Hancock opened a pale blue file in front of her. 'It's more to do with her account. The last two direct debits haven't gone through. I'm sure it's just an oversight.'

Sam sighed. 'It's probably the bank's fault,' she said. 'We've just opened a new savings account and I think some of the direct debit mandates went adrift. I'll give the manager a call this afternoon.'

Mrs Hancock smiled reassuringly and pushed her spectacles higher up her nose. 'I can't help but be aware of your present circumstances, Mrs Greene. Your husband . . . well, it was in all the papers.'

'Wasn't it just.'

'What I'm trying to say is, if you should be having problems of a financial nature, please let us know right away.'

'I will,' said Sam. 'Thanks.'

'Because if you are finding it difficult to meet the payments, we can help you find a place for Grace in a local authority institution.'

Sam's eyes hardened. 'Excuse me?'

'We can make alternative arrangements for Grace's care. I have extremely good contacts within the state sector. It won't be a problem, I can assure you.'

Sam stood up. 'Let's get one thing clear, Mrs Hancock – Grace is not going into the poor house.'

'Mrs Greene, you're over-reacting. I was simply pointing out that the private sector isn't for everybody.'

'You've been happy enough to take our money for the past three years. Now just because we're late with a couple of payments, you're threatening to throw an old woman out on the streets.'

'Mrs Greene, please . . .'

'You'll get your money, Mrs Hancock. Don't you worry.'

Sam hurried out of the office, tears of rage burning in her eyes.

* * *

Terry walked along the landing. A young prisoner slipped him two telephone cards and Terry nodded his thanks. Terry had made it known that he was prepared to pay twenty times the face value of telephone cards, the money being paid on the outside to family or friends. He'd been inundated with prisoners wanting to exchange their cards for cash and Terry had taken all he could get.

He slipped the cards into the back pocket of his trousers. Ahead of him two large prisoners, one black, one white, were lounging against a wall, their eyes scanning back and forth, taking in everything that was happening on the wing. Both were well over six feet, broad shouldered with bulging forearms. They straightened up as Terry got closer, and stood in front of him, their arms crossed, their faces set like stone.

'Hello, lads,' said Terry. 'Is he in?'

'You got an appointment?' said one of the prisoners in a thick West Country accent.

'No, just wanted to pay my respects, that's all,' said Terry.

The other prisoner knocked on the cell door behind them, then disappeared inside. A few seconds later he reappeared and nodded at Terry. 'You can go in,' he said gruffly.

'Thanks, lads,' he said.

The two men moved to the side and Terry walked into the cell. There was a single occupant, a black man in his late twenties with close-cropped hair and a runner's build, thin and wiry. A thick raised scar ran from his left eye down to the corner of his mouth. He wore a dark blue Nike T-shirt and tracksuit bottoms and a pair of gleaming white Nike training shoes. He acknowledged Terry with a slight nod of his head. 'Settling in, Terry?' he said.

Terry shrugged. 'You know how it is, Baz.' Baz Salter had

run a major drugs crew south of the river before being sentenced to life for an arson attack on a Brixton drinking club that left four Jamaicans dead and more than a dozen horrifically burned. Terry had never met him on the outside but he knew him by reputation. The four arson deaths were the tip of an iceberg – Baz was rumoured to be responsible for more than a dozen gangland slayings in the struggle for the dominance of the South London crack cocaine market.

'Have a seat,' said Baz, waving Terry to a chair by the single bunk. The cell was the same size as the one that Terry shared with Hoyle, but Baz had it to himself. There was a CD player and a selection of books on a shelf, and a green and black quilt on the bunk. Baz effectively ran the wing and was allowed privileges that reflected his status.

Terry sat down. 'I wanted to drop by and let you know I was here.'

'Jungle drums said you were coming,' said Baz.

'If there are going to be any problems down the line, I wanted to get them out in the open here and now,' said Terry. 'I don't want to keep looking over my shoulder.'

Baz nodded slowly, but didn't say anything.

'Jungle drums told you why I'm here, right?' continued Terry.

'It was in all the papers. Major celebrity, you are.'

Terry smiled thinly. 'So are there going to be repercussions?'

Baz leaned forward and put his head on one side. 'Of what nature?'

'Preston Snow was one of yours.'

Baz smiled. 'Ancient history.'

Terry nodded slowly. He looked into Baz's dark brown eyes, trying to see if the man was being honest with him or not.

'I didn't shed any tears over Snow,' said Baz. 'He went loco years ago. He needed killing.'

'Okay,' said Terry.

'So what are your intentions, then?'

'To get out of here as quickly as possible,' said Terry.

'That's easy to say. I was wondering more about your intentions on the wing.'

'It's your wing, Baz. There's going to be no boats rocked.'

'It'd be a difficult boat to rock,' said Baz.

'Absolutely,' said Terry. 'I just want to keep my head down.'

'You've been buying cards, big time. Pushing the price up.'

Terry nodded. 'I've things that needed sorting on the outside,' he said.

'You and me both,' said Baz. 'But pushing the price up is gonna piss me off.'

'Message received,' said Terry.

'Gambling, smokes, drugs, booze, I run them all,' said Baz.

Terry nodded.

'Any problems on the wing, you talk to me before sorting them.'

'Fine by me,' said Terry.

'Anything you need bringing in, you talk to me. I don't like contraband coming on to the wing without me knowing.'

'Okay,' said Terry.

Baz smiled. 'That's all the rules,' he said. 'Break them and I'll break you.'

Terry stood up. 'Thanks for your time, Baz.'

'Be lucky,' said Baz.

Terry left, closing the cell door behind him and nodding at the two heavies. He walked back down the landing to his own cell. He hated having to kowtow before a thug like Baz Salter, but he knew he had no choice. Terry didn't plan to stay behind bars for long and he didn't have time to wrestle for control of the wing. If Baz wanted his own little prison empire, all well and good. Terry had bigger fish to fry, and they were outside the prison walls.

* * *

The manager made Sam wait for almost an hour before his secretary ushered her into his office. It was austerely furnished, as if the bank was keen to demonstrate how little money it was spending on decoration. The manager was in his thirties with thinning sandy hair and a sprinkling of freckles across his nose and cheeks, and wore a suit that was slightly too small for him, so that he constantly pulled at the sleeves to cover his shirt cuffs. A wooden nameplate with black plastic letters announced his name as Mr Phillips. No first name. He even introduced himself as Mr Phillips when he offered Sam his slightly sweaty hand, the emphasis on the Mr, as if he was desperate to prove his gender.

He punched his computer keyboard with his index finger and frowned as he read what was on the screen. 'Ah,' he said. 'I see what's happened.' He tapped the screen even though all Sam could see was the back of the VDU and a tangle of wires. 'The account is still in the black, but there wasn't enough to cover the direct debit payments. So they weren't processed.'

'Why didn't anyone tell me?' asked Sam.

Mr Phillips squinted at the computer screen. 'Strictly speaking, you should have been told. I'll speak to our admin department.'

'So you can make sure the payments go through? It is important.'

Mr Phillips looked surprised at her suggestion. 'Oh, I couldn't do that, Mrs Greene. You don't have sufficient funds.' He peered at the screen again. 'In fact, as of today there is just under three hundred pounds in the account.'

'My husband and I have another joint account here, don't we? It pays the mortgage on the house and the household bills.'

The manager tapped on the keyboard and made a slow whistling noise through his teeth. 'That's also perilously close to being overdrawn, Mrs Greene. Up until a few months ago payments were made into the account on a regular basis from one of your husband's business accounts, but they appear to have stopped. In fact I'm glad you called, because I've been wanting to talk to you about your accounts for some time. Obviously with your husband now being, how shall I put it, indisposed, we were wondering what you propose to do with regard to your financial situation.'

Sam frowned and brushed a stray lock of hair away from her face. 'I don't follow you.'

'To put it bluntly, Mrs Greene, your income doesn't come anywhere near covering your present outgoings. In fact, you don't appear to have any income at all.'

'Since when?'

Another one-fingered tap on the keyboard. 'Since three months ago. That was the last time your husband transferred money into the accounts.'

Sam nodded hesitantly. That was about the time Terry was remanded. 'My husband has a number of business interests, Mr Phillips. You know that. He owns several clubs, a courier business, property development.'

'But we don't handle your husband's business accounts, Mrs Greene. Only his and your personal accounts. That's what I have to be concerned with.' He sat back in his chair and put his hands together like a child preparing to say his prayers. 'Do you think it would be possible for your husband to arrange a transfer of funds in the near future, considering his current predicament?'

'He's in prison, Mr Phillips. He's not dead.'

The manager's smile hardened a little. 'Even so . . .'

Sam remembered the accounts Laurence Patterson had showed her. There was nothing in them worth transferring to their joint accounts, and certainly not enough to cover the nursing home bills and Jamie's tuition fees. If she admitted that to Phillips, though, he'd have to move to protect the bank's position, and that would mean siezing the house. She tried to smile confidently, even though she could feel the bottom falling out of her world. 'I'm going to see my husband in a couple of days, I'll take the necessary papers with me.'

'Glad to hear it, Mrs Greene. You and your husband have been with the bank a long time, we'd hate to lose your custom.'

Sam stood up and held out her hand. What she really wanted to do was to slap young Mr Phillips' face, but she knew that she couldn't afford to antagonise him. She smiled sweetly. 'I'll be in touch, Mr Phillips. And thank you for your understanding.' She shook his hand across the desk.

★ ★ ★

Sam called Laurence Patterson on her mobile phone and arranged to meet him and Richard Asher in Asher's office. He didn't ask why, and she knew without a shadow of a doubt that he didn't need to and she hated him for that.

She stopped at a Starbucks on the way and had a double expresso and three Peter Stuyvesants, figuring that she'd need the caffeine and nicotine to get her through what lay ahead. 'Damn you, Terry Greene,' she muttered to herself as she sipped the rich brew at an outside table and blew smoke as she watched the city traffic crawl by.

Patterson and Asher were waiting for her. She sat on a leather and chrome chair opposite Asher's desk and took a handful of bills from her bag. 'I'm stuck between the devil and the deep blue, Richard, aren't I?'

Asher nodded.

'Terry's got me stitched up like a kipper, the bastard.'

Patterson snorted softly. 'I think given the choice, he'd rather not be in his current situation, Samantha. He's not doing this by choice.'

Sam tossed the bills on Asher's desk. 'These are going to have to be paid, and soon. What about getting Terry out? Then he can take care of his own dirty work.'

'It isn't going to be easy, Samantha,' said Patterson. 'The judge's summing up was fair, and I don't see any reasons to appeal on a point of law.'

'But they only had one witness and he was hardly credible.'

'We can't appeal just because the jury chose to believe a scumbag who sold drugs to schoolkids. There's the forensics.'

'They never found the gun.'

'They don't need to, not to get a conviction.'

'So are you telling me that we're not going to appeal? Is that what you're saying?'

Patterson held out a hand as if trying to soothe a wayward horse. 'What I'm saying is that we don't yet have solid grounds with which to approach the Court of Appeal. We need evidence of a miscarriage of justice.'

'Terry didn't do it.'

'Samantha, I'm on your side here. Look, the best way to get Terry out is to find out who did kill Preston Snow.'

'And how do we do that?' asked Sam.

'Private investigators. Professionals. I can recommend people.'

'Whatever I do, it's going to cost, isn't it?'

Patterson gave her a pained look, then the merest hint of a nod. 'I'm sorry,' he said.

'Pay peanuts, you get whatsits,' said Asher.

Sam stood up and paced up and down. She could feel herself being painted into a corner, and while she wanted to resist, she knew that she was clutching at straws.

'Look, is there any way we can untangle Terry's legitimate businesses from the dodgy ones? I could look after the property business and the courier firm. I've already arranged to sell the modelling company and I'm trying to find a buyer for Terry's football shares. There must be some way of generating some cash legitimately.'

Both men shook their heads.

'They feed off each other, Samantha,' said Patterson.

'It's symbiwhatsit,' said Asher.

'Symbiosis,' said Sam.

'That's it.'

'Shit,' said Sam. She sat down again. 'You know the

situation I'm in, don't you? I'm going to lose my house, Terry's mother is going to be put in a council home, our son's going to have to leave university. Unless I do what Terry wants.'

'Like I said before, Samantha, it's not really what Terry wants,' said Patterson. 'He's no choice in the matter either.'

'I had a thought on the way over. Why don't I remortgage the house? It's got to be worth three hundred grand, right? And the mortgage is what? A hundred and eighty?'

'A hundred and ninety-five,' said Asher.

'So I can get a bigger mortgage. Another hundred grand maybe.'

Asher shook his head. 'Won't work, Samantha. You've no income. The bank's not going to give you more money without a guarantee that they'll be getting it back.'

'But they'll have the house.'

'Thing is, Samantha, they've got the house already. If you default on the mortgage, they'll take it and sell it.'

Samantha realised he was right. She looked at them in turn. They waited for her decision, their faces impassive. Sam swallowed, angry at the unfairness of it all. 'Okay,' she said eventually. 'What do I do?'

Asher leaned to the side and opened a desk drawer. He took out a clear plastic file containing several typed sheets of paper. 'First we need you to sign a few papers,' he said.

Patterson appeared at her elbow, proffering a Mont Blanc fountain pen, its cap already removed. Sam took the pen and looked down at the first sheet of paper that Asher slid in front of her. 'I feel as if I should be signing this in blood,' she said bitterly as she scrawled her signature. Asher took the paper from her, dabbed it on his blotter, and gave her a second sheet. Sam didn't bother reading the legalese. She knew there was no point. Signing was the only choice she had. Terry had got what she wanted, by signing she was taking control of his companies. His bank accounts. There were more than a dozen in all. His life.

'Now what?' she said.

'Terry has a safe deposit box in South Kensington,' said Patterson. 'You'll need to see what's inside.'

'Can we do that tomorrow, yeah?' said Sam. 'I've had all the excitement I can stand today.'

* * *

Trisha was in the kitchen devouring a pizza when Sam got home. 'Did you buy that?' asked Sam, nodding at the box the pizza came in.

Trisha shook her head. 'You did,' she said. 'I used your credit card.'

'Trish! Why didn't you ask me first?'

'Because you weren't here. I thought you might be late again.'

'I was visiting your gran.' Sam took a triangle of pizza. 'And you know I hate pineapple.'

'Fruit's good for you. How is she?'

Sam sat down at the table opposite her daughter. 'The same, pretty much. She's not going to get better. It's not that sort of illness.'

'Yeah, I know. We did it in biology last year.'

Sam took a bite of pizza while Trisha went to the fridge and poured her mother a glass of milk. 'So how's school?' asked Sam.

'School's school. It's not going to get better either.'

'Soon be over. Then you'll be off to college or university.'

Trisha sighed. 'Don't start, Mum.'

'I'm not starting. It's just that an education's important. You know that.'

'You left school at fifteen and you did all right.'

Sam laughed and put down her slice of pizza. 'Oh, Trisha, come on. I've been a kept woman for almost a quarter of a century. That's hardly an achievement.'

'You're a wife and mother. You brought up three kids. You made a home.'

'And that's what you want to be? A housewife?'

Trisha grimaced. 'No bloody way. But I'm just saying there are options, that's all.'

'That's exactly what college will give you. Options. And don't swear.'

'Bloody isn't swearing, Mum.'

Sam arched an eyebrow and Trisha threw up her hands. 'Fine, I won't express myself.' She stood up. 'I've got homework. Don't stay up too late, you need your beauty sleep.'

'Thank you very much,' laughed Sam.

After Trisha had gone upstairs, Sam opened a bottle of white wine and sat on a sofa in the sitting room with an old Eagles CD playing on the stereo as she read through the file that Patterson had given her. The financial details didn't make any better reading the second time. The cheque that Warwick Locke had promised her would keep her creditors at bay for a week or so, but without a major injection of capital the whole house of cards was going to come tumbling down. The only salvation lay in the contents of Terry's safe deposit box.

Later she went upstairs and showered. As she stood in the bedroom, towelling her hair dry, she saw a flash of light through the curtains. She switched off the bedroom lights and peered through the window. A car was parked in the road outside the house. A big car.

* * *

Frank Welch popped two breath mints in his mouth and sucked on them as he stared at Sam Greene's house. Welch had been inside the house twice, both times with a search warrant. The first time, four years earlier, Welch had been gathering evidence against Terry Greene's drug-dealing empire, but the house had been clean and Welch and his team had walked away with Terry and Sam's insults ringing in their ears. The second time had been equally unfruitful – it was only when they went to the apartment where Terry was staying that they'd discovered a pair of Terry's shoes with spots of blood on them, blood that was later identified as being Preston Snow's. Not absolutely conclusively of course, but the police genetics expert gave evidence that there would have to be of the order of two hundred billion people on the planet for there to have been anyone else with the same DNA profile. That was good enough for Welch, and for the jury.

Welch cupped his hand over his mouth and exhaled, then sniffed cautiously. All he could smell was the mints. Sam's jibe at his bad breath had hit home. It had been a recurring problem since his school days. He wasn't a smoker, and it didn't seem to matter what he ate or how often he cleaned his teeth, he could see people turn away if he got too close, a look of disgust on their faces. Welch himself could never smell anything amiss, which made it all the worse because he never knew from one day to the next how serious his bad breath problem was. And he hated the taste of mint.

Welch settled back in his seat and tapped his fingers on the steering wheel. The light in the master bedroom had gone off half an hour earlier, and the daughter had switched her light off shortly afterwards. Welch knew Sam Greene had seen him: he'd deliberately flashed his hi-beams when she was in the bedroom. He wanted her to know that he was on the case, that he'd stay on the case until he'd closed down Terry Greene's entire operation. It wasn't as if Welch had anything better to do. There was no one waiting for him at home, and he'd already eaten, overcooked fish and chips in the staff canteen. All Frank Welch had planned was a few hours' sleep and an early start.

He rotated his neck, trying to ease the tension that was building up in the muscles there, then froze as he saw a figure standing by the side of his car. It was a second or two before he recognised the face. Andy McKinley, Terry Greene's former driver.

Welch wound down the window of the Rover. 'What the fuck are you doing here, McKinley? I thought you were working for George Kay.'

McKinley put a hand on the roof of the Rover and leaned down so that his head was level with Welch's. He smiled, showing slab-like teeth. 'Mrs Greene doesn't want you sitting outside her house,' he said in his broad Glaswegian accent. 'I'm sure you can relate to that, right? A woman and a girl on their own, big house. See, if this was official, you'd be twos up, so I'm guessing that this isn't official. There's a thin line between surveillance and stalking and it seems to me that you've crossed it, Chief Inspector Welch.'

Welch scowled at McKinley. 'I can do you for obstruction, McKinley. Now get the hell away from . . .'

Welch dried up as he saw the flicknife in McKinley's hand. McKinley thumbed the silver button on the handle of the knife and a six-inch-long blade snapped out.

'Don't do anything stupid, McKinley.'

McKinley looked at Welch with icy contempt, then bent down and stuck the knife into the front tyre. It hissed as McKinley pulled the knife out and retracted the blade.

'What the fuck did you do that for?' hissed Welch. 'I could arrest you for that.'

McKinley shrugged indifferently. 'So arrest me. Then we can go down to the station and talk to your boss about what you're doing sitting outside Mrs Greene's house in the middle of the night.'

* * *

The doorbell rang and Sam hurried to answer it, wrapping her silk dressing gown around her. It was Andy McKinley, wearing a large black overcoat with the collar turned up against the cold of the night. 'All sorted, Mrs Greene. He won't be bothering you again.'

'Thanks, Andy,' said Sam gratefully. 'I didn't know who else to call.'

'That's what I'm here for, Mrs Greene.' He gave a mock salute. 'Take care now, yeah?' He turned to go.

'Andy, the least I can do is give you a drink. Come on in.'

McKinley hesitated and then turned and smiled. 'Thanks, Mrs Greene. Never been known to turn down a dram.'

As Sam closed the front door and showed McKinley into the sitting room, Trisha appeared at the top of the stairs. 'Who is it?' she asked.

'It's business,' said Sam.

Trisha was only wearing a loose halter top and shorts, and Sam grinned as she saw how quickly McKinley averted his eyes. Trisha noticed, too, and she walked down a couple of stairs to get a closer look at the visitor.

'Trisha, bed!' warned Sam.

Trisha pulled a face, then went back upstairs.

'Come on, Andy, take off that coat.' McKinley put his overcoat on the back of a chair as Sam poured them both whiskies. 'You want anything in it, Andy?'

'Splash of water, Mrs Greene. Anything else would be sacrilegious.'

Sam added water to both glasses, then handed one to McKinley. She toasted him. 'Thanks, Andy. My knight in shining armour.'

'Aye, well, as my dad always used to say, once a king, always a king, but once a night is enough.' He smiled. 'You know, I was twelve years old before I realised what he meant.' He sat down in the centre of the sofa and Sam curled up in an easy chair by the fire. They sipped their whiskies. 'Thing is, Mrs Greene, Raquel's gone now, but I don't think he's going to give up. He's got a thing about you, you know?'

Sam nodded. 'Yeah. I can see it in his eyes. Like he's undressing me with them, you know?'

McKinley nodded. 'I can see how that might be,' he said and took another sip of his whisky.

Sam looked at him over the top of her glass, wondering if he was making a subtle pass at her, but then decided that he wasn't. There was an openness about McKinley that Sam instinctively liked, and she figured that if he ever were to make a pass he'd be up front and honest about it, probably go down on one knee and hand her a red rose. She smiled at the image.

'You all right, Mrs Greene? You look a million miles away.'

Sam's smile widened. 'I'm fine, Andy. Just glad you gave me your card, that's all.'

'I'm in the book, Mrs Greene. Ever you need me.'

'How do you get on with George Kay?' she asked.

McKinley shrugged but didn't answer. He looked down at the floor and Sam presumed that he didn't want to tell tales out of school.

'What do you do for him?'

McKinley shrugged again. 'Same as I did for Terry, pretty much.'

'Think you could do the same for me?'

McKinley raised his eyes and looked at her again. For the first time Sam noticed how blue his eyes were, a pale, cold blue that seemed to look right through her. 'You need protection, Mrs Greene?'

Sam ran a finger around the lip of her glass. 'Terry's asked me to take care of a few things for him. It's new territory for me, Andy. It'd be a big comfort to me to have you watching my back.'

'Mrs Greene, it'd be a pleasure,' he said. He reached over and clinked glasses with her. 'A real pleasure.'

* * *

The captain checked his position on the boat's global positioning system computer and grunted at his first mate. 'About another ten minutes,' he said in guttural Spanish. He took a small portable GPS handset from a plastic wallet and switched it on. It glowed with a faint orange light, hissed, and then figures flickered on its small screen. The captain checked that the handheld computer showed the same readout as the boat's.

The first mate tapped the radar screen. 'Nothing for miles,' he said. 'God's smiling on us.' He slipped a crucifix from under his reefer jacket and kissed it. 'I'll get the men ready.'

The first mate left the bridge and went out on to the heaving deck. His name was Lucero and he was being paid a hundred thousand dollars for the night's work. For that and for a brief trip to London.

It was a clear, cloudless night, but there was no moon and the four men huddled at the rear of the boat were little more than dark shapes as Lucero walked towards them, adapting his gait to the roll of the vessel with no more thought than a seagull gliding over the waves. Lucero was almost fifty and had been at sea since he was barely out of his teens. There wasn't a major port in the world that he hadn't visited, though his sailing days were now confined to trips from the Spanish coast to the North Sea in the fishing trawler. Not that Lucero was the least bit interested in catching fish.

There were eight plastic-wrapped bales attached to metal sleds lined up on the deck. At one end of each sled was a cylinder of compressed air connected to a plastic box. Lucero took a flashlight from his reefer jacket and knelt by the bales in turn, checking the mechanisms of each one. As he sealed the last box, the door to the bridge opened and the captain screamed over the howling wind that they were to dump the bales. Lucero slapped one of the men on the back. 'Get to it!' he shouted. The four men were also being well paid for the work, and like Lucero had done the trip many times. One by one they pushed the bales overboard and watched them disappear under the waves. Four tons of cannabis resin, consigned to the sea bed.

* * *

Trisha was checking herself in the hall mirror when Sam came downstairs. 'Are you allowed to wear that much make-up at school?' asked Sam.

'Mum, you say that every morning.' said Trisha, smoothing her eyebrows and, pursing her lips.

Sam stood behind her and put her hands on her shoulders. 'The teachers don't mind lip gloss and mascara?'

'It's not lip gloss, it's lip balm. I've got chapped lips.'

'Of course you have.'

'And my eyelashes are naturally long.'

Sam patted her daughter's shoulders. 'Of course they are. You know, in my day we weren't even allowed to show our knees at school. And hair had to be short or tied back. And we'd get sent home if there was even a hint of lipstick.'

'I know, I know, and dinosaurs roamed the earth, right?' Trisha turned and kissed Sam on the cheek. 'See you,' she said, and hurried out of the front door.

'Not if I see you first,' said Sam, heading for the kitchen.

'Oh my God!' shouted Trisha.

Sam stopped in her tracks. 'What? What is it?'

Trisha was standing on the threshold, her mouth wide open. 'Oh God, Mum, look what they've done to your car.'

Sam joined her daughter in the doorway. The words 'LYING BITCH' had been sprayed in yellow paint across the windscreen and bonnet of Sam's black Saab.

'Bastards,' said Trisha. 'It'll be that Snow family, that's who it was.'

'Maybe,' said Sam. 'I'll get it fixed.'

'Mum, you've got to call the police. You can't let them get away with that. That's vandalism, that is.'

'The police aren't our number one fans just now, Trish.'

'Mum!'

'It could have been worse, Trish. It'll come off. Go on, off to school.'

Sam closed the door and went through to the kitchen. She telephoned Andy McKinley and asked him to collect her at the house. She'd arranged to meet Laurence Patterson at ten o'clock in Kensington, outside the safe deposit box depository.

She made herself a cup of strong coffee and nibbled on a peach as she read the *Daily Mail*.

McKinley rang her doorbell at nine thirty. He was dressed in a blue blazer and black slacks with a white shirt and dark blue tie and he looked just like a holiday rep waiting to greet a planeload of tourists. He'd parked a grey Lexus behind Sam's Saab. Sam locked the front door and went over to the Lexus. 'Where did you get this from, Andy?'

'Terry left the keys with me,' said McKinley. He opened the back door for her and she slid into the plush interior. 'I thought it was more befitting your status.' He walked around to the front of the car and got into the driving seat.

Sam laughed. 'What, as a gang boss?'

McKinley eased the Lexus out of the driveway and headed for central London.

'Seatbelt, Andy,' said Sam.

'What?' McKinley frowned at her in the rear-view mirror.

'Seatbelt. I wouldn't want anything to happen to you while you were driving me.'

McKinley groaned. 'Och, Mrs Greene, seatbelts kill more people than they save.'

'I think that's airbags, Andy. And it's a spurious statistic anyway.'

McKinley groaned again and fastened his belt. 'Who do you think did that to your car, Mrs Greene?'

'One of Snow's relatives, I guess,' said Sam.

'The brother?'

'Maybe. I've been getting phone calls. And a chicken's head.'

McKinley twisted around in his seat. 'A chicken's head?'

'Don't ask. And keep your eyes on the road, Andy.'

Laurence Patterson was waiting for her outside the nondescript building that housed the depository. He was wearing a long black Burberry raincoat that flapped in the wind behind him, giving him the look of a demented crow. He waved as McKinley parked the Lexus, and rushed over to open the door for Sam. McKinley gave the solicitor a curt nod but said nothing.

'Everything okay, Samantha?' asked Patterson as he showed a plastic identification card to a uniformed security guard.

'Fine, Laurence. Considering that I'm about to embark on a life of crime.'

The security guard, a man in forties with a greying moustache, handed her a clipboard and she signed her name.

'She's joking,' Patterson told the guard.

The security guard's face remained impassive as he pressed a concealed button to open the reinforced door that led to the inner sanctum of the depository.

Sam followed Patterson along a grey-walled corridor covered by two closed-circuit television cameras, into a reception area where a young man in a grey suit checked Patterson's identification card. The man took a small key from Patterson and disappeared through a side door.

'Right, I'll leave you here, Samantha,' said Patterson.

'Aren't you staying?'

'Best not,' said Patterson. 'Terry said the contents of the box are for your eyes only.'

'You sure it's not because you don't want to get your hands dirty?' Patterson looked hurt and Sam patted him on the arm. 'Only joking, Laurence. Away you go.'

As Patterson left, the man in a grey suit returned with a large metal box which he placed in a booth. He nodded at a bell by the reception desk, and told her that when she'd finished she could ring it to have the box collected, then he left her alone.

Sam took a deep breath and opened the box. The first thing she saw was a bundle of fifty-pound notes, several inches thick. She whistled softly to herself and flicked her thumbnail along the edge of the notes. There must have been hundreds of them. More than ten thousand pounds. She put the notes in her bag and picked up a black leather Filofax. The alphabetical index section was packed with names and telephone numbers, and at the back a clear plastic pocket contained a single dollar bill, folded in half. Sam pulled it out. She tried to unfold the note and discovered that it had been torn in half. Sam frowned, wondering what its significance was. She flicked through the Filofax again and discovered a section of note-paper covered with Terry's cramped handwriting. The Filofax went into her bag with the money.

She took a large manila envelope out of the metal box. Underneath it were three passports. Sam picked them up, puzzled: the police had taken Terry's passport when they'd arrested him. Two of the passports were British and contained Terry's photograph, but not his name or date of birth. The third passport was American, and again the picture was Terry's but the details weren't. Sam put the passports back in the box and opened the manila envelope. Inside were half a dozen black and white photographs that had been taken with a long lens. They were of Terry with a man she didn't recognise, a large man with broad shoulders in a raincoat. Terry was giving the man an envelope, and in two of the photographs the man had opened the envelope and was examining a thick wad of banknotes. Sam put the photographs back in the envelope and dropped it into the box. She rang the bell and the grey-suited man reappeared and took away the box as Sam headed outside.

McKinley drove her home, then left the Lexus parked outside the house while he took the Saab away to get the graffiti removed. Sam made herself a coffee and sat at the kitchen table, reading through Terry's notes.

She was still reading when Trisha arrived home. Sam put the Filofax away and cooked a vegetarian chilli with wild rice, knowing it was one of Trisha's favourites. They sat and ate it in front of the TV, then when Trisha retreated to her bedroom to get on with her homework, Sam went back to the Filofax.

* * *

Lucero walked out of the arrivals terminal and took a courtesy bus to the airport hotel where he was booked in under an assumed name. He always pre-booked the same room, a suite on the seventh floor, and he never stayed more than twelve hours, though he always paid in cash for the full night. It was a trip he'd made half a dozen times over the past three years, and he'd never spent a minute more than necessary in the United Kingdom. It wasn't a country he particularly liked. He didn't like the climate, the food, or the people.

He opened his holdall, the only luggage he had with him, and checked that the portable GPS computer was functioning. It was. He put it back in the holdall and took out a Spanish football magazine and sat on the bed to read. He didn't bother switching on the television. English television was something else he couldn't abide.

He was halfway through the magazine when there was a knock on the door. It was the special knock, the knock he'd been waiting for. Two quick knocks, then a pause, then a single knock, then a pause, then three slow knocks. Lucero got off the bed and looked through the peephole in the door. He frowned. It was a woman. A woman in her late forties wearing sunglasses and with a headscarf tied around her head like Jackie Onassis used to wear. Like a filmstar who didn't want to be recognised. It had never been a woman before, but there was no faulting the knock.

Lucero put the security chain on and opened the door. The woman stood there, looking at him as if waiting for him to speak. Lucero stared back at her. He could see his own reflection in the lenses of her sunglasses, She groped in her handbag, and took out a half-dollar bill which she thrust at him. Lucero took it and closed the door.

He went over to his dressing table and picked up his wallet. He pulled out his Mastercard. Behind it was a piece of paper, folded several times. It was half a dollar bill. He unfolded it and placed it on the dressing table, next to the piece that the woman had given him. They matched. Lucero checked the serial numbers twice to be absolutely sure, then he picked up the holdall, opened the door and gave it to the woman. She walked away without a word and Lucero closed the door. He checked his watch. There were another four hours before his flight. Time for a drink. One of the reasons he used the hotel was because room service had bottled Spanish beer. He hated English beer.

* * *

Sam slid into the back of the Lexus and took off her headscarf and sunglasses. McKinley twisted around in his seat. 'How did it go, Mrs Greene?'

Sam forced a smile. Her hands were trembling. 'I thought I was going to pass out,' she said. 'God, I was so scared, and all I was doing was collecting a bag.' She let out a long sigh. 'But I did it! I bloody well did it!'

She opened the holdall and took out the GPS computer. 'How does this thing work, Andy?'

McKinley started the car and headed out of the hotel car park. 'Satellites,' he said.

Sam took the computer out of its plastic case and looked at it, bemused.

'It can tell its position to within a few feet anywhere in the world. If you lock in co-ordinates, you can find your way back to the exact same spot.'

'New technology,' said Sam, impressed. 'Probably Japanese, yeah?'

'American, I think. American military.'

'So the good old US of A is helping drug barons keep tabs on their gear, huh? Funny old world, innit?'

She lit a cigarette as McKinley drove to where she'd arranged to meet Reg Salmon. Salmon was an old friend of Terry's and Sam had met him socially more than a dozen times over the past five or six years. It had been a shock to discover from the Filofax that Salmon was more than just a drinking buddy of Terry's, that he was also a key player in the cannabis importation business. He was in his early fifties, an East End boy made good who lived in large detached house in Hampshire and who loved country pursuits – hunting, shooting and fishing – and even kept a couple of peregrine falcons which he'd reared from chicks. Sam had never asked her husband where Salmon's money had come from, and it was only after Terry's conviction that she realised how naïve she'd been. She'd always known that Terry and his friends sailed close to the wind, but that was to be expected considering the nature of some of his businesses – nightclubs, boxing promotion, property development. But she'd always assumed that while they might have bent the odd law, they weren't actually criminals. Now the veil had been lifted from her eyes and she realised what a fool she'd been.

McKinley brought the car to a halt. They'd stopped on a road that ran between two fields, the one on the right growing potatoes, the one to her left given over to pasture. Parked in front of them was a green Range Rover, speckled with red mud. 'Do you want me to come with you, Mrs Greene?' asked McKinley.

'No, it's all right, Andy. I won't be long. I just wish I'd brought my wellies.'

Sam got out of the Lexus and walked along the road to a wooden gate, the only way in through a barbed wire fence. A rutted path led to a line of trees and she walked down it carrying the holdall, weaving to avoid the many muddy puddles along its length. As she came closer to the line of trees she saw the river where Salmon had said he'd be fishing, and after a couple of minutes she spotted him, sitting on a large wicker basket with a rod in his hands, staring at a luminous orange float bobbing in the water. He was wearing an old Barbour jacket and a tweed cap, his trademark small cigar clamped between his lips. He stood up and waved as he saw Sam approaching.

'Sam, great to see you,' he said. He took the cigar out of his mouth and kissed her on the cheek.

'Hello, Reg. This is a turn-up for the books, isn't it?'

Salmon had the grace to look shamefaced. He shrugged and put the cigar back between his lips. Sam held out the holdall and he took it. He knelt down and opened the holdall and slid out the GPS. He switched it on, checked that it was working, and nodded up at Sam. 'Terry always gave me . . .'

Before he could finish, Sam held out an envelope. Salmon grinned and straightened up. He weighed the envelope in his hands but didn't bother counting the cash it contained. 'Thanks, Sam. You gonna be there on the night?'

'Wouldn't miss it for the world, Reg.' She turned to go, then stopped. 'How many times have you and Terry done this?'

'A few.'

'Ever go wrong?'

Salmon put the holdall into the wicker basket. 'You can reckon on about one in four going pear-shaped,' he said, 'but the problems are usually at the Spanish end. Getting ripped off by suppliers, or the Spanish cops boarding the boat before it gets into international waters. Once the stuff's at the bottom of the sea, all we've got to do is pick it up. It's gonna be fine, Sam. Don't worry.'

'Cheers, Reg.'

'How's Terry getting on?'

Sam grimaced. 'Seems to be okay.'

'He's gonna appeal, yeah?'

'Sort of.'

'Bloody liberty, the whole thing. Terry's not a killer.'

'Yeah, well, I never thought of him as a drugs baron, either. See ya, Reg. Be lucky.'

Sam walked back along the path to the Lexus. McKinley got out and opened the door for her. Sam smiled her thanks and checked her watch as she got into the car. 'We're going to have to get a move on, Andy. I've got to be at the prison by two.'

'We'll make it, Mrs Greene,' said McKinley, getting into the front seat and driving off.

'Seatbelt, Andy,' said Sam, lighting a cigarette.

* * *

McKinley pulled up outside the prison. Sam took a deep breath. She hated going inside, hated the smell, the noise, the people. 'I don't know how long I'll be, Andy.'

'Take all the time you want, Mrs Greene,' said McKinley. 'Give Mr Greene my regards.'

Sam got out of the Lexus and walked to the small metal door at the side of the large doors that allowed access to vehicles. She had to show the letter authorising her visit, and her passport as identification, and sign against her name on a list attached to a clipboard. She was given a small plastic badge with 'Visitor' on it to attach to her jacket.

She was shown into a waiting room where twenty or so people, mainly women, were sitting on orange plastic chairs. Sam didn't sit down. She reached into her bag for her pack of cigarettes, but then saw a large 'No Smoking' sign and a picture of a cigarette with a thick red line through it just in case she couldn't read English.

Another ten people wandered into the waiting room over the next twenty minutes, then they were taken as a group across a courtyard to the visiting room. A sniffer dog, a small black and white Collie with a hyperactive tail, ran back and forth between the visitors. The dog jumped up against a large black woman and started barking furiously at her bag. Two prison officers took an arm each and virtually frogmarched her away despite her protests. The dog followed, yelping happily.

Before they were admitted to the block containing the visiting area, their names were checked against another list and their belongings were searched by two female officers wearing rubber gloves. Sam waited patiently, though she desperately craved a cigarette.

When she reached the head of the queue, a bored prison officer asked her for her letter, then looked for her name on his list. He shook his head and tapped his pen against his thin lips.

'Don't see you on my list, Mrs Grey.'

'It's Greene,' said Sam. 'Like the colour. With an e.'

'Grey's a colour.'

He looked at her blankly and Sam couldn't tell whether he was being deliberately obtuse, or just stupid. Bearing in mind the prison officers she'd met on previous visits, she was quite prepared to believe the latter. 'I know grey's a colour, but my name is Greene,' she said patiently.

He handed the letter back to her. 'You're not on my list.'

'Well, I was on the list at the main entrance.'

'They have a different list.'

Sam waved the letter under his nose. 'What about this? It's written on prison letterhead, right? It says I have permission to visit, right? With today's date on it, right?'

The prison officer stared at her with total disinterest. 'You're not on my list,' he repeated.

A few of the visitors behind Sam started shouting for them to hurry up. Another uniformed prison officer walked over, his shoes squeaking as if they were new. He had a weasely face and was a good four inches shorter than his colleague.

'What seems to be the problem, Mr Bradshaw?' he asked.

'This woman's not on my list, Mr Riggs.'

Riggs took the clipboard and ran his finger down it. 'He's right.'

'How do you know he's right?' hissed Sam. 'You don't even know who I am.'

Riggs looked at her through narrowed eyes. 'You don't do

yourself justice, Mrs Greene. Your husband's quite the celebrity here.'

'So that's what this is about, is it? Getting back at Terry by giving me a hard time?'

Riggs smiled, showing uneven teeth. 'Come on now, Mrs Greene, we'd hardly be as petty as that, would we?' He showed her the clipboard. 'You can see for yourself.'

'I don't care what your list says. I've got a letter confirming today's visit and I'm damn well going to see my husband.'

There were more catcalls from behind her but Sam barely heard them, all her attention focused on the man who was denying her access to her husband.

'I could amend the list, of course,' said Riggs, barely managing to suppress a grin, 'but there's a procedure to go through first.'

'A procedure?'

He nodded over at a woman prison officer standing by a door marked 'Examination Room' and shrugged. 'Drugs are a big problem inside the prison system. Well, of course, you'd know that, being married to a drugs baron.'

'You have got to be joking.'

The smile vanished from Riggs' face. 'It's up to you, Mrs Greene. No search, no amended list, no visit.'

Sam swallowed. She wanted to scream at the man, to slap his self-satisfied face, but she knew that there was no way of fighting the system and winning. She forced herself to smile. 'Sure, why not,' she said.

Riggs took her over to the examination room door and the woman prison officer took her inside. There was an examination table covered with a sheet of white paper, a small sink with a wastepaper bin underneath it and a medicine cabinet. On the back of the door was a poster warning of the dangers of Aids.

The woman prison officer used a wooden spatula to check the inside of Sam's mouth. 'Stick out your tongue, please.' Sam did as she was asked. The woman checked around Sam's tongue and then nodded. 'Okay, now take off your clothes.'

'I suppose you get some kick out of this,' said Sam as she took off her jacket.

The woman prison officer snapped on a pair of rubber gloves. 'Oh yes, this is exactly what I told my careers officer I wanted to do with my life.'

'Do I look like I'd been carrying drugs inside my . . . inside myself?'

'You wouldn't believe who brings what in here, love. Just take off your skirt and pants, lie back and think of England. I won't be doing anything your gynaecologist hasn't done a hundred times before.'

Sam sensed that the woman wasn't part of the plan to make her life difficult, she was just doing what Riggs had told her to do. She took off her skirt and pants and climbed up on to the table and spread her legs. The woman prison officer inserted a gloved finger between Sam's legs and probed around.

'If you're looking for my g-spot, it's about another inch in,' said Sam.

The woman police officer chuckled. 'You've no idea how many times I've heard that one,' she said. She withdrew her finger.

'Are we done?'

'Just one more check.'

Sam tensed as she realised what the woman meant. 'Oh no. Come on.'

'I'm just following the rules, love. Believe me, I get no more pleasure out of this than you do. Close your eyes, it'll be over before you know it.'

Sam gritted her teeth and the woman inserted a finger inside her rectum, probed once, and then slid it out.

'All done,' she said. 'There's paper towels by the sink.'

'Thanks,' said Sam, fighting back tears of embarrassment and rage. 'Thanks a million.'

Terry was sitting at the same corner table he'd been at the

last time she visited. He stood up as he saw her walking across the visiting room. 'Hello, love,' he said and tried to give her a kiss on the cheek.

Sam pushed him away and sat down, crossing her legs away from him.

'What's wrong?'

Sam glowered at him. 'They fucking strip searched me, Terry.'

'Oh God. I'm sorry.'

'Pushed and probed me like I was a piece of meat. What's going on?'

Terry reached over and took her hand. 'Are you okay?'

Sam pulled her hand away. She didn't want Terry touching her. She didn't want anyone touching her, ever again. 'No. I'm not okay. I'm so far from okay that you'd need a fucking map to find it from where I am.'

To her left was an old couple, the man in his seventies in ill-fitting prison denims and a red vest that was several times too big for him. He had lined parchment skin and deep-set eyes that made his head look more like a gleaming skull. His wife was probably in her mid-sixties, about twice his size, plump and matronly, wearing a big woollen coat and a hat with a huge brown plastic handbag that she clutched in her lap with both hands. Sam could see that her fingernails were bitten to the quick. They sat in silence, occasionally looking at each other and smiling. Sam wondered if that was what lay ahead of her and her husband. Years of visits until there was nothing left to say, just a shared silence and single beds. She shivered.

'Are you cold?' asked Terry.

Sam shook her head.

Terry leaned forward, the concern clear on his face. 'There's a guy in here got it in for me, love. Guy called Riggs.'

'Chief Prison Officer? Yeah, he was there. Said my name wasn't on the list. Bastard.'

'I'm sorry.'

'Will you stop saying "sorry", Terry, it doesn't make me

feel any better.' She looked around the visiting room. At the far end a prisoner barely out of his teens was sobbing while his girlfriend or wife sat back in her chair, arms crossed defensively, a frown on her face. Children were running around and playing, while prison officers walked up and down, eyes forever on the move, looking for contraband. 'Christ, I wish I was a million miles away from here.'

'You and me both, love.'

Riggs walked into the room and sat at a table by the door, glaring at Terry. Terry smiled broadly and gave him a small wave. 'I'll fucking have you when I get out of here,' he said under his breath, still smiling.

Sam turned to see who he was looking at. When she saw that it was Riggs, she turned and scowled at Terry. 'Will you stop winning friends and influencing people? It's no wonder they're giving you a hard time.'

Terry raised his hands in surrender and settled back in his plastic chair.

'And don't say "sorry" again, Terry. All right?'

'All right.'

They sat in silence for a while, then Terry leaned forward. 'Everything's fixed up, yeah?'

Sam gave Terry a long, hard look. 'You're a bastard, Terry Greene.'

'Love . . .'

'Don't "love" me. Getting me to do your dirty work.' She shook her head, trying to clear her thoughts. 'The stuff was dropped off as arranged. I picked up the GPS gizmo from the hotel and gave it to Reg Salmon. I'm meeting Kay and the rest tomorrow.'

'Be careful with them, yeah? You've got to show them who's boss.'

'But I'm not their boss, Terry. I'm a wife and mother, not a bloody gang leader.'

'You mustn't show weakness, love. They'll turn on you.'

Sam sighed and nodded. 'Okay. I'll be okay.' She put a hand up to her forehead. 'I can't believe you've got me doing this for you.'

'Who else could I trust?'

'I'm not doing the counterfeit thing, Terry. I'll do this for you, but that's it.' Terry tried to hold her hand but she pulled it away. 'I mean it.'

'I know you do.' He put his hands on the table and interlinked his fingers. 'Andy McKinley's taking care of you, yeah?'

Sam nodded. 'He's a good guy.'

'Yeah. He's solid. None too bright, though.'

'Kay said that. Andy's not stupid, Terry. If anyone's stupid, it's me.'

Terry smiled and shook his head.

'Has Laura been to see you?'

'Not yet. I sent a request form. Takes time.'

A small boy fell at Sam's feet and she bent down and picked him up. He twisted out of her grip and ran back to his mother, crying.

'Remember how Laura was always trying to run before she could walk?' said Terry. 'Always falling over. But never cried. Tough kid.'

'Toughness isn't always a virtue, Terry.'

Sam watched as the mother picked up the boy and cradled him against her, whispering into his ear as her prisoner husband looked on anxiously. She turned back to look at Terry. 'Did you do it, Terry?'

Terry held her look. Then he slowly shook his head. His eyes never left hers. 'No,' he said. 'No, love, I didn't.'

She stared back at him, trying to see the answer in his eyes. Finally she shook her head, admitting defeat. 'I used to know when you were lying. You'd come back at all hours and tell me it was business kept you out, and I knew. I knew Terry Greene, knew you'd been out with one of your slappers because I could see it in your eyes. But this. I just don't know.

Why is that, Terry? Have you got better at telling lies, is that it? Better at covering your tracks.'

Terry hunched forward over the table. 'Find that slag Morrison, love. Find him and get him to tell you the truth.'

'He told the court, Terry. He told them everything. He said he saw you leaving Snow's house with a gun.'

'He was lying, love,' said Terry earnestly. 'On my mother's life.'

'Why would he lie, Terry?'

'Raquel must have put him up to it. Paid him. Offered him a deal on something else.'

'Terry . . .'

'You know what coppers are like. He was desperate to fit me up. Getting Morrison to roll over on me wouldn't have been much of a challenge. Now the trial's over, he might tell you what really happened. He might even know who really killed Snow.'

'So how do I find Morrison?' asked Sam.

Terry looked around as if he feared being overheard. Riggs was looking in their direction but he was too far away to eavesdrop. Terry put his hand up over his mouth as he talked. 'There's a cop on the payroll. Has been since the year dot. His name's Mark Blackstock. Detective Superintendent. His mobile's in the Filofax under Blackie. If he gives you any trouble, there's some pictures in the safe deposit box that'll gee him up.'

Sam shook her head in amazement. 'Bent coppers?' she said. 'Now you want me to deal with bent coppers?' Sam sat back in her chair, stunned. 'This is going from bad to worse.'

* * *

Luke Snow was in the back of a dark green Jaguar, sucking up dirt with an industrial Hoover, when he felt a tap on his shoulder. He turned around and saw a large man in a dark overcoat peering through the open door. 'Luke Snow?'

'Who wants to know?'

'I do, Luke. Now don't piss me about. Get out of the car, yeah?'

Luke found it difficult to understand the man's accent, but he sensed the menace in the man's voice.

The man stood back as Luke clambered out of the car and switched off the Hoover. 'What do you want?' He tried to sound confident, but he could see that the man was a good six inches taller than he was, and looked like he worked out. The man had a hard face, and cold blue eyes that stared unblinkingly at Luke. Luke found it difficult to meet the man's gaze and he kept looking away.

'My name's McKinley,' said the man. 'Just so you know who I am. I don't hide behind anonymous phone calls, Luke. I am who I am, right?'

'So?'

'So your brother was a scumbag. He sold drugs to kids. You wouldn't have caught *him* in overalls cleaning out the back of a rich man's car.'

'He didn't deserve to die like a dog.'

McKinley nodded. 'I understand that, Luke. I can see why you'd feel the way you do. But that's got to be between you and Terry Greene. Between men. Do you get my drift?'

Luke said nothing. McKinley's eyes continued to bore into him and Luke looked down. 'She lied, man. She fucking lied.'

'Everyone lies, Luke.'

'She lied in court.'

'So she won't go to heaven. You married, Luke?'

Luke narrowed his eyes, wondering if the big man was threatening his family. 'Yeah,' he said hesitantly.

'You love her, right? Your missus?'

Luke nodded again.

'You'd lie for her, right? Of course you would. Wouldn't matter if it was right or wrong, you do what you have to do to protect the ones you love. Look, your brother's dead and I can imagine how that must feel, but Terry Greene's behind bars for it. He's gonna be seventy before he gets out. You, you're a young guy, you've got a wife to go home to. Someone warm to sleep with at night. Be a man, Luke. If you want to take your grief out on someone, take it out on Terry Greene. Or me. But don't go frightening women. Okay?'

Luke raised his eyes and met McKinley's gaze for about the first time since he'd come into the cleaning bay. He stared at him for several seconds. McKinley stared back, totally relaxed, as if he didn't care one way or the other what Luke said. McKinley's physical superiority was intimidating, but there was something above and beyond that which made Luke Snow hesitate and think about what he'd said. McKinley was right. It had been wrong to take out his anger on Greene's wife and he suddenly felt ashamed. 'Yeah. Okay.' He nodded. 'It's over, yeah.'

McKinley nodded, satisfied. 'I appreciate that, Luke. I really do.' He turned to go, then stopped. 'Answer me one thing, Luke.'

'What?'

'That business with the chicken head? What was that, voodoo?'

Luke shook his head, puzzled. 'Voodoo? Give me a break, man. I'm from Brixton, not Haiti.'

'So why the chicken head?'

'Just wanted to gross her out.'

McKinley walked off chuckling, leaving Luke still shaking his head in bewilderment.

* * *

Sam Greene opened the front door within seconds of McKinley ringing the doorbell. She was dressed in a pale blue suit, the skirt just above the knee, and was carrying a large burgundy briefcase. McKinley reached out a hand for the case but Sam shook her head. 'I'm a big girl, Andy, I can carry my own case.'

'Fine by me, Mrs Greene.'

He opened the rear door of the Lexus for her and climbed into the front seat. He could feel her eyes on the back of his head, so he fastened the seatbelt before she had a chance to remind him. He glanced in the rear-view mirror and caught her smiling to herself.

McKinley kept checking in the mirror as he drove to Lapland. Sam was staring out of the window, deep in thought, the briefcase on her knees. It can't have been easy for her, thought McKinley. Terry Greene had a right cheek expecting his wife to start running things for him while he was inside. It was devotion above and beyond, especially when they'd been separated for more than a year. McKinley didn't think many wives would have been prepared to do what Sam Greene was doing. And if things went wrong, if Terry's carefully orchestrated plans fell apart, then there was a good chance that she would end up in prison, too.

She lit a cigarette and wound down the window halfway, the slipstream tugging at her hair. McKinley wanted to reassure her, to tell her that she was doing just fine, but he knew that it wasn't his place. He was just muscle, a hired hand, and besides, words of encouragement might sound patronising and he didn't want to run the risk of offending her.

Sam smoked three cigarettes during the drive, and didn't say a single word. McKinley parked at the back of the club in between a brand new BMW and a red Porsche. In all a dozen luxury cars were lined up behind the club, and at the rear entrance a group of large men in long coats were huddled, several of whom recognised McKinley and acknowledged him with offhand nods. One of them, whom McKinley didn't recognise, made a comment about Sam's short skirt. McKinley stopped and gave him a hard stare, but Sam carried on walking as if she hadn't heard. The man shrugged apologetically and McKinley let it go, but he made a conscious effort to imprint the man's face on his memory as he walked past him. There'd be another time.

'Sorry about that, Mrs Greene,' he said as he caught up with Sam. 'They're not usually hired for their table manners.'

'Andy, at my age I'll take compliments wherever I get them,' she said.

'Och, Mrs Greene . . .' protested McKinley. He pushed open the door to the club and followed her inside.

There were still three hours to go before the club was due to open, but the twelve men sitting around the bar weren't there to see girls dancing naked around silver poles. They turned as one to look at Sam as her high heels clicked across the dance floor. George Kay was in the middle of the group and he gave Sam a beaming smile.

McKinley watched impassively at the side of the club, his arms folded across his chest.

Sam waited until she had their full attention, then she swung the briefcase up on to the bar. 'Thank you all for coming, gentlemen. I know you've all been a bit disconcerted by Terry's sudden removal from the scene, but I'm here to reassure you that it's business as usual.'

There were mutterings from some of the men, but George Kay shushed them. 'Give the girl a chance,' he said.

His tone was patronising and Sam hated him for that, but at least the men went quiet and let her speak. 'Terry's asked me to take care of the delivery you're expecting,' continued Sam. 'That you've paid for.'

There were more mutterings and Sam held up a hand to quieten them.

'I know you'd rather have Terry in the driving seat, and I'm sure he'd have preferred to be here himself, but what's done is done. Tomorrow night everything goes ahead exactly as planned. Exactly as Terry planned.'

'Amateur hour,' whispered a thickset man with a mane of greying hair. He had his thumbs stuck into the waistband of his trousers and his belly thrust out in front of him. His name was Micky Fox and Sam had met him a few years earlier at a boxing match that Terry had been promoting.

'Well, Micky, I'll be sure to pass on your reservations to Terry.'

'Nothing personal, love, but I've a lot of money tied up in this.'

There were more mutterings from the group and a chorus of 'Yeah, me too.'

Sam nodded and held up her hands to calm then. 'Okay, okay,' she said, and gradually they fell silent again. 'Look, lads, no one here's got more at stake than me. Most of your cash is due on delivery, right? You've put a percentage on deposit, but the lion's share is still to come?'

Micky Fox nodded. So did the men around him.

Sam put her hand on the briefcase and tapped it with her blood-red nails. 'Anyone who wants out can say so now. I'll give you your deposit back and you can be on your way. I've got buyers lining up for the stuff.'

Micky Fox frowned. He looked across at George Kay and Kay shrugged. The other men looked equally confused.

'Well, Micky?'

'No need to be hasty, Sam. The stuff's on its way?'

'It just needs collecting. Reg Salmon's doing the business, but if you want to supply some of the manpower, you're more than welcome. You all are.'

Fox looked at the men around him. Several were nodding. Fox looked at Sam and grinned. 'What the hell, go for it, Sam!' he said. The men cheered and pumped their fists in the air.

Sam grinned over at McKinley and he smiled at her.

McKinley escorted Sam back to the Lexus. On the way she handed him the briefcase. 'You'd better take care of this from now on, Andy,' she said.

It was heavy. 'How much have you got in here, Mrs Greene?' asked McKinley as he dropped the briefcase in the boot.

'Two *Yellow Pages* and a stack of last year's *Vogue*,' said Sam, climbing into the back of the car.

McKinley grinned at her. 'Mrs Greene, you are a class act,' he said. He got into the front seat. 'Where to?'

'Trafalgar Square. I'm meeting that cop of Terry's.'

McKinley drove out of the car park and on to the main road and accelerated. 'Which one?'

'How many are there?' asked Sam.

'That's a good question.'

'And that's not much of an answer, Andy. Seatbelt.'

McKinley groaned and put on his seatbelt, annoyed at himself for being caught out again.

'Blackstock, his name is. Mark Blackstock.'

'Ah, Blackie. He's a chief super. One of the old school. Tough, no nonsense, and as bent as a nine-bob note.'

* * *

Sam sat at the front of the top deck of the tour bus. Behind her were half a dozen Japanese tourists, a German couple and a French family. They all wore headphones and looked around as the recorded commentary in their own language described the sights of Trafalgar Square. The bus had been Blackie's idea for a meeting place and Sam could see the sense of it. Hardly anyone on board the open-topped bus spoke English, there'd be no one who'd recognise either of them, and they'd be too busy listening to the recorded commentaries to overhear what was being said.

Blackie climbed on to the bus just before it crossed the Thames close to the Houses of Parliament. He was a big man, bigger even than Andy McKinley, and Sam had to squeeze herself to the side to give him enough room to sit down. He had close-cropped hair and a square face with thin lips that looked as if they rarely formed a smile. There were deep frown lines across his forehead and his fingernails were bitten to the quick.

'Thought you'd be sick of sightseeing by now,' said Sam. 'Eighteen years on the Met.'

Blackie scowled at her. 'Terry had no right to give you my name. No bloody right. And you can tell him that from me.'

'I'll be sure to do that,' said Sam, smiling sweetly. 'You remember the grass that gave evidence against him? Morrison? Ricky Morrison?'

'So?'

'So Terry would be ever so grateful if you'd find out where he is.' She paused for effect with a hand lightly touching her forehead as if trying to dredge up a long-forgotten memory. 'Actually, no, that's not how he put it. His exact words were "tell that wanker Blackstock to pull his finger out and get on the case." Something like that.'

All the tourists on the bus peered to the right as they drove by Lambeth Palace. Blackie shook his head and grimaced. 'Have you any idea how dangerous that's going to be?'

Sam patted him lightly on the shoulder. 'Compared to, say, fifteen years of taking bribes and kickbacks from my dear husband?'

Blackie looked like he was close to exploding. His face was red and eyes were wide and his breath came in short wheezy gasps.

Sam smiled. 'Come on, Blackie, let's not get off on the wrong foot here, hey? Terry just needs a bit of help, that's all. He's not asking you to do anything you haven't done a hundred times before.'

Blackie relaxed a little and settled back in his seat. Behind him there was a flurry of camera clicks but Sam and Blackie stared straight ahead as the bus drove alongside the Thames.

'What does he want?' asked Blackie eventually.

'He wants me to speak to Morrison. To get the truth from him.'

'The murder guys did that. He told them everything and repeated it in court. It's not like they had to strap electrodes to his balls. The way I hear it, they couldn't shut him up.'

'I just want to talk to him. That's all.'

'There's not just the witness, though. There's the forensic, too. The blood on Terry's shoes. The footprint on the dead man's carpet.'

'Terry says that Raquel stitched him up. First we discredit Morrison, then we'll see if we can show that he faked the forensic.'

Blackie shook his head in disbelief. 'For fuck's sake, Sam, this isn't an episode of *Murder She Wrote*. There were two dozen cops on that investigation, thousands of man hours. You're not going to overturn his conviction by a bit of do-it-yourself snooping.'

'It's no skin off your nose, though, is it, Blackie? All I need is an address for Ricky Morrison. Then you're free and clear.'

Blackie stood up and leaned over her. 'I'll see what I can do. Okay?'

'Can't say fairer than that,' said Sam.

Blackie went downstairs and got off at the next stop, close to Waterloo Station, and Sam settled back for the return trip to Trafalgar Square where McKinley was waiting for her. She needed time to think.

* * *

Sam sat on the sofa and lit a cigarette. She looked across at the bottle of White Horse whisky on the sideboard. She really wanted a stiff drink, but in view of what lay ahead, she figured she'd need a clear head. Her hand trembled slightly as she tapped the cigarette on the edge of an ashtray. The Filofax lay on the coffee table and she reached out for it, then pulled back her hand. There was nothing within its covers that she hadn't read a dozen times already. Terry had thought of everything, covered every eventuality. All she had to do was to follow his instructions and all their financial problems would be over.

She lay back on the sofa and blew smoke up at the ceiling. There'd be enough money to pay off the mortgage, Jamie's university fees and Grace's nursing home bills, and Patterson would have the funds to start the investigation into Terry's conviction. All she had to do was to bring four tons of cannabis ashore.

'Easy peasy,' she muttered to herself. She sat up as she heard a car pull up outside and was already halfway down the hall when Andy McKinley rang the doorbell. Sam heard Trisha moving around on the landing upstairs.

She opened the door. McKinley was wearing a thigh-length dark grey woollen coat and black leather gloves. 'It's a cold night, Mrs Greene, I'd wrap up warm if I were you.'

'I'll be with you in a minute, Andy. Thanks.'

Sam closed the door and went upstairs. Trisha's bedroom door was shut. Sam knocked on it. There was no answer.

'Trish?'

'What?'

Sam pushed open the door. Trisha was lying across her bed face down, reading a book that she'd placed on the floor.

'That'll ruin your eyes,' said Sam.

'You came all the way upstairs to tell me that?'

Sam sat down on the edge of the bed and stroked Trisha's long blonde hair. 'You've got beautiful hair,' she said.

'Where are you going?' asked Trisha, her voice loaded with resentment.

'Out.'

'Where?'

Sam smiled and played with Trisha's hair. 'Last time I looked in the mirror I was the mother.'

'Are you going out with him.'

'Who?'

'You know who. Him with the Lexus.'

'Actually, it's your dad's Lexus.'

'Actually, I don't give a shit.' Trisha rolled off the bed and went to sit in front of her dressing table.

'Hey, language!'

Trisha glared at her mother in the mirror. 'God, Mum, everyone says shit. I could have said—'

Sam silenced her with a warning finger. 'Watch your mouth, young lady. I'm warning you.'

Trisha held Sam's look for a couple of seconds, then looked away. She picked up a brush and started to comb her hair with long, slow strokes.

Sam rubbed her cheek. She didn't want to fight with Trisha, but she didn't have time to make it right. 'I'm going out for a while. Probably won't be back until late.'

Trisha whirled around as if she'd been stung. 'How late?'

'I don't know.'

'When *I* say I don't know, you hit the roof.'

'Which brings me back to my point about me being the mother and you being the dutiful daughter.' She took a deep breath, forcing herself not to raise her voice. 'Look, Trish, I might be all night.'

Trisha's upper lip curled back in a sneer. 'Slut!'

Sam felt as if she'd been slapped across the face. 'Trish, it's business.'

Trisha turned her back on Sam and started brushing her hair again.

'Trish . . .' implored Sam, but her daughter stared resolutely into the mirror. Sam looked at her watch. She was running late. 'Look, I've been getting some nasty phone calls over the past few days. If the phone rings . . .'

'What, I can't answer the phone now?'

'I'm just saying, if you get any hassle, leave the phone off the hook.'

'I'm not a child, Mum.'

'I know.'

'And if you need anything, there's someone sitting in a car outside. He's got a mobile and I've left the number by the answering machine. Okay?'

Sam hadn't liked the idea of leaving Trisha alone in the house, but when she'd suggested a baby-sitter, Trisha had refused point blank. They'd agreed on a compromise, a colleague of McKinley's from Lapland had agreed to park outside the house and keep an eye on Trisha.

'You're getting as bad as Dad,' said Trisha.

'It's not that. It's just that your dad's got enemies, people who'd like to get back at him.' Sam put a hand on Trisha's shoulder but Trisha shook her off.

'Has he got a gun?'

'Who?'

'This guy who's sitting outside the house.'

'Of course not.' Sam looked at her watch. 'I'm sorry, love, I've got to go. Be good.' She stood up, kissed Trisha on the top of her head and walked out, closing the door carefully behind her.

McKinley had the engine running and the heater on. 'All right, Mrs Greene?'

'Fine Andy.' She was wearing a dark blue padded jacket that she'd last worn on a skiing holiday in Austria with Terry. It seemed like a lifetime ago.

'Settle back, it's a long drive.'

McKinley nodded at a man sitting at the wheel of an Isuzu Trooper as they edged out onto the road. The man nodded back.

McKinley meant what he said. They headed up north, and even though the motorway was relatively clear he stuck religiously to the speed limit. The last thing they needed was a speeding ticket, a written record of where they were.

He drove up as far as Newcastle then cut eastwards towards the Northumberland coast. Sam dozed in the back until the roads began to twist and turn. The headlights of the Lexus picked out a sign and the name of a village. Alnmouth. McKinley turned left before they reached the village and in the distance Sam saw the rippling ocean nudging against the blackness of the night sky.

'Not far now, Mrs Greene.'

Sam peered out through a side window. There was the

merest sliver of a new moon, just enough to silver the edges of the waves. 'Andy. Change of plan.'

'What's wrong, Mrs Greene?'

'Nothing's wrong. I just don't want to be on the beach when the stuff comes ashore.'

'I'm not sure if that's a good idea, Mrs Greene. Terry always said it was best to be on the spot. Inspires confidence, he said. And there was less chance of the hired help ripping him off.'

'That's as maybe, but I'm not Terry. Find me somewhere where we can overlook the beach, but not be seen. Okay?'

'Whatever you say, Mrs Greene.'

Sam could sense that McKinley was disappointed that she hadn't taken his advice, but she couldn't explain why she'd had a change of heart. She'd had a sudden feeling of impending doom, and the only way of explaining it to was to say it was women's intuition. Somehow she didn't think McKinley would take her seriously.

McKinley drove along the coast for about half a mile, then turned westwards and drove up a hill before turning off on to a rutted track that was clearly only used by farm vehicles. He stopped in front of a five-bar wooden gate and switched off the headlights before getting out of the Lexus and opening it.

He drove carefully into the field and parked close to a stunted tree. Down below they could see a strip of beach.

'That's it?' asked Sam.

'Any moment now,' said McKinley, checking the dashboard clock. 'You can set your watch by Reg.'

Sam settled back in the seat. She lit a cigarette but couldn't wind down the window because McKinley had switched the engine off.

'You don't mind the smoke, do you, Andy?' she asked.

'Nah, not at all, Mrs Greene. My mum used to smoke forty a day. I think I can remember her smoking while she breastfed me, but I guess that could be one of those false memories.'

Sam bit down on her bottom lip to stop herself laughing

out loud. She inhaled smoke and blew it out slowly, enjoying the warmth of it as it flowed through her lungs.

'Who chose the place?' she asked.

'Terry. We used to spend hours driving up and down the coast, from Dover all the way up to Scotland practically.'

'That'd explain the nights he was away, I suppose.'

Sam caught McKinley looking at her in the rear-view mirror.

'Only joking, Andy.' She took another long pull on her cigarette and exhaled thoughtfully. 'The night Preston Snow was killed, Terry wasn't with you, was he?'

McKinley shook his head.

'Why not?'

'Said he had something to do on his own.'

'And he didn't say what?'

Another shake of his head.

'You know what he told me he was doing?'

'No, Mrs Greene. I don't.' It sounded from McKinley's tone as if he didn't want to know, either.

'You know he asked me to lie for him, to give him an alibi? Said there wasn't anyone else he could trust to come through for him.'

McKinley didn't answer.

'He said he was doing some work for some Irish guys. Money laundering. He was taking cash for them and running it through the clubs, returning it to them clean, paying them for goods and services never received, that sort of thing. He said that on the night Snow was shot, he was in Kilburn, picking up cash.'

'We'd be talking paramilitaries, do you think?'

'That's what he said, Andy.'

'Dangerous people.'

'Terry said that, too. Said they'd told him that if he told the police where he was, what he was doing, they'd terminate his contract. With prejudice. Which means that Terry couldn't give the police an alibi for that night. So I lied for him.' She blew smoke and sighed. 'Not that it did him any good, at the end of the day.'

McKinley jerked his thumb towards the beach down below. 'There's Reg, now,' he said. 'Sit back and enjoy the show.'

* * *

Reg Salmon switched off the engine and climbed out of the Transit van, carrying a waterproof duffel bag under one arm. His three passengers joined him at the back of the vehicle and helped him unload the inflatable off its trailer. Three other vans with inflatable dinghies on trailers drove up and parked alongside. More men piled out. Like Salmon and his team, they were all dressed in black and they moved like clockwork. Within minutes all four dinghies were being carried towards the water.

They paddled out a hundred feet or so into the swell before starting their outboards and roaring out to sea. Salmon took the portable GPS computer from his duffel bag and switched it on. It hissed and flickered and then glowed with its orange light. He checked the readout against a compass he had strapped to his right wrist and then pointed off to his left. The man on the outboard reacted immediately and turned to the new heading, and the three other boats followed behind.

The sea became markedly rougher as they got away from shore, and the men in black held on tightly to ropes as the inflatables bucked like angry bulls. Salmon kept checking the GPS and pointing out the correct course.

By the time they reached the rendezvous point, they were almost four miles from land and the waves were as high as a man. Salmon signalled for the boats to stop and the engines were cut back to idle. Salmon made one final check on the GPS, then took a transmitter from his duffel bag. There was an extendible aerial on it and he pulled it out as far as it would go. Set into the front of the transmitter were eight switches, with a light to show when the switch was activated. The transmitter was Terry's design, built by an electronics expert in Madrid, and Salmon had used it half a dozen times without fail.

One by one he flicked the eight switches. Down below, on the sea bed, relays clicked and compressed air hissed out of steel tanks into inflatable buoys. The buoys swelled and headed for the surface, pulling the plastic-covered bales and their sleds with them.

The first buoy burst through the waves over to their left and one of the inflatables buzzed over to it. The men on board grappled it and hauled it in. A second bale bobbed up just behind Salmon's boat. Within a minute all eight had surfaced.

One by one the bales were hauled in and the buoys deflated and fastened to the sleds and thrown back overboard. Five minutes later the inflatables were heading for the shore, Salmon's eyes narrowed against the wind, the GPS and transmitter back in the waterproof duffel bag.

* * *

McKinley flipped open the glove compartment and took out a pair of binoculars. He scanned the ocean, then checked his wristwatch. Sam spotted movement out at sea and she pointed. 'Andy, over there.'

McKinley put the binoculars to his eyes and looked where she was pointing. The four inflatables were charging towards the beach, the men in black barely visible against the night sky. 'Aye, that's them, Mrs Greene.'

The inflatables surged up on to the beach and the men began unloading the bales. They hauled them towards the Transit vans, four men to each bale, and even then it was a struggle to carry them.

'Sweet as a nut,' said McKinley.

Before McKinley had finished speaking, searchlights cut through the night, picking out the men on the beach. Six

Land Rovers roared on to the beach, kicking up plumes of sand behind them, and along the coast road a dozen police cars and vans appeared, sirens wailing and blue lights flashing.

Sam slumped back in her seat. 'Shit.'

McKinley put the binoculars down. 'We were set up. They knew we were coming.'

The men in black had dropped the bales and started running, but dog handlers had released Alsatians, and policemen in overalls were already piling out of the Land Rovers. A massive searchlight beam cut down from the sky, and even up at their vantage point, Sam and McKinley could feel the vibrations of the helicopter's turbine.

McKinley twisted around in his seat. 'We should be going, Mrs Greene.'

Sam nodded. McKinley started the car and drove back across the field, slowly because he didn't want to use the lights. He nudged through the open gate and out on to the road, and only switched on his lights when he was well away from the coast.

Sam lit another cigarette.

'Where do you want to go, Mrs Greene?' asked McKinley.

'Home,' said Sam quietly. 'Home, sweet home.'

* * *

Frank Welch popped a couple of breath-freshening mints into his mouth and sucked as he watched two men in black being locked in the back of a police van.

'Great night's work, boss,' said Simpson.

'Gotta be a commendation in this for you,' said Duggan, scratching his neck. 'Minimum. This is a promotion-getter, guaranteed. How much do you think there is?'

'Four tons,' said Welch emphatically. He walked down toward the shore, the downdraft of the helicopter tugging at his hair. Simpson and Duggan followed. Two of the men in black had tried to drag one of the inflatables back into the water, and had almost made it before half a dozen police reached them. The men had put up a fight and now the police were getting their own back, laying into them with boots and truncheons as the men tried in vain to protect themselves from the blows. A dog savaged the leg of one of the men in black while the handler stood over him, laughing. The man begged the handler to call the dog off, but the handler just laughed even louder. Most of the men had given up immediately when they'd seen how many police there were on the beach, dropping their bales and standing with their hands held high over their heads.

Clarke walked over, grinning, holding a waterproof duffel bag. 'Reg Salmon's in the van, boss,' he said, handing over the bag. 'We've ruined his day, I can tell you.'

'Ruined the next ten years of his life,' said Welch. He opened the bag and examined the transmitter and GPS computer.

A member of the Customs National Investigation Service walked over from the inflatables and Welch gave him the equipment.

'It's all hi tech these days, isn't it?' said the Customs officer, a stocky grey-haired man in his late forties and an old contact of Welch's. 'I remember when they used to wrap the bales in salt before they dumped them overboard. The salt would dissolve slowly, and twelve hours later they'd float to the surface. Nowadays it's all computers and satellites. They're better equipped than we are.' He hefted the transmitter in his hand. 'Okay if I keep hold of this for a while? And the GPS? Might get some clue as to who's behind it.'

'I know who's behind it,' said Welch. 'Terry fucking Greene.'

'He's banged up, isn't he?'

'Since when has that stopped them, Stuart? They use their cells like offices these days. But, yeah, keep the equipment. Doubt anyone here's going to be pleading not guilty.'

Welch gave the Customs officer the duffel bag and walked

down the beach towards the police van. Clarke hurried after him and showed Welch the van, where Salmon was sitting with his head in his hands. As Welch climbed into the van, the helicopter veered away and flew off down the coast.

Clarke attempted to follow Welch into the back of the van but Welch shook his head. Clarke backed out and closed the van door.

'Nice night for it, Reg,' said Welch cheerfully as he sat on the bench seat opposite the prisoner. 'Smooth seas, hardly any wind to speak of, the devil himself couldn't have planned it better.'

There was no reaction from Salmon.

'Third time unlucky, I'd say,' Welch continued. 'This time they'll throw away the key.' Welch leaned forward so that his mouth was only inches from Salmon's ear. 'Where is she, Reg?' he whispered conspiratorially.

Salmon said nothing, he continued to stare at the floor, his head in his hands.

'Come on, Reg. Do yourself a favour. You've got a family. Two kids, right? You'll be an old man by the time you get out. You help me and I'll pull a few strings, put in a good word for you. You'll be out in nine months.'

Salmon still didn't react. Welch slapped him across the top of the head, hard. 'Where the fuck is she?' he yelled. 'Where the fuck is Sam Greene?' He started punching Salmon in the face, but still Salmon made no sound.

Outside the van, the Customs officer and Simpson walked up to Clarke. The van was bouncing on its suspension and they could hear muffled blows as Welch laid into Salmon.

'What the hell's going on?' asked the Customs officer.

'Just questioning a suspect,' said Clarke laconically.

'Your boss doesn't seem over-thrilled about the bust.'

'That's because his date didn't turn up,' said Simpson.

'His date?'

There was a loud bang from inside the van, the sound of something – or someone – hitting the floor hard.

'The love of his life,' said Simpson.

'Yeah, unrequited love,' said Clarke. He exchanged a high-five with Simpson while the Customs officer looked at them, bemused.

Inside the van, Welch continued to lay into Salmon.

* * *

Dawn was breaking as Sam and McKinley drove down the road towards Sam's house. The Isuzu Trooper was still parked outside. The driver was pouring himself a cup of coffee from a flask and he raised it in salute as the BMW went by. McKinley turned into Sam's driveway and pulled up in front of the house. Sam rubbed her eyes and stared blearily at the front door.

'Shall I come in with you, Mrs Greene?' he asked.

'No, you go home, Andy. I'm sure you need your sleep as much as I do.'

McKinley smiled and nodded. 'Yeah, you're right. Try not to worry too much, okay?'

Sam pulled a face.

'I know, I know, things look the blackest just before the train hits you, but Reg and the boys won't say a word, you can trust me on that. They're pros. They won't drop you in it.'

'It's not just that, it's . . .' Sam left the sentence hanging. It wouldn't be fair to dump her financial worries on Andy, it wasn't his problem. She patted him on the shoulder. 'Go home, get some kip. I'll call you if I need you.'

'Thanks, Mrs Greene. Sleep well.'

As she got out of the car, McKinley yawned, showing a mouthful of perfect teeth. Sam knocked on the window. 'Come on, Andy, the least I can do is make you a coffee. You're gonna fall asleep at the wheel.'

McKinley nodded as he stifled another massive yawn. 'Aye, thanks, Mrs Greene. Wouldn't want to damage the Lexus.'

Sam fumbled in her bag for her keys, opened the front door and went down the hall to the kitchen. She stopped as she saw a teenager standing by the fridge wearing nothing but purple underpants and drinking from a bottle of milk.

'Who the hell are you?' she shouted. He spluttered and started to choke, spraying milk across the terracotta tiled floor. 'What the fuck are you doing in my kitchen?'

He bent double and coughed, and more milk peppered the tiles. 'I'm . . . I'm a . . . It's . . .' He couldn't catch his breath, and every time he tried to speak he started choking again.

'What's up, Mrs Greene?' McKinley came hurrying down the hall. 'Who's he?' he asked, as he saw the choking teenager.

Trisha came down the stairs wearing a T-shirt down to her knees, her blonde hair tousled. 'He's with me.'

'What do you mean he's with you?' snapped Sam. 'What's he doing in my kitchen?'

'I was thirsty,' gasped the boy.

McKinley took the half-empty bottle of milk from his hand and slapped him on the back, before he put it back into the fridge.

Sam glared at her daughter. 'Trisha, what's he doing here?'

'We were studying.'

Sam gestured at the boy's purple underwear. 'It looks like it.'

'He couldn't get a cab.'

'And he's lost the use of his legs, has he?'

The boy was regaining his composure. He straightened up and made a half-hearted attempt to smooth down his unruly hair. 'I'm Ken,' he said. He held out his hand to Sam, but she ignored the gesture. He offered to shake hands with McKinley, but McKinley just shook his head sadly.

'He lives miles away, Mum.'

'I just can't trust you, can I?'

Trisha narrowed her eyes. 'You were the one who stayed out all night.' She jerked a thumb at McKinley. 'With him,' she spat. She turned and ran out of the kitchen and scurried upstairs.

Ken smiled awkwardly at Sam and McKinley. 'I guess there's no use crying over it,' he said.

Sam frowned at him. 'What?'

Ken nodded at the milk. 'Spilled milk. No use crying over it.'

Sam looked at him in disgust. 'Get your clothes and get out of my house.'

Ken stood rooted to the spot like a rabbit caught in a car's headlights. It was only when McKinley took a step towards him that he finally moved, edging around Sam and then rushing into the sitting room.

Sam followed him. The boy's clothes were on a chair and there was a pillow and a sheet on one of the sofas. 'You slept here last night?' she asked him.

He nodded as he stood on one leg to pull on his jeans. Sam looked around the room. There was a pile of text books on the coffee table.

McKinley's mobile phone rang and he went out into the back garden to answer it as Sam went upstairs and knocked on Trisha's bedroom door.

'Trish?'

'Go away.'

'Trish, I just want to talk to you.' Sam pushed open the door.

Trisha was sitting on her bed, holding a hairbrush. 'This is supposed to be my room. I'm entitled to have some privacy, aren't I?'

'You're fifteen years old and I'm your mother.'

'So that means I don't have any rights, does it?'

Sam sat down on the bed next to her daughter. 'Of course you have rights. But I'm allowed to worry about you, aren't I?'

'You just assume the worst. You assumed that I slept with Ken.'

'What do you expect when I catch him in my kitchen in his Y-fronts?'

'Well we didn't have sex. He wanted to, but I said no. You should remember that you're the one who had unlawful sex. Right?'

'For God's sake, I was seventeen.'

Trisha nodded quickly. 'Which back in the dark ages was a year before it was legal. So let's not go throwing stones in glass houses, okay?'

'Trisha, I was just using that as an example of what not to do with your life. If I could turn back the clock . . .'

'What, you'd still have been a virgin when you'd met Dad? Would that have been better?'

'How did this conversation turn out to be about me? We were talking about you.'

'You accused me of sleeping with Ken. I'm just pointing out that you weren't exactly whiter than white when you were a teenager.'

'We didn't have teenagers back then. We were children one day, then suddenly we were adults.'

'And all it took was a couple of Babychams to make the transition . . .'

Sam sighed in exasperation. 'I told you that story because I thought it might help you understand the dangers,' she said. 'I didn't think you were going to throw it back in my face.'

'But you take my point?'

Sam nodded. 'Yeah. I'm sorry. I jumped to a conclusion, I should have given you the benefit of the doubt.'

Trisha smiled. 'Apology accepted.' She narrowed her eyes inquisitively. 'Where did you go?'

'It was business.' Trisha turned away and Sam put a hand on her knee. 'Really, it was.'

'Mum, what sort of business has to be done in the middle of the night?'

Sam hesitated. She didn't want to lie to her daughter, but

there was no way that she could tell her what she'd really been doing on the Northumbrian coast all night.

Trisha took the silence as an admission of guilt. 'See!' she said. 'You spent the night with him, and yet you slag me off because I let Ken sleep on the sofa. You're so hypocritical!'

'It's not that.'

'It's exactly that.' She stood up and headed for the bathroom. 'I've got to get ready for school.'

'Trisha . . .'

Trisha slammed the bathroom door, and Sam sat staring at her own reflection in the mirror on her daughter's dressing table. A number of photographs were stuck around the edge of the mirror: Trisha with Sam, with Laura and with Jamie. There were no pictures of Terry.

Sam sighed. She went downstairs just as Ken was heading down the hallway buttoning up his shirt. He opened his mouth to speak but Sam shook her head. She didn't want to hear anything he had to say. He ran past her and out of the front door, his backpack bouncing on his shoulder.

McKinley came in through the kitchen door, putting his mobile phone into his coat pocket. 'We've got a problem, Mrs Greene.'

'You can say that again, Andy,' said Sam, closing the front door.

'No. A real problem.'

'Compared with Customs seizing four tons of my husband's cannabis, this would rank how?'

* * *

McKinley parked in front of a weathered-brick warehouse not far from Paddington Station. The upper-floor windows had been whitewashed on the inside and those on the ground floor had been boarded up. It looked derelict, but outside stood three fairly new Transit vans and half a dozen cars.

McKinley got out and held the rear door open for Sam. She lit a cigarette and looked around. 'Salubrious,' she said.

'Not the sort of area where people ask a lot of questions, Mrs Greene,' said McKinley. 'Watch your step, the flagstones are a bit uneven.'

Sam followed McKinley to a delivery ramp. Grass and weeds had thrust their way up through the gaps between the concrete flagstones, several of which were broken in places. McKinley strode up the ramp and banged on the metal door at the top of the ramp. After a few seconds a voice from inside shouted, 'Who is it?'

'Who the fuck do you think it is?' McKinley shouted back. 'Now stop pissing about and open up.' He smiled apologetically at Sam. 'Excuse my French, Mrs Greene.'

The door rattled back and a stocky figure in a donkey jacket peered out.

'It's a bit late to be wary now, isn't it?' said McKinley. He turned to Sam. 'Mrs Greene, this is Kim Fletcher. He works for Terry.'

Fletcher grinned and held out his hand. 'Mrs Greene. Pleased to meet you.' Sam shook his hand. Fletcher was in his forties with greying hair and a cheerful smile marred by the fact that two of his front teeth were missing and there was blood on his lips. His left eye was almost closed and his right ear was swollen. 'Sorry about Terry and that. Should never have gone down for that, never in a month of Sundays.'

'This isn't a social call, Kim,' said McKinley. 'Mrs Greene's got a lot on at the moment, so let's get on with it, yeah?'

Fletcher nodded and ushered them inside, closing the metal door behind them.

The warehouse was piled high with metal shelving full of cases of alcohol of every description. Spirits, wines, beers, lagers. Sam wandered down an aisle, running her hand along cases of champagne. There was enough to stock a large supermarket. Several supermarkets.

McKinley came up behind her. 'This is all Terry's?' asked Sam.

'Yeah. He brings it in from the Continent and sells it on to off-licences and clubs. George Kay takes a fair whack of it, too. Terry didn't mention it?'

Sam shook her head and ground what was left of her cigarettes into the concrete floor. 'One of a million things my darling husband neglected to mention. How does it work?'

'It's a regular run, three times a week,' McKinley explained. 'Three vans, sometimes more, depending on the manpower. The booze comes over from France, we sell it in and around London. It's almost legit.'

'Almost?'

'Well, it's legit until the moment we sell it on. So long as our guys stick to the story that it's for personal consumption, there's nothing Customs can do.'

Sam smiled at the stacks of cases that almost reached the roof of the warehouse. 'Personal consumption?'

'Aye, well, you're seeing it all together. We've been stockpiling this for the last few months.'

'You keep saying "we", Andy.'

'I mean Terry. Terry's crew. Whoever's doing the driving says he's got a wedding or a birthday party or something, and that he's got a few dozen friends coming around. Customs can't touch him, he drives the stuff here, Robert's your father's brother.'

Fletcher came up behind them. 'The boys are in the office,' he said.

He led the way, down the aisle towards a plasterboard cubicle at the far end of the warehouse. Inside, three men stood around a fourth, who was sitting on a chair, his head back.

He was in his late thirties, with a mountain man's bushy hair, moustache and beard. He winced as one of the others dabbed at his face with a cloth.

'Stop your whinging, Ryser, it's just a cut,' said the man with the cloth.

'It fucking hurts,' said Ryser. His face was bruised, his lips were puffy and bleeding and he had a two-inch cut on his forehead.

'It's psychological,' said the man with the cloth.

'It fucking hurts,' Ryser insisted.

'What's going on?' Sam asked McKinley. The four men in the office looked around, surprised.

'We were robbed,' said Fletcher before McKinley could reply. 'Bloody liberty. Robbed on the open road. Don't know what this fucking country's coming to. Gave me and Steve a right seeing to.'

'There was six of them,' said Ryser. 'At least six of them. With fucking baseball bats.'

'Lads, would you mind moderating your language in the presence of a lady. This is Terry's wife.'

Ryser looked suitably chastened. 'Sorry, Mrs Greene. 'S'been a bit stressful, that's all. Steve Ryser,' he added by way of an introduction.

'Sorry, Mrs Greene,' said Fletcher. He took out a handkerchief and held it to his mouth.

'Yeah, sorry, Mrs Greene,' said the man with the cloth. He was short and balding with a small scar on his left cheek. He held out his hand, then realised that he was still holding the cloth. He tossed the cloth at Ryser. 'Roger Pike. Like the fish.'

Sam shook his hand. The other two men introduced themselves as Pete Ellis and Johnny Russell.

'Do you want to tell me what's going on?' she asked Ryser when the introductions were over.

'We came off the ferry, same as always, Mrs Greene. We got to the roundabout, then we split up as usual, the three of us taking different ways back here. Security. Terry's idea.'

McKinley made a 'hurry up' gesture with his hand and Ryser nodded earnestly.

'Okay, so we're driving along and all's well with the world, then this van pulls alongside. Blue, it was. Right, Kim?'

Fletcher nodded. 'Dark blue.'

'Okay, so there's a blonde in the passenger seat. Smile like butter wouldn't melt, right? And she's holding up a number plate. Our number plate. So I figure it must have fallen off, right? And she and her boyfriend are being good Samaritans, right? So I pull over.'

McKinley put back his head and closed his eyes, sighing in exasperation.

'Come on, Andy,' said Fletcher. 'You'd have done the same thing.'

McKinley just sighed again.

'Okay, so I stop, right?' continued Ryser. 'I get out and go to the back of our van, just to see if there's any damage. Fuck me but . . .' He grimaced as McKinley glared at him. 'Sorry, Mrs Greene. Anyway, you can imagine how surprised I was to see that the number plate is there. Just then the other van screeches to a halt and these guys in ski masks pile out with baseball bats and lay into us. It was a trap.'

'You don't say,' said Sam. She turned to McKinley. 'What did they take?'

'About ten grand's worth of booze, and the van.'

'And my wallet,' said Ryser. 'They took my wallet.'

McKinley gave Ryser a cold look, at which he looked away, mumbling and dabbing the cloth on his cut.

'Any idea who did it?' asked Sam.

'It's a competitive business, Mrs Greene,' said McKinley. 'We have run-ins with various firms from time to time, but this is something else. With Terry banged up, they reckon our doings are up for grabs. This has got be nipped in the bud before it goes any further.'

'Gardening isn't my thing,' said Sam. 'If there's any bud-nipping to do, my dear darling husband can do it.'

* * *

Terry was lying on his bed reading a copy of the Bible when Chief Prison Officer Riggs appeared at the cell door, with two prison officers behind him. 'Not getting all religious, are we, Greene?' he sneered.

'Just the bits where he tells you to go forth and multiply,' said Terry, his eyes still on the book. 'So why don't you do as God says, Mr Riggs. Go forth and multiply.'

'Very funny, Greene.' Riggs stepped into the cell and tore the Bible from Terry's hands. He handed it to one of the officers. 'Greene's reading privileges are revoked with immediate effect. For the next month.'

'That's okay, Mr Riggs. I know how it ends. The meek inherit, right? So you'll be all right.'

'Get off your bed and down to the interview room, Greene. Someone to see you.'

Terry sat up and swung his legs off the bed. 'Who is it?'

'I'm not your message service, Greene. Get your arse downstairs now.' Riggs walked away, leaving the two prison officers to escort Terry down to the ground floor and along the corridor to the interview room.

The officer on Terry's left was called Dunne, a former paratrooper who seemed to Terry to be a reasonable guy. Unlike Riggs, who took every opportunity to make his life difficult, Dunne was relaxed at his job, firm but courteous with the prisoners, though he had the size and build to react physically if needed.

'Who is it, Mr Dunne?' asked Terry out of the side of his mouth. 'Is it my brief?'

'Cops,' said Dunne.

'Terrific,' Terry muttered.

The door to the interview room was open, and two men in dark suits were waiting inside, standing with their backs to the corridor. They turned as they heard the booted footfall of the prison officers, and Terry saw that the shorter one was Welch, his companion Detective Inspector Simpson.

Welch grinned cruelly as Terry entered the room, a triumphant gleam in his eyes. Terry knew immediately that something had gone wrong with the cannabis deal and he felt a cold chill in his stomach.

'You're looking well, Terry,' said Welch. 'Prison food must be agreeing with you. Sit down.'

'I'd rather stand,' said Terry.

Welch's eyes hardened. 'Sit the fuck down, Greene.'

Terry held his stare for several seconds, then slowly pulled out one of the chairs and sat down. Welch gestured with his chin at the two prison officers and they left, closing the door behind them. Simpson went to stand with his back to the door. Terry folded his arms and waited for Welch to speak, but the detective just kept smiling, wanting to keep Terry in suspense for as long as possible. Terry yawned, loud and long.

'Reg Salmon sends his regards,' Welch said eventually.

Terry forced himself not to react. He kept a relaxed smile on his lips as he stared at a spot just behind Welch's head.

'Four tons,' said Welch slowly. 'That's got to hurt, Terry. That's got to really hurt. I tell you, my boss thinks the sun shines out of my arse.'

'Yeah, well, make sure you give whoever tipped you off his thirty pieces of silver.'

Welch tutted. 'The going rate's much more than that these days.' Welch glanced over at Simpson to check that his colleague was taking notes. 'So I can take that as an admission of guilt, can I, Greene?' said Welch.

'Since when have you cared about admissions of guilt, Raquel?'

Welch nodded thoughtfully. 'Fair point. It's always much more satisfying when they plead not guilty. Your face when the judge sent you down. It was a picture.'

'Are we done here?'

Welch sat down opposite Terry. 'How much would four tons fetch on the street, Terry? Millions. I mean, you'd have other investors, right? Spreading the risk? But a big chunk of the profits would have been coming your way, wouldn't it? Bet you were depending on that money, weren't you? The way I hear it, you've got big financial troubles. And no way to sort them out, either. Not while you're inside.' He grinned and rubbed his chin with the palm of his hand. 'Salmon's going to talk eventually. Then your name'll be in the frame and it'll be another ten years on your sentence.'

'What are you going to do, beat a confession out of him? That's your style, isn't it, Raquel? Why don't you pick on someone your own size?'

Welch leaned forward, still grinning. 'Like you, hey, Terry? Yeah, we could arrange that. Why don't you take a swing at me, here and now? Get rid of all the frustrations that are building up. You in here, the lovely Samantha out there. I guess you'll be missing a lot. Decent food, drinks with the lads, the footie. And the sex. You've got to be missing the sex. Regular sex, anyway. Sex between a man and a woman.'

Terry made a slow wanking gesture with his hand. 'As opposed to the sort you enjoy.'

Welch's eyes hardened, but he kept grinning. 'You'll be wanting to talk to Samantha, of course. Get her side of the story. Find out what went wrong.'

'Yap, yap, yap,' said Terry softly.

'Didn't think you'd be one to hide behind a woman's skirts. Getting your wife to do the dirty work.'

'Yap, yap, yap,' said Terry. 'Like a little dog bursting for a pee. Go cock your leg somewhere else.'

The grin vanished from the detective's face. 'You think you're so tough, don't you, Greene? A big man.'

'It's all relative, Raquel.'

'You're nothing, Greene. You're a fucking prisoner, slopping out like every other child molester, shoplifter and car thief in this place.'

Terry smiled easily. 'They've done away with slopping out, haven't you heard?'

'What are you now, Terry, fifty? Fifty-one? You'll be due your pension in fifteen years, and you know what? You'll still be banged up. By the time you get out you'll have a mouthful of dentures and a stainless steel hip and you'll be going to the loo half a dozen times a night.'

Terry stood up so quickly that his chair fell over backwards, the sound echoing around the room like a gunshot. Welch threw up his hands and flinched, thinking that Terry was about to attack him.

Terry smiled at Welch's display of fear. 'What do you think, Raquel, you think I'd give you a slap here with your man at the door and half a dozen screws outside waiting to drag me off to solitary?' He took a step towards the detective and Welch took a step back. 'When I slap you, it'll be outside and you'll stay slapped.'

Welch recovered his composure and pointed a warning finger at Terry. 'You threatened me.' He looked at Simpson. 'You heard him, he threatened me.'

Terry sneered at Welch, then turned his back on him. Simpson moved away from the door without a word and Terry walked out.

* * *

Later that morning McKinley drove Sam to the garage which had cleaned the graffiti off her Saab. She was pleased to see they'd done a good job, there wasn't a trace of the yellow paint. The mechanic who'd overseen the work was a small Irish guy with a limp, and he refused to let Sam pay, saying that he owed Terry a favour.

Sam told McKinley that she would go straight on to see her mother-in-law, now that she had her car back, and arranged to see him the following day. It felt good to be behind the wheel again, she realised, as she drove herself to Oakwood House. Being chauffeured around was all well and good, but Sam liked to be in control of her own destiny.

As usual, when Sam arrived Grace was sitting at the window, staring out, her hands clasped in her lap.

'Good morning, Grace,' said Sam, brightly.

Grace didn't react. On a side table was a tray with a plate of grilled fish and boiled new potatoes and a glass of orange juice.

'Grace, you haven't touched your lunch,' chided Sam. She pulled up a chair and sat opposite her mother-in-law. She picked up a fork and stabbed a piece of fish. 'This looks nice, Grace. Why don't you try some?'

Sam held the fork to Grace's mouth. Grace's lips parted and Sam pushed the fish in. Grace chewed mechanically, still looking out of the window.

'So, did you have a good night, Grace?'

There was no answer, and Sam hadn't expected one. It had been several years since Grace Greene had been able to have a sensible conversation with anybody.

'Didn't get much sleep myself, as it happens,' said Sam, putting another forkful of fish into Grace's mouth. 'Lost four tons of Terry's cannabis and came this close to getting arrested myself. Hell of a night.'

Grace smiled amiably as she looked out of the window, chewing slowly.

'See, without that deal, we're penniless, pretty much. The house, the car, this place. It's all going to have to go. Unless I carry on playing your darling boy's little games. Counterfeit money from Spain. All we've got to do is to get it into the country. What's a girl to do, Grace?'

Grace frowned. She turned to look at Sam and the frown deepened. 'Are you Laura?'

'No, Grace. Laura's my daughter. I'm Samantha.'

The door to Grace's room opened. A nurse, in a starched white uniform, was surprised to see Sam. 'Oh, hello, Mrs Greene. I was just coming for Grace's tray.'

'We're still working on it,' said Sam, showing her the fork.

'I'll come back later, then,' said the nurse. She started to leave, but hesitated and pushed the door closed. 'It's not really any of my business, Mrs Greene, but Mrs Hancock wanted to be told when you were on the premises. She said she wanted to talk to you about Grace's account.'

Sam's face fell. After the débâcle in Northumberland, she had no idea how she was going to be able to pay Grace's bills. Or any bills for that matter.

'She'll be doing her rounds in about fifty minutes. Okay?'

Sam smiled gratefully and thanked her. The nurse left and Sam continued to feed her mother-in-law.

Grace swallowed, then turned to Sam, a faraway look in her eyes. 'We had poached salmon, didn't we? Salmon in a watercress sauce.'

'That's right,' said Sam. 'We did.'

A huge smile spread across Grace's face. 'There was too much salt in the sauce,' she said. 'It was a lovely wedding, though. You and Terry looked so good together.'

'We did, didn't we? We did look good.'

Grace frowned and the blankness returned to her eyes. She tilted her head on one side and peered closely at Sam. 'Who are you?'

Sam sighed and held up a forkful of fish. 'I'm Samantha, Grace. Come on, chew your fish.'

* * *

Richard Asher was talking on his telephone headset and pacing up and down like a caged panther as the secretary showed Sam into his office. Laurence Patterson, who had been sitting on the edge of Asher's desk, came over and air-kissed Sam.

Asher said goodbye to whoever he was talking to, and took off the headset. 'Samantha, thanks for dropping by. I gather things went . . . awry.'

'You could say that, Richard,' said Sam. She sat down on one of the black sofas and lit a cigarette. Patterson hurried over with a crystal ashtray. 'They were waiting for us with open arms. They knew exactly where and when the gear was coming ashore.'

'You weren't . . . you know . . . compromised?' asked Asher.

'You mean caught red-handed? No, Richard, I wasn't. I'd hardly be here if I had been.'

A look flashed between the two men and Sam realised what it signified.

'You thought I'd come here to set you up? That I was working with the cops to cut myself a deal? Is that what you thought?'

Asher and Patterson shook their heads. 'Perish the thought,' said Patterson.

Asher went over to his desk and produced a small metal detector, the sort used by airline security people for personal checks. 'But just to put our whatsits at rest, yeah?'

'You have got to be joking,' said Sam.

'Samantha. Please,' said Asher. 'It's a formality.'

Sam sighed and stood up. She held her arms out to the side as Asher passed the metal detector over her body. 'You're not going to give me an internal, are you, Richard? Because I have to warn you, I've not had a chance to shower yet.'

Asher grimaced but didn't say anything. He finished the sweep then stood back. 'Sorry,' he said, 'but, you know, the filth have no morals these days.'

'Whatever happened to honour among thieves?' she asked them.

'Went out with AA salutes and beehive hairdos,' said Patterson. He slid open a glass door that led to a large terrace bedecked with plants. 'Let's get some fresh air, yeah?'

The terrace overlooked a large chunk of the city's financial district. There was a small fountain with water spraying from a dolphin's mouth and a white oval cast-iron table with six chairs. At one side of the patio was a small Japanese garden, its smooth rocks surrounded by perfectly raked sand, with more than a dozen bonsai trees on wooden benches. The perimeter of the terrace was lined with lush green plants connected to an automatic watering system.

In the distance Sam could see the NatWest Tower, dwarfing the rest of the City skyscrapers which clustered around it like chicks around a mother hen. She walked over to the edge of the terrace and looked out over the city. 'Hell of a view, lads,' she said.

'You get what you pay for,' said Asher, 'and this costs an arm and a leg.'

Sam turned to face them. Patterson had brought a briefcase with him, and he put it on the table. 'What's the financial position now, Richard . . . in view of last night's hitch?' asked Sam.

'There's money in two of the current accounts. Just about. And you're three months behind with the mortgage. The bank's not going to call in the mortgage straight away – they don't like repossessing unless they absolutely have to. However, Laurence is going to need funds to keep the case going.'

Sam turned to Patterson. 'Have you made any headway yet?'

'Samantha, there are basically two ways of getting Terry out of prison,' said Patterson, leaning back in his chair as though about to start a lecture.

'Not a helicopter, Laurence. I really can't afford a helicopter.'

Patterson smiled thinly, like an uncle humouring a favourite child. 'No, Samantha, not a helicopter. Hopefully it won't come to that. We need to discredit the forensic evidence, and we need to show that Ricky Morrison was lying when he said he saw Terry leaving Snow's house after the shots were fired. If we assume the forensic evidence was planted by one of the investigating officers . . .'

'Raquel . . .' Sam interjected.

Patterson nodded. 'Raquel. Quite. If we assume that the evidence was indeed planted, the easiest way of showing that is first to demonstrate that Morrison is lying. If it was the police who encouraged Morrison to lie, it follows that they could also have planted the evidence. Or at least an appeal court is likely to see it that way. The first step is to find Ricky Morrison, though, and I have to say that so far we've drawn a blank. Apparently he's under some sort of witness protection scheme. Finding him is going to cost, Samantha. It's going to cost big time.'

'I've got someone else working on that as we speak,' said Sam. From down below came the wailing siren of a fire engine.

'The more the merrier, obviously,' said Patterson, 'but the people I've got on the case are going to need paying. And as we stand right now, you don't have the resources for that.'

Sam lit a cigarette. 'Warwick Locke said he'd give me five grand for Terry's share of the modelling business. The cheque should arrive any day now.'

Patterson looked pained. 'Five thousand pounds is a drop in the proverbial, I'm afraid. Ten times that would just about cover what it's going to cost to get Terry's case reopened.'

Sam's face fell. Fifty thousand pounds? Where on earth was she going to get fifty thousand pounds from?

'I know that's a lot, Samantha. I'm sorry. But that's what it costs. That's not even including Richard's fees or mine. We're going to have to go over every court paper again, reinterview every witness, re-examine the forensics.'

Sam looked at them in turn. She could see the pity in their eyes and she refused to show how upset she was. She forced a smile. 'I'll get the money,' she said. 'Come hell or high water, I'll get it.'

Patterson tapped the briefcase that he'd brought with him. 'Terry's spoken to you about the other thing?'

'The counterfeit money? Yeah. I told him I wouldn't touch it with a bargepole, but that was before . . .' She left the sentence hanging.

'And now?' asked Asher.

'Now I don't think I've got any choice. Do you know exactly what he's got in mind?'

'Arm's length,' said Asher. 'Need-to-know basis.'

Patterson opened the briefcase. 'But he did say that we were to give you this if you did decide to go through with it.' He took out a notebook and handed it to her.

Sam took it and opened it. Asher walked over to the railing at the far end of the terrace as if wanting to distance himself as far as possible from the notebook and whatever was written in it. 'Why do I get the feeling that my strings are being pulled?' asked Sam.

'It's just Terry planning ahead, Samantha,' said Patterson, closing the briefcase and clicking shut the two locks. 'Anticipating problems before they arise.'

'Yeah? Causing them, more like.'

'Samantha, are you still driving the Saab?' asked Asher, peering down over the railing.

'Christ, now what?' said Sam. 'It's not been vandalised again, has it?'

'They're towing it.'

Sam cursed and rushed back into the office, shouting over her shoulder that she'd be in touch. She dashed to the lift and tapped the notebook impatiently against her leg all the way down.

By the time she reached the Saab it was already being lifted on to the back of a flatbed truck. A West Indian traffic warden in a too-tight uniform was punching the keys of a handheld computer. Sam hurried up to him. 'I'm sorry, I was in a meeting. I fed the meter, I guess I mustn't have put enough in.'

'Too late now, madam,' he said, not taking his eyes off the computer.

'I can't have been more than ten minutes.'

'Nothing I can do once the wheels have left the ground.' He finished tapping on the computer keys and slotted it into a leather holster, like a sheriff putting away his six-shooter. 'You can collect it from the pound in about an hour's time.'

'Can't you just pretend I got here a bit earlier? I really am having one hell of a day.'

'You and me both, madam.'

'Will you stop calling me "madam"? You make me sound like a brothel-owner.'

The Saab banged down on to the truck and two other West Indians in overalls began attaching chains to the wheels.

'Look, I need the car. I really need the car. Please don't do this to me.'

The traffic warden folded his arms and looked at her dispassionately. 'Madam, you're wasting my time. I just issue the tickets. Once the car is collected, it's out of my hands.'

Sam felt a surge of rage at the unfairness of it. 'Your mother must be proud of you. Her son in uniform. Must warm the cockles . . .' She could see from the look of smug indifference on his face that there was nothing she could say that would have any effect on the man. She figured that doing the job he did, he probably had the hide of a rhinoceros and had heard every possible insult there was. She turned and walked away, fuming.

She called Andy McKinley on her mobile. He said he'd be with her in thirty minutes, so Sam sat in a coffee bar with an espresso and read through the notebook while she waited.

Most of the notebook was blank: Terry's cramped handwriting filled only the first six pages. It was written in a chatty style and she could imagine him saying the words. It was peppered with loves and darlings and apologies, but the gist of it was that Terry had paid a quarter of a million pounds to a syndicate in Malaga who had access to top-quality counterfeit twenty-pound notes. Terry was getting a ten-fold return on the investment – a total of two and a half million pounds was being delivered to him in Malaga. Once the counterfeit money was ready, someone would have to go over to Spain, collect the notes, and bring them back to the United Kingdom. 'And with me banged up, love, I'm sorry to say it's going to have to be you,' Terry had written.

Sam shook her head. 'You bastard, Terry,' she whispered, and sipped her coffee. There was a phone number to call in

Spain to confirm that the money was ready, and details of how Sam was supposed to bring the cash back, along with a list of possible drivers and their contact numbers. Sam looked around nervously. What she had in her hands was a do-it-yourself guide to counterfeit currency smuggling, and she could only imagine what would happen to her if the police found it in her possession. She slid it into her handbag.

She smoked a cigarette and drank another coffee as she wondered what she should do next. Getting Terry out had to be her first priority. If Terry was out, he'd be able to do his own dirty work and she could go back to having some semblance of a normal life. It was, however, a huge 'if', one that depended on her getting fifty thousand pounds, and the only way to get the fifty thousand pounds was to go and collect the counterfeit money. It was a vicious circle, and the more Sam tried to come up with a way out, the more her head began to swim.

* * *

Frank Welch signalled that he was leaving the motorway and drove to the car park behind the service station. Welch hated informers. Hated them with a vengeance. And he hated even more having to give them money. Welch knew that they were a necessary evil, but he felt soiled by having to deal with them. He was late, although he knew that the man he was there to meet would wait. He drove slowly around the car park until he saw the Rover, and pulled up next to it.

George Kay wound down the window as Welch got out of his car. 'I thought we said two-thirty,' said Kay, holding out his hand.

Welch ignored the outstretched hand and got into the passenger seat. 'And I thought you said she was going to be there,' said Welch.

'That's what she told us,' said Kay, winding up the window.

'Yeah, well, she wasn't. And Reg Salmon and his team are saying nothing. I've got fuck all to pin on her.'

'That's not my fault,' said Kay. 'I told you when and where the stuff was coming ashore, gave you everything you needed.'

'What I needed, you fat fuck, was to catch Samantha Greene in the act.'

Kay's mouth fell open and he started to wheeze. He pulled his inhaler out of his coat pocket and took a long pull on it, his chest wheezing. 'There's no need to get personal, Mr Welch.'

Welch shook his head. 'This *is* personal, Kay. I'm not going to allow Samantha Greene to take the piss out of me. I want to know what she's up to. And I want you to tell me.'

Kay put away his inhaler. 'That's not going to be easy, Mr Welch. The cannabis, I was involved from day one. But whatever else he's up to, I'm not involved.'

'Well, get involved.'

Kay looked pained. 'I'll do what I can, Mr Welch, but Sam's not stupid. If I press her too hard, she's going to know I'm up to something.'

Welch looked at Kay contemptuously. 'What *are* you up to, Kay?'

'What do you mean?'

'How much did you lose on that cannabis deal? A hundred grand?'

Kay shrugged but said nothing.

'What I'm paying you isn't going to make up for that, is it?'

'I'm not doing it for the money, Mr Welch.'

'Oh, civic pride, is it? Do I have "fuckwit" tattooed on my forehead, Kay?' He patted his jacket pocket. 'Or are you saying I can keep this?'

'Mr Welch . . .' whined Kay.

Welch took the envelope out of his pocket and handed it to Kay.

'How much is there?' Kay asked, weighing the envelope in his hand.

'What we agreed,' said Welch. 'Though you don't fucking deserve it, not with Sam Greene footloose and fancy free.'

Kay put the envelope away as if he feared that the detective might change his mind. 'It wasn't a hundred grand, anyway,' said Kay. 'Nowhere near. Most of the money was put up by Terry and Micky Fox.'

'Still must have put a dent in your pocket, though.' Welch frowned. 'You want Terry short of cash, don't you? Why? So you can take over his team? See yourself as the new West London godfather, is that it? I do hope that's not your plan, Kay, because if it is, you'll end up behind bars with Greene. Being my grass doesn't mean you can act with impunity. Selling duty-free booze and profiting from prostitution is one thing – you pick up Terry Greene's reins and you'll be for the high jump.'

'I just want the clubs, Mr Welch. Swear to God, that's all. It's not as if I'm not asking for what's not mine. I'm the one who runs them, Terry just drinks there.'

'Not any more he doesn't,' laughed Welch.

'That's what I mean. With him behind bars, it doesn't seem fair that I should be shelling out half the profits every month. I just want what I'm entitled to, that's all.'

'So you fuck Terry over, he's short of cash, he sells out to you for a song? You're a devious bastard, Kay.'

'Coming from you, Mr Welch, I'll take that as a compliment.'

* * *

Terry wasn't in the prison visiting room when Sam arrived, and she had to wait almost fifteen minutes for him. He kissed her on the cheek and sat down. 'Sorry, love, they're still pissing me around.'

'What happened?'

'Strip cell, they call it. Went through everything.'

'Why?'

'They're supposed to be looking for contraband. Drugs, booze, telephone cards, stuff like that. But they weren't looking for anything, they were just turning the cell over out of badness. Ripped a few photos, smashed my mirror, dropped my toothpaste in the toilet.' He smiled. 'But what the hell, it's not supposed to be a holiday camp. How've you been?'

'Why didn't you tell me about the booze runs, Terry?'

'What booze runs?'

'What do you mean, "what booze runs"? Don't play the innocent with me, Terry Greene.' She told him about the attack on Ryser and Fletcher, and the theft of the van.

Terry cursed and banged his hand on the table. Heads swivelled in their direction and Terry sat back, his hands up to show that he wasn't being a problem.

'You know what I hate, Terry?'

'Fat men in high heels and suspenders?' Sam glared at him and he put his hands up in surrender. 'Okay, okay, I'm sorry. What do you hate?'

'I hate the fact that you're only giving me little pieces of the picture. A bit at a time. First you tell me about the cannabis, then I get the notebook about the counterfeit money. I only found out about the booze runs because something went wrong.'

'Yeah, well, I thought Russell and Pike had it under control. It was ticking over nicely.'

'That's not the point, Terry. It's like you only tell me what I need to know. What you want me to know. Everything else is hidden away. What is it, Terry? Don't you trust me?'

Terry reached for her hand but Sam wouldn't let him touch her. 'Of course I trust you. God, who else can I trust, hey?'

Sam put her hands up to her face. 'I don't know how much of this I can take,' she said.

Terry leaned forward, clearly concerned. 'Love, it's going to be okay.'

She snorted softly. 'That's what Jamie said when the jury came back.'

'It is. I promise.'

'You can't promise something like that, Terry.' Sam took a couple of deep breaths and composed herself. Terry looked genuinely worried, but Sam shook her head. 'I'm okay. Really. I'm okay.'

'You sure?'

Sam nodded.

'This booze thing, we've got to get it sorted,' said Terry. 'We've got to find out who did it and stamp on them, hard.'

'That'd be the royal we, would it?'

Terry shrugged and showed her the palms of his hands. 'There's only so much I can do in here, love. And like I said, you're the only one I can trust outside. Someone must have grassed us up on the cannabis.' He grinned. 'No pun intended. Seriously, love, if we let this go, they'll see it as weakness and they'll hit us again and again. I'll call Russell and get him started, but you'll have to keep an eye on them. Andy McKinley'll steer you right.'

Sam didn't say anything. She desperately wanted a cigarette, but smoking wasn't allowed in the visiting room.

'Did Richard and Laurence give you the notebook?'

Sam nodded.

'Piece of cake, Sam.'

'Yeah, well, you said that about the other thing. Terry, if they'd caught me with Reg and the rest, I'd be going down for ten years.' She leaned towards him and lowered her voice to a whisper. 'Now you want me to smuggle in counterfeit money. Can't it wait?'

'Thing is, it's not just my money tied up in the deal. There's other investors, too. Micky Fox for one. He's going to want to recoup some of his losses from that last fiasco.'

'Terry, you don't seem to understand how bad it is out there. They're going to repossess the house. Jamie's tuition fee hasn't been paid, Oakwood House is threatening to throw your mum out on the street. We need cash now. Not next week or next month. Now. All I've got is five grand coming from Warwick Locke.'

Terry frowned. 'Five grand? What for?'

'For your share of the modelling business.'

'What? For fuck's sake, Sam. My fifty per cent of the business is worth more than that.'

'Warwick says not.'

'Well, Warwick's talking through his arse.'

'I thought he was your friend.'

'Yeah. That makes two of us.' Terry shook his head. 'You can't trust anybody these days.'

'He said the business wasn't doing that well.'

'It was doing just fine last time I saw the books.' He put his hands flat on the Formica table. 'Okay. It's cash you need. George Kay is sitting on some for me. About ten grand.'

'He didn't mention it when I saw him.'

'Well, you can mention it now. Tell him you need it. Blackie's going to need a sweetener as well. Plus there'll be expenses for the Spanish thing.'

Sam slumped in her chair. She felt exhausted, as if all the strength had drained from her. 'This isn't fair,' she sighed. 'I had a life. I was over you.'

Terry smiled. 'You were never over me. Not really.'

Sam laughed harshly.

Terry bent towards her, his face suddenly serious. 'I know that my feelings never changed,' he said. 'Not deep down.'

'Your screwing around was just superficial, then?' she said sarcastically. 'That's a relief.' She took a deep breath. 'All I agreed to do was to give you an alibi for that night. Now you're dragging me into something that . . .' She shook her head, trying to organise her thoughts. 'This is all getting out of hand.'

'You can handle it,' said Terry.

'You'd better have told me everything.'

'On my mother's life.'

She looked at him coldly. 'Don't drag Grace down to your level, Terry.'

He shrugged apologetically.

'If there's anything else, any other deals you're not telling me about, I'll swing for you, Terry Greene.'

'Haven't you heard? They did away with capital punishment.'

'Yeah, and aren't you the lucky one.'

'Hey . . .'

He gave her a hurt look, but Sam wasn't mollified. 'You bastard.'

'I'll make it up to you when I get out, love,' said Terry, earnestly. 'I promise. Straight and narrow.'

'We'll see,' said Sam. 'We'll see.'

* * *

Lapland was a sad, seedy place during the day. All the lights were on, revealing how truly shabby it was. The purple velour seats in the booths were faded and torn in places, the tables were scratched and the carpets peppered with cigarette burns. A cleaner was running a Hoover over the carpet and whistling tunelessly while a man in overalls stood on a stepladder, changing one of the spotlight bulbs in the ceiling. Someone had sprayed lemon-scented air freshener around, but it did little to mask the smell of stale smoke.

George Kay was behind the bar, counting bottles of spirits. He turned as he heard Sam's footsteps. His face fell when he saw her, but he quickly smiled. 'Sam, what a lovely surprise.' He waddled around the bar and kissed her on the left cheek and gave her a arm a small squeeze. 'We didn't have a meeting arranged, did we?'

'Flying visit, George. How's things?'

'Fine.' He nodded at the spirits behind the bar. 'If I didn't count every bottle, they'd steal me blind.'

'Yeah, you can't trust anybody these days, can you?'

Kay's smile hardened a little. 'So what can I do for you? Social call?'

'Terry says you're holding some cash for him.'

Kay's eyes narrowed. 'Did he now?'

'Yes, he did. And frankly I'm a little disappointed that you didn't mention it last time I came to see you, George.'

Kay took his asthma inhaler out of his pocket and took a long pull on it. He patted his chest and put the inhaler away. 'Come on through to the office.'

Sam followed Kay to the office. His chest wheezed with every step and the material of his trousers whispered as his thighs rubbed together. He held the office door open for her and she squeezed past him, so close that she could smell his body odour.

Sam sat on the sofa and lit a cigarette as Kay went behind his desk. As he lowered himself into his executive chair he saw the cigarette in her hand. He frowned but didn't say anything.

'Terry said you had ten thousand pounds of his,' said Sam.

'Working capital, Sam. It's for the business.'

'That's not how Terry tells it. He says he left it with you for a rainy day. And believe me, George, it's pissing down outside.'

Kay put a hand up to his cheek, his brow furrowed. 'Sam, I'm sorry, but I don't have it. Not right now.'

'Where is it, George?'

'It's . . .' He struggled to find the words. 'It's in the business. The ebb and flow of capital. There's wages to be shelled out, suppliers to be paid.'

'George, how many thousands do you take each night? Last time I was here they were lining up outside.'

'Overheads, Sam.'

'Bollocks, George.'

'I don't want to fight with you, Sam. Please.'

'This isn't fighting, George,' said Sam coldly. 'This is conversation. Fighting is what Terry's going to be doing if you don't give me his money.'

Kay stiffened. 'That sounds like a threat, Sam.'

'You know Terry as well as I do.'

'Yeah, but Terry's not here, is he?'

'Very observant of you, George. But he's got friends on the outside.'

'Like McKinley. I hear he's working for you now.'

Sam didn't reply. She blew smoke up at the ceiling and kept looking at him.

Kay tapped his fingers on the desk. His face was glistening with sweat. Sam's eyes bored into his and eventually he looked away. 'I can let you have a few grand today,' he said, 'but the rest of the money is tied up in the business,' he said.

'Well, untie it. PDQ.'

Kay heaved himself up from behind his desk and went over to a framed poster of two blondes entwined around each other. He swung the poster to the side, revealing a wall safe. He flicked the combination lock and pulled open the door, then took out a bundle of twenty-pound notes. 'You know, I was thinking about what you said. About me buying out Terry's stake in the clubs.'

Sam held out her hand for the money and Kay took it over to her. She ran her finger along the edge of the bundle. 'How much is here, George?'

'Two thousand.'

'You said a few. Two isn't a few. Two's a couple. Two's two. Terry said ten.'

'I'll get you the other eight, Sam. As soon as I can. I'm down a bundle on that cannabis deal, remember.'

'You and me both.' She put the money in her handbag.

'I was thinking, maybe I could do a deal with Terry. Buy him out. That'd help your cashflow problem, right? I mean, I couldn't pay top dollar, not after what I lost on the cannabis thing, but I'm sure we could come to some arrangement.'

'I'll run it by Terry when I see him.'

'Do you know if he's got anything else planned?'

Sam narrowed her eyes. 'What do you mean, George?'

'You know. Any other . . . money-making opportunities. Recoup my losses.'

'You'd have to talk to Terry about that. You should go visit. I'm sure he'd love to see you.'

Kay nodded. He went back to the safe and locked it, then swung the poster back into place. 'I know it's a rough time for you just now, Sam. You've a lot on your plate.'

'Thanks for your empathy, George.'

Kay went behind his desk and dropped down into his chair. He took out his inhaler and toyed with it as he smiled ingratiatingly at Sam. 'It's from the heart, Sam. I've always had a soft spot for you. You know that. If you need someone to talk to . . .'

Sam crossed her legs and saw Kay's eyes follow the movement. Sam tried to contain her annoyance: she'd come to the club for Terry's money, not to be hit on by someone who was supposed to be Terry's friend. 'The only thing I want to talk about at the moment is the whereabouts of Terry's money.'

'There's more to life than money, Sam.' Kay took another long pull on his inhaler. 'You should come to the club one evening. Have a spot of bubbly. Some dinner. Let your hair down. Socialise, like you used to do. Woman like you, you shouldn't be on your own.'

Sam stood up. She felt suddenly dirty and didn't want to spend a minute longer in George Kay's presence. He was even seedier than the club. 'Call me when you've got the rest of Terry's money, yeah?' she said as she walked out of the door. Behind her, she heard Kay using the inhaler again.

* * *

Sam climbed into the car and sighed.

'How did it go, Mrs Greene?' asked McKinley.

'It was okay, I guess.' She closed her eyes and rested her head on the back of the seat. 'What's your take on George Kay, Andy?' she asked. When McKinley didn't answer, Sam opened her eyes. 'What is it, bodyguard's code of silence?

Don't want to tell tales out of school? Come on, I'm running out of clichés here.'

She saw him smile in the rear-view mirror. 'Let me put it this way, Mrs Greene. Did you shake hands with him?'

Sam shook her head. 'No.'

'That's okay, then, you don't have to count your fingers.' He started the car. 'Where to?' he asked.

Sam looked at her watch. It was just before noon. 'I want to go and see Blackie.'

'He'll be well pleased about you paying him a visit.'

'That's as may be, but I need to get Terry out, and Blackie's the only one who can help me.'

McKinley dropped her around the corner from the police station where Blackie was based, and she called the detective superintendent on her mobile as she walked towards the entrance. 'Blackie,' she said, 'it's Sam Greene.'

'What the hell are you doing calling me at the office?' he hissed.

'If you'd prefer it, I could get Terry to call you from prison, but wouldn't that be a bit awkward for you?'

'This isn't funny, Sam.'

'And I'm not laughing. I'm outside, Blackie. And if you're not here in five minutes, I'm going to be asking for you at the front desk.' She cut the connection and lit a cigarette. She'd only smoked half of it by the time Blackie stormed out of the front doors of the station, putting on his coat.

'What the fuck are you doing here?' he spat.

'If Mohammed won't go to the mountain . . .'

'You won't be happy until I'm behind bars with your husband, will you?' He looked left and right. 'Come on, we can't stay here.'

'Ashamed of me, Blackie?'

Blackie hissed in annoyance and walked off towards the main road, and Sam hurried after him.

Blackie turned off into a park. He kept looking around as if he feared someone might see them.

'Blackie, will you relax? You're making yourself look suspicious.'

'You're the wife of a convicted murderer. How's it going to look if I'm seen with you?'

'What, you never talk to criminals? What sort of cop are you? Just tell them I'm one of your grasses.'

Blackie hissed again and headed towards a small lake in the middle of the park.

Sam followed. 'Look, Blackie, I need to talk to Morrison. He said he saw Terry leaving Snow's after he was shot. I want to know why he lied. If I have to make your life a little uncomfortable to get to the truth, then tough shit.'

Blackie turned to face her. 'Morrison's in a witness protection scheme: new identity, the works.'

'You know where he is?'

'You can't see him. End of story. If I let you speak to him, word'll get back to Welch and I'll be in deep shit.'

'But you do know where he is?'

Blackie glared at her, then turned and walked off.

'You can't keep walking away, Blackie,' Sam called after him. She took a manila envelope out of her bag and held it up. 'Not if you want these destroyed.' Blackie didn't look back. 'You can be all macho if you like, but if these end up on your boss's desk, then your career's in the toilet.'

Blackie stopped. He slowly turned and stared at the envelope in Sam's hand. 'What the fuck's that?'

Sam didn't reply. They stared at each other like a couple of gunfighters, neither prepared to draw first. Blackie gritted his teeth and took his hands out of his overcoat pockets before slowly walking back to her. He snatched the envelope from her and ripped it open. Inside was the set of black and white photographs that Sam had found in the safe deposit box. Blackie looked through the pictures, his face reddening. 'You could get seven years for this.'

'Just a few holiday snaps.'

'This is fucking blackmail.'

'Oh, I didn't realise. Well, now that you've pointed that out, let's just forget about the whole thing. Grow up, Blackie. I know it's fucking blackmail. That's the point. Now, are you going to take me to Morrison or do I send the negatives to your boss?'

Blackie put the photographs back in the envelope. 'You're learning fast, Sam.'

'I'm having to.'

'Just be careful you don't get too smart for your own good, yeah?' He slid the envelope into his inside jacket pocket. 'You got a car?'

Sam took out her mobile phone and called McKinley. Two minutes later the Lexus pulled up outside the park and Sam and Blackie climbed in the back. Blackie told McKinley where to go and then settled back in a sullen silence.

They drove to a tower block in a rundown part of north-west London. Sam and Blackie got out of the car and Sam looked around at the boarded-up shopfronts sprayed with graffiti and pavements strewn with litter. 'You certainly look after your witnesses, Blackie.'

'Budget cuts,' said Blackie. 'Plus no one's going to bend over backwards to make life easy for a scumbag like Morrison.'

Blackie took her over to the entrance to the tower block. There was a keypad entry system on the rusty metal door, but the lock had been broken and the door swung gently in the wind. Inside, 'Out of Order' signs had been plastered across two of the three lifts.

'What floor's he on?' asked Sam.

'Third.'

'How about we walk up?'

'Good call,' said Blackie.

They walked up the stairs. The walls were covered in graffiti, mainly names and obscenities with the occasional anatomical drawing. 'How long's he been here?' asked Sam.

'Since about a month before the trial,' said Blackie.

'And this is part of his deal for grassing on Terry?'

'He didn't grass on Terry,' said Blackie, who was starting to breathe heavily with the effort of climbing the concrete steps. 'He was a witness at the scene of a crime. There's a difference.'

'Yeah, well, the devil's in the details,' said Sam. 'Why's he on the witness protection scheme?'

'He's helping the drugs squad with a couple of cases. Morrison is strictly smalltime, but he knows a few people higher up the food chain.'

'Presumably not too high up or he'd be in better surroundings.'

Blackie pulled a face. Someone had defecated in the stairwell, and they both gave the offending item a wide berth. Sam felt sick, and covered her mouth and nose with a handkerchief.

Blackie smiled at her discomfort. 'If you think this is bad, wait until you meet Morrison,' he said.

Morrison's front door was one of more than a dozen off a dimly lit corridor. It had three locks and a security viewer, and screwholes showed where there had once been a three-digit number. The numbers had been removed but the outlines could still be seen in the faded paintwork. Blackie rang the bell, and when they didn't hear anything from inside he knocked. They heard footsteps and Blackie knocked again.

'Come on, Ricky, I know you're in there.'

The security viewer darkened as Morrison scrutinised them from inside.

'Stop playing fucking games,' said Blackie.

'Who is it?' said a muffled voice.

Blackie took out his warrant card and held it up to the viewer. 'Police.'

The door opened a couple of inches. There was a security chain attached and the man inside kept his hand on the edge of the door. All Sam could see was a third of the man's face – a shock of unruly hair, a squinting eye and a cheek covered with stubble – but she recognised him from his time in the witness box.

'You're supposed to talk to my brief,' said Morrison. He had a slight lisp. 'You can't come here like this.'

'We don't have time to go through channels.'

'Who are you?'

Blackie pushed the warrant card closer to Morrison's face. 'Detective Chief Superintendent Blackstock.'

Morrison squinted at the card. 'Blackstock? You're not drugs, are you?'

'No, Ricky. I'm not drugs. Now, will you open the door or do you want me to kick it in?'

Morrison nodded at Sam. 'What's she doing here?'

'I just want to talk to you,' said Sam.

Blackie put the flat of his hand against the door and pushed. 'Come on, Ricky, your neighbours are going to start asking questions if we carry on like this.'

Morrison sniggered. 'Neighbours here don't give a toss about fuck all,' he said.

Sam took an envelope from her bag. 'I've got this for you,' she said.

Blackie threw her a threatening look but didn't say anything.

'What is it?' asked Morrison.

Sam smiled and tapped the envelope on the door. Morrison nibbled on his lower lip, then took off the security chain and pulled the door open. Sam walked into the flat first, handing the envelope to Morrison as she walked past him. He ripped it open. There was a wad of fifty-pound notes inside.

Blackie saw the money and put a hand on Sam's shoulder. 'You can't do that!' he said. 'He's a witness, you can't go bribing a witness.'

'She can do what she wants,' said Morrison. He was wearing a tartan dressing gown over grimy pyjamas. He hurried off to his bedroom as if he feared they might ask him for the money back.

Sam shook Blackie's hand off her shoulder. 'I'm just smoothing the way. Same as you do with your grasses, right? If this offends your sensibilities, maybe you should wait outside.'

'Maybe you're right,' said Blackie. He looked at his watch. 'Ten minutes, yeah? Then we're out of here.'

Sam nodded.

Blackie looked as if he wanted to say more, but he just turned and left.

Sam looked around the flat. There was a tired sofa, two worn leather armchairs and a brand new large-screen television and video recorder. Discarded fast food cartons lay on the floor, and dirty magazines were piled on a coffee table next to an opened can of lager. Sam walked over to the window and drew back a grubby net curtain. Down below a burnt-out car had been pushed on to its side, next to a skip overflowing with rubbish.

Sam turned around as Morrison came back into the room.

'I don't know what you think I can tell you,' he said.

'You know who I am, right?'

'Sure. Saw you in court. Mrs Greene, yeah?'

Sam nodded. 'Mind if I smoke?'

'Go ahead.' Sam took out a cigarette and then offered the pack to Morrison. He took a cigarette and she lit them both. She looked at the sofa. There was an opened magazine on the arm, next to a box of tissues. Morrison saw what she was looking at and pulled out a tissue and wiped his nose. 'I've got a cold,' he said. 'Can't shake it.' He tossed the magazine on to the pile and sat down, wrapping his dressing gown around him.

Sam decided not to sit. She stood with her back to the window and blew smoke at the floor. 'Ricky, I heard what you said in court, but I'm here to tell you that my husband didn't do it. He didn't kill Preston Snow.'

Morrison shrugged. 'I saw what I saw.'

'Which was what?'

'I already said. In court. I wasn't lying, Mrs Greene.'

'Tell me again, Ricky.'

Morrison sighed. He took a long pull on his cigarette, then sighed again as he exhaled the smoke. 'I've been through this a thousand times. With the filth, with the CPS, with the barrister.'

'Make it a thousand and one.'

Morrison picked a spot on his chin and put his feet up on the coffee table. 'I was asleep, right? I woke up. Then I heard two shots. Bang. Bang. I get up and I open the door. Your husband comes down the stairs putting something in his pocket. I see him, he doesn't see me. He goes downstairs and I close the door. I go back to bed. Couple of hours later the filth are knocking on my door and they tell me that Snow's dead. Shot twice.' Morrison threw his hands up, as if he'd just proved a complicated theorem. 'QAD.'

'I think you mean QED, Ricky.'

'QAD. QED. I saw what I saw.'

Sam nodded thoughtfully. 'You were staying at Snow's house?'

Morrison shook his head. 'Snow had the top two floors. There were bedsits on the ground floor.'

'And you knew Snow?'

'He wasn't a mate, if that's what you mean. He was just the Sooty that sold me gear from time to time.'

'Gear?'

'Bit of crack. Coke if I had the money.'

'You get high a lot?'

'If I can afford it.'

'You didn't tell the court that.'

'Wasn't asked.'

Sam paced up and down, and noticed a small kitchen off the sitting room. A gas cooker thick with grease, a stack of dirty plates in the sink, a dripping tap.

'You want a coffee or something, Mrs Greene?' Morrison asked.

Sam was taken aback by his sudden offer of hospitality, but there was no way she could bring herself to drink out of a cup from Morrison's kitchen. 'No, thanks, Ricky. Were you high the night Snow was shot?'

Morrison screwed up his face like a baby about to cry. 'I know what you're thinking, but I didn't imagine it.'

'I'm not saying you were, but maybe you were a bit woozy. A bit disorientated.'

Morrison shook his head. 'I saw what I saw.'

'It was night. There wasn't a light in the hallway.'

'Your husband's barrister said all that in court. There was enough light coming in from a skylight. I saw his face.'

'But only in profile. With his collar up.'

'It was him, Mrs Greene.' He took a drag on his cigarette, holding it between his thumb and first finger. 'You weren't with him that night, were you?'

'I'm the one buying information, Ricky.'

'Yeah, but we both know that if anyone was lying in court, it was you, right? He wasn't with you, was he?'

Sam didn't reply and Morrison grinned triumphantly. He jabbed his cigarette in her direction. 'See!'

'What woke you up?'

Morrison frowned. 'What do you mean?'

'You said you woke up and heard two shots. Why did you wake up?'

Morrison shrugged. 'Dunno. Wanted a piss maybe. Why does anyone wake up?'

'You didn't hear shouts? An argument?'

'I just woke up. Then I heard the shots. Then I saw your husband.'

Sam's cigarette had burned down to the filter. She looked around for an ashtray but couldn't see one. She went into the kitchen and stubbed it out in the sink. A cockroach scuttled across a dirty plate and Sam jumped back. 'Jesus, Ricky, don't you ever clean this place?'

'They said they'd send a cleaner around.'

Sam went back into the sitting room. 'Had you done business with Raquel before?'

'What?'

'Frank Welch. Were you involved with him before Snow was killed?'

Morrison still looked confused.

'Were you one of his grasses?'

Morrison rolled his eyes upwards. 'I can't tell you that. Do you know how many people want me dead?'

'Is that including me, Ricky?'

'If word gets out that I'm a grass, do you know what'll happen to me?'

'Ricky, you're on a witness protection scheme. Presumably every man and his dog knows that you're singing like a canary. All I'm asking is, were you one of Welch's grasses?'

Morrison nodded. 'Yeah,' he said. 'Yeah. I was.'

'See, I think Welch set my husband up. I think he faked the forensics.'

'And you think he got me to lie for him?'

Sam looked at him and nodded slowly. 'That's exactly what I think.'

He looked back at her steadily. 'Well, you're wrong, Mrs Greene. Dead wrong.'

* * *

The three white Transit vans drove off the ferry separately but regrouped just outside the terminal. All three had been waved through by a bored Customs officer in a yellow reflective jacket. They were just three among hundreds of vans taking advantage of the cheap beer and wine on the Continent, and the men in the vans had done the run enough times to have learned how to avoid attracting attention to themselves.

Kim Fletcher and Johnny Russell were in the first van to come off the ferry. Russell was driving, and Fletcher used a mobile phone to call Ellis, who was driving one of the other vans, and then Ryser, who was driving the third. They drove in convoy towards a large roundabout outside Dover, where they split up, taking different routes back to London. Each van was shadowed at a distance by two large motorcycles, the riders and passengers wearing leathers and full-face helmets.

Russell constantly checked his rear-view mirror while Fletcher kept his mobile phone in his lap. There was a burst of laughter behind them and Fletcher twisted around in his seat. 'Will you keep the fucking noise down,' he said.

Four big men sat in the back on cases of lager, cradling cricket bats. They wore leather bomber jackets and jeans and had holdalls containing cricket whites and pads in case Customs had stopped them. 'Sorry, boss,' said one of the heavies.

'We've got a tail,' said Russell.

Fletcher checked the wing mirror on the passenger side.

'Four cars back. Blue van.'

Fletcher saw the van. There was a blonde girl in the passenger seat and a big, balding man driving. 'You sure?'

'Changed lanes twice and so did he. Been matching our speed for the last two miles.'

'Okay, lads,' said Fletcher. 'This is it.' He called up the two other vans and told them that the pressure was off and that they were to tell their accompanying motorcycles to get over to Fletcher's van. He opened the glove compartment and took out a small radio transceiver. The two motorcyclists who were half a mile behind the van were turned to the frequency of the transceiver, Fletcher called them up and told them about the blue van, then he sat back in his seat and smiled. He began to hum quietly to himself.

The blue van kept its distance for another fifteen minutes, then made its move as they drove along a relatively quiet stretch of road. The blue van accelerated until it was just a car's length behind the white van, then it slowed and matched its speed. There was a traffic light ahead, and as it changed to red, Russell gently braked.

'This is it, lads,' said Fletcher. He leaned down and took out a large monkey wrench from under his seat. 'Brace yourselves.'

Russell brought the van to a stop. There was nothing ahead of them. The blue van banged into the back of them, but Russell had already taken his foot off the brake and the impact nudged them forward a few feet. Fletcher winked at Russell and climbed out.

The female passenger was already out of the blue van, apologising profusely in an East European accent. 'I so sorry,' she said, smiling and throwing her hands up in the air. 'We not see light.' She was pretty with a wide mouth and dyed blonde hair tied back in a ponytail. 'Everybody okay?'

Fletcher kept the monkey wrench behind his back as he smiled at the girl. 'We're fine. Are you all right? Not hurt?'

'We okay,' said the girl. 'But we have damaged the back of your van.' She pointed at the rear of the white Transit. 'See?'

Russell got out of the driver's seat and walked around to join Fletcher. As they approached the back of the Transit, the rear doors of the blue van flew open and four heavily built men jumped out wielding crowbars. The girl ran to them, shouting in a language Fletcher didn't recognise.

'Fuck me,' said Russell. 'It's a stick-up.'

'A cock-up, more like,' said Fletcher, producing his monkey wrench. Russell brought a length of chain out of his jacket pocket and stepped to the side, swinging it around as he walked towards the four heavies. Fletcher banged his monkey wrench against the side of the van and the doors burst open. The four men inside leapt out, their cricket bats at the ready, yelling obscenities.

The four heavies stood rooted to the spot, their mouths open. The driver of the blue van had climbed out by now, but he stood by the van door, transfixed, his eyes wide with surprise.

Suddenly there was a roar of engines and two motorcycles screeched to a halt behind the blue van. The riders and passengers dismounted and advanced towards the heavies, brandishing a variety of weapons.

Fletcher continued to hum as the motorcyclists and the men with cricket bats laid into the heavies from the blue van. Barely had the fighting started when another two motorcycles arrived with four more of Terry's footsoldiers.

The mêlée was over in minutes: the four men from the back of the blue van lay bleeding and moaning at the side of the road, and the girl was running back down the road, screaming. One of the motorcyclists grabbed her by her ponytail, but Fletcher shook his head and told him to let her go. This wasn't about fighting girls.

Russell and one of the cricket bat wielders grabbed the driver of the blue van, a big, balding thirty-something with a lazy right eye and a scar on his left cheek. In heavily accented English, he pleaded with them not to hurt him. 'I innocent standbyer,' he kept repeating, much to the amusement of his captors. They threw him into the back of the white Transit van and pulled a sack over his head.

Fletcher and Russell climbed into the front of the Transit as the rear doors slammed shut, and they drove off. Fletcher was still humming as the men in the back went to work on their captive.

* * *

Sam picked up the mail from the doormat and took it through to the kitchen where Trisha was wolfing down a bowl of Alpen. 'Anything for me?' asked Trisha.

'Not unless you want to take care of the electricity bill,' said Sam, dropping one of the manila envelopes down on the kitchen table.

'Aren't you going to open it?' asked Trisha.

'What's the point? It's not as if I'm in a position to pay it.'

Trisha looked suddenly worried. 'Is everything okay, Mum?'

Sam smiled thinly. 'Money's a bit tight, love. That's all.'

'How tight?'

Sam shook her head. 'It's nothing for you to worry about.'

'What do you mean it's nothing for me to worry about? I'm a part of this family, what's left of it.'

Sam ruffled her daughter's hair. 'I was making a bad joke, I'm sorry. Your dad being away has just made it a bit difficult, that's all. But it's temporary. There's money on the way and everything'll be okay, I promise.'

Trisha still looked concerned. 'I guess I can cut back on stuff. If it'll help.'

Sam laughed. 'Like what? You want we should go on a diet of bread and water?'

'It'd be okay, so long as it was Evian, I guess.'

They both laughed and Sam hugged her daughter, then kissed her on the forehead. 'You'll be late for school.'

Trisha picked up her backpack, blew Sam a kiss, and headed down the hall. Before she reached the front door the doorbell rang. Trisha opened the door to find McKinley in a dark overcoat buttoned all the way up.

'Morning, Trisha,' he said.

'Yeah,' she said, brushing past him.

Sam came out of the kitchen and saw McKinley on the doorstep. 'Andy? What's up?'

'We've got one of the guys who ambushed the van, Mrs Greene. The lads are having a word with him now.'

'You think I should be there?'

'I think it'd be best.'

Sam nodded. She picked up her coat and followed McKinley out to the Lexus.

McKinley drove her to the warehouse in Paddington where they stored the duty-free booze brought in from the Continent. He banged on the metal door, and after a couple of minutes it rattled open. It was Johnny Russell, the front of his denim shirt soaking wet.

'Mrs Greene,' Russell said. 'You're just in time for the fun.'

Sam and McKinley followed him through the warehouse. A hosepipe snaked across the floor from a tap on one wall. In the middle aisle Fletcher and Pike were standing around a barrel full of water. Above them, a man was suspended head first from the rafters, his head and shoulders underwater. A chain had been tied around his ankles and thrown over a rafter high above, and Ryser and Ellis had hold of the other end of the chain. The man in the barrel was struggling, but with his legs tied and his head underwater, all he could do was thrash around.

'What the hell's going on?' shouted Sam.

'We're making him talk,' said Pike.

'How's he going to talk with his head under water?' asked Sam.

Pike and Fletcher exchanged a worried look. Pike shrugged. The man in the barrel went suddenly still. All the men looked at Sam as if wondering what she wanted them to do.

'For God's sake, were you all bullied at school or something?' said Sam. 'Get him down.'

* * *

Zoran Poskovic took a swig from the bottle of vodka on his desk, wiped his mouth with the back of his hand and went back to counting the stacks of banknotes on his desk. From where he was sitting he could watch his men preparing the day's hot dogs, opening cans of brown-skinned sausages and pouring them into metal trays, cutting rolls open and chopping onions. Like Poskovic, they were all Kosovans. About half had entered the country as refugees and were waiting for their asylum applications to be processed, the rest were illegals, brought in by Poskovic, usually hidden in specially built compartments in lorryloads of fruit shipped over from the Continent. More men arrived every week, and most ended up working for Poskovic. If they refused, they were beaten or betrayed to the authorities. Or both.

Poskovic usually started the new arrivals on his hot dog trolleys. He had more than fifty with pitches around central London. Poskovic would watch them carefully, and those who proved themselves he'd move on to his more illicit activities. He already had a dozen Kosovan prostitutes working for him in a chain of apartments on the Edgware Road, and he'd started using some of the women as drugs couriers, bringing in small amounts of heroin from his contacts back home.

Two men in their twenties pushed out a trolley and Poskovic nodded at them. His face fell, however, when he saw Petko stagger in through the door. He was soaking wet and his face was cut and bruised.

'Where the fuck have you been?' he shouted. 'The rest got back hours ago.'

Petko shook his head. 'They beat the shit out of me,' he said.

'Who did?'

A woman in a raincoat with the collar turned up walked in, flanked by two large men, one wearing an overcoat, the other a leather jacket. 'That would be me,' she said.

Poskovic stood up. 'Who the fuck is she?' he shouted at Petko in his own language. 'You brought her here?'

Another four men appeared behind the woman, all wearing long coats. They all stood glaring at Poskovic.

Poskovic shouted over at his men and they stopped work. They came over carrying their knives and stood at his desk as Poskovic continued to stare at the woman, wondering who she was and why she had walked into his warehouse. Most of the men with her had their hands deep in their pockets. Poskovic had a gun, but it was in the drawer of the desk and he didn't want to risk getting it out, not until he knew what exactly he was up against.

'Don't blame Petko, here,' said the woman. 'It's not his fault. The boys got a bit heavy with him. You must be Zoran Poskovic, yeah? I'm Samantha Greene. It's my husband's vans you've been playing fast and loose with.'

She stepped forward and held out her hand. Poskovic frowned at the hand. She smiled patiently, her hand outstretched. Poskovic slowly wiped his right hand on his trousers, then shook hands with her. She had a surprisingly strong grip for a woman, though her hand was small and her fingers long and delicate.

Sam noticed the cases of beer and cigarettes and nodded at them. 'That's probably his stuff there, is it?'

Poskovic shrugged his massive shoulders but didn't say anything. His men looked at him, wondering what he wanted them to do, but he continued to look at the woman.

'Petko says you're Kosovans?'

'Petko talks too much,' said Poskovic. 'What do you want?'

'What I want is for you to leave my husband's booze runs alone, that's what I want.'

Poskovic smiled, showing four gold teeth at the back of his mouth. 'It's a free market economy,' he said. 'The strong prosper at the expense of the weak.'

He looked across at his men, wanting them to be impressed by his use of English, but none of them had understood and they looked at him blankly.

'Yeah, but you see that's where your hypothesis starts to fall apart,' said Sam. 'My husband's not weak. He's in prison, I'll grant you that, but he wouldn't want you calling him a softie. And I wouldn't want you thinking I was a pushover either.' She looked at him with unblinking green eyes.

Poskovic had faced hundreds of men over the years, more often than not intimidating them by the mere threat of violence, with a long stare or a menacing look, but he could sense that Sam Greene wasn't scared, and that it would take more than posturing to beat her down. He could see that she had been a very pretty woman in her youth, stunning maybe. She was still a beautiful woman, with high cheekbones and a sensuous mouth, long eyelashes and flawless skin, but the prettiness had given way to an elegance and self-confidence that Poskovic found even more of a sexual turn-on than mere looks.

'Terry's going to defend what's his,' she said. 'And so am I.'

Poskovic nodded slowly. She had eight men with her. Poskovic had almost twenty. Plus a dozen others who could be summoned within minutes. She was outnumbered and she knew it, but she was still unafraid as she faced him. Poskovic looked at the men behind her and wondered if they had guns in the pockets of their overcoats. And if they'd be prepared to use them.

Sam gestured at the bottle on Poskovic's desk. 'That vodka?' she asked.

Poskovic nodded. 'The real thing. Got it from a friend in St Petersburg. You are a vodka drinker, Mrs Greene?'

'Zoran, I'll drink whatever you've got right now.'

Poskovic grinned and told his men to fetch another glass, then he poured two shots and handed her one. They both knocked them back and Poskovic watched her closely to see how she'd react, to see if she really was a drinker or if it had just been bravado.

She licked her lips thoughtfully, then nodded. 'Nice,' she said, and held out her glass for a refill.

Poskovic laughed. He gave her another shot of vodka and toasted her. 'I think you and I are going to be friends, Mrs Greene.'

She held up her glass. 'That depends on whether or not you leave my husband's vans alone.' She drained the glass again. 'Have you got anywhere to sit, Zoran, or do you do all your negotiating on your feet?'

Poskovic called for chairs to be brought over, and he and Sam sat facing each other. Their men were visibly more relaxed, but they still stood warily by, and Sam's men kept their hands in their pockets.

'So what's Kosovo like, Zoran?' Sam asked.

'It's a hard country,' said Poskovic. 'Poor like you would not believe. Everyone wants to get out.'

'And come to England? To make a new life?'

'To America. America is best. But if they cannot get to America, London will do.'

'And that's what you did? Got out and carved a new life for yourself here?'

Poskovic nodded.

'I can understand that, Zoran. My family were economic refugees, if you go back a couple of generations. My great-great-grandfather was Hungarian.'

Poskovic nodded appreciatively. 'Good people, Hungarians.' He help up his vodka glass. 'Good drinkers.'

Sam shrugged. 'Yeah, maybe that's where I get it from.' She drank another shot of vodka. 'So what are we going to do, Zoran? We don't want to go to war over this, do we?'

'War?'

'Because that's what'll happen if we don't get something sorted. You'll keep on hitting my vans, my guys will hit yours, we'll spend so much time fighting each other we won't either of us be in a position to make any money. Doesn't make much sense, does it?'

Poskovic shrugged. 'It's business, Mrs Greene. We have to take what we can, no one is going to give us a living.' He waved over at the hot dog trolleys. 'We had to fight the Bosnians for this business. And they're hard bastards. If we'd just walked up and said please can we share your business, what do you think they would have done?'

Sam smiled. 'It's a dog eat dog world,' she said.

Poskovic frowned. He didn't understand.

'It's an expression, Zoran. It means things are so bad that even the dogs fight each other.'

Poskovic nodded. 'Nothing to do with hot dogs?'

Sam threw back her head and laughed, and so did her men. Poskovic laughed too, though he wasn't quite sure what she found so funny.

When she'd finished laughing, Sam took out a pack of cigarettes and offered one to Poskovic. He accepted and she lit it for him, then lit one for herself. 'Why did you choose my husband's vans, Zoran?'

Poskovic blew a cloud of smoke and waited for it to disperse before he spoke. 'We thought that because your husband was in prison . . .' He left the sentence unfinished.

Sam nodded. 'And what was it you were after? A few grand's worth of booze. You must have bigger fish to fry.'

Poskovic frowned again. His English was fairly good, especially compared with his compatriots, but he didn't have a particularly good grasp of British slang.

Sam smiled at his confusion. 'It's smalltime, Zoran. A vanload of booze? It's nothing, right?'

'If you didn't have the goods, your customers would look for alternative suppliers. They would become our customers.'

'That's what I thought,' said Sam. She took several sheets of paper from inside her coat and handed them to Poskovic. 'These are the places we supply at the moment, and a list of places we don't. You can see for yourself, the list of places we don't sell to is a hell of a lot longer than the list of places we supply.'

Poskovic bit down on his lower lip as he scanned the lists. She was right.

'They're in the same geographical area, same sort of businesses. Indian restaurants, corner shops, drinking clubs. There's plenty of scope for you there, Zoran. You don't have to go poaching my business.'

'But you will be expanding,' said Poskovic.

Sam shook her head emphatically. 'Oh no we won't,' she said. 'I promise you that. As soon as my husband gets out of prison, we're walking away from all this.'

Poskovic looked at her carefully, wondering if she was being totally honest with him.

She looked back at him, unfazed. 'Oh, there are a couple of other conditions,' said Sam.

Poskovic raised an eyebrow.

'We'd like our van back. And the booze.'

Poskovic chuckled, then held out his hand. Sam accepted it. His hand dwarfed hers, but he shook gently, then stepped forward and gave her a bear hug, again using only a fraction of his strength as if he feared she might break. 'You have a deal, Mrs Greene,' he said, planting a kiss on her cheek. Sam's feet were almost off the floor.

'That's a relief, Zoran, I was worried you might want to arm wrestle me for the van.'

Poskovic laughed even louder as he set her down. He walked her to the door, McKinley and the rest of Sam's heavies following.

One of Poskovic's men dropped an opened can of sausages on to the floor. He bent down and picked them up, putting them one by one on to his trolley, grunting apologetically at Poskovic.

'Do people really buy those?' asked Sam as the man wiped one of the sausages on his overalls.

'We make a fortune,' said Poskovic. 'Japanese tourists pay ten quid for a hot dog. Germans'll pay five quid. That's why the Bosnians fought so hard for the business. We had to break a lot of heads, Mrs Greene. A lot of heads.'

Sam and McKinley headed for the Lexus while Pike, Fletcher, Russell and the rest went to their cars.

'I didn't realise your family were from Hungary,' said McKinley.

Sam gave him a withering look. 'Andy, do I look in the least bit Hungarian to you? Give me some credit, will you?'

McKinley stopped dead in his tracks and began to chuckle, shaking his head in wonder at Sam's audacity.

* * *

Frank Welch showed his warrant card to the young constable standing guard in the foul-smelling lift lobby. 'Third floor, sir,' said the constable.

'I know where it is, son,' growled Welch. He stabbed a

finger at the lift call button and popped in a couple of breath mints while he waited for one of the three lifts to arrive. He stared at the floor indicators. Two of the lifts weren't working and the third showed the lift was on the third floor and not moving. Welch decided to walk up.

Two more uniforms stood in the hallway outside Morrison's apartment, and a scene of crime officer in white overalls was taking fingerprints from the front door.

Welch showed his warrant card again and walked into the flat.

He found Simpson and Clarke in the sitting room. Simpson was flicking through a pornographic magazine, and he dropped it on to the sofa when he saw Welch.

'Shouldn't you be wearing gloves?' asked Welch.

'Sorry, guv,' said Simpson. He took out a pack of plastic gloves and ripped it open with his teeth.

'This way, guv,' said Clarke. 'Bedroom.'

Welch followed Clarke through to the bedroom, where two more SOCO technicians were taking samples from the floor and walls. Morrison was hanging on the back of the bedroom door. Naked. The rope around his neck was looped over the top of the door and tied to the handle on the outside of the door.

'Who found him?' asked Welch, peering at Morrison's neck.

'His handler came around when he didn't check in. Forced the door.'

'Where is he now, the handler?'

'Went to talk to his boss.' Clarke gave Welch a card with the name and phone number of a police sergeant working with Paddington Green's drug squad. 'Morrison was supposed to be giving evidence in a drugs case tomorrow.'

'This was supposed to be a fucking witness protection scheme,' said Welch. 'They shouldn't have left him on his own.'

Simpson came up behind him. 'One of the SOCOs said it

might be an auto-erotic thing,' he said. 'Cutting off his air supply and playing with himself.'

'Bollocks,' said Welch.

'There were no signs of a struggle,' said Simpson. 'Dirty magazines on the floor.'

'And no note, so it doesn't look like he killed himself,' said Clarke.

'He was murdered,' said Welch emphatically.

'Come on, guv, we don't know that for sure,' said Simpson.

'I do,' said Welch. 'Somebody murdered the little shit. Question is, who? And how did they know where to find him?'

* * *

Sam was on her hands and knees cleaning the oven when the phone rang. She cursed and stood up, stripping off her rubber gloves. It was Blackie. 'Remember the park near the office?' he snapped. 'Be there in thirty minutes.'

'Why? What's happened?'

'Just be there.'

The line went dead. Sam frowned and put the phone back. Wondered whether or not to call McKinley, but decided against it and drove the Saab to the park.

Blackie was already at the lake, pacing up and down, his face set like stone. 'Have you heard what happened?' he said.

'What? Is it Terry? Has something happened to Terry?'

'No, it's not Terry. It's Morrison. He's dead.'

Sam's jaw dropped. 'Dead? How?'

'They found him hanging on the back of a door.'

'He didn't look suicidal when I saw him,' said Sam.

'It wasn't suicide,' said Blackie. 'That's what it looked like, but a lowlife like Morrison isn't going to kill himself. Jesus H. Christ. Twenty-four hours after he talks to you, he's dead. That strike you as a coincidence?'

'What do you mean?'

'What do you think I mean? Christ, if they ever find out that I gave you Morrison, I'll be in so much shit they'll need a submarine to find me.'

'You're a big boy, Blackie. I'm sure you covered your tracks.'

'Did you tell anyone else where Morrison was?'

'Of course not.'

'What about Terry?'

Sam shook her head. 'I haven't spoken to Terry for a week.'

Blackie put a hand up to his forehead. 'This is the last time I put myself in the firing line for you. Or Terry.'

Sam walked up close to Blackie so that her face was only inches away from his. 'It's the last time when I say it's the last time,' she said, her voice ice cold. 'You've been on Terry's firm since you were a woodentop pounding the beat. You do as you're told or your career's over and you'll be spending your retirement on Rule 43 with the rest of the bent coppers behind bars.'

'Who the fuck do you think you are?' hissed Blackie.

'I think I'm the woman who's got photographs of you taking bungs from my husband. And I think I'm the woman who can walk into your boss's office and tell him that you took me to see Morrison.'

'Then you'd go down with me.'

Sam smiled thinly. 'Really? You don't think I could cut myself a deal, Blackie? Who do you think they'd rather put behind bars? A housewife and mother, or a detective superintendent? I mean, think of the pension money they'd save for a start.'

Blackie stared at her in near disbelief, his jaw set tight as the colour visibly drained from his face. 'You're a bitch,' he said eventually.

'I'm having to be, Blackie. I'm fighting for my life here.'

Blackie shook his head and walked away, keeping to the edge of the lake.

'Look, Terry tells me that when he gets out, he's going legit,' said Sam.

'Bollocks.'

'I think he means it. He's had a taste of prison and he won't want to go back. Once he's out, he won't need you any more. You'll be home free.'

'Terry Greene isn't ever going to go straight. Take my word on that.'

'I'm just telling you what Terry told me. And I believe him.'

Blackie shook his head. He kept his eyes on the ground as he followed the path around the lake. Two well-dressed women with prams were walking their way, so they stopped talking until they'd gone by.

'Terry said he was with some Irish heavyweights the night Snow was shot,' said Sam.

Blackie frowned, then realisation dawned. 'Paramilitaries? For fuck's sake.'

'That's why he couldn't say where he was. That's why I had to lie for him.'

'Have you any idea how dangerous those people are? What was Terry doing?'

'Best you don't know, Blackie.'

Blackie continued to shake his head.

'Look, I need a name,' said Sam. 'Someone I can talk to.'

'Talk to? Why?'

'Seems to me that the more you know, the more you worry. Just give me the name of someone in London I can speak to. Then you can leave the worrying to me.'

Blackie looked at her as if she were mad, then he took a small black notebook out of his jacket pocket and scribbled a name and address. He ripped out the page and handed it to her. 'For fuck's sake don't mention my name,' he said, and walked away, still shaking his head.

* * *

Sam drove from the park to Oakwood House. She made her way to Grace's room, but was surprised to find it empty, the bed freshly made. Sam frowned. Grace had been in the same room since her arrival at the home – it didn't make sense that they'd move her after three years. She noticed that the framed photographs that Grace kept on her bedside table had gone, as had all her personal belongings. Sam rushed over to the wardrobe and opened it. All her clothes were missing. A sudden chill gripped her heart.

'Mrs Greene?'

Sam whirled around. It was the friendly nurse who'd tipped her off about Mrs Hancock on her last visit. The nurse stood in the open doorway, her hands clutched in front of her. Her lower lip was trembling.

'Where's Grace?' snapped Sam. 'What've they done with her?'

'I'm sorry, Mrs Greene.'

'Sorry? What for?'

The nurse took a couple of steps into the room. 'Grace is dead, Mrs Greene. I'm so sorry.'

Sam felt as is she'd been kicked in the stomach. The strength drained from her legs and she sat down heavily on the bed. 'She didn't look too bad last time I saw her.'

The nurse looked away, still wringing her hands, and Sam sensed that there was something wrong. 'What happened?' she asked.

'You really should speak to Mrs Hancock,' said the nurse.

'Tell me,' said Sam.

The nurse shook her head. 'I can't, Mrs Greene. Really, I can't.'

Sam looked up at the nurse. 'Did something happen to her?'

The nurse closed the door and went down to sit on the bed next to Sam. 'She went out. She went out and there was an accident.'

Sam took a handkerchief from her bag and wiped her eyes.

'What do you mean she went out? Grace hasn't been out for two years.'

'She walked out,' said the nurse. 'No one seems to know when, no one saw her go. She went across the field and onto the road. Oh God, Mrs Greene, I'm so, so sorry.' The nurse started to cry. Sam gave her the handkerchief and the nurse dabbed at her eyes. 'She was run over. They said she died right away.'

The strength drained from Sam's legs and she sat down on the bed. 'When?' she gasped. 'When did it happen?'

'This morning.' The nurse blew her nose and wiped her eyes again. 'I brought her lunch and she wasn't here.'

Sam closed her eyes. She'd always known that Grace would never be going home, that she would be in Oakwood House until the day she died, and that there was no cure for her illness. But death, death was something in the far-off future. She'd never expected Grace to be snatched away suddenly, the life smashed out of her on a lonely country road.

The nurse gave her back the handkerchief. 'She was a real lady, Mrs Greene. Always gentle, always kind. I'll miss her.'

Sam nodded. 'Yeah, I'll miss her, too.'

On the way out, Sam went to the administrator's office, brushing past the secretary's desk and opening the door unannounced. Mrs Hancock was tapping on her computer keyboard, and the look of annoyance which flashed across her face when she saw Sam was quickly replaced by a professional smile. 'Mrs Greene, I am so sorry about what happened.' She spoke slowly and the smile never left her lips, but Sam could see the insincerity in the woman's eyes.

'What the hell was Grace doing outside?' asked Sam.

'Excuse me?' said Mrs Hancock, icily.

'I said, what the hell was my mother-in-law doing outside?'

'This isn't a prison, Mrs Greene. There are no bars on the windows, we don't have armed guards on the gate. Residents are free to come and go as they please.'

'Why didn't anyone tell me what had happened?'

'We tried to contact you, Mrs Greene, but there was no one home. I left two messages on your answering machine myself. And we asked the police if they would send someone around to leave a written message.'

'I wasn't home,' said Sam quietly. 'I had to see someone.'

'There you are then,' said Mrs Hancock. 'It's not as if we didn't try.'

'Didn't try!' echoed Sam. 'It was a bit bloody late to be trying, wasn't it? Why was nobody trying when she walked out?'

'I don't think I like your tone, Mrs Greene,' said the administrator, sitting back in her chair.

Sam walked up to the desk and glared down at the woman. 'And I don't think I like the fact that you let an eighty-year-old woman with Alzheimer's go walkabout.'

'Mrs Greene . . .' protested the administrator, but Sam cut her short by pointing her finger at her face.

'She needed looking after,' shouted Sam. 'Twenty-four hours a day. That's why she was here. That's what we were paying for.'

Mrs Hancock sneered at Sam. 'Actually, you weren't,' she said.

Sam frowned. 'What do you mean?'

Mrs Hancock stood up. 'You haven't paid your mother-in-law's account for more than three months.'

'Yeah, well, you can whistle for your money now.'

Mrs Hancock reached for the phone on her desk. 'I'm going to have to ask you to leave, Mrs Greene. Or you'll force me to call security.'

'Security? If you had any security, Grace wouldn't have got out in the first place.'

Mrs Hancock started to dial, and Sam turned her back on the woman and stormed out of the office.

* * *

Terry was whispering into one of the landing telephones when he saw Chief Prison Officer Riggs flanked by Dunne and another guard walking up the metal stairway. Riggs paused at the top of the stairway, looked around, then headed towards Terry.

Terry hung up as soon as Riggs came within earshot. 'Your missus sends her regards, Mr Riggs,' Terry said.

Terry moved to get past Riggs and the two other guards, but Riggs stepped to the side, blocking his way. 'I'll miss your sense of humour when you leave, Greene,' said Riggs. He smiled coldly. 'In about thirty years.'

Terry could sense something was wrong. He looked at Dunne, but the guard looked away quickly, unwilling to meet his gaze.

Riggs had a triumphant look in his eyes. 'Your mother's dead,' he said quietly. Riggs stared at Terry, wanting to see how he'd react.

Terry felt as if his stomach had turned to ice. He couldn't breathe and his heart was racing, but he forced himself to keep looking at Riggs.

Riggs's eyes hardened. 'She was hit by a fucking ice cream van,' he said. 'Had to scrape her off the road with a wafer.'

Terry took a step towards Riggs and the three guards tensed. Terry took a deep breath. Losing his temper wouldn't get him anything other than a period in solitary. Or worse. He kept his hands at his sides and clenched his jaw as he stared at Riggs. Riggs stared back, a smile flickering across his lips, wanting Terry to lash out. Terry refused to give him the satisfaction.

When Riggs realised that Terry wasn't going to react, he turned and walked away, his shoes squeaking.

Dunne pulled a sympathetic face. 'Sorry, Terry,' he said, his voice a soft whisper so that Riggs wouldn't hear.

Terry didn't say anything, but he acknowledged Dunne

with a curt nod as he glared at the back of Chief Prison Officer Riggs.

* * *

Sam parked the Saab outside Laura's house and walked slowly to the front door. She rang the doorbell several times but there was no answer, so she went around the side of the house and opened the wooden gate that led to the rear garden. Laura was at the far end of the lawn, clipping roses. Sam walked across the grass towards her daughter. 'Laura?'

Laura flinched and turned around. She was wearing sunglasses even though the sky was overcast and threatening rain. 'Mum, what are you doing here?'

'Thanks for making me feel so welcome,' said Sam.

Laura smiled but Sam could see that she was far from happy to see her. 'You should have called, Mum.'

'I did call. Lots of times. But I keep getting your machine.'

Sam went to kiss Laura on the cheek but Laura backed away as if she didn't want to be touched. Sam frowned. 'What's the matter?' There was a small cut on Laura's chin and a bruise on her left cheek.

'Nothing,' said Laura, too quickly.

'Laura . . .'

'Mum, it's nothing. I'm just busy, that's all.'

'You're pruning roses, Laura. It's not brain surgery.'

'Please, Mum, just go. I've got a headache.'

Sam reached out and slowly took off her daughter's sunglasses. She gasped as she saw the black eye.

'I fell,' said Laura. She saw the look of disbelief on Sam's face. 'Honestly. I fell.'

Sam folded up the sunglasses, shaking her head sadly.

'It's not his fault. He's under a lot of pressure. At work.'

Sam put an arm around her daughter and guided her towards the house. 'Come on, I'll make you a coffee.'

They walked to the house as tears began to run down Laura's face.

'Maybe hot chocolate'll be better,' said Sam. 'Like we used to, yeah? Hot chocolate and EastEnders. Remember?'

'Yeah, Mum,' sniffed Laura. 'I remember.'

Sam sat Laura down in the kitchen and made two mugs of hot chocolate while Laura dabbed gently at her eyes with a piece of kitchen roll.

'How long has this being going on?' asked Sam as she poured boiling milk on to the chocolate powder. Laura shook her head but didn't reply. 'Laura . . .' insisted Sam.

'They're giving him a tough time at work.'

'That's no excuse.'

'Because of Dad.'

Sam handed Laura her mug and sat down opposite her. 'What do you mean, because of Dad?'

'They wind him up,' sniffed Laura. 'Father-in-law's a drug dealer and a murderer. Not the normal sort of pedigree of a merchant banker, is it?'

'Hitters always hit, Laura. There's no changing them.'

'I love him, Mum. He loses his temper, that's all. He's always sorry afterwards.'

'Oh, that makes it all right, then.' Sam leaned over and brushed a lock of Laura's hair behind her ear.

Laura kept her head down as if trying to hide her bruises. 'He doesn't mean it,' she whispered. 'If he didn't love me so much, he wouldn't do it.'

'That's what he says, is it?'

Laura looked away, embarrassed.

'Laura, in all the time I was with your father, no matter how much we argued, no matter how we rowed, he never, ever, laid a finger on me.'

'I know,' said Laura quietly. She put her hands around her mug of hot chocolate.

'Real men don't hit women,' said Sam. 'They can make your life a misery in a million different ways, but they don't hit.' Laura started crying again and Sam hurried around the table to sit next to her. She put her arm around Laura's shoulders and tried to comfort her. 'It's all right, Laura. Don't cry. Please don't cry.'

Laura wiped her eyes. 'I'm sorry, Mum.'

'There's nothing to be sorry about. You don't have to apologise for anything. Drink your chocolate.'

Laura sipped her hot chocolate. 'Did you see Gran today?' she asked.

Sam's face fell and Laura stiffened. 'What? What's happened?'

Sam cupped her hand around her daughter's cheek. 'She's had an accident. I'm sorry, love. That's why I came around. Your gran's . . . your gran's dead.'

'Oh God, Mum! No!'

Laura's look of disbelief turned to one of horror and Sam hugged her.

* * *

McKinley was waiting for Sam as she drove up to the house in her Saab. He'd parked the Lexus in front of the double garage and stood by the front door, his gloved hands clasped in front of him, his face a sombre mask. He walked over to her as she got out of the car and closed the door for her.

'I'm so sorry about your loss, Mrs Greene,' he said.

'How did you . . .'

'Terry phoned me,' McKinley said, before she could finish. 'Called me from the landing. He's been trying to call you on the mobile.'

Sam frowned and took her mobile phone out of her handbag. The battery was dead. She showed it to McKinley.

'Aye, he's been trying to get through for hours, he said. Prison authorities notified him about his mother.'

'How's he taking it, Andy?'

'He's not one for showing his feelings, Mrs Greene. But it's hit him hard.'

'Yeah, he's not the only one.' She took out her door key. 'Come on in, Andy, we could both do with a drink.

McKinley held out a business card. 'A WPC was here a while back. Came to tell you about Mrs Greene. I said I'd be talking to you but she gave me this and said if there were any questions, you could call her.'

'You keep it, Andy,' she said. 'I know all I need to know.'

The message light on the answer machine was flashing accusingly. The digital read-out showed two messages. Sam pressed 'play'. It was Mrs Hancock from the nursing home. Sam deleted both messages without listening to them.

They went through to the sitting room and Sam poured them both brandies.

'Were you close?' asked McKinley. 'You and your mother-in-law?'

Sam nodded. 'Yeah, since my own mum died. That was about fifteen years ago. Car crash.' She smiled. 'Which is why I'm so picky about seatbelts, I guess.' She took a sip of brandy. 'Grace was always there for me. When I needed someone to talk to, you know?'

McKinley nodded. He was a great listener, looking at her with his pale blue eyes as if he were hanging on her every word. It would be very easy for a girl to get romantically involved with Andy McKinley, Sam realised. He was attentive, thoughtful and kind, but he was tough, too. Sam never felt anything other than completely protected when she was with him. If she'd been twenty years younger, she'd probably have been tempted, but the age difference being what it was, she felt more like his elder sister. Or worse. His mother.

'Even when the Alzheimer's kicked in, I still used to enjoy talking to her. There was a stillness about her. I used to feel so much better getting things off my chest, you know?'

McKinley nodded. 'Its good to have someone to talk to,' he agreed.

'What about you, Andy? Who do you talk to?'

McKinley shrugged but didn't answer. Sam didn't press it. She had known McKinley long enough to know that he didn't like personal questions, and she respected his desire for privacy.

'Do you know what Terry wants me to do about the currency thing?' she asked.

'He mentioned it. Just the basics.'

'You don't mind helping me?'

'I'll do what I can.'

Sam sipped her brandy. 'Thanks, Andy. I don't know what I'd do without you. Really.'

McKinley leaned forward and clinked glasses with her. 'It's a pleasure, Mrs Greene.'

Sam held his look. He was a good-looking man, was Andy McKinley. Tall and strong with a confident air, the sort of man you knew you could rely on, who'd never let you down. Sam wondered again if he had anyone special in his life. He'd never mentioned being in a relationship and he seemed to be on call twenty-four hours a day.

'How old are you, Andy?' she asked.

'Old enough, Mrs Greene,' he said with a smile. 'Why do you ask?'

'I was just wondering if I'm old enough to be your mother, that's all. You can't be much older than Laura.'

McKinley grinned. 'I've had a rough life, Mrs Greene,' he joked.

'Really?'

McKinley shrugged, then he became serious. 'I've had my moments, but it's worked out all right.'

'You an only child?'

McKinley flashed her a slightly embarrassed smile. 'Five sisters,' he said.

'My God! Older or younger?'

'I was the youngest.'

Sam started laughing, and McKinley looked hurt. 'Oh, I'm

sorry, Andy,' she said, reaching out and patting him on the back of the hand. 'It was just the thought of you and five older sisters. I can just imagine them dressing you up, treating you like a little doll, you know.'

McKinley's face reddened. 'That was pretty much what it was like.'

'I'm sorry, I didn't mean to laugh.'

He took a long drink of his brandy then put down the glass. 'Our dad disappeared when I was about eight. He had some pretty heavy debts and no way of covering them. One night he packed a suitcase and legged it. Left my mother to bring up six kids.'

Sam sipped her brandy, not sure what to say. She knew that any words of commiseration would sound trite.

McKinley settled back in his chair. 'It was too much for her. Burned her out before her time. She had a heart attack. Died in the kitchen while I was school. Got back home and she'd gone.'

'Andy . . . that's terrible,' said Sam.

McKinley shrugged again. 'It was a long time ago. It was hard at the time, I guess, but my sisters shielded me from the worst of it. They wanted to put me and two of my sisters into care but my older sisters wouldn't have it. They insisted the family stayed together and they got their way.' He picked up his brandy and took another drink. 'Tough cookies, my sisters.'

'Like their brother.'

'Aye, maybe. Certainly toughened me up. We were always short of money. I left school first chance I got and became the breadwinner.'

'You still in touch with them?'

'Sure. They never left Glasgow, but I try to get back whenever I can. They're all married now.' He grinned. 'I've got more than a dozen nephews and nieces, can you believe that?'

Sam nodded. 'Yeah, Andy, I can.'

They sat in silence for a while, then McKinley looked at his watch. 'Okay if I push off, Mrs Greene? I've got things to do.'

'Sure. Can you pick me up tomorrow? About ten? There's something I've got to take care of.'

'I'll be here, Mrs Greene. It's okay, don't get up, I'll see myself out.' He stood up. 'Thanks for the drink.' He hesitated as if he were about to say something else, but then he shook his head.

Sam reached up and touched his hand as he walked by. She'd had a sudden urge to give him a hug, but knew that to do so could easily be misinterpreted. She made do with a gentle brushing of the back of his hand with her fingertips. McKinley didn't react and Sam wondered if he'd even noticed the brief physical contact.

Trisha was walking up the drive as McKinley drove away.

She stormed into the sitting room and gave Sam's brandy glass a disparaging look. 'What was he doing here again?' asked Trisha.

'Business.'

Trisha rolled her eyes. 'Yeah. Sure.'

'Come into the kitchen, Trish.'

'I've got homework.'

'We've got to talk.'

Trisha sighed. 'Now what?'

Sam took a deep breath and told Trisha about Grace.

* * *

McKinley brought the Lexus to a stop outside the modern glass and steel tower that housed the offices of the merchant bank where Jonathon Nichols worked.

'Are you sure this is a good idea, Mrs Greene?' he asked.

'Good idea or not, I'm doing it, Andy. You wait here.'

A security guard in a uniform more befitting a rear admiral told Sam that Nichols worked on the twelfth floor. She went up in the lift and walked up to a sour-faced receptionist. 'I'm looking for Jonathon Nichols,' she said.

'He's in a meeting,' said the woman. 'Can you tell me what it's in connection with?'

'It's in connection with him beating the shit out of my daughter,' said Sam. 'Now where is he?'

The receptionist looked to her left, down a corridor. 'He's busy,' she said. She turned to look back at Sam, but she was already walking purposefully down the corridor.

Through a panel of glass next to one of the doors, Sam could see Jonathon Nichols on his feet, talking to a group of half a dozen suits. A blonde woman in a short skirt was taking notes.

Sam threw open the door and stormed in.

Nichols stopped mid-sentence. 'Sam?' he said, confusion written all over his face. He was standing next to an overhead projector, and on the wall was a series of financial calculations.

'Don't fucking "Sam" me,' she shouted, walking up to him. 'If you ever lay a finger on my daughter again, I'll kill you. As sure as I'm standing here, I'll kill you.'

Nichols took a step back and bumped into the projector.

'I don't know where you get the nerve to think it's okay to hit a woman!' continued Sam, pointing her finger at his face. 'Any woman! But to beat your wife black and blue, to have her living in fear of you, that's not being a man.'

Sam took another step towards Nichols, and he raised his hand as if to push her away.

'You want to hit me?' she shouted. 'Go on. I fucking dare you.' She glared at him, her face contorted with rage.

Nichols lowered his hand.

Sam turned to look at the suits sitting around a rosewood table, their mouths wide open. 'How does it feel, doing business with a wife-beater?' she said. Several of them looked embarrassed. 'He knocks my daughter around. His own wife. Beats her up and he's twice her size. She's wearing dark glasses to hide the black eye he's given her. Think about that, yeah. Think about the sort of man you're dealing with.' Sam walked out, her head held high.

The receptionist was waiting in the corridor. 'Security are on their way,' she said, but Sam ignored her and carried on walking.

McKinley had the door of the Lexus open for her. 'How did it go, Mrs Greene?' he asked.

'Just fine, Andy,' said Sam. 'I feel much better now.'

* * *

Terry sat on the one chair in the cell, staring at the wall, while Charlie Hoyle lay on his bunk. Ever since the death of Terry's mother had become public knowledge, Hoyle had barely said a word to him. Prison was a pressure cooker, and inmates who received bad news were generally left alone in case they exploded. Not that Terry was in danger of lashing out. His mother's death had been an accident, but he'd known for some time that she didn't have long to live. In many ways the accident had been a godsend: at least it had been quick compared with the gradual deterioration that the Alzheimer's had caused.

It was almost time for lock-up. Terry heard booted footsteps coming along the landing, and looked up as the door opened. It was Riggs, carrying a clipboard, with another prison officer behind him.

'On your feet, Greene,' he said.

The springs of Hoyle's bed springs squealed as he sat up.

'You stay where you are, Hoyle. Don't want your bunk collapsing, do we?'

Hoyle settled back in his bunk with another squeal of springs.

Terry stood up.

Riggs made a play of looking at his clipboard, even though he obviously knew what he was going to say. 'Your request to attend your mother's funeral . . .' he kept Terry in suspense for several seconds, a sly smile on his face . . . 'has been denied.' Riggs drew himself up to his full height and sneered.

Terry had his hands clasped behind his back, and he dug his nails into his palms so hard that he could feel the flesh tear. He gritted his teeth, refusing to show Riggs his pain and anger. He forced himself to smile. 'Oh well,' he said, 'there's always next year.'

Riggs glared at Terry, hatred pouring out of him. The atmosphere was so charged that Terry felt the hairs stand up on the back of his neck, but he continued to smile as if he hadn't a care in the world. Riggs turned on his heel and marched out of the cell. The other prison officer closed the door and locked it.

Terry turned and slammed his fist against the wall. 'Bastard!' he hissed, refusing to shout because he didn't want anyone on the landing to hear him. He hit the wall again and again until his knuckles were bruised and bloody.

Hoyle said nothing, just turned over and lay facing the wall, leaving Terry alone with his grief.

* * *

The taxi office stood in a row of rundown shops near Kilburn High Street, a yellow light flashing above the door, which was propped open with a rolled-up newspaper. The windows of the first-floor office had been whitewashed so that no one could see in, and 'Murphy's Cabs' had been stencilled in black paint.

McKinley squinted up at the windows. 'I think I should come up with you, Mrs Greene.'

'What, and leave the Lexus on the street? It'd be stripped in minutes.'

'Aye, but even so . . .'

'Andy, I'll be fine.'

She climbed out of the back of the Lexus and up the bare wooden stairs to the first floor. An anorexically thin man with a mop of red hair was talking into a radio mike and eating a cheeseburger at the same time. On the wall behind him was a chart of drivers and their call signs next to a large-scale map of London.

'Where do you want to go, love?' he asked.

'Brian Murphy?'

The redhead jerked his thumb towards a flight of stairs leading up to the second floor as he took a large bite out of his cheeseburger.

Sam went up the stairs, which led on to a small landing. One door was open, revealing a foul-smelling toilet, the other, with a frosted-glass window, was shut. Sam knocked, and a gruff Northern Irish voice told her that the cab office was downstairs.

Sam opened the door. A large man with a receding hairline sat behind a desk, reading the racing pages of the *Daily Telegraph*, pen in hand. 'Brian Murphy?' she asked.

'Who wants to know?'

'Sam Greene. My husband's Terry Greene.'

'So?'

Sam closed the door behind her. 'So I'd appreciate a word.'

Murphy waved her to a chair. Sam took an envelope from her handbag and put it down in front of Murphy before sitting down. She crossed her legs and waited while Murphy picked up the envelope and opened it.

Murphy raised his eyebrows when he saw the thick wad of fifty-pound notes.

'A donation,' said Sam. 'For the Cause.'

Murphy smiled thinly. 'Haven't you heard? There's no cause any more.'

Sam held out her hand for the envelope. Murphy held her look for several seconds, then opened the bottom drawer of his desk, dropped the envelope in and took out a bottle of Bushmills whiskey and two glasses.

He showed the bottle to Sam and she nodded. 'Might I ask where you got my name from, Mrs Greene?' said Murphy as he poured two large measures.

'I'd rather not say,' said Sam, 'but it's not public knowledge, I can tell you that.'

Murphy offered her one of the glasses and she took it. '*Slainte*,' he said.

'*Slainte*,' said Sam. They both drank, then Murphy waited for Sam to speak.

'My husband's doing life for a murder he says he didn't do,' she explained. 'He says that on the night of the murder, he was doing business with some of your people. Laundry business. But your people being the way they are, Terry says he couldn't tell the cops.'

Murphy topped up their glasses. 'Sounds a bit fanciful, truth be told.'

'Can you check?'

Murphy looked at her for several seconds, then held out his hand. Sam assumed he wanted more money and she fumbled for her purse. Murphy shook his head. 'Your handbag, Mrs Greene.'

Sam gave him the bag. Murphy opened it and took out her purse. He went through it, examining her credit cards and identification, then took her driving licence out of its wallet and copied down the details on a notepad. He didn't have to explain to Sam the significance of what he was doing: he knew where she lived. He put everything back in the purse, put the purse back in the handbag, and gave it to her. 'I'll ask around, but hackles might be raised.'

'I'll have to risk that,' said Sam.

* * *

Terry walked down the landing towards the phone. He had six phone cards in his pocket that he'd bought from various inmates on the wing, men who valued tobacco or drugs more than contact with the outside world.

Prison Officer Dunne was standing at the top of the stairs that led down to the ground floor, his face impassive as he watched two prisoners playing chess. Terry stood next to him and Dunne acknowledged his presence with a slight nod of his head.

'What do you think?' asked Dunne. 'The bishop, yeah? Mate in three for white?'

Terry shrugged. 'Not my game, Mr Dunne.'

'Strategy,' said Dunne. 'It's all about planning ahead.'

'Yeah, well, if I was a bit better at planning ahead, I wouldn't be in here, would I?' said Terry.

Dunne smiled.

'I think that's the first time I've ever seen you smile, Mr Dunne,' said Terry. 'You wouldn't want to make a habit of that. People might think you're human.'

'We're all human, Terry.'

'Even Riggs?'

'Yeah, well maybe there's the odd exception. About the only time he cracks a smile is when he talks about his Morris.'

'What, he's got a gay lover, has he?'

Dunne's jaw tensed as he tried not to grin. 'A Morris Traveller. One of those cars with wooden bits on the side. It's his pride and joy. Rebuilt it from scratch. Spent thousands on it. Bores us rigid in the canteen showing us photographs. Relates more to the car than he does to people, if you ask me.'

They stood watching the game for a while. The prisoner playing white put his finger on his queen and Dunne tutted.

'Do you know if the governor got my request for a pass to my mum's funeral, Mr Dunne?'

Dunne pulled a face as if he had a bad taste in his mouth. 'Between you and me?'

'Sure.'

'I think Riggs blocked it.'

Terry cursed under his breath.

The prisoner took his finger off the queen and scratched his head.

'The bishop, you twat,' Dunne muttered.

'Could you put in an application for me?' Terry asked quietly. 'Direct. Go around Riggs.'

'Wouldn't be easy,' said Dunne, out of the side of his mouth.

'There's a monkey in it for you on the outside.'

Dunne's face hardened, and for a moment Terry wondered if he'd crossed the line, if he'd managed to misjudge the prison officer. Eventually Dunne slowly nodded. Down below the prisoner moved the queen and Dunne hissed softly. 'Moron,' he said. He turned to look at Terry as if seeing him for the first time. 'Have you put any noses out of joint on the wing?' he asked.

'Not that I know about,' said Terry. 'Why?'

'Word is there's someone gunning for you.'

'You know who?'

Dunne shook his head and started to walk away. 'Just watch your back, yeah?' he whispered. 'A death on the wing's going to look pretty shitty on my CV.'

* * *

Sam looked at her watch. It was a Cartier, a gold one that Terry had bought for her after Trisha had been born. 'Mum, we're going to have to go in,' said Jamie, putting a hand on her shoulder.

'I know. I just thought . . .'

'It's not likely they'd let him out, Mum. Even for this.'

Sam nodded.

Trisha linked her arm through Sam's. 'Are you okay, Mum?'

'I'm fine, love. Just give me a minute to catch my breath.'

They were standing outside a church in West London, a modern church with a squat spire and wire mesh over the stained-glass windows to protect them from vandals. It wasn't an especially pretty church, but Grace's husband, Terry's father, was buried in the graveyard next to it, and before

Alzheimer's had robbed her of her mind, Grace had always insisted that she wanted to be buried next to him.

Andy McKinley was close by in a black suit and a black overcoat, his hands clasped in front of his groin as though he were standing guard outside a nightclub, shoulders squared and chin up.

Sam, Jamie and Trisha were also dressed in black, and all wore thick coats to protect themselves from the cold. The sky was almost white overhead, and a chill wind blew across the churchyard, swirling dead leaves and empty crisp packets and faded confetti.

The vicar appeared at the door to the church. He was in his sixties with a mane of white hair. The flecks of red in his cheeks and nose suggested to Sam that he had more than a passing acquaintance with strong drink. Sam nodded at him. 'Okay,' she said to her children. 'In we go.'

Barely had she finished speaking than a black van with darkened windows came screeching around the corner and pulled up in front of the church. The back door opened and half a dozen armed policemen wearing bulletproof vests piled out and took up positions around the churchyard.

Sam smiled. 'That'll be your father,' she said. 'Always liked a grand entrance.'

A second, larger, van arrived, this one white, with 'Securicor' written on the side. The rear door opened and a uniformed prison guard stepped out, followed by Terry, blinking in the light. Terry tried to lift his hand to shield his eyes, but he was handcuffed to the guard and there wasn't enough chain to get his arm up. As Terry got out of the van, a second guard followed him, handcuffed to Terry's other wrist. Terry was wearing the same clothes he'd had on in court: the dark blue Armani suit, a white shirt, and the dark blue tie with yellow stripes.

The three men walked towards the church. Trisha muttered something but Sam couldn't hear what it was.

'Hiya, love,' said Terry, grinning at Sam.

'Thought you weren't going to make it,' said Sam.

'Couldn't keep me away from my mum's send-off. Hiya, Jamie.'

'Hiya, Dad.' Jamie went over and hugged Terry.

Terry winked at Trisha over Jamie's shoulder. 'How's it going, Trish? Got a hug for your old dad?'

Trisha tutted and looked away. 'We're holding everybody up,' she said to Sam.

Jamie let go of his father. Terry saw McKinley and nodded at him, then he took a step towards Sam. He reached for her, but the handcuffs held him back. Terry raised his eyes. 'How about it, Mr Dunne?' he said to the prison officer on his right. 'Let me give the missus a hug?'

'No can do, Terry,' said Dunne.

Terry nodded over at the armed police who were scanning the surrounding buildings. Sam wondered what they were looking for. Snipers? A crack team of mercenaries waiting to rescue her husband? The stupidity of it made Sam smile. 'It's not as if I'm going to make a run for it, is it?' said Terry.

'Regulations, Terry,' said Dunne. 'Sorry.'

'More than your job's worth, is it?' said Sam, bitterly.

'He's okay, love. If it wasn't for Mr Dunne I wouldn't be here. Come on, let's go in. Vicar's looking a bit testy as it is.'

They headed as a group towards the entrance to the church, with McKinley bringing up the rear. As they reached the threshold, a car pulled up in a squeal of brakes. They all looked over to see who it was. Terry sighed as he recognised the man in the front passenger seat. Frank Welch.

'The vultures are gathering,' said Terry. 'Come on, let's get inside. I heard he can't enter holy ground.'

'That's vampires,' said Sam, smiling and shaking her head.

They walked into the church. The vicar had taken up position behind a large wooden lectern and was wearing the same sort of fixed smile that Sam had last seen on the face of the administrator of Grace's nursing home.

There were about a dozen people scattered along the varnished pine pews. George Kay was there, sucking on his asthma inhaler. He put the medication away and gave Terry a thumbs-up. The nurse who'd looked after Grace was there, and she flashed Sam a tight smile. Sam gave her a small wave, grateful that she'd come. Three women in their early eighties whom Sam vaguely recognised were deep in conversation at the back of the church. They were old schoolfriends of Grace, and before her illness they'd played bridge together every Sunday evening. That had been one of the first signs that there had been something wrong with Grace: she began to lose her concentration and couldn't remember the order of bidding. A year after she'd given up playing bridge, she was in Oakwood House.

Sam heard rapid footsteps behind her and she turned to see Frank Welch and his sidekick Simpson tearing down the aisle towards them.

Welch rushed up to Dunne. 'What the hell is he doing here?' shouted Welch, stabbing a finger at Terry.

Dunne stared back at Welch from under his black peaked cap, unfazed by the detective's outburst. 'Who are you?' asked Dunne quietly.

Welch took out his warrant card and held it inches from Dunne's nose. 'You can read, can you?'

'Yes, Chief Inspector Welch. I can read.'

Welch put his warrant card back in his pocket. 'So let me repeat the question. What the hell is he doing here?'

'The governor approved his pass.'

'He's a convicted murderer, he's only just been sent down, for God's sake.'

'It's his mother's funeral,' said Dunne firmly.

Terry took a step forward, his arms held back by the handcuffs. 'Yeah, so why don't you respect the sanctity of the church and fuck off, Raquel,' he said.

Welch looked like he might explode. He stared at Terry for what seemed a lifetime, then glared at Dunne. Dunne stared back at the detective, refusing to back down. Welch turned and walked away. Simpson followed.

Dunne turned to look at Terry, his face a blank mask. 'Cops,' he said, 'what can you do with them, huh?'

The service was mercifully brief. Terry had to sit with a prison officer on each side, but Dunne let Sam reach across him to hold Terry's hand. Dunne stared straight ahead as if trying to make himself invisible.

Afterwards, Dunne and the other prison officer stopped by the rear of the van so that Terry could say goodbye to Sam.

Terry leaned forward and kissed her on the cheek. 'Thanks for today,' he said. 'For taking care of everything.'

'I wish I could have made it more . . . you know . . . special.'

'This is what she wanted,' said Terry. 'She wanted to be buried next to him. God knows why, the way he treated her.'

'Married for life. That's how it was back then.'

'Till death us do part.'

'That's the point, Terry. I don't think they believed that even death would part them. In spite of everything, it was for ever. For eternity.'

Terry looked around. 'Laura couldn't make it?'

'I guess not.'

'I'm sorry, love. For everything.'

Sam shrugged, not sure what to say.

'We're going to have to go, Terry,' said Dunne.

'Just a minute, yeah?'

Dunne nodded.

Terry leaned closer to Sam. 'It won't be much longer, love.'

'What do you mean?' she asked.

'I mean, hang on in there. It's going to work out.'

'That's easy to say, Terry.'

'I'm serious, love,' he said. 'There's light at the end of the tunnel. Keep your chin up. I'm expecting good news.'

Sam laughed. 'Christ, Terry, you sound like a cheap horoscope.'

'Just wait and see.' Terry reached for her but the handcuffs held him back. He turned to look at Dunne. 'Come on, Mr Dunne. Can the cuffs come off for a second? I just want to hold my wife, that's all. I'm not going to be seeing her for weeks.'

Dunne gave Terry a long stare, then he slowly nodded and reached for his keys. 'Just the one wrist, Terry.'

'Thanks, Mr Dunne.'

Dunne was inserting the key into the handcuff lock when Welch hurried over, his face contorted with anger. 'What the fuck do you think you're doing!' he shouted.

'He's just saying goodbye,' said Dunne.

'Which is what you'll be saying to your pension if you touch those locks!' shouted Welch, flecks of saliva peppering the prison officer's uniform. 'Get him in the van, now!'

Dunne's cheeks reddened and he put the key away. The other prison officer opened the back of the van.

George Kay waddled over, wiping his forehead with a white handkerchief. 'Don't you worry, Terry, we'll get you out of there,' he said.

Welch pointed his finger at Sam's face. 'You're next. I know you put that drug deal together for him.'

'Yeah?' sneered Sam. 'Prove it.'

Jamie glared at Welch. 'Can't you leave us alone?' he said. 'This is a funeral, for God's sake.'

'What about Preston Snow's funeral? I didn't see you there.'

The two prison officers stood with Terry at the back of the van, watching the altercation.

'Just piss off, Raquel,' said Sam vehemently. 'This is private grief, it's got nothing to do with you.'

'We'll see about that.' Welch glared at Sam, his face only inches away from hers.

Trisha pushed the detective. 'Leave her alone, you!' she shouted.

Welch took a step back. 'I'll have you for assault,' he said to Trisha.

'It's our grandmother's funeral!' protested Jamie.

Welch ignored Jamie and tried to grab Trisha, but Sam pushed his arm away. 'Don't you dare touch her!' she shouted.

Terry struggled to get to his wife, but the two prison officers held him back. 'Sam! Leave it!' he shouted. 'He's not worth it!'

Welch pointed a finger at Dunne. 'Get him in the van! Now!' Before the prison officers could react, mud splattered across Welch's face. He whirled around and saw Trisha standing with a muddy hand held high. 'Right, that's it!' Welch shouted.

He lunged forward to grab Trisha but Sam stepped in front of him. 'I told you, leave her alone,' said Sam. 'You shouldn't be here. Not at a funeral.'

Jamie stepped forward to stand next to his mother. 'You're out of order and you know you are,' said Jamie, putting an arm around Sam. 'If we complain to the police complaints authority, it'll stay on your record, proven or not.'

Welch looked at Jamie scornfully. 'Boy lawyer, huh?'

'Or we could go to the papers. Either way, your superiors are going to wonder why you didn't handle the situation better.'

Welch glared at Jamie, who stared back, and Sam was suddenly immensely proud of her son. Welch gritted his teeth, then turned to look at the prison officers. They were grinning at Welch's discomfort, as was Terry. 'What are you looking at!' he snapped. 'Get him in the van. Now!' He took out a handkerchief and wiped the mud off his face.

The prison officers ushered Terry into the back of the van. 'Chin up, love!' Terry shouted as the doors slammed shut.

The armed police piled back into their van and Welch and Simpson went over to their car, Welch continuing to wipe his face with the handkerchief.

Trisha turned her back on the van and walked off to the Lexus where McKinley was waiting with the door open.

Jamie and Sam stood together watching the van drive away. She ruffled his hair. 'Thanks, Jamie,' she said.

'Bastards,' said Jamie.

'Hey,' said Sam. 'Watch your language.'

Jamie laughed and hugged her. 'Can't wait until I'm a barrister,' he said. 'Can you imagine how much fun I'm going to have with them in the witness box?'

They walked together to the Lexus, Jamie's arm still around her.

Sam had decided against any sort of reception. It hadn't seemed right, not with Terry having to go straight back to prison. Besides, she'd known that very few mourners would turn up, though she hadn't expected that what mourners there were would be outnumbered by the police.

McKinley drove them home, but Sam stayed in the car when Trisha and Jamie got out.

'Where are you going?' Trisha asked sullenly.

'Something I've got to take care of, love,' said Sam. 'I won't be long.'

Trisha stomped away, and Jamie shrugged at Sam. 'I'll talk to her,' he said.

'Why don't you do what you used to do when you were kids?' said Sam. 'Put her head in the toilet and flush it.' She patted her son on the back. 'I won't be long. What time are you going?'

'I'll leave at five. I'd stay but I've got a stack of revision to get through.'

Sam blew him a kiss and McKinley drove off. Sam told McKinley to drive to Laura's house, then sat back in her seat and lit a cigarette.

The curtains were drawn on the ground-floor windows, but Sam kept ringing the doorbell until she heard footsteps. The door opened on its security chain.

'Laura? What are you playing at?'

'Mum, you can't come in,' said Laura, her voice subdued as if she were close to tears.

'You should have been there,' said Sam.

'I know,' said Laura. She began to cry. 'I'm sorry.'

'Let me in, love. Come on.'

'I can't, Mum. I'm sorry. Please go.'

Laura started to close the door but McKinley moved quickly, jamming a foot in the gap. He pressed the flat of his hand against the door. 'Do as your mother says,' he said quietly.

Laura turned and hurried down the hall. McKinley looked at Sam and she nodded. He put his shoulder against the door and pushed, hard. The wood around the security chain splintered and the door flew open. McKinley stood to the side to let Sam in first.

Laura was sprawled on a sofa in the sitting room, crying her eyes out. Sam sat down next to her and stroked the back of her neck. 'What is it, love?' she asked. 'What's the matter?'

'I wanted to go, Mum, really I did,' sobbed Laura.

'I know you did,' soothed Sam.

'He said I couldn't. He said if I did . . . he'd . . .' She mumbled incoherently as her body was wracked by sobs. Sam rolled Laura over. Laura looked up at her, her face wet with tears. There was a cut on her nose and a bruise on her neck.

Sam gasped and covered her mouth with her hand. 'Oh God, Laura.'

'He didn't mean it, Mum. He was really sorry afterwards.'

Sam looked at McKinley, who was standing in the doorway, his arms folded. 'Do you want me to take care of this, Mrs Greene?' he asked.

Laura looked at McKinley in horror as she realised what he meant. 'Mum, no!'

Sam stroked Laura's neck. The bruise was fresh, the skin still red in places. 'You can't let him do this to you, Laura.'

'I can handle it, Mum. Honest. I can.'

'Mrs Greene?' said McKinley.

Sam smiled gratefully at McKinley but shook her head.

Laura started to cry again and Sam cradled her in her arms.

* * *

'This is a waste of my fucking time,' said Frank Welch as he got out of the car and walked to the prison gate.

'Frank, I'm just telling you what he told me,' said Welch's companion, a detective chief inspector in his late fifties with close-cropped snow-white hair and a slight stoop.

Welch turned up his collar against the drizzling rain that was blowing from behind them. 'Does it always rain in Manchester? Last time I was here it was pissing down as well.'

'This? This is a good day.' The man pressed a small button and a couple of seconds later there was a buzzing noise and he pushed open the metal door, allowing Welch through first.

'It's bollocks,' said Welch.

'Don't get angry at the messenger, Frank. If I hadn't passed on the information, what would that make me?'

Welch snorted as he showed his warrant card to the prison officer manning the reception desk.

'Detective Chief Inspector Frank Welch and Detective Chief Inspector Bradley Caine to see prisoner Sean Kelly,' said Caine, showing his warrant card to the prison officer. 'We're expected.'

'We're wasting our time is what we're doing.'

'Jesus, Frank, you're like a stuck record. Listen to the man then piss off back to London, why don't you?'

Welch said nothing else until they were standing in the interview room, facing a tough-looking man in his early thirties. He had receding sandy hair and a boxer's nose, a square chin and a cracked front tooth. He looked at the two detectives without a trace of apprehension. 'Got any fags?' he asked in a Birmingham accent.

Caine tossed a pack of Silk Cut on to the table in front of the prisoner. 'Sean, this is Detective Chief Inspector Frank

Welch from the Met. He's had a long drive and he doesn't like the weather here, so let's keep it short and sweet, shall we? Just tell him what you told me.'

Kelly took out a cigarette, put it to his lips, and raised an eyebrow. Unfazed, Caine took out a slim stainless-steel lighter and lit it for him. Kelly blew a thin plume of smoke at the ceiling, then fixed Welch with his cold grey eyes. 'I killed Preston Snow,' he said.

'Like fuck you did!' exploded Welch.

'Frank . . .' said Caine with a pained look on his face.

'Shot him twice. Once in the chest. Then the head.'

'Bollocks!'

Kelly shrugged. 'Fine. Don't believe me.' He took a long pull at his cigarette and leaned back in his chair.

'Why? Why did you kill him?'

Kelly shrugged carelessly. 'He owed me money. Wouldn't pay and he bad-mouthed me all over the manor. Had to teach him a lesson, didn't I?'

'And you're telling me this, why?'

Kelly shrugged again. 'It's on my conscience.'

'Like fuck it is,' said Welch. 'You've been in prison longer than you've been outside. Armed robbery, GBH, theft, you're a fucking career criminal, Kelly, you don't have a conscience.'

Kelly looked at Welch. He slowly pulled up his sleeve, revealing a tattoo of Christ on the cross. 'I've been born again,' said Kelly. 'I've seen the light.'

Welch snorted and faced Caine. 'He's taking the piss. Terry Greene killed Preston Snow. We had a witness, we had the forensics.'

'Yeah,' said Kelly, grinning, 'but I had the gun, didn't I?'

Welch stiffened. His eyes narrowed as he turned to stare at Kelly.

Kelly grinned up at him. 'A twenty-two. Serial number filed off it but you'll get a match on the bullets. You got the bullets, right? Dug 'em out of the little shit before you buried him, yeah?'

Welch had a sick feeling in the pit of his stomach, but he kept his face impassive as he sat down on one of the chairs opposite Kelly.

'Got your attention now, haven't I, Chief Inspector?' said Kelly. He leaned forward. 'You know the canal, the one that goes through Regent's Park? Goes to Camden Lock. There's a path you can walk along. Nice walk of an evening, before they shut the gates. Last bridge before Camden Lock. Look under there.' He sat back and watched Welch with amused eyes. 'Praise the Lord,' he said, and waggled his hands.

* * *

Sam walked down the escalator and turned left on to the Tube platform. The electronic board said that there was a train due in two minutes. She checked her watch then walked to the far end of the platform. There were four seats there, little more than individual plastic mouldings on a metal frame, designed so that the homeless couldn't sleep on them. There was only one man sitting there, and Sam sat next to him. She was holding a copy of the previous day's *Evening Standard* and she placed it on her lap, headline uppermost.

The man glanced sideways at the paper. He was in his mid-forties, his brown hair flecked with grey, and he wore a green anorak over a black polo-neck sweater. 'You know that's yesterday's paper?' he said.

'Yes, I know,' she said.

Two Japanese tourists walked by deep in conversation, studying an *A to Z* street directory.

'There was an interesting article that I missed,' said the man. 'About cars.'

Sam passed the paper to him. 'You can have this one,' she said.

The man took the paper. Inside was an envelope. He thumbed open the envelope flap and flicked through the wad of fifty-pound notes. 'Thought maybe you wouldn't be needing me,' he said, 'Terry being inside and all.'

'Terry says it's business as usual,' said Sam. 'The cars are both Mercs, the registration numbers are on the envelope.'

The man closed the paper. Air rushed along the platform, warning of the approaching train. He stood up. 'Let me know when they're coming over,' he said. 'Just in case I've got to juggle the rosters.'

The train arrived. It disgorged its passengers, and the man boarded without a backward look.

Sam sat and watched as the train pulled away. The man she'd just given two thousand pounds to was a senior Customs officer based at Dover who would ensure that the cars containing the counterfeit money weren't searched as they entered the country. Terry had explained how and when the man was to be paid, that the car registration numbers had to be written on the envelope, and that Sam wasn't to refer to the man by name. Everything, even down to the out-of-date newspaper, had been planned by Terry. Sam sighed as the train disappeared into the tunnel. She felt like a puppet, and Terry was the one pulling her strings. It wasn't a pleasant feeling. She stood up and went back up the escalator.

There were double yellow lines all around the Tube station, so McKinley had parked about a hundred yards away. He saw her walking to the car and had the door open for her by the time she reached it.

'How did it go, Mrs Greene?' he asked as he climbed into the car and started the engine.

Sam lit a cigarette. 'I don't believe that Terry's got me doing this,' she said. 'Fixing up drug deals, threatening corrupt detectives and paying off bent Customs officers. He's turned me from a housewife and mother into a gang boss in a matter of weeks.'

McKinley grinned at her in the rear-view mirror. 'You're doing fine, Mrs Greene,' he said. 'It's like you were born to it.'

Sam took a long pull on her cigarette. 'That's what scares me, Andy.'

* * *

Searchlights played across the surface of the canal, the water splintering the light into a thousand shards. It was a bitterly cold night and Frank Welch wore a sheepskin jacket and woollen hat, his gloved hands thrust deep into his pockets. He stamped several times on the canal towpath like a racehorse impatient for the off. 'This is bollocks,' he said.

Simpson, Duggan and Clarke stood at the mouth of the tunnel, their shoulders together as if they were huddling together for warmth. 'Sounds far-fetched to me, guv,' said Simpson. 'Kelly's never used a shooter before.'

'Sawn-offs,' said Duggan, taking a hip flask from his back pocket. 'He's used sawn-offs before.' Welch frowned at the pewter flask and Duggan put it back in his pocket, unopened. Welch was a stickler for his people not drinking on duty. Not in view of civilians anyway, and there were a dozen or so onlookers peering over a police line on the other side of the canal.

'Snow wasn't killed with a shotgun,' said Welch acidly. 'He was shot with a handgun. A twenty-two.'

'That's what I'm saying,' said Simpson. 'Kelly never used a twenty-two.'

There were two divers in the water, and two more on the side of the canal checking their gear. Other members of the diving team held ropes tied to the men underwater, and another diver waited with an assistant in a rubber dinghy in the middle of the canal. They had been searching the bottom of the canal for more than eight hours and had decided to continue through the night rather than starting again the following day. Welch suspected that overtime payments were the prime consideration of the diving team, but he hadn't argued. He wanted the farce to be over as quickly as possible so that he could get back to Superintendent Edwards and tell him that Kelly was a lying bastard who should be prosecuted for wasting police time.

'How about I go get coffees?' suggested Clarke.

'There's no coffee places around here,' said Welch.

'There's a pub back up the road,' said Clarke.

Welch gave him a withering look. 'Do I look like I was born yesterday?' he asked.

'Worth a try, guv,' said Clarke, unabashed.

The canal was only about fifteen feet deep and they could see the underwater flashlights of the divers as they moved slowly along the bottom. Welch stamped his feet again. Another hour, he decided. Another hour and he was going to call off the search. They'd started at the point Kelly had described and worked out from there. Now they'd searched the full length of the tunnel and ten feet outside either end.

One of the spectators on the other side of the canal was holding a camera with a long lens and a large flashgun. It looked like a professional set-up and Welch said a silent prayer that the man wasn't a newspaper photographer. That would just about make his week, his photograph on the front page of one of the tabloids. Welch could imagine the headline. 'POLICE REOPEN TERRY GREENE CASE.' He shivered.

There was a flurry of bubbles in the canal and then a gloved hand appeared, holding something aloft. Something glossy and wet, glistening in the searchlights. Something that looked disturbingly like a handgun.

'Fuck,' said Welch.

'Looks like a twenty-two to me,' said Duggan.

* * *

Terry hung his towel on one of the hooks by the entrance to the shower room and walked under the steaming jets of water. There were only three other men in the showers and they acknowledged Terry with nods.

Terry soaped himself down, relishing the hot water as it coursed over his body. One of the many things he missed in prison was being able to take a shower whenever he wanted. The three prisoners finished showering and left, their feet slapping on the green-tiled floor. Terry closed his eyes and let the water play over his face.

He turned around under the water, raising his arms. He heard footsteps and opened his eyes. Two men had walked into the shower room, fully dressed. Terry recognised one. Rodney Hobson, shaven headed and heavily tattooed, was serving a life sentence for a double murder. The man with him was shorter and more squat with a frog-like face, wide lips and bulging eyes. His name was Byrne, and like Hobson he was a lifer. Hobson had a home-made shiv in his right hand, a razor blade embedded in a toothbrush handle. Byrne was holding a wicked-looking metal spike, at least nine inches long. They moved towards Terry, ignoring the water cascading over their prison-issue denims.

Terry stepped to the side, away from the water. He knew there was no point in saying anything: Hobson and Byrne weren't there to talk. Calling for help was out of the question, too. No prisoner would respond, and he doubted that the two men had got into the showers unseen by a prison officer. The staff must know what was going on. Terry was on his own.

Hobson slashed with his shiv and Terry took a quick step back. Hobson grinned. Terry moved to the side and Hobson moved, too. Hobson stepped into a shower stream and his eyes blinked against the torrent of water. Terry seized the opportunity and stepped forward, kicking Hobson between the legs. Hobson managed to twist to the side and Terry's foot caught his thigh. Hobson grunted in pain and lashed out with the shiv, almost catching Terry's leg.

Byrne lunged forward with his spike, and Terry managed to deflect it with his hand. He tried to grab Byrne's wrist but Byrne was too quick for him.

The two men regrouped, breathing heavily. Terry ducked

down to his left to a drainhole in the floor. He reached inside and pulled out a foot-long piece of lead pipe. He'd hidden the pipe in the drain soon after Dunne's warning, knowing that there was a good chance that if he was attacked it would be in the showers. He slapped it against the palm of his left hand, a cruel grin on his face. 'Okay, boys,' he said. 'Let's dance.'

Hobson and Byrne exchanged a quick look. Byrne looked apprehensive but Hobson gestured with his chin. 'Get the bastard,' he hissed.

Byrne raised the spike and stepped forward, but he was too slow, Terry lashed out with the pipe and it cracked against Byrne's elbow. Byrne yelled and the spike fell from his nerveless fingers and clattered to the floor.

Terry tried to kick the spike away but Hobson moved in, slashing his shiv from side to side. Terry jumped back.

Byrne was nursing his injured elbow. 'For fuck's sake, man, use your other hand,' said Hobson. He forced Terry back with slashes of the shiv and back-kicked the spike to Byrne. Byrne knelt and picked it up with his left hand.

Hobson kept forcing Terry back until he was in a corner. Byrne came up behind Hobson, a manic gleam in his eyes, his right arm hanging uselessly by his side.

Hobson grinned triumphantly. 'You're dead meat, Greene!' he hissed.

Terry said nothing. He swung the lead pipe slowly, his feet shoulder width apart, waiting to see who would attack first. Byrne would have to use a stabbing movement, and it was the end of the spike that would do the damage. Hobson would have to slash to use the edges of the blade. Different weapons, different methods of attack, different defences. Terry fought to keep his breathing calm and relaxed, knowing that if he hyperventilated he'd lose concentration. Hobson and Byrne were both breathing like bulls at stud, their chests rising and falling, their lips drawn back in savage snarls.

Is was Hobson who moved first, slashing at Terry's stomach. Terry breathed in and swung his pipe at Hobson's head, clipping him in the mouth and breaking a tooth. Blood spurted from Hobson's lips and he grunted and stepped back. Byrne stabbed the spike at Terry's face and Terry ducked to the side. He felt a stinging sensation across his chest and realised that Hobson had cut him.

Terry dropped on one knee and swung his pipe at Byrne's shin as hard as he could. He heard a satisfying crack and Byrne pitched forward, screaming. Terry stood up and pushed him away, then he charged at Hobson, bringing the pipe down on the back of the man's shaven head. Hobson's eyes rolled back and he slumped to his knees. Terry hit him again on the back of the head and Hobson pitched forward, unconscious. Byrne was moaning and trying to get to his feet. Terry stamped on him over the kidneys, and he kept stamping until Byrne lay still.

Terry stood over the two injured men, panting. He wiped his face, then put the lead pipe back in its hiding place. Drops of blood plopped on to the tiled floor and streaked towards the drain. Terry examined the cut on his chest. It was about six inches long and ran just above his stomach. It wasn't too deep and by the look of it wouldn't require stitches.

Terry took his towel off the hook, wrapped it around his waist and walked out of the shower room.

Chief Prison Officer Riggs was standing in the toilet area, leaning against one of the cubicles. He straightened up when he saw Terry, a look of surprise on his face. He stared open-mouthed at the blood on Terry's chest.

Terry put his hand on the cut and showed his bloody fingers to the officer as he walked past him to collect his clothes. 'Must have cut myself shaving, Mr Riggs,' said Terry.

* * *

Superintendent Edwards stood in front of the window, his hands clasped behind his back. 'I'm not sure I understand this aversion to gift horses, Frank,' he said.

Welch was pacing up and down, shaking his head. 'Terry Greene killed Preston Snow. End of story.'

'You're off the case, Frank.'

Welch stopped pacing. 'Like fuck I am!'

Edwards stiffened. He looked at Welch coldly and Welch realised that he'd overstepped the mark.

'I'm sorry,' he said.

Edwards nodded, accepting the apology.

'But I'm telling you,' Welch continued, his tone more conciliatory this time, 'Sean Kelly didn't do it. No way. He's lying.'

Edwards moved away from the window and sat behind his desk, steepling his fingers under his chin. 'Look at the facts, Frank. Why would Kelly lie his way into a life sentence? He's doing seven years for armed robbery, probably be out in four. Kelly says he killed Snow and he's given up the gun. It is the gun, right?'

Welch nodded. Forensics had shown that the bullets that had killed Preston Snow were fired by the twenty-two they'd found in the canal.

'And we never had a motive for Greene killing Snow.'

'Drug dealers falling out. Happens all the time.'

'But we had nothing concrete, Frank. Kelly has a motive. Solid gold.'

Welch shook his head, refusing to accept what the superintendent was saying.

'So Terry Greene's going to be out before you can say "miscarriage of justice", Frank.' Edwards put his hands on his desk. 'Your best bet would be to keep your head down and avoid the flak.'

Welch snorted and turned to leave.

'I'll do what I can, but . . .'

Welch stormed out of the office before the Superintendent could finish.

* * *

Sam was loading the dishwasher when the phone rang. It was Laurence Patterson. 'Samantha, good news,' he gushed. 'The best. Terry's going to be released.'

'What?' said Sam.

'Terry's going to be out. A few days, a week at most.'

Sam felt her legs start to tremble and she put a hand against the fridge to steady herself. 'What's happened, Laurence?'

'Someone else has confessed to the murder. And given the murder weapon to the police. It's an open and shut case.'

'That's what they said about Terry.'

'This is different, Samantha. The only real evidence against Terry was the witness, and Morrison's dead—'

'What about the forensics?' interrupted Sam.

'Called into question,' said Patterson. 'Welch could be out on his ear after this.'

'I don't believe it,' said Sam.

'Believe it,' said Patterson. 'It's on the fast track with the Court of Appeal. We'll be suing for compensation, the works. We've won, Samantha! Terry's coming home.'

'That's great news, Laurence,' she said hesitantly.

'I've already spoken to him, and he says he can't wait to see you. And he says to hang fire on the other thing until he's out.'

Sam frowned. 'The other thing?'

'You know. The thing you were arranging for him. The business thing.'

Sam realised what he meant. The counterfeit money. 'Right, Laurence. Sure. Thanks.'

She hung up, her mind in a whirl, and sat down at the kitchen table. She wondered why she didn't feel elated. It was what she'd been working towards, getting Terry out of prison, but she didn't feel the least bit happy about the solicitor's news. In fact she had a sick feeling of dread in the pit of her stomach. An image sprang into her mind and she realised why she was so apprehensive. It was Terry, outside the church as he was being led to the van in handcuffs. 'Keep your chin up,' he'd said. 'There's light at the end of the tunnel.'

How had he known? How had Terry known that someone else would be confessing to Preston Snow's murder?

* * *

The next few days passed in a blur. There were congratulatory phone calls from most of Terry's friends. George Kay, David Jackson, Warwick Locke. Even Micky Fox called from Spain, where he'd rushed off to following the cannabis fiasco. They were all coming out of the woodwork now that they knew Terry was going to be released. Sam accepted their congratulations and good wishes without warmth, unable to forget how unhelpful they'd been when she needed them.

The day before Terry was due to appear in the Court of Appeal, the Press laid siege to her house and she kept the curtains closed and the phone off the hook. Trisha didn't want to go to school and Sam couldn't blame her, so they stayed at home watching television. Journalists kept shoving pieces of paper through her letterbox offering money for an interview, and the doorbell rang so often that Sam disconnected it.

The Press became increasingly obtrusive during the evening, presumably because their deadlines were approaching. Earnest men and women trampled over the garden and knocked on her windows, and once a reporter from one of the tabloids pretended to be delivering a bouquet of flowers and shouted a barrage of questions when Trisha opened the door.

When she peered through the curtains and found a television crew climbing over the garden wall, Sam decided that she'd had enough and phoned Andy McKinley. He arrived within thirty minutes, accompanied by half a dozen burly bouncers from Lapland. They forced the Press pack off the property and stood at the entrance to the driveway, glaring menacingly at any reporter who came near them.

Sam let McKinley into the house and made him coffee. 'I called the police, but they said there was nothing they could do.'

'Nothing they wanted to do, more likely,' said McKinley, sipping his coffee. 'They're going to look pretty stupid when Terry is released.'

'I can't believe it's all happened so quickly,' said Sam. 'A few weeks ago it looked as if he'd never get out. Now . . .' She shook her head. 'I just don't know, Andy.'

McKinley said nothing as he studied her over the top of his mug.

'Do you think this is . . .' She couldn't finish the sentence. She lit a cigarette. 'I'm sorry. I'm not making much sense.'

'You're under a lot of stress, Mrs Greene.'

'Yeah. Maybe.' From upstairs came the sound of Trisha's stereo. Sam smiled ruefully. 'Trisha's not exactly over the moon at the thought of her dad getting out.'

McKinley looked uncomfortable and Sam realised that she was putting him in a difficult position. While McKinley had been a tower of strength for her, Terry was still his boss.

'Thanks for coming, Andy.'

'Absolutely no problem, Mrs Greene. I'll stay the night, yeah?'

'Are you sure?'

'I think your husband would want me to. And you'll need me to drive you to the court in the morning.'

Sam felt a lot safer knowing that McKinley was in the house. He slept in Jamie's room and was up half an hour before her, cooking scrambled eggs and bacon. Trisha turned up her nose at the food but Sam ate gratefully and drank two cups of strong coffee.

Most of the journalists had gone by the time they left the house. Two of McKinley's friends still stood guard at the gate, and a man and a woman stood next to a car watching the house. The man made a half-hearted attempt to shout a few questions at the Lexus as it drove by, and the woman produced a camera with a motor drive and snapped away. Sam kept her head down until they were well away from the journalists.

'There'll be more at the court, Mrs Greene,' warned McKinley, fastening his seat belt as he steered with his right hand. 'It's a big story.'

'They're parasites,' said Sam, putting on a pair of dark glasses.

McKinley waited with the car while Sam went inside the Court of Appeal. Terry was brought up by two prison officers, and he waved at Sam and grinned. Pike and Russell were in the court and they started cheering until a court officer hissed at them to be quiet.

Of the three judges, only one spoke. Sam barely heard his words, and was surprised at how brief the procedure was. Two minutes, three at the most, then a cheer went up from the people in the court.

Terry walked out of the dock and hugged her. 'Told you,' he whispered in her ear. 'I told you it would be okay.'

Laurence Patterson clapped him on the back, and Terry's barrister, John Orvice shook his hand. Terry put his arm around Sam and they walked out of the court together.

Welch and two of his detectives were sitting at the back of the court and they glared at Terry as he walked by. Terry grinned over at Welch. 'Drinks in the pub later, yeah, Raquel? I'm buying.'

'Leave it, Terry,' said Sam, and he hugged her.

Outside, cameras started clicking and TV crews ran forward, their lights blinding. Sam put her dark glasses on as Terry launched into an impromptu speech.

'I just want to thank my legal team, and for all the support I received during my incarceration,' he said. 'I always knew I was innocent, but this isn't the first miscarriage of justice in this country and it won't be the last. Someone should take a closer look at the way the police are conducting investigations. It was obvious to a blind man that I wasn't guilty.'

Several reporters started shouting questions, but Terry held up his hand to silence them. 'It's the Snow family that I feel sorry for. What they've been through. Now I just want to go home and get on with my life. I hope you'll all respect my privacy. I'm happy to answer a few questions now, but then I hope you'll leave me and my family alone.'

There was another flurry of questions. Sam pulled at Terry's arm but he wouldn't budge, as if he was relishing being the centre of attention.

* * *

McKinley sat in the Lexus watching Terry talk to the assembled journalists. He tensed as he saw someone he recognised, walking purposefully along the road to the court. It was Luke Snow, his dreadlocks tucked in a black woollen hat, his shoulders hunched inside his green Army surplus jacket.

McKinley got out of the car and hurried to intercept Snow, who was so fixated on Terry and the Press pack that he didn't see McKinley until he was right in front of him. 'Don't even think about it, Luke,' said McKinley quietly.

Snow's right arm tensed. McKinley caught a glimpse of something metallic in Snow's pocket. A knife. McKinley was almost relieved. A knife he could handle. A gun would mean problems.

'He killed my brother and got away with it,' whispered Snow through clenched teeth.

McKinley looked steadily at Snow, his hands swinging freely at his side. He didn't want to make any movement that might antagonise Snow, but he wasn't going to be caught unawares either. 'The court said he didn't do it,' said McKinley.

'Fuck the court,' spat Snow. He tried to get past McKinley, but McKinley moved with him, blocking his way.

Snow started to pull the knife from his pocket and

McKinley clamped a hand on his arm. Snow fought against him but McKinley was by far the stronger man. 'I'll break it,' said McKinley.

'He killed my brother!' hissed Snow. There were tears in his eyes and his lower lip was trembling. 'Now look at him, mouthing off to the fucking Press.'

'He's not doing this to be famous, Luke.' McKinley felt Snow stop struggling against his grip and let go off his arm. 'Go home.'

'I'll kill him.'

'No you won't, Luke. Not here. Not with so many cops around.' There were three uniformed police officers standing outside the court, and Raquel and two of his detectives were walking out, surrounded by reporters holding out tape-recorders and scribbling in notebooks. 'You won't get within ten feet of Terry Greene. And you'll end up doing time. For what?'

'For my brother. For my fucking brother.'

Over at the court, Terry and Sam moved away from the TV crews, flanked by Pike and Russell. Fletcher was at the wheel of a large BMW and they all piled in.

Snow stared after the car as it roared off down the road. A tear ran down his cheek and he pulled his right hand out of his pocket to wipe it away, revealing a six-inch long-bladed hunting knife.

'For God's sake, Luke, put that away!' said McKinley, looking around to check that the police hadn't seen the weapon.

Snow realised what he'd done and hurriedly put the knife away. 'Sorry,' he said.

McKinley patted him on the shoulder. 'Go home.'

Snow nodded and walked slowly away, his head down. McKinley watched him go, then went back to the Lexus.

* * *

George Kay had closed Lapland to the public and broken open several dozen cases of his best champagne to celebrate Terry's homecoming. Most of the dancers had been invited, though they were under orders to dress conservatively out of respect for the large numbers of wives who were expected to be in attendance.

More than two hundred people shouted and cheered as Kay walked out on to the stage, where a banner reading 'WELCOME HOME TERRY' had been strung between two of the silver poles. Kay tapped the microphone, whispered, 'Testing, testing,' and then shouted for quiet.

The crowd gradually quietened, albeit for the occasional popping of a champagne cork.

'It's true what they say, isn't it? You can't keep a good man down,' said Kay, loosening his tie. 'And they don't come any better than Terry Greene. Come on, Terry. Get up here!'

Terry climbed up on the stage, accompanied by a loud cheer. He raised both his arms in the air in a victory salute. The crowd burst into applause. Kim Fletcher fell back off his chair and crashed to the ground. Pike and Russell pulled him to his feet and Fletcher waved apologetically at Terry and mouthed, 'Sorry.'

Terry laughed out loud. He stood basking in the applause for a full minute before waving his arms for silence. 'Shut up, I've got something to say!' he yelled.

The audience cheered all the more and Terry grinned across at Sam, who was sitting at a table with Richard Asher and Laurence Patterson. She smiled back and raised a glass of champagne to him.

Eventually the audience stopped applauding and Kay handed his microphone to Terry, who walked to the centre of the stage, picked out by a spotlight. 'I really want to thank you all for your support,' he said. 'There were times over the last few weeks when I thought I'd be spending the rest of my life behind bars.'

There were shouts of 'No way' from Fletcher's table.

'Seriously. It's at times like that when a man finds out who his friends really are. And I found you lot.' The audience started to applaud and Terry had to shout to make himself heard over the clapping. 'I guess that means I'm fucking stuck with you!'

Everyone cheered and glasses were raised in salute.

Terry waited for them to go quiet again. 'And for those of you that are wondering . . .' He paused and patted his backside. 'Yes, I'm still very much a virgin.'

The audience burst into laughter and there was more applause.

Terry waved for silence, then pointed a finger at Patterson. 'And to you, Laurence, I can't thank you enough.'

Patterson raised his glass to Terry. 'My bill's in the post!' he shouted.

'Yeah,' said Terry, 'and my cheque's in your mouth.'

There was more laughter and again Terry called for silence.

'But there's one person here I owe everything to. Without her, well, she knows what she did. And how much I owe her. Sam, get on up here. Come on.'

Sam shook her head.

'Come on!' shouted Terry. Sam smiled but shook her head again. There were cries of 'Go on, Sam' from all around her table. She waved her hands in front of her face.

Terry walked towards her, wagging his finger at her. The spotlight moved to pick her out, and she shaded her eyes with one hand.

'Don't make me come down there and get you!' warned Terry.

Sam stood up amid thunderous applause. She threaded her way through the tables towards the stage and Terry helped her up. He stood with his arm around her, acknowledging the applause and cheers.

'I want you all to know that I love this woman. She stuck by me when I needed her, she kept the family together, she did what she had to do.' Terry put his hand on his heart and looked into her eyes. 'I know that I haven't been the easiest man to live with over the past few years, Sam, and hand on heart I apologise for that. I'm going to make it up to you, I promise.'

Sam looked at him, still embarrassed at being on the stage. He reached over and stroked her cheek as if trying to coax a smile from her. Slowly she began to shake her head, then a smile broke across her face. Terry leaned towards her and kissed her, full on the lips, and the audience went crazy, shouting and clapping as if the curtain had just gone down on a West End show.

'I've one last request,' said Terry.

'I thought that was only for the condemned man!' shouted Fletcher.

'Will someone put Kim on the next bus home,' said Terry. 'Seriously, Sam, how about a song? How about a song for me?'

Sam shook her head.

'Come on,' he said. He dropped down on one knee and offered her the microphone. 'Please. Sing.'

'No,' she hissed. 'It's been ages.'

The audience started shouting for her to do as Terry asked, and she reluctantly took the microphone from him. 'You'll pay for this,' she whispered, but Terry just grinned. A backing track started. George Kay gave her a thumbs-up from the side of the stage where he was standing by the sound system. Terry stood up and left her alone on the stage.

Sam fluffed the first few words but she was soon on top of the song, amazed at how quickly the phrasing came back to her. She hadn't sung professionally for more than twenty years, though she'd often been made to perform at social occasions. Luckily her audience were usually so inebriated they never noticed when she forgot the words or lost the tune.

Terry went to sit with Asher and Patterson and he raised his glass to her from the table. Sam walked to the edge of the stage and stood singing to him. It was almost like the old days, she thought. The days before she'd caught him having one affair too many. The days before she'd kicked him out, the days before he'd gone to prison on a murder charge. The days before she'd become a drug importer and gang boss.

As she sang she caught sight of Andy McKinley standing at the bar at the back of the club. He was looking at her, his face impassive as if his mind was elsewhere. Sam flashed him a smile and winked but McKinley didn't react. He seemed to be looking straight through her. It was an uncomfortable feeling and Sam felt a cold shiver run down her back.

She was on the last verse when suddenly the lights went on and the music died mid-note. A uniformed policeman and two policewomen walked through the club towards Terry's table. There were jeers and catcalls from the audience but the police made straight for Terry. Sam's heart sank as the heavily built male officer walked up to Terry and put a hand on his shoulder. Terry sat transfixed, a look of horror on his face.

'Mr Terrence Greene?' said the officer. The two female officers, one blonde, the other a redhead, stood behind him. The blonde took out a pair of handcuffs.

'What the fuck's going on?' said Terry.

'Terrence Greene, I have a warrant here for your arrest . . .'

Terry tried to get to his feet, but the blonde policewoman pushed him back in his seat and clamped the handcuffs to his left wrist.

'I have to caution you,' said the male officer, 'that anything you say may be taken down . . .'

At that, the policeman turned to the redheaded policewoman, grabbed the bottom of her skirt and ripped it off, revealing stockings and a suspender belt and bright red panties.

'. . . and rubbed against you!'

George Kay fiddled with the sound system and stripping music blared out across the club. The three officers stripped off the rest of their clothing, and the blonde sat in Terry's lap, rubbing her breasts across his face as the redhead handcuffed his hands behind his back. Warwick Locke stood up at his table and shouted something at Terry, and Sam figured that it was probably Locke who'd arranged the surprise. The blonde whispered something into Terry's ear, but Terry shook his head.

Sam watched from the stage. Terry looked across at her, grinning apologetically, and Sam smiled back even though she didn't feel like smiling. Seeing Terry surrounded by his cronies, the centre of attention, she wondered if the leopard truly had changed its spots. She looked over to the bar to see how McKinley was reacting to the interruption, but he'd gone.

* * *

The taxi dropped them outside the house and Terry slipped the driver a twenty-pound note and told him to keep the change. 'Our financial problems are over, are they, Terry?' asked Sam, climbing out of the taxi.

'Nah, I'm going to take it out of McKinley's wages,' said Terry. 'I told him he was supposed to drive us home tonight. He had no right disappearing like that.'

The taxi headed down the driveway as Sam fumbled for her doorkey. Terry came up behind her and tried to kiss her neck.

'I meant what I said, Terry,' she said, firmly. 'A nightcap and then you're on your way.'

'Nothing like making a man feel wanted,' said Terry.

Sam opened the door and Terry followed her inside.

'Great night, though, wasn't it?' said Terry, closing the door.

'It was. One hell of a night.'

'Yeah. I should get freed from prison more often.'

Sam went into the sitting room and poured large brandies. As she turned to hand a tumbler to Terry, he surprised her by grabbing her and kissing her. With a tumbler in either hand, she wasn't able to push him away, and his mouth stifled her protests. She fought against him, but then started kissing him back. He caressed the back of her neck as his tongue probed hers and his other hand cupped her breast. She felt her nipple stiffen and she moaned softly.

Terry broke away, grinning. He took the brandy from her and raised it to her. 'Cheers, love,' he said.

'You bastard,' she said.

'You're my wife, Sam. Kissing isn't against the law.'

'We're separated.'

'I know.'

'We've been separated for almost a year and a half.'

'I know.'

'So maybe you don't understand the meaning of separation.'

Terry sat down and sipped his brandy, watching her with amused eyes. 'Oh no, I understand it. Laurence Patterson spent a great deal of time explaining it to me. What it meant and what the financial implications were.'

'You've still got the flat?'

'Are you asking, or telling?'

'I'm asking, Terry.'

'Yes, I've still got the flat.'

'So it's not as if you're on the street, is it?'

'Sam . . .' groaned Terry.

'Don't Sam, me,' she said. 'If you want, I can get Trisha's dictionary, just to refresh your memory on the definition of separation.'

'That was then, Sam. This is now.'

'You want to move back in, is that it?'

Terry held her look. 'Do you want me to move back in?'

Sam smiled sadly. 'Terry, you can't just storm back into my life as if nothing's happened.'

'I know.'

'You betrayed me. I lost count of the number of times you let me down.'

'I know, I know. And I'm sorry.'

'You're not sorry, Terry. I can see it in your eyes.'

'Bloody hell, Sam, the amount of champagne I've had to drink, I'm amazed you can see anything in my eyes.'

'I can see it, Terry.' Sam drained her glass and looked at her watch. 'I've got to get to my bed. I'll call you a cab.'

Terry lay back in his chair and loosened his tie. 'Sam, love, we're not going to get a cab this time of night.'

Sam shook her head. 'We got a cab here without any problems.'

Terry looked at her plaintively and made little puppy noises.

'You are pathetic,' she laughed. She stood up and put her empty glass on the sideboard. 'Okay, you can stay.' She pointed a warning finger at him. 'You can sleep in Jamie's room.' She bent down and kissed him on the top of the head. Terry tried to grab her waist but she was too quick for him and slipped away. 'And I'm warning you, Terrence Greene, I sleep with a knife under my pillow.'

Terry closed his eyes and rested his head on the back of the chair. Sam stood watching him. His hair was tousled and there was lipstick on both cheeks where the strippers had planted kisses. He was one hell of a good-looking man, and if anything he'd become even better looking over the years. Sam knew why so many women found him attractive; she'd known from the first time she went out with him that she'd always have competition for his affections. They'd gone to an Italian restaurant in Soho and the waitress who'd served them had batted her eyelashes and flashed her cleavage for all she was worth. Terry didn't seem to notice, his eyes never seemed to leave Sam's face all the time they were in the restaurant and Sam had loved him for that. A wedding ring on his finger hadn't made him any less attractive to other women, but, in the early years at least, Terry had always been faithful. It was only after the birth of Jamie that Terry had started to stay out late and Sam had begun discovering the telltale signs that perhaps her husband was succumbing to the temptations on offer. At first Sam had tried to convince herself that it was all in her mind, but she found too many scribbled phone numbers in his pockets, too many unexplained restaurant and hotel receipts, to blame an overactive imagination.

Terry smiled, his eyes still closed. 'You're watching me, aren't you?'

'No,' said Sam, and walked out of the room, annoyed that he was still so able to predict her actions.

She went upstairs and showered, and watched herself in the mirror as she towelled herself dry. She dabbed perfume behind her ears as she smiled at her reflection, then stopped, wondering why the hell she was making herself smell good. She put the perfume bottle down. 'Damn you, Terry,' she whispered to herself.

She went through to the bedroom, turned off the light and got into bed. She lay on her back, staring up at the ceiling, listening to her own breathing.

She heard the whisper of the door against the carpet and she rolled on her side. Terry was standing in the doorway, wearing his old bathrobe. 'Found it in the kids' bathroom,' he said.

'Never got around to throwing it out,' said Sam. 'Go back to bed, Terry.'

'You don't mean that.' Terry kept his eyes fixed on hers. He took a step forward. Then another.

'Terry . . .' Sam could hear the indecision in her voice, and as he took another step forward, she felt the resistance flow out of her. She sighed and lifted the duvet. Terry slipped off the robe and got into bed with her. Sam rolled on to her back and Terry reached for her, kissing her hard and sliding his hand between her legs. She opened for him, gasping as he touched her, ashamed at herself for being so ready for him and yet wanting him with all her heart. He moved on top of her and she cried out his name as he entered her, hard and forcefully, but his lips were gentle on hers and his hands never stopped caressing her.

She turned her head away so that she could speak. 'Don't

hurt me again, Terry,' she whispered, wrapping her legs around him.

'I won't,' he said, thrusting into her so strongly that she cried out. 'I promise,' he said, and then he pushed his mouth on to hers and she surrendered herself to the kiss. It was as if they'd never been apart, Sam realised. Terry knew exactly how to move, how to touch her, how to do everything she craved until she was his, his alone, calling out his name and never wanting it to stop.

* * *

Sam opened her eyes. Terry was looking at her, a sly smile on his face. 'You still snore, then,' he said.

'You bastard,' she laughed, and tickled him.

They kissed and Terry put his arm around her. Sam stroked his stomach. She frowned as she felt the scar on his stomach and she pulled the quilt down to see what it was. 'Christ, Terry, what happened?'

Sam stared at the wound. It was almost four inches long and there were surgical stitches spaced along it at regular intervals. It had almost healed but there was still a thick ridge of red tissue. 'That's a knife wound,' she said.

'What, you're a doctor now?' laughed Terry.

'It's not funny, Terry. Doesn't it hurt?'

Terry shook his head. 'It itches a bit, that's it. It'll be fine in a few days. Superficial, the doc said.' He grinned. 'Come on love, you didn't pay it any attention last night.'

Sam grinned and slapped his chest. 'You didn't give me a chance,' she said. 'I barely had time to draw breath.'

Terry snuggled against her. 'You've got time now,' he said. He pulled her close and kissed her. As he rolled on top of her, the bedroom door opened.

'Mum, do you want a cuppa?' asked Trisha. She froze as she saw Terry. 'What's he doing here?'

Sam looked pained. 'Trisha . . .'

'Morning, Trish,' said Terry, unabashed.

'You slut!' Trisha yelled at Sam, then ran out of the room.

Sam pushed Terry off her. 'Terry . . .'

'Leave her, she'll be okay.'

Sam got out of bed and pulled on her dressing gown. She went to Trisha's bedroom and knocked on the door. 'Go away,' said Trisha.

Sam pushed the door open. 'Trish . . .'

'Go away!'

Trisha was lying face down on her bed, holding her pillow tightly. Sam sat down next to her and put a hand on her shoulder. Trisha shook her away. 'Leave me alone,' she said.

'Trisha . . .'

'How could you?'

'Trish . . . he's my husband.'

Trisha rolled over and looked at Sam tearfully. 'He walked out on us. He didn't give a shit about you or me or any of us.'

'He didn't walk out. I told him to go.'

'So you say,' said Trisha, her voice laden with bitterness.

'That's right. That's what I say. But whatever the circumstances, he's back now,' said Sam firmly.

'He's not back, Mum,' said Trisha. 'He's visiting. First bimbo he meets, he'll be off again.'

Trisha dropped back on the bed and rested her chin on her pillow. Sam patted her on the back, but Trisha shook her off again.

Sam went back to her bedroom. The bed was empty. She heard running water. Terry was in the shower. She sat down on the bed and put her head in her hands.

* * *

Frank Welch nodded at Clarke and the detective flashed a slide up on to the wall. Welch strode over and tapped his finger in the middle of Sean Kelly's forehead. More than a dozen detectives were gathered for the briefing, and Welch knew that they were all familiar with the Greene case so he didn't have to cover the basics. 'Greene walked free yesterday because this little shit confessed to the shooting of Preston Snow. Sean Kelly. Blagger doing a seven stretch in the Scrubs.'

Welch nodded at Clarke and a second slide flashed up on to the wall. Terry Greene. 'We all know that Terry Greene killed Snow. So first things first, I want to know why Kelly confessed.'

'Didn't he give up the murder weapon?' asked a young detective constable who had recently joined the team.

Welch frowned at the man, who couldn't have been more than twenty-five years old. 'What's your name, son?' asked Welch.

'Wright,' said the detective hesitantly, realising that he'd offended the chief inspector.

'Why don't you speak when spoken to, Detective Constable Wright?' said Welch. 'Unless you'd rather go back to being plain old Constable Wright.'

The detective nodded and flushed beetroot red.

Welch turned back to the huge projected photograph of Terry Greene. 'So, before I was so rudely interrupted, I want Greene under twenty-four-hour surveillance. He's just lost four tons of top-grade cannabis, so he's going to be hungry for a deal. Any deal. Could be drugs, could be a robbery, but it'll be something big and it'll be soon. We put him under the microscope until we find out what it is.'

The lights flickered on and Welch scowled over at the door, wondering who had the temerity to interrupt his briefing. It was Superintendent Edwards. 'Can I have a word, Frank?'

'I'm actually in the middle of something, sir,' said Welch.

'I'm sure it can wait,' said Edwards. He left without giving Welch the chance to say anything else. Welch cursed under his breath and followed Edwards to his office.

Edwards went behind his desk and stood there, his back ramrod straight. 'There's no easy way of saying this, Frank. You're suspended.'

Welch was stunned. 'What?'

'I'm sorry, Frank.'

'Sorry? You're sorry?'

'It's the forensics, Frank. With Kelly confessing to the Snow killing, the forensic evidence is called into question somewhat.'

Welch shook his head angrily. 'There was a bloody footprint in Snow's hall, and we found Snow's blood on one of Greene's shoes.'

'Exactly my point,' said the superintendent.

Welch's eyes hardened. 'You're saying I planted the evidence?'

Edwards groaned as if that was the last thing on his mind. 'Frank, please,' he said. 'You're over-reacting. There's to be an investigation, that's all. Until then, it's only prudent for you to catch up on a little gardening.'

'My flat's on the twelfth floor,' said Welch. He could see from the look on the superintendent's face that there was no point in arguing. He turned to go.

'Frank?'

Welch stopped. 'What?'

'Your warrant card.'

Welch took out his wallet, tossed his warrant card on to the superintendent's desk, and walked out.

* * *

A young West Indian prisoner was on the landing phone, but Byrne clipped him on the back of the neck, and when he looked around, Hobson pulled out the man's phone card and threw it over the railing. It fluttered to the ground. 'Now fuck off or you'll follow it,' said Byrne.

Byrne's arm was in a sling, but he was almost twice the size of the West Indian, so the man scurried down the stairs in search of his telephone card.

Hobson slotted in his own card and dialled a number. The phone was answered on the eighth or ninth ring. Hobson's grandmother was deaf in one ear and it often took her a while before she realised that her phone was ringing.

'Nan? It's me,' said Hobson.

'Hello, love. How are you?'

'I'm fine, Nan,' said Hobson. Byrne moved away, out of earshot, knowing that Hobson didn't like anyone listening in when he spoke to his grandmother. It wasn't that he ever said anything confidential, but he was well aware that sweet-talking his grandmother wouldn't do much for his hardman image. 'Did you get my birthday card?'

'I did, love. Thank you.'

Hobson had made the card himself, and had spent hours copying the flowers from a picture in a book he'd found in the prison library. 'I'm sorry I couldn't send you any flowers.'

'Oh, that's all right, love. Your friend brought some around.'

Hobson stiffened. 'What?'

'Your friend Terry.'

Hobson put his hand over the receiver and cursed loudly. Byrne looked over anxiously, but Hobson waved him away.

'Do you want to talk to him?' asked Hobson's grandmother. 'He's still here.'

'Okay, Nan, yeah. Put him on.' Hobson gripped the receiver so hard that his knuckles whitened.

Terry Greene came on the line. 'Hello, mate,' he said cheerfully. 'How's the old place without me?'

'You touch one hair on her head and you're dead, Greene!' hissed Hobson.

'Of course I am,' said Terry. 'Your nan's fine. I love the card. Didn't realise that you could do joined-up writing.'

'Get the fuck out of her house!'

'I was just telling your nan, she should get a smoke alarm. Old houses like this, they can be death traps.' Terry's voice faded as he covered the mouthpiece. 'I'm just saying, Mrs Hobson, you should get a smoke alarm.'

'You bastard!' hissed Hobson.

'You know what I want,' said Terry calmly. 'The name. Then I'll be on my way. Who paid you for that business in the showers?'

Hobson slammed the flat of his hand against the wall. He took a deep breath. 'Don't hurt her,' he said.

'The name,' said Terry.

'Kay. George Kay.'

'See?' said Terry. 'That wasn't so hard.' The line went dead.

Hobson yelled and hit the wall again.

Byrne came up behind him. 'What's up?' he said, putting a hand on Hobson's shoulder.

Hobson yelled in frustration. He turned and headbutted Byrne then laid into him with his feet before two prison officers pulled him off and dragged him away, still screaming.

* * *

Terry twisted around and looked out of the back window of the BMW. 'Fuck,' he said. Three cars back was a brown Rover. Welch's car.

'What's that tosser playing at?' asked Fletcher in the driving seat. Pike was in the front passenger seat, noisily chewing gum.

'Fucked if I know,' said Terry. 'Maybe he thinks he'll catch us robbing a post office.'

'Do you want me to lose him?' asked Fletcher.

'Nah, let's have some fun with him.' Terry peered out of the side window. 'Hang a left, then drive on to the estate there, yeah?'

Fletcher did as he was told. The council estate was a series of eight-storey buildings linked by walkways. Fletcher parked the BMW and the three men ran for a stairway.

* * *

Frank Welch slowed as he saw the BMW pull into the council estate. It wasn't a pleasant place, graffiti covered and home to drug dealers and prostitutes. It was a place the police visited in vans, never on foot.

He saw the BMW and braked sharply. It was parked near a skip overflowing with broken furniture and rolls of stained linoleum. The car was empty.

Welch climbed out of his Rover and looked around. He didn't like leaving his car unattended, but he didn't have a choice if he wanted to find out what Terry Greene was up to. He headed towards the nearest block, but kept looking over his shoulder to check that his car wasn't being vandalised.

As Welch walked around the block he saw Greene on one of the overhead walkways. Greene raised a hand in salute and Welch cursed. He'd been spotted.

'Oi, Raquel, over here!' shouted Greene.

Welch stepped forward. As he did, water trickled down over his head and over the front of his coat. He looked up and it splashed over his face. His stomach turned as he realised that it wasn't water pouring over him. It was urine. Fletcher and Pike were standing on the walkway above, urinating on him.

Welch jumped back, cursing. Fletcher and Pike roared with laughter and zipped up their flies.

'Now piss off!' shouted Greene.

Welch flushed with embarrassment. He took off his coat and went back to his car, wiping his face with his handkerchief.

* * *

Sam was loading bags of groceries into the back of her Saab and thinking about Laura, which was why she wasn't aware of the man's approach until he was standing next to her. 'Mrs Greene?' he said, with a soft Irish lilt.

Sam looked up, frowning. The man was in his twenties, good looking with jet-black hair and piercing-blue eyes. He was wearing a well-cut black leather jacket and brown corduroy trousers. 'Yes?' she said, hesitantly.

'My boss would like a word with you, if you've got the time.' He smiled easily and brushed his hair away from his eyes. He had a boyish look about him that reminded Sam of Terry.

'Your boss being . . .' said Sam.

'The guy who wants a word with you,' he said.

'That's it?'

'I think you know what it's about, Mrs Greene,' he said.

Sam nodded slowly. 'Okay,' she said.

'My car's over there,' he said, nodding at an old Ford Escort.

'I'd rather follow you in mine, if it's all the same to you,' said Sam. 'I've already been towed away once this month.'

'Suit yourself, Mrs Greene,' said the man. He went over to the Escort and Sam got into the Saab. He drove out of the supermarket car park and Sam followed. He kept below the speed limit and indicated well in advance of every turn so that Sam could stay close to him. They drove through West London, then headed north.

The Ford Escort slowed and drove into a breaker's yard, piled high with rusting cars, most of them with no tyres or windscreens. The carcass of an old Jaguar was being loaded into a crushing machine by a bored-looking man sitting at the controls of a crane.

The Escort pulled up in front of a battered Portakabin with cracked windows. A man in his fifties wearing a donkey jacket and a yellow hard hat came out of the Portakabin. 'Thank you for coming at such short notice, Mrs Greene,' said the man as Sam got out of her car. He had a kindly, weatherbeaten face and his eyes crinkled as he smiled. He waved at the driver of the Escort, who reversed his vehicle, turned, and drove away.

Behind her, the crushing machine began to devour the Jaguar in a squeal of tortured metal. 'I wasn't sure if I had a choice,' said Sam, extending her hand.

The man shook it. He had a strong grip and Sam could feel the callouses on his palms and fingers. It was the hand of a man who was used to hard manual labour. 'Of course you had a choice, Mrs Greene.' His accent was also Irish, but it was harder and more guttural than that of the man who'd led Sam to the breaker's yard. 'The name's McEvoy. Martin McEvoy. I'd try to be a bit more devious about it, but as it's written in foot-high letters over the entrance to this place, I don't see that there's much point. Having said that, I think it would be best if you forgot my name immediately you leave the premises, okay?'

'Okay,' said Sam.

They walked together through the yard, between stacks of stripped cars. 'Now then, I'd be grateful if you'd tell me what you told Brian Murphy.'

Sam had almost forgotten about going to see Brian Murphy, and her request for confirmation of Terry's whereabouts on the night that Preston Snow was killed.

'It's not important any more,' said Sam. 'My husband's been released.'

'Oh, it's important, Mrs Greene,' said McEvoy.

Sam looked at him sideways. The man had a pleasant-enough manner, but there was a hard edge to his voice. Sam realised that she and McEvoy were alone, that no one would be able to hear her over the sound of the car-crushing machine, and that a breaker's yard would be the perfect place to dispose of her Saab. And her body. She shivered. If McEvoy noticed her discomfort, he showed no sign of it. Sam took a deep breath. 'My husband was accused of killing a drug dealer. A man called Preston Snow. He told me that on the night that Snow was killed, he was with some of your people, arranging to launder money for them.'

'I don't suppose your husband gave you any names?'

Sam shook her head.

McEvoy stopped and turned to look at her. 'He wasn't laundering anything for us, Mrs Greene. We don't do business with people we don't know. And we don't know your husband.'

Sam felt as if a cold hand had gripped her heart. She could barely breathe and her head swam with the realisation of what she'd just been told. Terry had lied to her about where he was when Snow was killed. And there was only one reason for him to have lied.

'I'm sorry, Mrs Greene,' said McEvoy. He reached out and gave her arm a small squeeze. She could see in his eyes that he knew the significance of his revelation, and that made it all the harder for Sam to bear. She felt tears sting her eyes and she turned and walked away quickly, not wanting McEvoy to see how much pain she was in.

* * *

There were two women on the king-sized bed, a blonde with shoulder-length hair and pneumatic breasts and a brunette who couldn't have been more than a couple of months past her sixteenth birthday. The blonde kissed the brunette and her hand moved between the younger girl's legs, easing them apart. The younger girl moaned and caressed the blonde's breasts, then arched her back as the blonde's fingers moved inside her.

'For fuck's sake, Maddy, at least look as if you're enjoying it!' shouted Warwick Locke. 'You're not exactly giving me a hard-on here.'

The blonde redoubled her efforts, tossing her hair from side to side and moving down the brunette's lithe body, kissing and licking and talking dirty to her.

Locke turned to Terry. 'Fucking amateurs,' he whispered. They were sitting in director's chairs next to a cameraman and sound man who were filming the two women.

Terry grinned. 'They look good to me, Warwick.'

'Yeah, well, it's what they look like on screen that matters,' said Locke. The cameraman was licking his lips, his eye glued to the viewfinder as he moved in for a close-up of the blonde as she started kissing the brunette between the legs.

'All right, Allan, get stuck in there, mate,' said Locke.

A heavily built man with hair almost as long as the blonde's slipped off his bathrobe and went over to the bed.

'Bloody hell,' said Terry, eyeing the man's genitalia. 'That's enough to give anyone an inferiority complex.'

'He is a big 'un, isn't he?' said Locke. 'Wait until you see it erect. Trouble is, Allan shoves so much coke up his nose, it takes him about an hour before he can get a hard-on.'

Allan slid between the two girls. The brunette started to give him oral sex while the blonde rubbed her breasts back and forth across his chest with a look of bored disinterest on her face.

'Maddy, if you don't stop fucking around you're off this set!' shouted Locke. 'And Allan, start to think happy thoughts, will you? You're supposed to be enjoying every man's fantasy here.' Locke pulled a face at Terry and shook his head. 'Bloody artistes,' he said.

A door opened at the far end of the warehouse where they were filming the blue movie, and a large figure ambled in. It was Mark Blackstock, wearing a long, shabby overcoat over his rumpled suit. He walked over to Terry, and nodded at him sullenly. 'I don't like being summoned like I'm some sort of lapdog,' he said.

Terry grinned amiably. 'You'd rather I came around to your office?'

'You know what I mean.' He watched in disgust as the blonde climbed on top of the well-endowed man and began bouncing up and down. 'And why here?'

'It's private,' said Terry. He jerked a thumb at the trio on the bed. 'And there's sloppy seconds if you feel like it.'

Blackie wasn't amused. He turned his back on the bed. 'Don't waste my time, Terry.'

Locke leaned over. 'Please, we're trying to make a movie here,' he said.

Terry stood up, put an arm around Blackstock and shepherded him away from the film crew. 'Look, Blackie, Raquel's still on my case.'

'He's suspended.'

'That's as may be, but he's being a bloody nuisance. I want him off my back.' Terry took an envelope from his suit pocket and handed it to the detective superintendent.

Blackie didn't open it. 'I'm not on candid camera again, am I?' he glowered.

Terry patted him on the back. 'You're getting paranoid in your old age,' he said.

Blackie opened the envelope and flicked his thumb across the banknotes inside.

'Thing is, Raquel I can handle,' said Terry, 'but I need to know if SO11 or the NCU are sniffing around.'

'Doubt if criminal intelligence would be bothered with you,' said Blackie. 'Bigger fish to fry.'

'Thanks for the vote of confidence, Blackie.'

'I'll ask around,' said Blackie, putting the envelope away.

'There's something else,' said Terry.

Blackie sighed. 'There always is.'

'I think George Kay is stooling for Raquel. Check it out, yeah?'

'You don't ask for much, do you?' Blackie shook his head despondently. 'Sam said you were retiring. Going legit.'

'That's the plan,' said Terry, cheerfully.

'When?'

Terry shrugged carelessly but didn't answer.

* * *

Sam had her head in the oven when she heard Terry calling her name. 'In here,' she shouted.

Terry walked into the kitchen. 'Didn't think things were that bad,' he said when he saw what she was doing.

She took her head out of the oven and took off her rubber gloves. 'Ovens have to be cleaned from time to time,' she said. 'Not that you'd know.'

'Any chance of a coffee?' he asked, sitting down at the table.

'What's wrong, Terry?'

'Why should anything be wrong?'

'Because you've got that look on your face.'

Sam made coffees for them both and sat down opposite him.

Terry sighed. 'The thing is, Raquel's been following me around like a lovesick spaniel,' he said. 'He's been suspended, but with him on my back I can't get on with business. And if he sees me going to Spain, he'll start alarm bells ringing. You've got to help me, Sam.'

Sam put down her coffee mug. 'Oh no.'

'The money thing's got to be sorted this week.'

Sam sighed with exasperation. 'So get Micky Fox to do it. Or McKinley.'

'They're footsoldiers, Sam. I need you.'

Sam gave Terry a long, hard look but didn't say anything.

'Sam, it's a one-off.'

'Another one-off?' She sipped her coffee, then lit a cigarette. 'Jamie's up from Exeter on Sunday,' she said. 'I was going to cook. Lamb. It's always been his favourite. Be handy if you were there to carve.'

Terry smiled and nodded.

Sam leaned forward. 'This has to be the last time, Terry. You can't keep asking me to do your dirty work.' She sat back in her chair and shook her head. 'I hate Spain,' she said.

* * *

Emma Riggs rolled over and prodded her husband. He snored loudly and she prodded him again. 'Oliver. Wake up!'

Riggs opened his eyes sleepily. 'What?' he murmured.

'There's someone outside.'

'It'll be those bloody cats again,' groaned Riggs, rolling over and wrapping the quilt around himself.

Riggs' wife shook her head. 'I don't think so,' she said. 'It sounded like the garage.'

At the mention of the garage, Riggs sat up. He strained to listen but all he could hear was traffic on the nearby main road. 'Are you sure?'

'I heard something, Oliver,' she said archly. 'I'm not senile.'

Riggs swung his legs off the bed and picked up his dressing gown.

'Are you going to call the police?' asked his wife.

'Don't be stupid,' scowled Riggs. 'I can handle this myself. It'll be kids, that's all.'

Riggs hurried downstairs and went out through the kitchen door, leaving all the lights off so as not to alert whoever was outside. He'd left a garden spade leaning against the rear wall of the house and he grabbed it.

The garage had been built against the side of the house in matching brick with a sloping slate roof, but there was no connecting doorway leading directly into the house. There was the upward opening metal door at the front and a wooden door at the rear that opened into the garden. Riggs headed towards the rear door, hefting the handle of the spade in both hands. The garage didn't have any windows so there was no way of seeing inside. Riggs pressed an ear against the wooden door. He jerked his head away and swore. The wood was hot. Burning hot. And Riggs could smell smoke.

The door was locked so Riggs rushed back into the kitchen to retrieve the key from its hook by the fridge. He unlocked the door and gingerly opened it. A sheet of flame whooshed out and Riggs ducked back, cursing. He slammed the door shut and hurried around the side of the garage to the front.

He stopped and his mouth fell open. Someone had spray-painted the word 'WANKER' in green paint across the metal door. Riggs reached out and felt the surface of the door. It was also hot to the touch. Riggs stared at the lock. It had been broken, drilled out by the look of it. He carefully twisted the chrome handle and swung up the door. Black smoke billowed out. The Morris Traveller was in flames. The heat was intense and Riggs had to move back as more smoke and fumes poured out of the garage.

He watched in despair as his pride and joy burned. He'd invested thousand of hours in the car, rebuilding it from a rusted wreck that he'd found in a breaker's yard. Every weekend for the past five years had been spent working on it or taking it to classic car shows where he would stand by the open bonnet proudly showing off the results of his restoration to other enthusiasts. Now it was all gone, and the amount it was insured for wouldn't even come close to replacing it.

Riggs knew who'd destroyed his beloved car. The green paint graffiti was enough of a clue. Terry Greene. Terry bloody Greene.

* * *

Sam caught a taxi at Malaga airport and settled back for the drive to Marbella. According to Terry, Micky Fox was staying at a large villa about a mile from the city. The taxi driver didn't know the area and twice had to stop and ask for directions, but eventually they pulled up in front of a pair of wrought-iron gates set in a ten-foot-tall stone wall.

The taxi driver pointed at the gates. 'This is it?' said Sam.

The driver nodded. Sam paid him and got out. An intercom was set into one of the gateposts, and Sam pressed it. After about thirty seconds a Spanish voice said, *'Qué?'*

'It's Samantha Greene to see Micky. He's expecting me.'

There was silence and Sam wondered if the man had understood her, then the gate buzzed and opened electronically. Sam walked up a long, winding drive that zigzagged through well-tended gardens to a huge villa with large balconies on the upper floors and terraces on the ground floor, and a massive white satellite dish in one corner.

A Spanish boy who couldn't have been out of his teens was waiting at the front door. He had jet-black hair, flawless mahogany skin and dark brown eyes and was wearing only a towel wrapped around his waist, revealing a tight stomach and hairless chest. He didn't say anything, but as Sam reached the front door he turned and walked inside the house.

Sam followed the boy through an ornately decorated hall that reached up two storeys, then through two large gilded doors into a sitting room packed with the most tasteless furniture she'd ever seen. There were life-size statues of African natives holding spears, next to Chinese vases with pictures of flowers painted on them, Louis XIV chairs and footstools and overstuffed sofas with tasselled cushions. Thick rugs covered most of the wooden floor space. Large chandeliers dripped from the ceiling, and the walls were hung with portraits of nineteenth-century grandees and their wives in massive gilt frames. The windows were covered with thick green velvet curtains and several lamps were switched on, giving the room a warm glow. There didn't appear to be any air-conditioning and the overall effect was so stifling that Sam was beaded with sweat within seconds of entering the room.

At the far end of the room french windows led out on to a terrace, and Sam blinked as she walked back into the bright Spanish light.

'Sam, over here!' shouted Micky Fox.

Sam shielded her eyes with her hand and peered around the terrace. It overlooked the Mediterranean, which stretched out in front of her, a clear blue that was almost painful in its purity.

'Here, Sam!'

Micky Fox was sprawled on a flight of white marble steps that led down to the shallow end of a large swimming pool, a Spanish boy either side of him. The boys were as young and pretty as the one in the towel who'd guided Sam through the house and who was now showering next to the pool, quite naked. Fox had a champagne glass in his hand, a silver ice bucket containing a bottle of Dom Perignon on the step behind him.

'Sam! Great to see you. Come and have some shampoo.' He gestured with his chin at his two young companions in turn. 'This is Jesus. And Pablo. Come on, get a costume on and join us.'

Sam smiled. 'They're a bit young for me, Micky. Besides, a bit of privacy would be nice.' She lifted the briefcase up so that he could see it. 'I'm here to talk business.'

'Talk away,' said Fox. 'They don't speak English. Do you, Pablo?'

Pablo frowned and put his head on one side. *'Qué?'* he said.

Fox beamed at Sam. 'See?' He leaned over to the ice bucket and refilled his glass. 'So how's Terry, then?'

'Out and about.'

'I knew they wouldn't be able to keep him inside for long,' said Fox, climbing out of the pool and slipping on a peach towelling robe. 'I gather you're getting more involved with the business.'

'Word gets around,' said Sam. It was sweltering by the pool and Sam took off her jacket and rolled up the sleeves of her white silk shirt.

'Not much else to talk about over here, truth be told,' said Fox. He steered her towards a flight of steps that led down to the beach.

'Micky, I'm wearing high heels here,' Sam protested.

'Kick 'em off,' said Fox. 'Get some sand between your toes.'

'I'm also wearing tights.'

Fox laughed and came back up the steps. He sat down on a wooden lounger and Sam dropped down on to the one next to him. Pablo rushed over with a large umbrella and he positioned it to shade Sam before jumping into the pool.

'How's the timeshare coming on?' asked Sam.

Fox pulled a face. 'Like pulling teeth. Bone idle, the Spaniards. Bloody siestas will be the death of me.'

'What are you saying, Micky?'

'They're dragging their feet. The builders. The utility companies. The Spanish bureaucrats.'

'So no cashflow?'

'If I said there's light at the end of the tunnel, I'd be lying, Sam. But we're thinking about changing the design, making them top-end apartments. Marbella is attracting the high-rollers again, we could make a killing.'

'When?'

Fox shrugged carelessly. '*Mañana*,' he said in a bad imitation of a Spanish accent. 'Terry been asking about his investment?'

'Doesn't sound like much of an investment to me.'

'It'll come good eventually, Sam. But you can tell Terry I could put something else his way, if he's interested.'

'That's nice of you, Micky, but Terry's set on retiring.'

Fox laughed. 'Terry Greene settling for a pipe and slippers?'

'I'm serious, Micky,' said Sam. 'He means it.'

Fox stopped laughing, not wanting to offend Sam. 'What are you drinking, Sam?'

'Something cold and non-alcoholic,' she said.

'Orange juice? They grow 'em down the road. They were hanging on trees this morning.'

'Sounds great, Micky. Thanks.'

Fox shouted over at Pablo, who was swimming lengths in a slow, relaxed breaststroke. Pablo waved and swam to the side.

'The cars are ready, yeah?' said Sam.

'Will be by tonight,' said Fox.

'I want a look-see, okay?'

'Sure, Sam. Wouldn't have expected otherwise.'

Pablo padded over, carrying a tray on which was balanced a jug of iced orange juice and a glass. He put the tray down on a table next to Sam's lounger. Sam and Micky said nothing as Pablo poured orange juice into the glass.

'What are you doing out here, Micky?' asked Sam as Pablo walked back to the pool. 'I don't see this being your scene.'

'Pablo, you mean? He's a bit gauche but he's got a lovely arse.'

'I meant the Costa del Crime. I assume there's Pablos all over the world.' She gestured at the villa. 'Don't get me wrong, this is nice, but it's not London, is it?'

Fox gulped his champagne, then wiped his mouth with the back of his hand. 'Something rotten in the state of Denmark,' he said.

Sam frowned.

'That cannabis bust,' explained Fox. 'Someone grassed. I couldn't take the risk of staying. Not until we know who the rotten apple is. Fact is, Sam, I'm surprised you're hanging around there. You never know when the other foot's gonna fall, do you? Tell Terry to watch his back as well, yeah?'

Sam shrugged. 'I figured if they were going to pull us in, they'd have done it already.' She sipped her orange juice.

Fox leaned over conspiratorially. 'I meant what I said about putting something Terry's way,' he said. 'There's a Russian guy here who can get us gear from Afghanistan. Good stuff.'

Sam put her glass back on the table. 'Heroin?' she said. 'Give me a break, Micky. All I'm doing here is putting the finishing touches to Terry's counterfeit thing.'

Fox sighed and loosened his robe. 'It's where the real money is, Sam,' he said. 'Tell Terry if he needs a sweet deal . . .'

Sam gave Fox a hard look and he shrugged and stopped talking.

'Tell you what, Micky. Let me have a shower and a lie down, then you can take me to dinner, okay?'

'Sure thing, Sam. What do you feel like?'

'Oh, I don't know, Micky. What about Spanish?'

* * *

Micky Fox had the good grace not to mention heroin again during dinner. He took Sam to a seafood restaurant, high up on a peninsular overlooking the sea, where he was clearly a regular customer. The *maître d'* greeted him like an old friend, and as they were escorted to their table Sam saw a photograph of Fox and several other London faces sitting at a table raising champagne glasses.

Sam let Fox order, and he chose lobsters and more champagne. Sam wondered why men always ate lobster when they wanted to impress. Warwick Locke had done the same when she'd gone to see him about Terry's share of the model agency. There was something primeval about the way they pulled the crustacean apart, cracking the shell and sucking out the meat. Terry had never liked lobster. He always said that they were nothing more than big insects that happened to live in the sea, and that if they weren't so expensive no one would ever eat them.

After the meal, and more handshakes and pats on the back from the *maître d'*, Fox drove them to a garage on the outskirts of the city. Inside, two Spanish mechanics were packing black plastic-covered packages into the wings of two large Mercedes saloons.

Fox picked up one of the brick-sized packages and took a small silver penknife from his jacket pocket. He cut a slit in the black plastic and handed the package to Sam. It was full of brand new fifty-pound notes. Sam pulled one out and gave the package back to Fox. She held the note up to a light. It looked perfect in every detail, including the silver foil strip and watermark. She whistled softly. 'Bloody hell, Micky. These are good.'

'The best,' said Fox, tossing the package to one of the mechanics.

'Thing is, I can't work out why I had to fly over with a briefcase full of real money to pay off the drivers and the rest.' She held up the counterfeit note. 'Why didn't we just give them these?'

Fox laughed. 'Sam, they're not going to go through all this for funny money. They want real readies.'

Sam smiled ruefully. 'I obviously don't have a criminal mind,' she said. 'Where did you get them?'

'Russian guy.' He smiled. 'Not the heroin guy, don't worry. This guy's former KGB. He used to make counterfeits for the Russian government. Stole a bunch of plates when the wall came down. Now he's freelance.'

'And why take them to the UK? Why not just change them here?'

'No one really checks notes in the UK. They might do what you just did, give them a quick squint, but they don't really check them. Here it's foreign currency, so they give them a good going over. And they're good, but they're still counterfeit.' He walked over to one of the cars and peered over the shoulder of the man who was packing notes into the panels. 'Besides, we don't want to shit on our own doorstep, right?'

'Your doorstep, Micky.'

'For the time being, yeah.' Fox gave the mechanic a thumbs-up and said something in Spanish. The man laughed and Fox patted him on the shoulder. 'You'll stay in the villa tonight, Sam?' he asked.

'Sure.'

'We'll try to keep the noise down,' said Fox with a grin.

'Don't hold yourself back on my account, Micky,' laughed Sam.

* * *

Terry flicked through the channels of the large-screen TV, idly looking for something to watch. He'd just settled down to watch football on Sky Sport when he heard a key in the front door. He hit the mute button on the remote control then stood up and went over to the sitting-room door. He put his ear against it and frowned as he listened. He heard voices. Trisha, and a man's voice.

'She'll be asleep but keep quiet, yeah?' Trisha said. Then she giggled.

Terry eased open the door. Trisha was in the hallway, closing the front door. A teenage boy in a tight white T-shirt and military-style trousers was running his hands through Trisha's long, blonde hair. Trisha locked the door and they headed for the stairs. They both jumped with fright when they saw Terry leaning in the doorway, his arms folded across his chest.

'What the hell are you doing here?' asked Trisha defiantly.

'Babysitting,' said Terry quietly.

'Where's Mum?'

'Out running errands.'

'It's nearly midnight.'

Terry smiled. 'Isn't it just.' He peered at Trisha's eyes. The pupils were dilated and the whites were tinged with red. 'Have you been drinking?' He walked towards her and she moved to get around him. Terry was too quick for her and he grabbed her by the shoulders.

'I'm going to bed,' she said.

'What are you on, Trish?'

'Nothing.'

'It's nothing,' said the boy.

Terry looked at him as if seeing him for the first time. His skin was almost as soft and pink as Trisha's, and it looked as if he didn't have to shave more than once a week. He had grey eyes, and like Trisha the pupils were dilated and seemed to be having trouble focusing. He had a small gold earring in his left ear. Terry reached over, grabbed the earring and pulled it, hard. Blood spurted from the boy's earlobe and he screamed.

'Fucking hell!' he shouted.

'Ken!' shouted Trisha.

Ken took his hand away from his ear and stared at the blood on it. 'I'm bleeding!' he said.

'Better get off home, then,' said Terry. 'Let Mummy have a look at it.' He tossed the earring at Ken's face.

'You can't do that!' yelled Trisha. 'I'm not a baby!'

'Then stop acting like one. Get up those stairs, now!' Terry turned to Ken, who was holding his ear, the colour draining from his face. 'Close the door on your way out, Ken. And don't get blood on the rug.'

Terry followed Trisha up the stairs and bundled her into the bathroom.

'You can't do this to me!' she said.

'I'm your father.'

'Only genetically,' she said.

Terry pushed her into the shower cubicle fully clothed and turned on the cold tap. She started crying and bent double under the torrent of cold water. 'This isn't fair,' she sobbed.

Terry closed the cubicle door and waited until Trisha was soaking wet, then he opened the door and handed her a towel. 'Downstairs,' he said. 'I'll make you hot chocolate.'

Terry went downstairs. Ken had gone. Terry went to the kitchen and boiled milk and made two mugs of hot chocolate. He was stirring them when Trisha appeared wearing a bathrobe.

'You've no right to be here,' she said.

'The mortgage is in my name. And I pay the bills.' He handed her one of the mugs and she took it, reluctantly. 'Sit down, Trish.'

Trisha did as she was told, but she refused to look at her father. 'Does Mum know you're here?'

'Yes, Mum knows I'm here.' Terry sat down opposite her. 'What is it, Trisha? Ecstasy? Dope? Speed? What did that little shit give you?'

'No one calls it ecstasy any more. It's E, and I had one tablet. It's nothing.'

'You've got school tomorrow.'

She lifted her head and looked at him. 'So if it was Friday, it'd be okay?' she sneered.

'That's not what I meant and you know it. How do you think your mum'd feel if she knew?'

'How do you think she felt when the papers were calling you London's biggest drugs dealer?' she retorted angrily.

'How do you think she felt about that? And what about when you were sent down? If anyone's let this family down, it's not me.'

Terry looked at his daughter for several seconds. She was staring at him with a mixture of anger and hatred, and he realised for the first time how much he'd hurt her. He wanted to reach over and hug her, to hold her and tell her that he was sorry, but he could see in her eyes that she was in no mood to be mollified. 'I do what I do to keep this family together,' he said.

Trisha's face contorted with anger. 'You left us, Dad! You didn't keep us together, you broke us apart. What fucking planet are you living on?'

Terry pointed a finger at her. 'Hey!' he shouted.

'Don't tell me to mind my language!' she yelled. 'Don't you dare tell me to mind my language!'

Terry said nothing. Trisha grabbed her mug with shaking hands and raised it to her lips. She sipped her hot chocolate slowly and gradually her hands stopped trembling. She put down her mug. There was a chocolatey moustache on her upper lip and Terry put out a hand to wipe it away. Trisha flinched and Terry took his hand back.

'You've got chocolate,' he said. 'On your lip.'

She wiped it away with her hand. 'Thanks.'

'Is it okay? The chocolate?'

'I guess. Mum makes it better. But this is okay. Thanks.'

Terry watched her take another sip of hot chocolate. 'Why drugs, Trisha? Why do you need them?'

Trisha shrugged. 'Why do you drink? Why does Mum smoke?'

'That's not the same.'

'Says you.'

'It's not just me.'

'Dad, you can count on the fingers of one hand the number of people who've died from ecstasy. Yet cigarettes kill hundreds of thousand every year. Cancer. Heart attacks.

You don't see them banned, do you? Thousands of road deaths caused by drunk drivers. But booze isn't banned. How many times have you driven home drunk?'

'I have people drive me, Trisha. I don't drink and drive.'

Trisha looked away as if she didn't want to argue with him.

'I don't understand what you get from ecstasy, though. Why do you need it?'

'It makes me feel good, Dad. That's all. You feel . . . different. More confident. Happier.' She looked suddenly serious. 'I'm not an addict, Dad.'

'I know. I know you're not.'

'And I can handle it. It's not a hard drug.'

Terry could feel that he was losing the argument.

'Anyway, it's a bit like the pot calling the kettle black, isn't it?' she said. 'Considering.'

'Considering what?'

'Considering how you earn your money.'

Terry stood up. 'Bed,' he said.

Trisha grinned in triumph. 'You don't have an answer to that, do you?'

'I don't want an argument, Trisha,' said Terry.

'No, you don't want to *lose* an argument,' said Trisha. 'There's a difference.'

Terry walked out of the kitchen and back into the sitting room. He sat down in front of the television and turned up the volume.

* * *

Sam arrived at Heathrow just after midday. Andy McKinley was waiting to meet her. He took her bag and walked with her to the multi-storey car park. 'Terry says he's sorry he can't be here to meet you himself, Mrs Greene,' said McKinley. 'Said he had some business to take care of.'

'Like what?' asked Sam.

McKinley shrugged but didn't answer.

'Hear no evil, see no evil?' teased Sam.

'He honestly didn't say, Mrs Greene.'

'But if he had said, would you have told me?'

McKinley looked uncomfortable. 'That's not a fair question to ask me,' he said.

'And that's you being evasive, as usual,' said Sam.

McKinley screwed up his face as if he were in pain, and Sam linked her arm through his.

'I'm only teasing you, Andy. I'm sorry. I'm sure my dear darling husband is behaving himself.'

McKinley looked across at her and Sam burst out laughing at the look of incredulity on his face. 'Teasing again,' said Sam. 'Sorry.'

* * *

Kim Fletcher swung the cricket bat along the shelf, and dozens of bottles of white wine crashed to the floor. 'You just haven't got the message, have you?' he shouted. He swung the bat again and smashed a display of magnums of champagne.

The owner of the off-licence pleaded with Fletcher to stop. He was an Indian in his late forties, his black hair flecked with grey, his moustache almost white, and he bore a passing resemblance to a young Omar Sharif. Fletcher had remarked on the resemblance, and had just asked the man if he was related to the filmstar, when Roger Pike and Johnny Russell had grabbed his arms and Fletcher had started to demolish the shop.

Steve Ryser popped the tab on a can of strong cider and helped himself to a packet of crisps. He was slotting a handful of cheese and onion into his mouth when Terry strode in, his feet crunching on broken glass.

'This isn't a fucking picnic, Steve,' warned Terry.

'Sorry, boss,' said Ryser, spraying crisp crumbs as he spoke. He brushed pieces of crisps out of his beard.

'Terry, please, there's no need for this,' said the Indian. 'My heart. I was only in hospital last year. Any stress and the doctor said it could kill me.'

'Don't fucking talk to me about stress,' said Terry, stepping to the side to avoid a pool of créme de menthe.

Fletcher opened a chilled display case and started dropping bottles of wine on to the floor. The Indian winced as each one smashed.

'For God's sake, Terry,' he whined. 'What am I supposed to do?'

Terry walked over to the man. The Indian struggled to get away but Pike and Russell held him firm. 'You're supposed to buy your booze from me, like we agreed.'

'But the Kosovans . . .' began the Indian.

Terry cut him short with a warning look. 'Fuck the Kosovans.'

'Terry . . .'

Terry raised a hand and the Indian fell silent. 'Don't Terry me,' he said through gritted teeth. 'I'm fed up with being Terryed. Just do as you're told.'

'But . . .'

Before the Indian could continue, Terry grabbed him by the throat and pushed him back. Pike and Russell kept hold of the Indian's arms so that he was spreadeagled against a rack of wine bottles. 'I don't want to hear any buts,' hissed Terry. 'I don't want to hear you say "but" and I don't want to hear you say "Terry". Okay?'

'But Terry . . .'

Pike and Russell grimaced. Terry grabbed a bottle of red wine and the Indian cowered and closed his eyes, whimpering like a scared dog. Terry was just about to bring it crashing down on the Indian's head when he noticed the label. 'This okay, yeah?'

The Indian opened his eyes fearfully. 'What?'

'This wine. Is it okay?'

The Indian swallowed nervously. 'Yeah. It's a fruity red. Full bodied. Blackberry aftertaste.'

Terry pursed his lips as he studied the label. He nodded. 'It'd go with lamb, yeah?'

'Perfect,' said the Indian.

The Indian flinched as Terry reached out with his free hand. Terry smiled and took another bottle of the wine.

* * *

Jamie turned away from the sitting room window. 'Dad's here,' he said.

'Hooray,' said Trisha. 'Let's hang out the flags.' She was arranging knives and forks on the table.

'Be nice, Trisha,' said Laura.

'It's so false, that's all,' whined Trisha. 'Playing at happy families.'

'Dad's back, isn't he?' said Jamie. 'He's back with Mum, yeah?'

'If you can call it back,' said Trisha. 'His toothbrush is in the bathroom, but that's about the extent of his commitment.'

'That's not fair, Trish,' said Laura, putting placemats between the knives and forks.

'How would you know what's fair. You don't live here any more.' She pointed a knife at her brother. 'And neither do you.'

'What are you saying?' asked Jamie. 'Is he back or not?'

Trisha sighed. 'He says he is, but he keeps coming and going at all hours. I don't know why she stands for it. And he's still got his flat. The one he moved into before.'

'How do you know?' asked Jamie.

'I just know,' said Trisha. 'It's his safety net.'

'It's a rented flat,' said Laura. 'He's probably just waiting for the lease to run out.'

'You always take his side,' complained Trisha.

Laura shook her head but didn't say anything.

Jamie put a hand on Trisha's shoulder. 'Come on, Trish.

This means a lot to Mum. Just make an effort, yeah?' Trisha opened her mouth to reply but Jamie held up a warning finger. 'Or I'll flush your head down the toilet.'

Trisha laughed. 'I'm not two years old any more,' she said.

Jamie looked at her seriously. 'I know you're not,' he said.

Trisha narrowed her eyes. 'You are going to be such a good lawyer.' Jamie grinned. 'That's not meant to be a compliment,' she said.

Jamie patted her on the back and went off to the kitchen, where Sam was basting a huge joint of lamb, her hair tied back in a ponytail. 'Dad's here,' he said.

'Table set?'

'Almost.'

They heard the front door open. 'That's a good sign,' said Jamie. 'You've given him a key.'

Sam grinned and pinched his arm. 'He's always had a key, Jamie. It is his house. The mortgage, anyway.'

'How are things? Between the two of you.'

'We're getting there. I did miss him. More so when I thought he was going to be behind bars.' She shuddered. 'One day at a time, yeah?'

The kitchen door opened and Terry walked in with two bottles of red wine. He hugged Jamie and kissed Sam on the cheek. 'Smells lovely,' he said.

'Me or the lamb?' joked Sam.

'Both,' said Terry, trying to kiss her again. She flicked him away with a tea towel.

Terry went into the dining room. Laura rushed over and hugged him, and he kissed her on the top of the head. 'Long time no see, love,' he said.

'I'm sorry,' she said. 'I've just been busy.'

Terry looked closely at her face. 'Is that a bruise?' he said.

'Ages ago. I bumped my head on a cupboard door.'

Before Terry could say anything else, Jamie pushed

open the door and Sam came in carrying the lamb joint on a huge plate. 'Trish, Laura, can you bring in the veggies?'

'How about a hug first, Trish,' said Terry. Jamie gave Trisha a warning look and mimed flushing a toilet. She grinned despite herself and gave her father a perfunctory hug and a peck on the cheek before heading off to the kitchen with Laura.

Terry handed one of the bottles of wine to Jamie. 'Open that, kid,' he said.

Jamie nodded approvingly at the label. 'Didn't know you were a wine buff.'

'Got advice from an expert,' said Terry.

Trisha held out her glass and Jamie looked at Sam. Sam shook her head. 'No way.'

'Mum, I'm fifteen.'

'Come on, Sam,' said Terry. 'A little wine's not going to hurt her.'

Trisha looked across at her father, surprised that he'd stuck up for her. He winked.

'Yeah, the French let babies drink wine,' said Jamie, pouring some into Trisha's glass.

'I'm not sure that's true,' said Sam. 'Come on, sit down, Terry.' She pulled out the chair at the head of the table for Terry. He took his place and began carving the massive joint.

'Lovely,' he said, carving off a large slice.

'Better than bread and water, hey, Dad?' said Jamie.

'Jamie!' said Sam, shocked.

Terry grinned amiably. 'Nah, he's right, love. A few weeks behind bars makes you appreciate home-cooked food.'

'Well, thank you very much.'

'That's not what I meant,' said Terry. 'Your grub's always been top notch.' Terry heaped meat on to Jamie's plate and nodded across at Laura. 'So where's that husband of yours?' Terry asked her.

Laura shrugged. 'He had a golf game he couldn't get out of,' she said.

'Too good for us?' said Terry.

'It's not that.'

'When was the last time he set foot in this house, hey?'

Laura looked plaintively at Sam.

'He works hard,' said Sam.

'We all work hard. He was keen enough to take our money for the reception.'

'That was four years ago. And you insisted,' said Laura.

'I don't remember threatening to break his legs if he didn't take it.'

'We've only got your word for that,' said Trisha. Sam flashed her a warning look. 'Well, we haven't,' muttered Trisha under her breath.

'The lamb's lovely,' said Laura.

'Yeah, great,' said Jamie.

Terry raised his glass. 'We don't do this often enough,' he said.

'Being in prison didn't help,' whispered Trisha.

Terry grinned and raised his glass to her. 'You're right, love, it didn't,' he said. 'But I'm out now, and we're a family. So come on, everyone raise their glass.'

They did as he asked.

'To family,' he said.

'To family,' they echoed, though Jamie kicked Trisha under the table when he saw that she was only miming the words.

Terry helped himself to vegetables. Sam watched him pile carrots and sprouts on to his plate and wondered whether they were truly a family again. Straight and narrow, he'd promised, but Terry didn't appear to be doing anything to distance himself from his criminal associates or activities. And there was still the question of where Terry had been the night that Preston Snow was shot. Terry had lied to her about that – so what else had he lied about?

Terry looked up and smiled at her, and she smiled back, trying to push the dark thoughts to the back of her mind.

* * *

The framed photograph crashed into the wall and fell to the ground in a shower of broken glass. Jonathon Nichols walked over to it and stamped on the broken frame, grinding the bits into the carpet. It was a photograph of Laura and Sam, holding each other and smiling. 'I said I didn't want you to go around to his house!' shouted Nichols.

Laura was curled up on the sofa, crying. 'It's my mum's house,' she sobbed.

Nichols stood over her, his hands on his hips. 'Oh, I misunderstood,' he said. 'Your father wasn't there, then?'

Laura didn't reply. She reached for a cushion and hugged it to her chest.

'I knew it,' said Nichols triumphantly.

Laura curled up into a ball. Nichols grabbed her by the collar and shook her.

'They're my family!' cried Laura.

'I'm your family,' hissed Nichols, pulling her to her feet.

'No, you're not,' said Laura, glaring up at him. 'You don't know anything about families. Your mum and dad sent you away to boarding school first chance they got. You know nothing about families!'

Nichols sneered at her and pushed her. She staggered back, lost her balance and screamed as she crashed through the glass-topped coffee table. She lay on the floor surrounded by bits of wood and glass, her arm over her face. Blood trickled down the side of her neck and she moaned softly.

Nichols knelt down next to her. 'God, Laura. I'm sorry.' He pulled out a handkerchief and held it against the worst of her cuts. 'Laura, listen to me. Can you hear me?'

Laura's eyes fluttered, then closed.

'Laura, you mustn't tell anyone I hit you, okay? You

have to say you fell. Do you understand? You mustn't say I hit you.'

* * *

Terry walked down the hospital corridor, his footsteps echoing like pistol shots off the tiled walls. Sam looked up as he walked into the intensive care unit. Laura was lying on her back, hooked up to monitoring equipment. Terry rushed over to his daughter and looked down on her. Her face was black and blue and so swollen that he barely recognised her.

'She's okay,' said Sam. 'It looks worse than it is.'

'What happened?' asked Terry. He put out a hand and gently stroked Laura's hair. The monitoring equipment bleeped slowly and regularly. Her right forearm was bandaged, and there were several dressings on her left arm and on her neck.

'She tripped, she said,' said Sam, standing up and walking up behind him. 'Tripped and fell through the glass coffee table, the one in the sitting room.' Tears welled up in Sam's eyes and she brushed them away with the back of her hand. 'He hits her, Terry.'

Terry frowned. 'What do you mean, he hits her?'

'He loses his temper.'

'He hits her? I'll kill him.'

'You can join the queue.'

'Where is he?' said Terry.

'He's gone home.'

Terry's face contorted with rage. 'I'll fucking kill him!'

Sam put her hands on his shoulders. 'Calm down, Terry.'

'Calm down? How long has this been going on, Sam?'

Sam shrugged. 'A while, I guess.'

'Why didn't you tell me?'

'You were in prison, remember.' Terry glared at her and Sam pulled an apologetic face. 'I'm sorry,' she said. 'That wasn't fair.'

Terry put his hands on her face and kissed her forehead. 'I know, love. It's not you and me should be fighting. We should just be glad it wasn't worse, yeah?'

Sam hugged him and they stood listening to the bleep of the monitoring equipment.

'What does the doctor say?' asked Terry.

'She's lost some blood. Not enough to need a transfusion. And he doesn't think that she'll be scarred.'

Terry tensed again. 'Scarred? For fuck's sake!'

'Terry, can you watch your language?'

'It's a fucking hospital here, not a church.'

'Terry!'

Terry softened. He kissed her on the forehead again. 'I'm sorry, love. Good as gold, I promise.'

'I'll hold you to that, Terry,' said Sam, looking deep into his eyes.

Terry smiled down at her. 'Yeah, I bet you will, too,' he said.

They stayed with Laura for an hour, but she didn't wake up. A doctor examined her and said that she was asleep, she wasn't unconscious or in a coma, that she just needed rest. She'd be out of intensive care the next day and probably home within forty-eight hours, he said. At nine o'clock a nurse came in and said that they'd have to go, that visiting hours were over.

When they got home, Trisha was sitting on the stairs, her face with streaked with tears. 'How is she?' she asked.

'She'll be fine,' said Sam, closing the front door.

'What happened?'

'She fell,' said Sam, flashing Terry a warning look. 'It was an accident.'

Terry went through to the sitting room and poured himself a Scotch.

'Has Jamie gone back to Exeter?' asked Sam.

Trisha nodded. 'Yeah, he said he's got exams tomorrow. He'll call you tonight, he said.' She nodded towards the sitting room. 'Is he staying the night?'

'He's your father, Trisha. And he's still my husband.'

'He'll let you down again, Mum. You know he will.' Trisha stood up. 'It'll end in tears. It always does.' Trisha went up to her bedroom. Sam watched her go, wondering if her daughter was right. Would it end in tears? And would she ever know the truth about where Terry had been the night that Preston Snow was murdered?

She went into the sitting room. Terry handed her a tumbler of whisky. Sam shook her head. 'Take it,' said Terry.

Sam was too tired to argue. She took the tumbler from him and sat down on the sofa in front of the fireplace. Terry sprawled in an easy chair and put his feet up on the coffee table. They sat in silence, listening to the tick of the brass carriage clock on the mantelpiece.

* * *

Sam rolled over and opened her eyes. Terry was sitting on the edge of the bed, pulling on his trousers. 'What time is it?' she said, sleepily.

'Go back to sleep, love,' said Terry. He stood up and zipped up his trousers.

Sam peered at the alarm clock on her bedside table. It was just after two o'clock in the morning. 'Where are you going?' she asked.

'Duty calls,' said Terry, slipping on a black polo-neck sweater. 'Mountains to climb, rivers to cross.'

'It's starting again, isn't it?' said Sam, trying to sit up.

Terry sat down on the bed. 'It's business, love,' he said, and moved to kiss her.

Sam pushed him away. 'Just go,' she said. She rolled over in the bed and turned her back on him.

Terry reached out to stroke her but she shrugged him away. He put on a jacket, went downstairs and let himself out of the front door.

Pike and Russell were waiting for him, standing next to the

BMW. Ryser was in the driver's seat, wearing a baseball cap the wrong way around.

Terry climbed into the back seat. 'What are you waiting for?' he asked. 'And when are you going to shave off that beard, Ryser? It gives me the willies.'

They drove for half an hour to a warehouse in Clapham. A car was waiting for them, and it flashed its headlights. It was Fletcher and Ellis. 'Right, let's get this over with,' said Terry.

They piled out of the BMW. Pike opened the boot and handed out axes and pickaxe handles.

Fletcher and Ellis walked over, Fletcher carrying two red cans of petrol and Ellis holding a cardboard box with a mobile phone taped to the side. They were all wearing gloves.

'You sure that thing'll work?' asked Terry, nodding at the box.

'I just hope we don't get a wrong number while we're setting it up,' said Ellis.

'I hope you are fucking joking, Pete.'

Ellis grinned. 'Yeah, boss. It's switched off.'

'Yeah, well, make sure it stays that way until I'm well out of it, okay?' He looked around the team. 'Okay?'

They all nodded.

'Let's do it, then.'

They walked together to the wooden door at the side of the main delivery area. Pike swung his axe and the wood around the lock splintered. Another whack with the axe and the door hung on its hinges and Ryser booted it open. They rushed in and fanned out. Two Kosovans were sleeping on camp beds among the hot dog trolleys. Ellis and Ryser set about them with pickaxe handles while Pike started smashing up the trolleys.

Terry and Ellis walked to the middle of the warehouse and put the cardboard box on a shelf surrounded by bottles of whisky. 'Seems like a terrible waste of booze, boss,' said Ellis as he checked the mobile phone on the side of the box.

'We'll get a bigger bang,' said Terry. 'Besides, this isn't

about stealing booze, it's about teaching that bastard Poskovic a lesson he won't forget.'

Fletcher began slopping petrol over the shelves. The two Kosovans had been beaten unconscious and Ellis and Ryser dragged them outside.

Terry went over to the office in one corner of the warehouse and kicked in the door. Checking through the drawers of the two desks inside, he found a wad of twenty-pound notes which he stuffed into his pockets.

By the time Terry went back into the warehouse, Fletcher had emptied the two petrol cans and the air was thick with fumes. 'Right,' said Terry, 'everybody out.'

They got back into their vehicles. Ellis leaned in through the window of the BMW and handed a mobile phone to Terry. 'Just press send,' he said, grinning.

As the BMW pulled away from the warehouse, Terry pressed the send button. The phone at the other end rang twice, then there was a dull thudding noise that they felt as much as heard, followed almost immediately by a loud explosion that tore up through the roof of the warehouse and blew out the windows.

Ryser, Pike and Russell all ducked involuntarily, but Terry didn't even flinch. He laughed uproariously and slapped Ryser on the back. 'That'll let the bastards know that Terry Greene is back,' he said. 'Come on, let's go get us a drink.' He tossed the mobile phone out of the open window as the BMW sped away.

* * *

Sam opened her eyes sleepily. 'Terry? Is that you?' she asked. There was no answer. She rolled over and saw that the door was open. She couldn't remember whether or not Terry had closed it when he'd left. She squinted at the bedside alarm clock. It was just before four o'clock. 'Damn you, Terry,' she muttered to herself and closed her eyes.

She heard a rustling sound and jerked awake. 'Terry?' No answer. She sat up. 'Trish?' A figure stood by the window and Sam widened her eyes, trying to accustom them to the dark. The figure moved towards her, and Sam still half thought that it might be Terry, fooling around, but as the man moved closer she recognised his features. It was Luke Snow, wearing a long black leather jacket and brown trousers that had faded at the knees, and a shapeless peaked leather hat from which his dreadlocks dangled like bits of old rope. And he was holding a sawn-off shotgun.

'Where is he?' hissed Snow. He pointed the shotgun at Sam's face and she flinched.

'He's not here,' said Sam, pulling the quilt around her.

'I can see that. Where's he gone?' He was sweating, and looked around nervously as if expecting Terry to appear at any moment. He waved the shotgun back and forth, his finger tight on the trigger.

'I wish I knew,' said Sam.

Snow glared at her. He lifted the butt of the shotgun to his face and aimed it at her chest, squinting along the stubby barrel. 'You're his wife, aren't you?' he snarled.

Sam didn't say anything. She swallowed, but her mouth was so dry she almost gagged. She put a hand up to her mouth, but dropped it and held on tightly to the quilt when she realised how much it was shaking.

Snow took a step towards her, the butt of the shotgun pressed against his cheek. 'When's he coming back?' he whispered.

Sam stared at the twin barrels. They seemed huge enough to swallow her up. She could barely imagine the damage the weapon would do if Snow fired it at short range, and her heart was now pounding so hard she feared it would burst. She took a deep breath and tried to calm herself. 'I don't know if he is,' said Sam. She could see the look of disbelief on his face. 'I'm serious, I'm not sure where I stand with him at the moment. He says he's back—'

'I'm not interested in your marital problems,' interrupted Snow, taking another step towards her. He raised the shotgun as if to strike the butt against her face, and Sam threw up her hands defensively. 'Don't lie to me,' said Snow. 'If you lie to me I'll blow you away, I swear to God I will.'

'I'm not lying,' said Sam, her voice trembling. 'Why would I lie? You can see he's not here.'

Snow aimed the shotgun at her again. 'Yes, I can see he's not fucking here. Now I'm going to ask you one more fucking time, when's he coming back?' Sweat was pouring down his face and he wiped his forehead with his sleeve.

'I don't know,' said Sam. 'Look, you're Preston Snow's brother, aren't you? Luke Snow?'

Snow jabbed the end of the shotgun at her. 'Shut the fuck up!' he hissed.

'This is about your brother, isn't it? It's not me you want to hurt, is it, Luke?'

'Shut up!' he repeated. 'I'll use this. I will.'

Sam stared at the barrel of the gun. Her legs were shaking under the quilt and her mouth was so dry that every breath hurt her. She kept picturing the explosion and the blood and the mess, and she held the quilt tighter even though she knew it offered no protection. She brought her knees up towards her chest in an attempt to stop them shaking. 'Look, my daughter's asleep down the corridor,' she said quietly. 'I don't want her woken up. She's got school tomorrow.'

Snow's dreadlocks swung from side to side under his leather hat as he shook his head. 'What?'

Sam nodded at the shotgun. 'They go bang if they go off.' She forced a smile, trying to put Snow at ease.

'Don't fucking patronise me!' he hissed. 'I'll shoot you and I'll shoot your slag of a daughter.'

Sam narrowed her eyes. 'Just because you're angry at my husband doesn't give you the right to take it out on his family,' she said quietly.

'I'm the one with the gun,' he hissed, taking a step towards her, his eyes wide and staring.

Sam glared back at him. 'That's right. You are.'

Snow looked down at the shotgun as if seeing it for the first time.

'What do you think you're doing, Luke?' asked Sam quietly.

'I'm gonna kill him,' said Luke. He held the shotgun with his right hand, and began to stroke the stubby barrel with his left. 'He killed my brother so I'm gonna kill him.'

'Aren't you forgetting something?' asked Sam.

Snow frowned. 'What?'

'The Court of Appeal released him. Someone else confessed. That guy in prison said he shot your brother.'

Snow's face contorted with rage. 'Just because someone else confessed, doesn't mean your husband didn't kill Preston,' he said. 'He shot my brother then he got someone else to say that they did it.'

'That doesn't make sense and you know it,' whispered Sam. 'Why would someone confess to a murder they didn't do?'

Snow shook his head. 'I don't know, but he did. Your husband got away with murder.' He shook the shotgun in her face. 'And I'm gonna give him what he deserves.'

'Then you'll be in prison, too,' said Sam. 'Is that what you want? You want to spend the rest of your life behind bars? How does that help your brother?'

Snow paced up and down at the foot of the bed. 'I'm not stupid, I know nothing's going to bring Preston back. This isn't about bringing him back, it's about teaching your husband a lesson.'

'If you shoot him, he's not going to learn anything, is he?'

Snow stopped pacing and pointed the shotgun at her again. 'You're patronising me again!' he hissed.

'I'm just saying, that's all,' said Sam. 'Revenge isn't going to get you anywhere. It doesn't help anyone.' She pushed the quilt to the side and swung her legs over the side of the bed.

'What are you doing?' said Snow, stepping back. He waved the shotgun at her.

Sam ignored him and reached for her dressing gown. 'Do you want a coffee?' she said, tying the belt of the robe.

'What?'

'Look, you obviously came here to shoot Terry,' said Sam patiently. 'He's not here, and you don't look as if you're going to hurt me. Not deliberately, anyway. So we might as well be civilised.'

Snow stood holding the shotgun and shaking his head as if not sure how to react. 'No. Stay here. We're going to stay here and wait for him to come back.' He aimed the shotgun at her stomach.

'I already said, he might not come back. He might stay out all night. It wouldn't be the first time. At least let me make you a coffee. Okay? We can wait for him downstairs just as easily as here.'

Snow stared at her for several seconds, then he let the shotgun swing down to his side. He shrugged. 'Yeah. I guess.'

Sam nodded and headed downstairs. Snow followed her. He walked on tiptoe, and Sam realised he was trying not to disturb Trisha. She smiled to herself. Snow was a hurt, disturbed young man, but he didn't appear to be a cold-blooded killer.

Sam switched on the kettle and took instant coffee and sugar out of a cupboard while Snow paced up and down. 'I'd offer you decaff, but I haven't got any,' she said.

Snow frowned. 'What?'

'Sit down, Luke, you're wearing a hole in the floor.'

Snow took off his hat and more dreadlocks tumbled around his neck. He sat down at the kitchen table and put the shotgun on the chair next to him, taking care that it wasn't pointing towards Sam. 'Where did you get that from?' Sam asked, gesturing at the gun.

'Guy in a pub,' said Snow. 'Three hundred quid.' He

pulled an apologetic face. 'I didn't mean to scare you, you know.'

'That's sweet of you, Luke,' said Sam, smiling thinly. 'Sweet, but bullshit. What if my husband had been in bed with me? What if you'd shot him? Sugar?'

The last bit threw Snow and he frowned. 'What?'

'Sugar?' repeated Sam. 'Do you take sugar, because we haven't got any. We've got sweetener, though.'

'No. No sugar. Just milk.'

'Sweet enough, huh?' said Sam, but Snow just frowned again.

The kettle boiled and Sam made two mugs of coffee. She handed one to Snow, who nodded his thanks and cupped his hands around it, blowing on the surface to cool it.

'I probably wouldn't have done it,' he said, his voice little more than a whisper. 'I didn't know what else to do.'

Sam sat down opposite him. 'Why are you so sure that my husband killed your brother?' she said.

Snow shrugged. 'The police said. That detective, Welch.'

Sam shook her head. 'Welch has had it in for my husband for years, Luke. The Met's full of bent coppers. And your brother was a drug dealer, right? He must have had lots of enemies.'

'Yeah, I tried to tell him he was heading for trouble . . .'

'Wouldn't listen?'

'Nah. You can only do so much, right? Alicia was always trying to keep him on the straight and narrow, but he wouldn't listen to her, either.'

Sam frowned. 'Alicia?'

'Preston's wife.'

Sam put her mug down. 'She wasn't mentioned in court.'

'Nah. They were separated. She'd left him long before he . . .' Snow couldn't finish the sentence. He sipped his coffee. 'Moved to Bristol, I think.' Snow looked at his watch. 'I'd better be going. My wife's gonna go mental if I stay out all night.'

He stood up and reached for the shotgun. Sam put her hand on it. 'Why don't you leave that with me?' she said.

Snow smiled apologetically. 'Guy I bought it off said he'd give me half the money back if I didn't fire it,' he said. Sam took her hand away and Snow picked up the shotgun, carefully as if he feared it might break. 'I won't be back,' he said. 'Don't worry.'

Sam put a hand on his elbow and squeezed gently. 'I am so sorry about what happened to your brother,' she said.

Snow nodded. 'Thanks,' he said.

* * *

Sean Kelly frowned as he saw who was waiting for him in the interview room. He turned to the prison officer who had escorted him down from the landing. 'I've fuck all to say to him,' said Kelly.

'Sit down and shut up,' said Frank Welch. Welch tossed two packs of cigarettes on to the table in front of him. They were Kelly's brand. Kelly sneered at the cigarettes, but he sat down opposite Welch. The detective gestured at the prison officer to leave them alone.

As the prison officer opened the door, Kelly twisted around in his seat. 'Oi, don't leave me alone with him,' he said.

'Don't worry, Sean,' said Welch. 'You're not my type.' Welch waited until the door was closed before speaking again. 'How do you feel?' he asked.

Kelly looked confused. 'What do you mean?'

Welch stared coldly at Kelly. 'You know what I mean.'

Kelly opened one of the packs, took out a cigarette and lit it with a safety match.

'I spoke to your doctor,' said Welch, quietly.

Kelly tensed. 'Like fuck you did.'

Welch smiled and raised an eyebrow. 'Always getting parking tickets, doctors.'

Kelly narrowed his eyes as he scrutinised the detective, then he looked away. 'Fuck,' he whispered.

'Pancreatic cancer's a bitch, isn't it?' said Welch, his voice almost a whisper. Welch sat in silence for a few seconds, then he leaned forward. 'Went around to see your missus, too. Nice car she's got. New stereo, as well. I know it doesn't mean much to you, putting your hand up for the Preston Snow murder. Not when you've only got a year or so. But I bet Terry Greene was really grateful. Who paid over the money, Sean? McKinley, was it? Kay? Or did his wife pay out? Was it Sam Greene?'

Kelly picked up the two packets of cigarettes and stood up.

'Was it Sam Greene?' shouted Welch. 'Was it?'

Kelly turned his back on the detective and hammered on the door to be let out.

* * *

Sam walked slowly through the graveyard. Leaves swirled around her feet as she arrived at Grace's grave. She knelt down and placed a small bouquet of lilies against the stone. Lilies had always been Grace's favourite flower.

Sam brushed dead leaves away from the bottom of the stone, then stood up, wiping her hands. 'I miss our little chats, Grace,' she said. 'I really do.'

Two small boys ran alongside the brick wall that bordered the pavement, laughing and kicking a soft-drink can. Sam smiled at their youthful exuberance, all their lives ahead of them.

'Well, your darling boy's out,' she said, shoving her hands deep into the pockets of her coat. 'He's still got me doing his dirty work, though. He's back in the house. He's even back in my bed. But I've got this horrible feeling that something's not right. What's a girl to do, Grace? What's a girl to do?'

Sam sighed. The bunch of lilies fell over and Sam knelt down and propped them up again. She ran her hand along the cold smoothness of the polished marble. 'He told me he was with some Irish heavyweights the night Snow was shot, but he was lying. So where was he, Grace? Where was he?'

Sam put her head on one side as if expecting the gravestone to answer, but the only sound was the wind whipping around the church.

'Laura's in hospital. She's on the mend. Still says she tripped. I don't know why she stays with him.' She laughed harshly. 'That's not true, is it?' She nodded at the adjoining gravestone. Grace's husband. 'You of all people know that, don't you? You either love 'em or you don't. What do I do, Grace? The more I dig, the more I think he's been lying to me.'

* * *

It was early evening and Sam was lying down in her bedroom with a cold compress on her eyes. Trisha was out at a concert – it was Friday, so Sam had said she could stay out late, so long as she was back before midnight. Terry was out too, but he'd been less specific about where he was going, and even vaguer about when he'd be getting back.

She was drifting in and out of sleep, relishing the chance of being alone. No arguments, no decisions to be made, no verbal jousting. Just silence and solitude.

She stiffened as she heard a noise on the landing, followed by the swish of the door rubbing against the carpet. Images of Luke Snow and his shotgun flashed through her mind and she ripped off the compress and struggled to sit up. Someone was moving towards her, someone in black, someone with a hand outstretched. Sam opened her mouth to scream, but then her eyes focused and she realised it was Terry.

'For God's sake, Terry, what are you playing at?' she shouted.

Terry sat down on the edge of the bed. 'Now what's wrong?'

'Creeping up on me like that.'

'I didn't creep.'

Terry looked genuinely concerned at her reaction. Sam hadn't told him about Snow's nocturnal visit to the house, and she didn't intend to.

She sat up and brushed the hair away from her eyes. 'I was asleep,' she said.

'I didn't mean to scare you,' he said.

'You should have knocked. Or rung the bell.'

'I live here, Sam.'

'I wonder about that.'

Terry frowned. 'Okay, and I wanted to surprise you.'

'Well, you did that.'

Terry grinned and picked up a nylon holdall. He unzipped it and emptied the contents on to the bed. There were bundles of fifty-pound notes. Dozens of bundles. Hundreds. The bundles that Sam had last seen in the Spanish garage with Micky Fox. Terry ripped the paper wrapper off one of the bundles and threw the notes into the air. They fluttered around Sam like massive snowflakes.

'It got here?' said Sam. She grabbed a handful of the notes and looked at them.

'Every last one,' said Terry, beaming. He picked up a second holdall and emptied it on to the bed. 'Both cars straight through. Unpacked them at the warehouse, paid off the other investors, this is all ours.' He dropped the empty holdalls on to the floor and kissed Sam, full on the mouth.

Sam pushed him away. 'How much is there?' she asked.

'Here? About half a million.'

'Half a million!'

'Don't get too excited. It isn't real, remember. It's got to be cleaned. Through the clubs, through some people I know. We can't just pay it into the bank.'

Sam pressed a handful of the banknotes to her face and drew in the fragrance. 'I love the smell of new money,' she said.

'We can't spend it, Sam,' said Terry.

'But they're perfect.'

'They're perfect, but they're not real. Get caught with one and we'd be for the high jump. We clean them, get the clean money into the bank, then we can spend it.'

Sam dropped the notes on to the bed. Five hundred thousand pounds. She had seen Terry with wads of banknotes in his free-spending days, but she doubted that she'd ever seen more than a few thousand at one time. Five hundred thousand pounds. It was lottery money. 'How long will it take, to launder it?'

'A few weeks. And whichever way we do it, we lose about twenty-five per cent. Maybe more. We'll probably end up with about three hundred thousand when we're all square.'

Sam nodded. That was still big money. At least their short-term money problems would be over.

Terry moved on to the bed, reaching for her.

'Terry!' she scolded.

'Come on,' he said, pushing her back on to the thick layer of fifty-pound notes. 'How often do you get to make love on half a million quid, hey?'

'You tell me,' laughed Sam.

Terry looked down at her. 'I couldn't have done it without you, Sam,' he said. 'Any of it.'

She held his look, and when he moved down on her she reached up for him, her mouth opening to receive his. They kissed, slowly at first, then passion overtook them and Sam rolled over on top of him, pulling at his clothes as he undressed her, panting and urging each other on.

Later, they lay together on top of the money, Sam pressed against his side, her hand gently stroking his chest. 'Did you mean it?' she whispered. 'Straight and narrow?'

'Absolutely.'

'So this is the end of it? You're going to be legit from now on?'

Terry groaned. 'God, you choose your moments, don't you?'

'What do you mean?'

'You know what I mean. You make love to me like there's no tomorrow, then you hit me with the "when are you going to retire?" speech.'

'That's not what happened. I just want to know where I stand, that's all.'

Terry ran his fingers down her spine. 'You're not standing, love.'

Sam smiled coldly. 'This isn't a laughing matter, Terry.'

Terry cupped her breast and tried to kiss her but she turned her head to the side. 'Terry . . .'

'That's my name . . .' He kissed her and this time she didn't turn away. He slipped his hand down between her legs and she moaned softly. He rolled on top of her, but as she opened her legs there was a ringing from the floor.

Terry cursed and groped for his mobile phone.

'Leave it,' said Sam, trying to pull him back.

'I'd better get it, love,' he said. 'It might be important.'

'*This* is important,' she said.

He kissed her on the cheek, then picked up the phone and swung his legs off the bed. 'Yeah?' He listened for a few seconds. I'll be right there. Yeah.' He cut the connection and smiled ruefully at Sam. 'I've got to go, love.'

'Terry, we need to talk.'

He grinned and ruffled her hair. 'We've been doing more than talking, love.'

'There's things we have to discuss.'

Terry stood up and began dressing. 'Sure, but not now, okay? I've got things to do.'

'Mountains to climb?' said Sam, sarcastically.

'Later, I promise.'

Terry finished dressing, kissed her on the cheek, and left. 'Take care of the money, yeah?' he said as he closed the bedroom door.

* * *

Terry drove into the rugby club's car park and pulled up next to Kim Fletcher's car. Fletcher was in the driving seat, Roger Pike beside him. Terry climbed out and went over to Fletcher. There was one other car in the car park. A red Porsche.

'Just him in there,' said Fletcher. 'Through that door then first on the left.'

Terry nodded and held out his hand.

Fletcher reached into his inside pocket and took out a handgun. 'You sure about this, boss?' he said.

Terry took the gun off Fletcher. 'You stay in the car. I won't be long.'

Fletcher looked across at Pike. 'Sure you don't want us with you?' asked Pike.

Terry checked the action of the gun. 'Think I can't handle myself, boys?'

'It's not that, boss,' said Fletcher. 'It's just that if you're going to get heavy, the more the merrier, yeah?'

Terry shook his head and slipped the gun into his jacket pocket. 'This one's all mine,' he said. He headed towards the entrance to the club's gym.

Jonathon Nichols was lying on his back lifting weights, and he didn't see Terry walk into the gym.

'Working off excess energy, are we?' said Terry. 'Now that you haven't got my daughter to beat up.'

Nichols froze, the weights on his chest. 'Terry . . . I . . . she fell . . .' he stuttered.

'Oh, an accident, was it?' said Terry. He bent down and picked up a two-kilogram weight. 'Accidents do happen, don't they?'

Terry tossed the weight at Nichols and it hit him in the chest. 'For fuck's sake!' exclaimed Nichols, scrambling to his feet. He dropped his weights on to the floor and stood rubbing his chest. 'You could have broken my fucking ribs.'

He was wearing a rugby shirt and baggy black shorts. Terry jerked a thumb at the shirt. 'Bit of a poofter's game, rugby,' said Terry. He jabbed Nichols in the chest with his finger. 'All that touching, all that groping, putting your head between other men's legs.' He jabbed him again, hard enough to make Nichols take a step back. 'Gotta be a bit suspect, that. Soccer, now that's a man's game. But then, you're not really a man, are you?'

Nichols took a swing at Terry, but Terry swayed back and the punch went wide. Terry grinned. 'Was that an accident too? I mean, I wouldn't want to misinterpret a perfectly harmless gesture of affection.' He slapped Nichols on the side of the face.

Nichols grunted and threw another punch, but Terry blocked it and hit Nichols twice in the solar plexus. Nichols bent forward, gasping for breath, and Terry elbowed him in the face, hard. Nichols staggered backwards, blood pouring from his broken nose.

'Different, isn't it?' said Terry. 'When they fight back.'

Nichols wiped his bloody mouth. 'I'm sorry,' he muttered.

'No, you're not,' said Terry. 'Not yet you're not.'

He punched Nichols in the face and Nichols fell back, tripping over a set of weights. As he crashed to the floor, Terry started kicking him in the kidneys, grunting with each kick. Nichols curled up into a foetal ball, but that only left his back even more unprotected and Terry laid into him with a vengeance.

Nichols rolled over, trying to protect his back, and Terry dropped down on top of him, trapping the man's arms with his legs and punching him with both fists, left, right, left, right, until his son-in-law's face was a bloody pulp. Terry stopped, panting heavily, and stared down at Nichols. The man's eyes were puffy and half-closed, and as he coughed up blood and phlegm, two teeth slid down his chin and fell on to the floor.

Terry bent down and grabbed Nichols by the collar of his rugby shirt and hauled him to his knees.

'Can you hear me?' said Terry.

Nichols groaned and nodded.

'Open your fucking eyes,' hissed Terry.

Nichols did as he was told and stared up at Terry fearfully. Terry took the gun from his pocket, pressed the barrel hard against the man's forehead and cocked the hammer with his thumb. 'You're a dead man,' said Terry.

'Please don't . . .' gasped Nichols.

'You're a wife beater and a coward,' said Terry. 'No one's going to shed a fucking tear for you.' Terry's finger tensed on the trigger.

Nichols began to sob. There was a bitter smell of urine and the front of his shorts darkened. Terry wrinkled his nose in disgust.

'Don't kill me,' sobbed Nichols. 'Please don't kill me.'

Terry stared down at his son-in-law, a look of loathing on his face. Nichols closed his eyes, still sobbing. Terry took the gun away and pushed Nichols down on to the floor. He stood over Nichols, the gun pointing down at the man's head. 'She's lying in hospital, tubes in her, her face all cut up,' hissed Terry. 'You came this close to killing her. Give me one fucking reason why I shouldn't just put a bullet in your head right now.'

The wet patch around Nichols' groin widened.

'You are fucking disgusting,' spat Terry.

'I'm sorry,' sobbed Nichols.

Terry was breathing heavily. He aimed the gun at a point between his son-in-law's eyes. He thought of Laura and what Nichols had done to her, and the anger flared again. His finger tightened on the trigger. Nichols curled up into a tight ball, his tears smearing across his bloodstained face.

Terry sneered at his son-in-law. 'This is what you're going to do, and if you don't do it, you're dead, do you understand me?'

Nichols nodded quickly. He spat bloody froth from between his puffy lips.

'Go home, get your passport and whatever else you need, and fuck off out of the country. I don't care where you go or what you do, but if I find you're still in the UK, you're dead. I will kill you. As sure as I'm standing here, I will fucking kill you.'

Nichols closed his eyes, still nodding. His breathing was ragged and uneven. Terry grabbed his hair and banged his head against the floor.

'Don't pass out, you bastard!' Terry shouted. 'Open your fucking eyes!' He rammed the gun against the man's nose.

Nichols did as he was told, but his eyes were unfocused and he was close to passing out.

'You don't ever talk to my daughter again. You write her a letter, telling her you're leaving. You get a lawyer to handle the divorce. I find you've ever talked to her again, you are dead, do you understand me?'

'My job . . .' moaned Nichols.

'Fuck your job!' shouted Terry. 'Tell them whatever you want, you little shit. Do you understand? Twenty-four hours, and if you're still in the country, you are a dead man.'

Nichols nodded. He coughed up more blood and spat out another tooth. Terry let go of his hair and stood up. He put the gun back into his pocket, wiped his hands on his son-in-law's towel and threw it down on top of him with a look of disgust.

Terry walked out of the gym and back towards Kim Fletcher's car. Fletcher wound down the window. Terry took the gun and slipped it to Fletcher with a wink.

'You didn't . . .' said Fletcher.

'Not yet,' said Terry, 'but it's still an option.'

Fletcher nodded and handed the gun to Pike, who put it into the glove compartment.

Terry patted the roof of the car. 'Right, lads, have the rest of the night off. I've got someone to see.'

* * *

The staff nurse was in her fifties with the build of a prop forward and the confidence born of years of telling patients what to do. She heard Terry's rapid footfall before she saw him, and stood in the middle of the corridor waiting for him, holding up a hand like a policeman stopping traffic. 'Where do you think you're going?' she asked.

'Laura Nichols,' said Terry. 'I'm her father.'

'Visiting hours are over, Mr Nichols.'

'I just want a few minutes with her. And it's Greene. Terry Greene.' Terry took out his wallet and handed the nurse four twenty-pound notes. 'Two minutes, yeah?' He walked on, leaving the staff nurse staring at the notes in amazement.

Terry sat on the plastic chair next to Laura's bed. She was asleep and didn't react as Terry reached over and held her hand. 'Hiya, love,' he said softly. 'It's your dad.' Laura's monitors continued to bleep quietly and her eyes remained closed. 'Everything's okay. I've taken care of it. There's nothing to worry about any more.'

Terry smiled at Laura. He took her hand and kissed it, then pressed it against his cheek.

'My dad used to hit your gran,' he said. 'Never put her in hospital, he was too clever for that. That's why I left home when I did. He got handy with his fists once too often and I smacked him in the mouth.'

Laura moved in her sleep and she squeezed Terry's hand, then relaxed again.

'I've always done what I've had to do to support this family, Laura,' said Terry. 'Yeah, I've broken a few laws along the way, but who hasn't? I never hurt anyone who didn't deserve it, though.'

Terry looked down at his hand on the hospital bed. The knuckles were bruised and bloody from beating Nichols. He let go of Laura's hand and bent over her, kissing her on the forehead. 'Anyway, it's all sorted now. He won't ever bother you again. Night, love. Sleep well.'

Terry walked out of the room, licking his injured knuckles.

* * *

Sam took off her jacket and slung it over her shoulder. It was in the mid-eighties and humid, the conditions necessary to maintain the good health of the hundreds of tropical plants and trees in the greenhouse. It had been one of Grace's favourite places. She had spent hours at Kew Gardens, sketching the lush vegetation and talking to the gardeners, most of whom she was on first-name terms with.

The door at the far end of the greenhouse opened and Blackie walked in. He kept his overcoat on as he strode along the path to Sam, and his face was bathed in sweat by the time he reached her.

Sam smiled at his obvious discomfort. 'Hot enough for you, Blackie?' she said.

'This is a bloody liberty, Sam,' said the detective superintendent. 'I'm on Terry's payroll, not yours.'

'It's all in the family, though, isn't it?' said Sam. 'Have you got it?'

Blackie took a piece of paper from his pocket and slipped it to her, looking left and right to check that there was no one else near by. 'I just hope that she doesn't decide to top herself after you've spoken to her.'

'Morrison's suicide was nothing to do with me,' said Sam.

Blackie shrugged. 'We'll probably never know,' he said. He gestured at the piece of paper. 'Don't say where you got that from, okay?'

'Give me some credit, Blackie.' She read the name and address on the paper and put it into her handbag. 'Why wasn't she called as a witness?'

'She'd already left Snow. No suggestion that she was anywhere near the house on the night. And Terry's name was in the frame from day one. They weren't looking for anyone else.' Blackie wiped his forehead with his overcoat sleeve. 'I thought you told me Terry was retiring?'

'He is,' said Sam emphatically.

'I'd check your facts if I was you, Sam.' Blackie turned to

leave. 'Stay here for a few minutes, I don't want anyone to see me leaving with you,' he said.

Sam smiled thinly. 'God forbid I should sully your good name, hey?'

Blackie snorted softly, put his hands in his pockets, and walked away.

Sam walked around the greenhouse for five minutes, deep in thought, then went out the same way Blackie had gone.

McKinley was waiting for her in the car park, standing next to the Lexus. He opened the rear door for her, then climbed into the front seat.

'Fancy a drive, Andy?' said Sam.

'Whatever you say, Mrs Greene.'

'Bristol,' said Sam. 'And fasten your seatbelt, yeah?'

* * *

Sam said nothing during the drive west, the piece of paper clutched in her hand. From time to time McKinley looked at her in the rear-view mirror, but he didn't intrude on her thoughts.

As they reached the outskirts of Bristol, Sam read out the address and McKinley nodded. 'I'll find it, Mrs Greene,' he said.

He didn't have to stop to ask for directions, and twenty minutes later they pulled up in front of a pretty detached house with a neatly tended garden. A gleaming blue MGB was parked in the driveway. Sam nodded at the car. 'The girl done well,' she said to herself. She sat in silence, staring at the house. 'You been here before, Andy?' she asked quietly.

'What makes you ask that, Mrs Greene?' he said.

'Just a thought,' said Sam.

McKinley twisted around in his seat. He looked at her with his cold blue eyes. 'What are you getting at, Mrs Greene?'

Sam shrugged. 'You seemed to know the way, that's all.'

'It's not that big a city.'

Sam lit a cigarette. She wound down the window and blew smoke out of the car. 'I don't know, Andy. Maybe she might've been a witness, maybe Terry might've wanted you to warn her off.'

McKinley turned back in his seat and stared silently through the windscreen.

'Andy?'

McKinley put his big hands on the steering wheel. 'Bit of a headache, Mrs Greene. That's all.'

Sam opened the door.

'Mrs Greene?'

'What?'

'Do you think this is a good idea?'

'Is there something you want to tell me, Andy?'

McKinley sighed, then slowly shook his head.

Sam got out of the car, dropped her cigarette and twisted it into the pavement with her heel, then strode up the path and rang the doorbell. She turned to look at the Lexus. McKinley was still staring straight ahead, his hands gripping the steering wheel.

The door opened and Sam turned her head. A pretty black girl stood on the threshold, looking quizzically at Sam. She was in her mid twenties, flawless black skin, high cheekbones and large dark brown eyes framed by shoulder-length hair. 'What?' she said, in a south London accent. 'What do you want?' A baby was crying somewhere in the house.

'You're Alicia Snow, yeah?'

The look on the girl's face hardened and she tilted her chin. 'What are you doing here?'

Sam frowned. 'Do you know me?'

'How did you find me?'

'You know who I am, don't you?' said Sam.

Alicia went to close the door but Sam was too quick for her. She used her shoulder to force her way in.

'Hey! You can't do that!' shouted Alicia.

Sam stormed down the hallway and into a large living

room. The baby was in a playpen, holding the bars and crying her eyes out. Sam stared at the child. She was about fifteen months old, maybe a month or two younger, with paler skin than her mother and lighter coloured hair. She stopped crying and stared back at Sam.

Alicia came up behind Sam. 'You shouldn't be here,' she said.

Sam didn't reply. She barely heard Alicia, it was as if the girl's voice was at the end of a long tunnel. Time seemed to have stopped as she stood staring at the baby. There were toys in the playpen. A Winnie the Pooh soft toy. Some plastic balls. A cuddly caterpillar. Blocks of wood with animals painted on them.

'I'll call the police,' said Alicia.

'No you won't,' said Sam quietly.

A group of framed photographs on a sideboard showed Terry and Alicia, holding champagne glasses, in what looked like Lapland, George Kay grinning behind them. A photograph of the two of them on a beach, Terry in swimming trunks, Alicia in a black bikini that left little to the imagination. The beach could have been in Spain. It could have been the beach close to Micky Fox's villa. One of the photographs was of Terry, holding a baby, a month or two old. Terry beaming at the camera. The proud father.

Alicia put a hand on Sam's shoulder but Sam shook her off. 'Don't you touch me!' hissed Sam. 'Don't you dare touch me!'

The baby started crying again and Alicia went over and picked her up. She made shooshing noises as she stared defiantly at Sam, the baby in her arms.

Sam shook her head, unable to accept what she was being faced with. The enormity of it all took her breath away.

'I think you should go,' said Alicia.

Sam turned and ran from the room. She fumbled with the lock on the front door and staggered out of the house, gasping for breath. She felt as if she'd been punched in the chest, every breath an effort. Her heart was pounding and she could barely stand.

Sam put a hand out to steady herself. The door slammed shut behind her. She didn't know if it had been the wind or if Alicia had done it. She didn't care. She had to get away from what she'd seen, away from the child and the photographs and everything that they signified. She took deep breaths, trying to calm her racing heart, then walked slowly down the driveway past the MGB.

McKinley hadn't moved, and was still staring fixedly through the windscreen.

Sam opened the rear door of the Lexus and slid on to the back seat. 'Drive,' she said.

'Where to?' said McKinley. He looked at her in the rear-view mirror, but averted his eyes as soon as he saw that she was staring at him.

'Just drive,' she hissed. Sam groped in her handbag and lit a cigarette with trembling hands.

McKinley drove slowly, flashing looks at her in the mirror. They drove past a children's playground.

'Stop here,' said Sam.

She scrambled out of the car and walked across a patch of grass to a set of swings. Tears ran down her face as she blew a plume of smoke that was whisked away by the wind. Terry had lied to her. It had all been a lie. Everything. He'd told her what she'd wanted to hear, he'd used her, lied to her. And she'd let him. She had been so bloody stupid. So unforgivably stupid.

She heard the door of the Lexus open and slam shut but she didn't turn around as McKinley walked across the grass.

'Mrs Greene . . .' he said haltingly.

Sam whirled around and slapped him, hard. McKinley didn't flinch, so she slapped him again. And again.

'I'm sorry,' he said.

'You bastard!' said Sam. She turned her back on him as tears trickled down her cheeks. Sam refused to wipe them away. She took a long pull on her cigarette and shivered. 'How could you?' she whispered. 'You knew, all the time. Right from day one. He did it, didn't he? Terry killed him. Shot him dead, just like the police said.'

She looked over her shoulder and McKinley nodded.

Sam turned away from him again. 'What happened?'

'I wasn't there, Mrs Greene,' he said.

Sam sighed.

'I wasn't, Mrs Greene. I only know what Terry told me. He said it was self defence.'

'He was shot twice. The chest, then the head.'

'I'm just telling you what Terry told me. Snow said he needed cash. A lot of cash. When Terry went around to pay him off, Snow pulled a gun.'

'Pay him off? Because of her? The wife?'

'Ex-wife,' said McKinley. 'Snow said Terry owed him. Said Terry had stolen his wife and had to pay.'

McKinley moved to stand next to Sam. 'It was self defence, but who was going to believe him? Raquel was gunning for him, the filth weren't going to listen to Terry.'

'So you helped him?'

'Terry gave me the gun. I got rid of it. Dumped it in the canal.'

'Then Terry came to me for an alibi?'

McKinley nodded.

'And you paid off Sean Kelly?' said Sam. 'Got him to confess to the murder?'

'Kelly's got cancer. Jumped at the chance to take Terry's money. Asher and Patterson gave his wife ten grand. Kelly put up his hand to the shooting.'

'They paid off Snow's wife, too?'

McKinley nodded.

'So you all knew?' said Sam bitterly. 'You, Asher, Patterson, you all knew that Terry had knocked up Alicia Snow, and that's why he killed her husband?'

'It was self defence, Mrs Greene.'

'So you keep saying.' Sam had reached the end of her cigarette. She flicked away the butt and lit another. 'You bastards. You must have thought I was so fucking stupid.'

'No, Mrs Greene. It wasn't like that.'

'You bastards,' repeated Sam. She walked away from the swings and climbed on to a wooden roundabout. She sat down, blew smoke and looked scathingly at McKinley. 'There's more, isn't there?'

McKinley stood looking at her, his hands clasped at his groin.

'Terry knew about Morrison, didn't he? Knew that there was a witness, knew that Morrison would put him at the scene. And he knew that there was no way he could get to Morrison while he was under police protection. No way he could get to him before the trial. Right?'

McKinley nodded.

'But afterwards, after the trial, with Terry behind bars, Morrison would be easier to get to.' She shook her head sadly. 'He used me, didn't he? He used me to get to Morrison?'

McKinley didn't say anything, but Sam could see by the look on his face that she was right.

'I was so bloody stupid,' she said. 'Why didn't I see it? Why didn't I see that he was using me?' She drew on her cigarette and exhaled slowly. 'Did you kill him?' she asked eventually. 'Did you kill Morrison for Terry?'

'No, Mrs Greene. I didn't.'

'But you know who did?'

McKinley's jaw tightened, then he nodded slowly. 'Pike and Russell.'

'Killed him and made it look like suicide?'

McKinley nodded.

'You told them where to find Morrison, didn't you?'

McKinley said nothing.

'Didn't you?' shouted Sam, her voice echoing around the deserted playground.

'Mrs Greene . . .' McKinley shook his head sadly. 'I'm sorry.'

'Sorry?' said Sam. She put her cigarette to her mouth with a trembling hand. 'You're sorry?'

* * *

Russell checked the driving mirror. 'He's still there, three cars back,' he said.

Terry laughed out loud from the back seat of the BMW. 'What is it with Raquel?' he said. 'Does he think if he puts two cars between us and him that he's fucking invisible?'

'They learn it at woodentop school,' said Pike, who was in the front passenger seat.

Terry settled back. 'Plan B it is, then,' he said. All three men laughed.

Pike took out his mobile phone and tapped out a number. 'Kim? Yeah, you in position?' Great. Be with you in five, yeah?' He cut the connection and gave Terry a thumbs-up.

Terry grinned and settled back in his seat.

They drove on to a motorway, keeping well below the speed limit, until they reached an underpass. Russell brought the BMW to a stop and Terry and Pike got out and scrambled up the embankment.

They stood at the top and waved at Frank Welch as he went by in his Rover. 'Wanker! shouted Pike.

Welch glared at them, but he was powerless to do anything, boxed in by the fast-flowing traffic.

Russell drove off as Terry and Pike climbed up to the top of the embankment. Kim Fletcher was waiting for them at the wheel of a Toyota four-wheel drive. Terry and Pike got into the Toyota and Fletcher drove off.

'You got it, Kim?' asked Terry.

Fletcher reached into the glove compartment and took out a handgun, which Pike passed back to Terry.

'Lovely,' said Terry, checking the gun's action.

* * *

Lapland was just about to close. Two blondes were making a desultory attempt to keep a group of suited businessmen interested, but the men were looking at their watches and draining their glasses.

Terry walked in, flanked by Fletcher and Pike.

George Kay was sitting alone at a table with a half-empty bottle of champagne in front of him. He frowned as he saw Terry, then hauled himself to his feet and waddled over, hand outstretched. 'Terry, you should have called. Half the girls have gone home.'

Terry shook Kay's hand and slapped him on the back. 'Just wanted to drop by and say hello, George.'

'Always glad to see you, Terry. You know that. Bottle of bubbly?'

'Yeah, why not?' Terry sat down at Kay's table and motioned for Pike and Fletcher to sit. 'So how's business?' asked Terry.

'Bit slow tonight, but it's midweek. We'll be jumping on Friday.' He waved at a pretty waitress and mouthed 'champagne' to her. 'Sam not with you?'

Terry shook his head. 'Boys' night out.' The blondes had perked up when they saw Terry, and were now doing some heavy-duty hair-tossing and creative polework, but Terry didn't appear to notice. 'You know what I fancy, George? Poker. I haven't played poker for years. Got any cards?'

Kay looked confused. 'Cards?' He took out his inhaler and took a long pull on it. 'Might have some in the office.'

'Go get them, yeah? And might as well close the door and let everyone go home. I feel like a long night.'

He looked at Pike and Fletcher, and they both grinned and nodded. The waitress returned with a bottle of champagne in an ice bucket and four glasses. Kay frowned at the bottle. 'Not the Moët, dear,' said Kay. 'Get us a bottle of the good stuff, will you?'

Two hours and three bottles of Christal later, the four men were alone in the club, sitting around a pile of banknotes. Kay won the pot, and he grinned as he pulled the money towards him.

'Bloody hell,' said Pike, sitting back in his chair. 'That's your third pot on the run, George.'

'Yeah, your luck's in tonight, Georgy boy,' said Terry. 'Wish I had your luck.'

'Just the way the cards fall,' said Kay. He opened a fourth bottle of champagne as Fletcher dealt the cards.

'Nah, your guardian angel is on your case,' said Terry. He grinned. 'Let's put her to the test, yeah?'

Kay frowned as he poured champagne for the four of them. Terry reached into his pocket and pulled out the revolver. Kay's hand trembled and champagne slopped over the card table.

'Steady, George,' said Terry.

'Fucking hell, Terry!' said Kay.

'What, you've seen a gun before, haven't you?' said Terry.

'If the filth find that here – Christ, my licence, the club . . .' He put the champagne back in the ice bucket with trembling hands.

'Relax, George,' said Terry, caressing the barrel of the gun. 'Why would the cops be here, huh? Not been serving afters, have you?'

Pike and Fletcher laughed loudly, but Kay looked uncomfortable. He sat down and wiped his forehead with a large white handkerchief, staring at the gun with wide eyes. 'What are you doing with that?' he asked.

Terry's grin widened. 'Ah, that's for me to know . . .'

Kay took another pull on his inhaler.

Terry popped out the cylinder and peered down the barrel. 'Smith & Wesson thirty-eight,' he said. 'Can't beat it. Automatics look flash, but they spit shells all over the shop.' Terry tipped the shells out of the cylinder and they clattered on to the table.

Kay stared at the bullets. He held his inhaler with both hands and his chest wheezed with every breath.

'Number of twats that have ended up behind bars because they forgot to wipe their prints off the shells.' Terry put a single shell in the cylinder and clicked it closed.

'Remember that movie, George? The Vietnam one?'

Kay swallowed. '*Apocalypse Now*?'

Terry shook his head. 'Nah, that was the one with Marlon Brando. I mean the one with De Niro. The one where they played Russian roulette. Christopher Walken was in it.' Terry spun the cylinder.

Pike sniffed. '*The Deerhunter*, wasn't it?'

Terry nodded approvingly. 'Yeah, that's it. *The Deerhunter*. Fucking great movie.' He put the gun down on the table and spun it. They all watched as it gradually slowed, then stopped, the barrel pointing directly at Terry. Terry smiled laconically. 'See. It's just not my night.'

Terry slowly raised the gun and pointed it at his temple.

'Terry!' shouted Kay.

Terry's eyes hardened, then he pulled the trigger. Click.

'Jesus Christ!' exploded Kay.

'Maybe my luck's changing, George,' said Terry. 'What do you think?'

Terry put the gun back on the table and spun it again.

'Terry, what are you doing?' asked Kay.

Terry didn't reply. They all watched as the gun came to a halt. This time it pointed at Fletcher.

'Come on, Kim,' cajoled Terry.

'Terry, this is fucking crazy,' said Kay.

'What's wrong, George? Sense of humour failure?'

Fletcher picked up the gun. He looked at Terry. Terry nodded encouragingly. Fletcher slowly put the gun against his temple, closed his eyes, and pulled the trigger. Click. Fletcher sighed, then opened his eyes and grinned. 'Fuck me, what a rush,' he said.

'Better than sex,' said Terry. Kay stood up, and Terry pointed a warning finger at him. 'Sit the fuck down!' he said, his voice loaded with menace, then nodded at Fletcher.

Fletcher put the gun down and spun it. It whirled around half a dozen times then stopped. It pointed at Kay. Kay stared at the gun in horror.

'Your shot, George,' said Terry.

'Yeah, come on, George. We're behind you,' said Fletcher.

'You won't feel a thing, George,' said Pike.

Kay picked up the gun. The blood had drained from his face and his breath was coming in ragged gasps. Terry stared at him coldly as he raised the gun to his head. Kay looked at Terry with pleading eyes. He was close to tears. 'Terry . . .' he said.

'Come on, George,' said Terry. 'Be lucky.'

Kay's finger tightened on the trigger. The gun was shaking in his hand and he bit down on his lower lip.

'Come on, George,' said Terry. 'You can do it.'

Kay's finger was white on the trigger, and his whole body shook as though he'd been plugged into the mains supply. Fletcher and Pike sat transfixed, tight grins on their faces, silently urging him on.

Kay eventually broke. 'I can't,' he said, slamming the gun down on the table. Tears streamed down his face. 'I'm sorry, I can't. I just can't.' His body was wracked with sobs.

Terry slowly smiled. He held out his left hand and opened it. On his palm lay a single bullet.

Kay frowned, not understanding. Then realisation dawned.

Terry, Pike and Fletcher laughed out loud.

'Your face, George,' Terry said. 'A fucking picture.' He leaned over the table and gently patted Kay on the cheek.

Kay started laughing, too, but it was a nervous, disjointed sound.

★ ★ ★

Terry, Fletcher and Pike left Lapland, laughing and joking. 'He damn near pissed himself, did you see him?'

'He's an arsehole,' said Pike.

'Yeah, well, it's like they said in *The Godfather*, right? Keep your friends close and your arseholes closer.'

'What is with all these movie references, Terry?' said Pike.

'It's his new DVD player,' laughed Fletcher.

Terry tried to slap the back of Fletcher's head, but he ducked away, chuckling. Terry pushed him, and as Fletcher staggered against a wall, three men in donkey jackets and ski masks rushed from behind a parked four-wheel drive. They had guns. Automatics.

'Down on the ground, now!' hissed one.

'What the fuck is this?' said Terry, a gun jammed against his throat.

'Do as you're told or we'll end it here,' said the man. He had wide shoulders and cold brown eyes that stared out of the two holes in the mask. Terry could smell garlic on the man's breath. He had an Irish accent. Northern Irish.

'Who the fuck are you?' asked Terry.

The gun was jammed harder against Terry's neck. The man was wearing leather gloves and Terry watched his finger tense on the trigger.

'Okay, okay,' said Terry. 'Keep cool, yeah?'

One of the other two men pistol-whipped Pike and kicked him to the ground. 'I said get on the fucking floor!' he snapped. Like the man with brown eyes, he had an Irish accent, but harder and more guttural.

Fletcher got to his knees, then lay down with his hands outstretched. He turned his head towards Pike. 'You okay?' he whispered.

'Shut the fuck up!' shouted one of the men.

Terry started to kneel down, but the man with brown eyes kicked him in the stomach and pushed him to the ground. He kept the gun pointing at Terry's face. Terry stared up at the man, refusing to show fear. The brown eyes glared back at him, unblinking, and Terry realised that he was looking into the eyes of a killer.

One of the other two men tore strips of insulation tape off a roll and used them to gag Fletcher and Pike, then he wound the tape around their wrists and ankles, binding them securely.

The man with brown eyes kept the gun aimed at Terry's face as he roughly searched through his pockets. He found the Smith & Wesson and stuck it into the belt of his trousers.

Terry relaxed a little. If they were going to kill him, there'd be no point in searching him first. 'What do you want?' he asked. 'What is it you're after?'

The man backhanded Terry across the mouth. 'Shut the fuck up, Greene, or I'll put a bullet in your head here and now,' he hissed as he went through the rest of Terry's pockets.

One of the other men came over and slapped a piece of insulation tape across Terry mouth, and another across his eyes. His arms were twisted behind his back and he was bundled into the four-wheel drive. He tried to struggle but a gun was pushed against the back of his neck. 'Be still now,' said an Irish voice. The doors of the four-wheel drive slammed shut and the vehicle sped off, leaving Fletcher and Pike on the ground, bound and gagged.

Terry lay with his face pressed against the floor of the vehicle. He had trouble breathing through his nose so he used his tongue to push the insulation tape away from his mouth. He sucked in air gratefully.

The four-wheel drive accelerated. They drove in a straight line and Terry figured they were on a motorway. He had no idea where they were going, or who the men where. When he'd first seen the men in ski masks, his first thought had been that it was the Kosovans, but the Irish accents put paid to that notion. So who were they? The only Irish that Terry had crossed swords with were a group of Liverpool-based gangsters who'd tried to double-cross him a few years back, but they'd ended up behind bars after they'd been caught with a container-load of cannabis *en route* to London.

Whoever these men were, it wasn't a case of mistaken identity. The brown-eyed man had called him by name, and they'd snatched only Terry. Whatever it was about, it was personal.

They drove along the motorway for the best part of half an hour, then along rougher roads, twisting and turning. Eventually the four-wheel drive came to a halt and Terry was dragged from the vehicle and half carried, half dragged across rough ground. He was thrown forward, and he pitched on to wet grass and dead leaves.

'On your knees,' said an Irish voice.

Terry struggled to get up. He could feel the dampness of the ground soaking through his trousers. The tape was ripped from his mouth and eyes and he blinked. All around were trees, the wind rustling through them like restless spirits, whispering and taunting.

A man stood at either side of him, and when he looked up one of them hit him on the top of the head. 'Eyes on the ground,' said the man.

Terry looked down, clenching his fists. There were three of them and they had guns, but if they really were going to kill him Terry was determined to go down fighting.

The third man, the one who'd spoken in the vehicle, walked to stand in front of Terry. He was wearing brand new Timberland boots and Terry stared at them. 'Big mistake, using our name in vain,' he said.

Terry looked up at him. In the darkness all he could see was a large, dark shape. 'What the fuck are you talking about?' said Terry.

The man pistol-whipped Terry. 'Spreading the word you were doing business with us,' he said in his guttural Belfast accent. 'Like we'd even piss in your pot.' He pointed the gun at Terry's forehead. 'Any prayers to say?'

Terry stared up at the masked man. Off in the distance, a fox barked, then there was only the sound of the wind in the trees. Terry slowly smiled. He knew now that the men had no intention of killing him. If they were going to shoot him, there'd be no need for the lecture. 'Fuck you, Paddy,' he said, enunciating every syllable. 'If you were going to do anything heavy, you'd've done it back there. So why don't you do what you were told to do, give me the verbal and piss off back to Ballygobackwards.'

The gloved hand tensed on the gun, but Terry didn't flinch. The hammer was already cocked and the man pressed the barrel against Terry's forehead. Terry glared at the masked face but his insides went cold. One tug of the finger on the trigger and his brains would be splattered over the grass. He swallowed nervously, but resolutely forced himself to keep staring up at the gunman. No matter how this ended, he was determined not to show any weakness. If he was going to die, he'd die like a man.

Slowly the man took the gun away. Terry grinned in triumph as he realised he'd called it right. 'How about a lift back, then?' he asked.

The man smacked the gun hard against Terry's temple. Everything went red, then black, but even as he passed out Terry was still grinning, knowing that he'd won.

* * *

McKinley slowed the Lexus and put his headlights on full beam. The tunnels of light picked out Terry at the edge of the forest, waving. McKinley stopped next to Terry, and he climbed into the front passenger seat, holding a handkerchief to his head.

'You took your fucking time,' growled Terry.

'Got here as soon as I could,' said McKinley. 'I was in the bath when you called. Are you okay?'

'Of course I'm not fucking okay. I've been pistol-whipped by the IRA and left in the fucking woods. That sound okay to you, McKinley?'

McKinley grimaced and didn't say anything.

'Just drive. Take me home.'

McKinley headed back to London.

'How did the fucking IRA get my name, Andy?'

McKinley looked pained.

'I figure it was Sam, making waves,' said Terry. 'Think I'd be right?'

'Not while she was with me, Terry.'

'I thought I told you to stick with her. Watch her, I said.'

'I did do.'

'Well, she must have spoken to them some time. How else could they have known what I'd told her?'

'She could have phoned.'

'The IRA aren't in the *Yellow Pages*,' said Terry.

'I'm just saying—' began McKinley.

'Don't say,' interrupted Terry. 'I don't fucking pay you to say. I pay you to keep an eye on my missus, end of story. And right now I don't seem to be getting my money's worth.' Terry took his handkerchief away from his head and examined the bloodstains on it. 'Fucking Paddies,' he said. He turned to look at McKinley. 'Anything else I should know?'

McKinley frowned. 'What do you mean?'

'You know what I mean,' said Terry. 'Did she talk to anyone else that's gonna cause me grief?'

'No,' said McKinley.

'You sure?'

McKinley nodded but didn't reply.

* * *

Sam was in the kitchen making herself a cup of hot chocolate when she heard Terry let himself in. She poured more milk into the saucepan. He walked into the kitchen, holding a blood-stained handkerchief to his head.

'What happened?'

'Don't start,' said Terry.

'What do you mean, "don't start"? You're bleeding.'

'I've had a shitty day, love.'

'Whereas my life's a bed of roses?' she said. 'I'm making hot chocolate. Want some?'

'I want a beer,' he said. He tossed the handkerchief into the bin and took a bottle of lager out of the fridge. He popped off the cap and sat down at the kitchen table, drinking from the bottle.

Sam tried to examine the cut on his head but Terry shook her away.

'What happened?' she asked.

'I knocked my head getting into the car.'

'You need something on it.' She opened a kitchen cupboard and took out a bottle of TCP and a pack of cotton buds. She dabbed some antiseptic on his wounds.

Terry winced. 'For God's sake, Sam. I'm not a kid.'

'Yeah, and you're a bit too old to be fighting, aren't you?'

'I told you,' said Terry. 'It was an accident.'

'Yeah, you tell me a lot of things.'

Terry twisted around to look at her. 'What's that supposed to mean?' he asked.

Sam pushed him back and carried on dabbing TCP on the cuts. 'Keep still.'

'My wife, the nurse,' complained Terry.

'Where were you tonight?'

'The club. Taking care of business.'

Sam finished treating his cuts and put the antiseptic and cotton buds away. 'Jonathon's left Laura,' she said, pouring hot milk into her mug and stirring in spoonfuls of chocolate powder.

'Good riddance,' said Terry.

'More than that,' said Sam. 'He's left the country. He called her from Toronto. Canada.'

'Yeah, I know where Toronto is.'

Sam sat down at the table opposite Terry. 'Did you do something to him?'

Terry raised his eyebrows. 'Like what?'

'You know what like. Did you hurt him?'

Terry said nothing.

'Answer me, Terry.'

'What do you want me to say?'

'I want the truth,' said Sam. 'Did you do something to Jonathon?'

Terry held her look and put down his lager. 'I had a word with him,' he said. 'That's all.'

Sam looked into Terry's cold blue eyes, trying to tell if he was lying. He looked back without blinking.

'What did you say to him?'

'I told him that if he ever laid a finger on Laura again, he'd have me to answer to. I think he got the message.' He drank from the bottle of lager and wiped his mouth. 'He won't be bothering her any more.'

Sam sipped her hot chocolate. 'Laura said he sounded scared. He said that she should divorce him, that she could have the house and everything.'

'Small price to pay for what he did to her.'

'Yeah, but why did he leave the country? Was that your doing, Terry?'

'Don't be stupid. Anyway, she's better off without him.'

'The truth, Terry. Did you hurt him?'

Terry shook his head. 'No, love. I talked to him, that's all. God's honest.'

Sam stood up. 'I'm going to bed.' She washed her mug in the sink.

'I'll be up in a minute,' said Terry.

'Whatever,' said Sam.

Terry watched her go, then he went to the fridge for another lager.

* * *

Fletcher and Pike were waiting with the BMW when Terry left the house next morning. They both looked shamefaced as Terry shut the front door behind him. 'Thanks for your help last night, guys.'

'Sorry, Terry,' said Fletcher.

'Yeah, they snuck up on us, boss.'

'Yeah, and they were tooled up.'

'Did they get heavy with you?' asked Pike.

Terry got into the back of the BMW. 'I think it best we draw a veil over events, lads. In case I get all emotional.' His mobile phone rang and he answered it.

Pike and Fletcher got into the car as Terry grunted into the phone and cut the connection.

'Change of plans, lads,' said Terry. 'We're going to Bristol.'

Terry sat in silence during the drive west. Pike and Fletcher kept exchanging looks, wondering if they should start up a conversation, but it was clear that Terry didn't want to talk. At one point Pike reached over to switch on the radio, but Fletcher shook his head.

When they arrived outside Alicia's house, Terry told the two men to stay in the car. He went up to the front door and rang the bell.

Alicia opened the door wearing a tight dress that was cut low at the top and barely covered her backside. 'Terry!' she squealed.

'Don't act so surprised. You called me,' he said. 'Are you going to open the door, or what?'

As soon as Terry was in the hall, she plastered herself against him and kissed him full on the lips. The baby started crying in the sitting room and Terry pulled away from Alicia.

'The baby,' he said.

'She's been crying all day,' said Alicia. 'She'll be okay.' She dropped down on her knees and unbuttoned his trousers.

'Alicia . . .' said Terry. 'Come on, stop that.' He gasped as she took him into her mouth, her eyes on his as she moved her head back and forth. 'You bitch,' he whispered as he stroked her hair.

She took away her mouth and smiled up at him. 'Your bitch,' she said. 'I'm your bitch, remember.' Terry pulled her up, kissed her, and unzipped her dress. She wasn't wearing underwear and she smiled when she saw the look of surprise on his face. 'I was waiting for you,' she said. She took his hand and pressed against it herself. 'Feel how wet I am,' she whispered.

Terry pushed her against the wall and she drew her legs up around him as he entered her, so hard that she gasped. 'Yes,' she whispered into his ear. 'Yes, Terry, come on, love. Come on.'

Terry thrust into her, harder and harder as she called out his name.

'Upstairs,' she moaned. 'Take me upstairs.'

Terry picked her up and carried her upstairs and made love to her on her double bed.

Afterwards, he lay with an arm around her, staring up at the ceiling. The baby was still crying downstairs.

'Why've you been staying away, Terry?'

'Alicia . . .' groaned Terry. The last thing he wanted was an argument.

'Too much pressure?'

'It's not that. I told you. If the filth see me with you . . .'

'I know, I know. But it's been months.'

'Leave it out, Alicia.'

Alicia ran her hand down his chest to his groin, then down to his thighs. Terry smiled and kissed her as she stroked him.

'Your wife was here,' she said.

Terry froze. 'What?'

'Your wife. That's why I wanted to see you. She came here.'

Terry sat up abruptly. 'Why the hell didn't you tell me?'

'What do you think I'm doing?'

'Why didn't you tell me on the phone?'

'Because if I did, you wouldn't have come. Would you?'

Terry got out of bed and started dressing.

'See!'

'What do you mean, "see"?' said Terry, buttoning his shirt.

'You still love her, don't you?'

'Don't be stupid. What did she want?'

'Why do you care what she wanted?' Terry glared at her, and she shook her head in frustration.

'I don't know what she wanted,' said Alicia. 'She wasn't here more than a minute. She forced her way in, saw Rosie, stared at me like she wanted me dead, then walked out.'

'She saw the kid?'

'That's what I said.'

Terry swore under his breath. 'Did she drive here?'

'Someone drove her. A guy in a big car.'

Terry swore again. McKinley. It had to have been McKinley. He finished buttoning his shirt and headed for the stairs.

Alicia grabbed her robe and hurried after him. 'Terry . . . she doesn't matter. You can stay here . . . with us.'

Terry found his shoes in the living room and slipped them on. Alicia tried to put her arms around him but he pushed her away. 'You know that's not going to happen,' he said.

She smiled at him seductively. 'I'll be good for you . . . you know how good I can make it for you.'

'Leave it out, Alicia.'

Alicia tried to kiss him, but he turned his back on her and put on his jacket. She slapped him on the back. 'You bastard!' She slapped him again and again but Terry barely felt the blows.

'Grow up,' he sneered as he headed for the front door.

'You killed Preston for me!' she shouted. 'You shot him so you could have me.'

Terry whirled around, his eyes blazing. 'I killed him

because he pulled a fucking gun on me.' he hissed. 'Because he would've killed me.'

'You say.'

'Yeah, I say. He asked for it.'

'He was my husband,' said Alicia, her voice trembling.

'Ex-husband,' said Terry. 'And your marital status didn't stop you shaking your tits at me.'

'Neither did yours,' said Alicia. Terry stood staring at her, breathing heavily. Alicia smiled and rubbed herself against him. 'You want me, you know you do.' Terry shook his head, but Alicia reached between his legs and stroked him.

Terry pushed her away and opened the door.

'It's me you want! You can't go back to her!' Alicia screamed as he slammed the door behind him. 'You can't!' she shouted as she kicked the door.

* * *

Sam took Laura's arm as they walked out of the hospital. 'Don't fuss, Mum,' said Laura. 'I'm fine.' She was wearing dark glasses and a scarf around her head to cover the fading bruises and still-healing cuts.

'I know you're fine, I just want to hold my daughter,' said Sam. 'Nothing wrong with that, is there?'

They walked together towards the Lexus. McKinley stepped forward and took Laura's bag from Sam. He put it into the boot as the two women got into the back of the car.

'What's he going to do in Canada, Mum?' asked Laura.

'I don't know, love.'

'He's a merchant banker, there's nothing for him to do in Canada.'

'Didn't he say when he phoned?'

'He just said he wanted a divorce and that I could have the house and everything. He was only on for a minute. He sounded scared stiff, like someone had a gun to his head. It's Dad, isn't it? Dad's run him out of town.'

McKinley got into the driving seat.

'Your dad says no,' said Sam.

'Well, he would, wouldn't he?'

McKinley's mobile phone rang and he answered it.

'How is Dad?' Laura asked Sam.

Sam sighed. 'I'm not sure,' she said.

'Is he back for good?'

Sam pulled a face. 'I wish I knew, love.'

McKinley put his mobile phone away. He looked worried.

'Everything okay, Andy?' asked Sam.

'Mr Greene wants to see me later,' said McKinley. He started the car.

'Seatbelt, Andy,' reminded Sam.

* * *

It was dark when McKinley arrived at the football stadium. As he walked out on to the pitch, the floodlights came on and McKinley shaded his eyes against the searing light. Terry was standing at the penalty spot in front of one of the goals, a bulging sack at his feet.

'What's this about, Terry?' called McKinley.

'Just fancied a kickabout,' said Terry. He nodded at the goalmouth. 'Get in goal, will you?'

McKinley walked slowly to the goal. Terry picked up the sack and emptied out a dozen footballs. He was wearing a knee-length leather jacket over his suit, and his Bally shoes gleamed under the floodlights. McKinley wasn't dressed for football either, in a woollen coat over his jacket and cord trousers.

Terry took a short run-up and pounded a ball into the back of the net. He stood looking at McKinley with his hands on his hips. 'You're not trying, Andy,' he called.

McKinley adjusted the fingers of his black leather gloves one by one. 'What's going on, Terry?' he asked.

Pike and Fletcher appeared from the shadows behind the

goal. They stood on the edge of the pitch, their faces stone hard. McKinley looked over his shoulder at them, then back at Terry.

Terry kicked another ball and it whistled past McKinley into the back of the net. 'Make an effort, hey!'

'And if I don't want to play?' asked McKinley.

'Then it'll stop being a game,' said Terry. He trapped a ball and dribbled it around in a circle, flipped it up on to his chest and then dropped it back at his feet. 'I had a trial for West Ham when I was a kid, did I tell you that?' He knocked the ball up into the air and juggled it on his knees, then dropped it at his feet again. 'Nothing came of it, but there was a time when I was in with a chance. That's what life's all about, innit? Chances. Chances and opportunities. Some you grab, some you miss.'

Terry kicked the ball, hard, towards the top right-hand corner of the net. McKinley shuffled to the side and stuck out his hand, deflecting the ball over the crossbar. Terry grinned. 'Better . . .' he said.

He dribbled a ball to the penalty spot and took a few steps back. 'I'm going to give you one last chance, McKinley. If I were you, I'd grab it with both hands.' He smiled without warmth, then pretended to kick the ball. McKinley moved, then straightened up as he realised that Terry was faking him out. 'Why didn't you tell me about my wife going to Bristol?' said Terry, taking a step back.

McKinley didn't reply. Terry dashed forward and kicked the ball, hard. It curved through the air and slammed into McKinley's chest, knocking the wind from him. He stood panting as Terry got another ball ready.

'Well?' asked Terry.

'I didn't want to . . .' McKinley left the sentence hanging.

'What? You didn't want to what?'

'I didn't want to get her into trouble.'

Terry looked over at Pike and Fletcher. 'Is it me or is the whole fucking world going crazy?' he shouted. Pike and

Fletcher shrugged. Terry pointed at McKinley. 'Remind me again, McKinley. Who pays your wages?'

'You do.'

'So you do work for me, right?'

McKinley nodded.

'Because if there's some misunderstanding on that point, might be best to clear it up here and now.'

Terry kicked another ball. McKinley took a swift step to the side and caught it, snatching it from the air in his gloved hands and clutching it to his chest. Terry nodded, impressed.

'So what the hell are you doing running my wife down to the West Country to talk to the ex-wife of the guy I was accused of killing? Didn't that seem a bit on the disloyal side?'

'She asked me to,' said McKinley. 'What could I say?'

'You could have called me. You could have told me. Fuck me, McKinley, how stupid are you?'

McKinley stared at Terry, his mouth a tight line.

Terry kicked again and sent a ball winging into the bottom right-hand corner of the net. 'Yeah,' said Terry. 'He shoots, he scores, the crowd goes wild.' He bowed to the stands, then put another ball on the penalty spot. He stood facing McKinley. 'What did she say, afterwards?'

'She wanted to know if you'd killed him.'

'And?'

'And I said it was self defence.'

'She believe you?'

'Seemed to.'

'And Morrison. She knows I used her to get to him?'

McKinley nodded slowly.

Terry paced around the ball. 'So thanks to you, my wife now knows that I'm a lying killer who got the victim's wife pregnant and who used her to dispose of the only witness to my crime,' said Terry. 'Doesn't that strike you as being a tad detrimental to the stability of my marriage, McKinley? Not to mention my prospects of staying out of fucking prison?'

McKinley said nothing.

Terry put his foot on the ball and rolled it backwards and forwards. 'What the fuck am I going to do with you, McKinley?' he said. 'Yellow card? Red card? What do you think?'

'Terry . . . I . . .'

Terry motioned with his hand for McKinley to shut up. 'How about we put it down to a penalty shoot-out?' said Terry. 'Next shot, you save it and you're on probation. Let it in and we go and take a walk in the woods.'

'Terry . . .'

Terry walked backwards as McKinley prepared himself. Pike and Fletcher shifted uneasily behind the goalmouth. Terry looked at McKinley, nodded, and then gently kicked it. The ball arced through the air and McKinley caught it easily. Terry grinned. 'Probation it is, then.'

Terry walked off the pitch and headed for the car park. Pike and Fletcher hurried to catch up with him and they walked together to the BMW.

'That's it, then?' said Pike.

'My missus can be bloody persuasive when she puts her mind to it,' said Terry. 'McKinley wouldn't have stood a chance against her. If she'd set her mind on finding Alicia, there's bugger all he could have done to stop her.' He looked over at McKinley, who was heading towards the Lexus. 'He's all right, he's just none too bright, that's all.'

A blue Transit van drove into the car park, its headlights off. Terry turned to look at the van, frowning.

'What's up boss?' asked Pike.

Before Terry could reply, the rear door of the van was thrown open and two burly masked men piled out, wielding shotguns. Two explosions followed quickly, and a car window behind Terry exploded into a thousand cubes of glass. Terry dived to the ground. Pike and Fletcher followed his example, swearing loudly.

* * *

Andy McKinley flinched at the sound of the gunshots. He whirled around just in time to see Terry, Pike and Fletcher crawling around the back of a silver-grey Honda. Two heavily built men were advancing on the car, their pump-action shotguns held aloft, and one of the men pumped another shell in as he walked.

The blue van followed slowly behind the two gunmen, the driver also wearing a ski mask.

McKinley cursed. The only weapon he had on him was a flicknife. Even if he had been carrying a handgun, it wouldn't be any use against two shotguns. He looked around. There was no one else in the car park.

McKinley already had the car keys in his hand, and he rushed to open the door of the Lexus. He slid in and slotted the key into the ignition. The engine roared into life and McKinley blipped the accelerator. He cursed again. There were a million places he'd rather be just then, a million things he'd rather be doing, but he knew there was only one course of action open to him.

* * *

Terry took a quick look around the back of the Honda, but jerked his head away when one of the gunmen pointed his shotgun at him. There was another explosion and lead shot ripped through the rear indicator light, smashing the red and orange glass into a dozen shards.

'What the fuck's going on?' asked Fletcher.

'Just a guess, but maybe they're fucking shooting at us,' said Terry. He rolled to the side and scuttled behind a Toyota. There was another loud bang and the sound of running feet.

'Fucking hell, I'm hit,' said Pike, holding a hand to his shoulder. 'They fucking shot me.'

'Don't suppose either of you two are carrying?' said Terry. Pike and Fletcher shook their heads and Terry cursed.

Terry looked cautiously over the boot of the Toyota. The

two masked men were standing by the van, pumping the shotguns. Terry frowned. Who the hell was it? It couldn't be the Irish again. Besides, the Irish heavyweights had been carrying automatics, not shotguns. He snatched a quick look around the car park and cursed. Other than the Honda, the Toyota, his BMW and a couple of others saloons, there was no other cover. All the men had to do was to walk over to the Toyota and it'd be all over. Terry cursed again. Then he heard the roar of an engine and the Lexus surged across the car park with McKinley at the wheel.

* * *

McKinley gripped the steering wheel with both hands. He had the accelerator pressed hard against the floor, and his back was pressed against the seat. Everything seemed to slow down, as if all his senses had gone into overdrive. He saw the driver of the van turn to look at the Lexus, his mouth open in surprise. One of the masked men was about to fire his shotgun from the hip, the other had stopped and was reloading. Neither had noticed the Lexus. He saw Terry, crouched behind the Toyota.

All McKinley's instincts were to turn the wheel, to avoid the impact, but he knew it was the only way to stop the gunmen. He began to howl, a scream of defiance that blended with the roar of the engine into a single animal-like sound, and he pushed his head back into the headrest, extending his arms fully, bracing himself for the inevitable impact.

Time started to speed up again and then he hit the van full on.

* * *

Terry stared in disbelief as the Lexus crashed into the side of the van. The impact pushed the van to the side and it clipped the two masked men, throwing them to the ground. One of the shotguns clattered along the tarmac. McKinley kept his foot hard down on the accelerator, grinding the Lexus into the van, the engine screaming like a dying animal.

The two masked gunmen lay on the ground, shaking their heads, confused.

'Get them!' shouted Terry. He charged around the Toyota and lunged at the driver, who was trying to scramble out of the passenger door. Terry grabbed him and punched him in the face, grinning with satisfaction as he felt the man's nose break. Behind him, Pike and Fletcher began to kick the two men on the ground, cursing and yelling.

Terry swung the driver around by the hair and kicked him in the stomach, then kicked him again, letting go so that he flew backwards and hit the ground. Pike turned away from the man he'd been kicking and stamped on the driver's chest, cursing loudly. The other man was unconscious, blood seeping through the ski mask. Fletcher picked up the two shotguns and hurled them away.

Terry went over to the Lexus. McKinley was still in the driving seat, shaking his head and breathing heavily like a weightlifter about to go for a personal best.

'You okay?' said Terry.

'Yeah,' said McKinley. He exhaled deeply.

'Good job you had your seatbelt on,' said Terry.

He walked around to the front of the car and inspected the damage. He whistled softly and pointed at the crumpled wing. 'This is coming out of your wages, McKinley.' He stared at McKinley for a few seconds, then a smile spread across his face and he winked. 'Thanks, Andy. I owe you one.'

McKinley nodded, acknowledging the thanks, but he didn't smile.

Pike knelt down and ripped off the ski mask of one of the injured men. 'It's the fucking Kosovans!' he said.

* * *

Sam opened her eyes. There were voices downstairs. Male voices. She sat up, rubbing her eyes, then looked at the alarm clock on the bedside table. It was two o'clock in the morning. Sam got out of bed, pulled on a robe and went downstairs.

Roger Pike was sitting on a chair, while Andy McKinley and Kim Fletcher were standing over him, looking at his left shoulder. 'That fucking hurts,' whined Pike.

'It's your own fault for not moving quick enough,' said Fletcher.

Terry was looking through one of the kitchen cupboards. 'Will you two keep the noise down?' said Terry. 'If Sam hears us . . .'

He tailed off as he heard Sam walk into the kitchen. Fletcher and Pike exchanged guilty looks. 'Sam's already heard you,' she said coldly. 'And if you wake up Trisha and Laura, there'll be hell to pay.'

'Sorry, love,' said Terry.

Sam went over to Pike and examined the wound on his shoulder. 'What happened?' she asked. McKinley moved away as if he wanted to distance himself from Pike and Fletcher.

'They had shotguns, Mrs Greene,' said Pike.

Terry flashed Pike a warning look, but the damage had been done. Sam turned to him, wide eyed. 'Shotguns?' she said.

'Small ones,' said Terry. 'Where's the first aid kit?'

'Same place it was yesterday when you came home like a wounded soldier.' Sam sighed and got a first aid kit from the cupboard. 'Get his shirt off,' she said to Pike.

Fletcher helped Pike strip off the shirt.

'That hurts,' complained Pike.

'Of course it hurts, you've been shot,' said Terry.

Sam bent down over Pike and dabbed at the wound with a damp cloth. 'You could have been killed,' she said.

Pike looked quite pleased at Sam's verdict. He looked up at Fletcher. 'See?'

Fletcher slapped the back of Pike's head. Sam pushed him away. 'Would you act your age, Kim?' she said.

'Kim, go check the car,' said Terry. 'Make sure there's no blood on the seats, yeah?'

Fletcher pulled a face and left.

Sam cleaned the wound and used a pair of tweezers to remove pieces of lead shot from the bloody flesh. The damage was mainly superficial and the bleeding had already stopped. 'Who did this?' Sam asked Terry.

'Your Kosovan friends.'

'What?' Sam looked across at McKinley but McKinley turned away, not wanting to get involved.

'The Kosovans that you let encroach on our territory,' said Terry. He went over to the fridge and took out a beer. 'That bastard Poskovic and his crew.'

'I thought I'd sorted that.'

'You thought wrong, love,' said Terry, popping the cap off the bottle of beer.

'They tried to kill you?'

'No, love, this was just their way of sealing our business relationship,' said Terry. He took a swig from the bottle and wiped his mouth.

'You must have done something to set them off,' said Sam, dabbing antiseptic on to Pike's injured shoulder.

'This isn't the school playground,' said Terry.

'You could have fooled me,' said Sam. She nodded at Pike and screwed the cap back on the bottle of TCP. 'Okay, you're done,' she said. 'Take two aspirins and don't bother me again.' She put the first aid kit back in the cupboard. 'I'm off to bed,' she said.

'I'll come with you,' said Terry. He jerked a thumb at Pike. 'Off you go, lads.'

Pike picked up his shirt and he and McKinley left. McKinley didn't look at Sam as he walked past her.

Terry went into the bathroom, took off his clothes and showered. Sam stood at the bedroom window and watched

Pike, Fletcher and McKinley drive off. As she turned away from the window, she caught sight of herself in the mirror. She looked tense and drawn, dark patches under her eyes and tight lines around her mouth. Sam knew it wasn't just lack of sleep. Terry was draining the life from her. He'd lied about Preston Snow. He'd lied about giving up his criminal activities. He'd used her to get rid of Ricky Morrison. And God only knew what else he had planned for her.

She went into the bathroom. Terry was lathering himself and humming under the torrent of hot water. 'You said you were finished with all this,' said Sam, leaning against the door.

'Don't nag, love.'

'This isn't nagging. This is conversation. You said you were going to retire, remember? Or are you coming down with early Alzheimer's?' Sam stopped as she realised what she'd said. Terry turned to face her, water pouring over his chest. 'I'm sorry, Terry. I didn't mean that. Alzheimer's isn't . . .' She cursed.

'It's all right, love. I know you didn't mean anything.'

'I just . . .' She shrugged. Grace was never far from her thoughts.

'I know. Forget about it. Slip of the tongue.' Terry smiled slyly. 'Don't suppose you'd scrub my back, would you?'

Sam picked up a flannel and threw it at him. He grinned and carried on showering.

'Why do you keep at it, Terry?' asked Sam. 'It can't be the excitement of being shot at.'

'We're not out of the woods, money-wise.'

'Those counterfeit notes you brought in. Three hundred grand, you said.'

Terry turned off the water. Sam held out a towel as he stepped from the shower, dripping wet. 'I had investors to pay off,' he said. 'Debts to settle. We've got cashflow now, but we're not on easy street. Far from it.'

'Terry, you promised me,' said Sam. 'Straight and narrow, you said.'

'What about one last deal?' said Terry, wrapping the towel around his waist and picking up another to dry his hair with. 'A big one?'

Sam tutted and walked out of the bathroom.

Terry followed her, drying his hair. 'Hear me out, Sam,' he said.

Sam sat at the dressing table, brushing her hair. 'I don't believe I'm hearing this,' she said.

Terry sat down on the bed. 'Remember Micky told you he could put something big our way?'

Sam glared at him in the mirror. '*Your* way. Not our way.'

'He knows someone who's got access to some top grade heroin. From Afghanistan.'

Sam waved the brush at him angrily. 'You want to put together a heroin deal? For God's sake, don't you ever learn? They'll throw away the key.'

'Only if we get caught.'

'There's that "we" again.'

'Look, love, I'm not over the moon about this, but if you want me out, we've got to have one last big score. Enough money to walk away with.'

Sam gave him a frosty look and went back to brushing her hair.

'What?' said Terry. 'What's that look for?'

'You've been giving this a lot of thought, haven't you? This hasn't just come out of the blue.'

Terry wrapped the towel around his shoulders. 'I guess so, yeah.'

Sam narrowed her eyes. 'You weren't using Micky to plant the idea, were you? Pave the way?'

Terry pulled a pained face as if nothing could have been further from the truth. 'Sam, come on,' he said. 'You were the one who mentioned it to me. Look, we're not going to be able to live worrying if the next knock on the door is the bailiff. But if we put together one big deal we can take the money and run.'

'Terry . . .' said Sam plaintively.

'That's where everyone goes wrong, don't you see? They get greedy, they keep doing what they're doing until their luck runs out. We do it once, then we walk away.'

'The cannabis deal was a one-off, and that went belly up,' said Sam.

'Too many cooks, that's why. This time, I'll keep it simple.'

Sam shook her head, confused. Terry had an answer for everything. 'Heroin is big time, Terry. You don't need me to tell you that.'

'Compared with four tons of cannabis?'

Sam sighed. He had a point. 'How would we get it into the UK?' she asked.

Terry smiled and raised an eyebrow and Sam realised that she had said 'we' again. She threw her brush at him but it was a half-hearted throw and he easily dodged it.

'I've got a plan,' said Terry.

'I just bet you have,' said Sam.

Terry sat grinning at her.

Sam finished brushing her hair and climbed into bed. 'Go on, then,' she said. 'Tell me.'

'We bring it in on the booze run,' said Terry. 'The vans normally go to Calais to pick up the lager and stuff, but this time we drive down to Spain first. We get Micky's mechanics to put false compartments in the vans and we pack them with the gear. Then we drive them to Calais and load up with booze. Our drivers never get stopped, and if they are, the worst that'll happen is that the booze'll be confiscated. Customs won't be looking for drugs.'

'Where do we get the money from to buy the heroin?' asked Sam.

'We use the cash we've got. I'll get some from Kay, from the clubs. And Asher and Patterson can chip in.'

Terry tossed his towels on to the back of a chair and slipped under the quilt.

'You've got it all planned, haven't you?' said Sam.

'I've been giving it some thought, yeah.' Terry put his arm around her and drew her closer to him. He kissed her on the neck.

'Then what?' she said. 'We get the stuff into the UK, what do we do then? You're going to be on street corners selling it, are you?'

'I'll sell the lot to one guy. I've a few names, but I'll put out feelers first. See who's interested. We'll be wholesalers, Sam, that's all. Bring it in and sell it on.'

'I don't know, Terry.'

Terry rolled on top of her and kissed her. 'It'll be fine, Sam. Trust me.'

Sam looked up at him. Can I, Terry? she thought. Can I trust you?

'Now what's wrong?' he asked.

'What do you mean?'

'You've got that look.'

'What look?'

'That suspicious look.' Terry grinned, then kissed her again.

Sam twisted her head to the side. 'And that'll be it,' she said. 'One deal and it's over?'

'I promise. Straight and narrow. We'll set up a business, a pub maybe.'

'Terry Greene, pulling pints?'

'We'll see, yeah. One step at a time.' He tried to kiss her again but Sam pushed him away.

'I've got a headache, Terry. I'm sorry.'

Terry slid off her and lay with his arm around her.

She kissed him on the cheek. 'Goodnight,' she said. She turned her back on him and lay with her eyes open, listening to his breathing. No, she decided, she couldn't trust him. She couldn't ever trust him. There were just too many lies between them. Too many lies, and a baby in Bristol.

* * *

Richard Asher paced up and down in front of his desk. 'Have you lost the plot or what?' he asked.

Terry smiled up at him from the sofa. He crossed his legs and adjusted the crease of his trousers. 'It's a good offer, Richard,' said Terry. 'Chance of a lifetime.'

'We're professionals,' said Laurence Patterson, who was standing by the door, looking equally as indignant as Asher.

'Whereas I'm just an enthusiastic amateur?' asked Terry.

Patterson went over to stand next to Asher's desk. 'I meant professional as in members of a profession, Terry,' he said patiently. 'I'm a solicitor, Richard's a chartered accountant. We offer advice, we don't get involved.'

Terry smiled easily. 'Look, this is a one-off, Laurence. It's a straightforward investment. You get your money back threefold within the week.'

Asher stopped pacing. 'But Terry, it's a drug deal. Heroin, for God's sake.'

'Richard, how much money have you earned from me over the last ten years?' said Terry. He stood up. 'Where do you think that money comes from?' Terry pointed a finger at Patterson. 'And you know damn well what pays *your* fees.' Terry walked behind Asher's desk, sat down in the brown leather executive chair, and swung his feet on to the desk. 'Let's get this straight. This is my last deal. After this, it's over. No more padded fees, no more retainers, no more commissions. The fat lady will have sung. I'm offering you a chance for one last hurrah.'

Patterson and Asher exchanged a look and Terry could see that they were almost convinced.

'How much?' asked Asher.

'How much have you got?' said Terry.

* * *

Frank Welch picked up his camera as soon as he saw Terry leave the building. He focused the long lens and clicked away as Terry walked towards the BMW parked in the road, Kim Fletcher gunning the engine.

Welch saw a movement out of the corner of his eye and turned to see Steve Ryser and Roger Pike standing by the window of his Rover. Pike made a wanking gesture, and grinned. They both laughed at Welch, then ran over to the BMW.

Pike climbed in the front and Ryser got in the back with Terry. The BMW drove off and Welch pulled away from the curb in pursuit. There was a bump from his offside rear tyre and Welch slammed on the brake. He got out of the car. A piece of wood studded with nails had been pushed under the tyre.

Welch cursed and glared after the departing BMW. Terry waved from the back seat.

* * *

Terry walked through Lapland, flanked by Pike and Fletcher. The club was in near darkness, the only light coming from the open door to George Kay's office.

Kay was sitting at his desk, stacks of banknotes in front of him. He looked up when he heard Terry at the door.

'You got it, then?' said Terry, nodding at the money.

'I'm not happy at being threatened, I can tell you,' said Kay.

Terry dropped down into the chair opposite Kay and swung his feet up on to the desk. Pike closed the door and stood with his back to it. 'What say we play poker for it, hey, George?' Terry laughed.

Pike made a gun with his hand and mimed shooting Kay. 'Bang, bang!' he said, joining in the laughter.

'It's not funny, Terry,' complained Kay. 'There's three hundred grand here, I think I should know what you're planning to do with it.'

'I told you, George. It's the deal of a lifetime.'

'I'd like specifics. I think I deserve it.'

Terry nodded at Fletcher. 'Check it, Kim.'

Fletcher started counting the notes.

Kay fumbled in his desk drawer and took out his inhaler. He took a long pull at it.

'Not allergic to money, are you?' asked Terry.

Kay put the inhaler on the desk but kept his hand on it. 'What do you want it for, Terry?'

Terry looked coldly at Kay, his face hard. 'What's it to you?'

Kay looked confused. 'It's my money. Three hundred thousand pounds of it.'

Terry took his feet off the desk and leaned forward. 'It's the business's money,' he said, 'and I own half the business. Plus, there's the money you've been skimming over the years.'

Kay sat back in his chair and threw up his hands. 'Terry, Terry, Terry, that's not fair.'

Terry stood up and leaned over the desk. 'George, George, George, I don't give a flying fuck what's fair and what's not fair.'

Kay picked up his inhaler with a trembling hand and sucked on it like a baby feeding.

'They say it's caused by stress, asthma,' said Terry.

Kay nodded. 'Had it since I was a kid.'

Terry straightened up and looked at him scornfully. 'Fat, asthmatic and ugly. It can't have been an easy childhood.'

Kay looked wounded, as if he couldn't understand why Terry was being so hostile.

Fletcher finished counting the stacks of money. 'It's all here, Terry,' he said.

Terry nodded and Fletcher put the money into a nylon holdall.

'Good to see you didn't try to short-change me, George,' said Terry.

Kay looked pained. 'Terry . . .'

Terry cut him off with an impatient wave. 'I know you've been Raquel's grass for donkey's, George,' he said.

Kay looked shocked. The inhaler fell from his hands.

Terry lunged forward and grabbed Kay's wrists, forcing them down on to the table.

'I know you gave up the cannabis deal,' Terry continued, his voice a dull monotone. 'I know you had me attacked in the prison showers. I know everything.'

Kay's mouth moved soundlessly, like a badly operated ventriloquist's dummy.

'Now it's time to pay the piper . . .' said Terry.

Kay fought to pull his hands back but Terry was too strong for him. Fletcher stepped forward and grabbed Kay's hair. To his amazement, it came away in his hands. He stared at the hairpiece, his mouth open in astonishment. Terry's face broke into a grin and he let go of Kay's hands. Pike roared with laughter at Kay's embarrassment, and Kay put his hand up to cover his bald spot. Fletcher waved the wig back and forth over Kay's head. Kay began to giggle nervously, and soon all four men were laughing.

Terry shook his head. 'Nice syrup, George,' he said. He nodded at Pike, who moved away from the door, pulling a plastic bag out of his jacket pocket. He thrust it down over Kay's head. Fletcher grabbed hold of Kay's arms and grunted at him to hold still.

Pike twisted the bag around Kay's neck. Kay's eyes began to bulge and the bag pulsed in and out in time with his breathing.

Terry stood up and stared down at Kay. 'Goodbye, George,' he said. He picked up the holdall full of money and walked out of the office. Kay's feet started to thrash around under the desk but Terry didn't look back.

* * *

Sam poured milk into her coffee and popped in a sweetener. She handed a coffee to Laura who was sitting at the kitchen table in her bathrobe. 'Thanks, Mum,' said Laura.

Trisha walked into the kitchen in her school uniform and helped herself to orange juice from the fridge. She sneered at the mug of coffee in Sam's hands. 'You're digging yourself an early grave, Mum,' she said. 'Coffee knocks years off your life.'

'Trisha!' said Laura. 'Be nice.'

Sam grinned at Trisha. 'Frankly, love, I'm looking forward to the rest.' She sat down at the table with Laura and sighed despondently.

Trisha looked suddenly concerned. 'What's wrong, Mum?'

Sam ran a hand through her hair. 'Oh, nothing,' she sighed. 'I'm a bit tired, that's all.'

Trisha put a hand on Sam's shoulder. 'Is it Dad?'

Sam frowned and looked up at her. 'What makes you think that?'

'Well, for a start he didn't come home last night.'

'It's business.'

'Yeah, right.' Trisha sat down and held Sam's hand. 'Mum, he's up to his old tricks again, can't you see that?'

'You don't know what he's doing, Trish,' said Sam.

'I can guess.'

'Where is he, Mum?'

'He didn't say. But it's business.'

Laura and Trisha exchanged looks.

'Stop that, you two,' said Sam.

'He's using you, Mum,' said Trisha. 'You cook for him, you clean for him, you let him into your bed, but he's using you.'

'Trisha!'

'She's got a point, Mum,' said Laura. 'He shouldn't be staying out all night.'

'He's not a kid,' said Sam.

'Then he shouldn't act like one,' said Trisha.

The door opened and they all looked up. It was Terry. He stood in the doorway, smiling easily. 'Hen party, huh?' he said.

'Speak of the devil,' said Trisha. She drained her glass of orange juice, picked up her backpack and pushed past Terry.

'Hiya, Trish.'

Trisha snorted but didn't say anything.

'Bye, Trish.' Terry sat down at the kitchen table. 'She still mad at me, then?'

Laura sighed and stood up. 'I'm going to have a bath,' she said.

'You're not mad at me as well, are you?' asked Terry.

'Jury's still out on that,' she said, wrapping her bathrobe around her.

'Did Jonathon call again?'

Laura shook her head.

'Have you thought about what he said? The divorce?'

'I don't know, Dad. I just want to talk to him.'

'You should talk to Laurence Patterson,' said Terry. 'Find out where you stand. Divorces can be messy if you don't get the right legal advice.'

'Dad . . .' protested Laura.

'I'm just saying, if he's done a runner, you've got to protect your position.'

'Yeah. Maybe.' Laura shook her head. 'I'm just confused, you know.'

'Talk to Laurence,' repeated Terry. He tried to pick up Sam's coffee but she batted his hand away.

'You know where the kettle is,' she said.

Terry got up to make a cup of coffee as Laura went upstairs to the bathroom.

'How did it go?' said Sam.

'Asher and Patterson are in for a million. They're dipping into their clients' accounts, which is a bit naughty of them, but they know it's going to be a quick deal. And I got three hundred from Kay.'

Sam raised her eyebrows. 'You got three hundred grand from George Kay? That must have been like getting blood out of a stone.'

'Sort of.'

Sam sipped her coffee. 'Who are you going to sell it to once you've got it into the country?' she asked.

Terry took his coffee over to the kitchen table and sat down. 'There's some North London guys that Micky and I did some deals with a few years back. The governor's Geoff Donovan. He's up for it. It's going to be C.O.D. all round. He's putting together a syndicate to come up with the readies. It's going to work, Sam.'

Sam put down her mug and wiped her face with her hands. 'Are you sure about this, Terry?'

'It's the only way, love. It's either this or we sell up and move into a one-bedroom flat in Clapham. And I don't know about you, but I couldn't face that.'

'But heroin . . .'

'Don't think of it as heroin. Think of it as a commodity. We buy it on the Continent, we sell it for five times the price here. Just like we do with the cheap booze.'

'It's not the same, Terry. You know it's not.'

'Because it's illegal? Because the government has decided that alcohol is a legal drug and heroin isn't?'

'It's heroin, Terry.'

'You keep saying that, love, but we're not forcing anyone to be a junkie. We're supplying a need, that's all. People choose to use heroin, no one forces them. Same as you and your cigarettes. No one forces people to smoke, but millions do.'

Sam reached out for the pack in front of her, then stopped. Suddenly she'd lost the need for a cigarette.

Terry reached over and tapped the pack. 'How many people do these kill every year, Sam? Tens of thousands? Hundreds of thousands? You know how the kids are always moaning at you to stop. But does the government make them illegal? No. Why not? Because it makes millions from the tax on them.' Terry sat back in his chair and stretched. 'I tell you, as soon as the government works out how it can tax drugs like cannabis and heroin, they'll be legal.'

'But what if we get caught, Terry?'

Terry smiled. 'We won't, love. Trust me.'

* * *

McKinley brought the Saab to a halt outside the brick-built warehouse. 'Better if I went in with you, Mrs Greene,' he said.

'I don't want to spook him, Andy,' said Sam. She grinned. 'Just don't crash my Saab while I'm inside, yeah?'

McKinley groaned. 'It was an accident with the Lexus, Mrs Greene. I told you.'

'Yeah, well, Terry tells it different.'

McKinley grimaced. 'Terry told you what happened?'

'No secrets between a husband and wife, Andy,' said Sam. She took a deep breath and smiled at McKinley. 'That's what they say, isn't it?' She stared out of the window, psyching herself up.

'You're sure about this, Mrs Greene?' asked McKinley.

Sam sighed. 'No, not really, but I don't see that I've a got a choice.' She got out of the Saab and winked at him. 'If I'm not out in ten minutes, send in a search party, yeah?' She walked towards the entrance, feeling McKinley's eyes on her all the way.

The door leading into the warehouse was open, and as she approached, two men appeared, both well over six feet tall with rough skin and badly cut hair. She recognised one of them from the last time she'd spoken to Poskovic, and she nodded at him. He turned and shouted something in Kosovan into the warehouse. Sam heard Poskovic shout back, and the two men stepped to the side to allow Sam in.

There was a dank, musty odour in the warehouse, overlaid with the smell of stale fried onions. There were up to twenty hot dog trolleys being prepared, and heads swivelled as Sam walked by.

Poskovic stood at the far end of the warehouse, supervising two men stacking cases of lager. He was wearing a battered leather jerkin over a tatty multi-coloured pullover. His face hardened as Sam walked up to him. 'What are you doing here?' he snarled.

'I came for a chat,' said Sam.

'I've nothing to say to you,' said Poskovic. 'You should go, before I forget that you are a lady.'

'Why, Zoran, that's almost a compliment,' said Sam. She nodded at a table and a couple of chairs. 'How about we sit down?' she said.

'Better you go,' he said. 'My men are still angry at what your husband did.'

'The way my husband tells it, you went after him with shotguns,' said Sam.

'Have you any idea how much your husband cost me? He burnt out my last place. Burnt it to the ground.'

'I'm sorry, Zoran,' said Sam. 'It wasn't my doing, I can promise you that.'

Poskovic shrugged. 'Two of my men were badly beaten. One of them is still in hospital. He is an animal, your husband.'

'I hear what you're saying, Zoran. Honestly I do. But you gave as good as you got, didn't you? Guns blazing, Terry said.'

'He beat them up. And smashed our van.'

'And his Lexus was almost written off. Zoran, it's tit for tat.'

Poskovic frowned. 'Tit for tat?'

'It means, what he does to you, you do back to him.'

Poskovic nodded. 'Next time, we will hit him harder.'

'And he'll hit you harder. Tit for tat.'

Poskovic shrugged. 'I did not expect to see you again,' he said.

Sam smiled thinly. She looked around the warehouse. 'This is bigger than the other place. Every cloud, hey?'

Poskovic frowned. 'What?'

'Every cloud has a silver lining. It's an expression. It means something good can come out of something bad.'

'So you are saying I should be grateful that your husband burnt me out?'

'No, that's not what I meant, Zoran.'

Poskovic glared at her. 'Do you think I had insurance, Mrs Greene?'

Sam shook her head. 'No, I don't suppose you did,' she said. 'Have you got any booze, Zoran? I've got a terrible thirst. What about that vodka we had last time?'

'That went up in the fire,' he said.

'Pity,' said Sam.

Poskovic slowly smiled. 'But I had more sent over from St Petersburg.' He waved towards a metal desk against one wall. 'Bottom drawer,' he said.

Sam went over to the drawer and took out the bottle of vodka.

Poskovic picked up two large glasses off a shelf and took them over to her.

'What do you want, Mrs Greene?' he asked as she poured two large measures of the clear spirit.

* * *

Laura and Trisha were in the kitchen when Sam got back to the house, loaded down with supermarket carrier bags.

'Come on, give me a hand,' chided Sam. Laura and Trisha took the bags off Sam and started putting the provisions away. 'Do you think you two can take care of yourselves for a couple of days?' asked Sam.

'Why?' asked Trisha.

'Your dad and I want to go away for a bit, that's all.'

'What, like a second honeymoon?' asked Laura.

'Sort of.'

Laura hugged Sam. 'Mum, that's great. Where's he taking you?'

'Spain. Just a few days in the sun.'

'You should go for longer. Go for a couple of weeks. Trisha and I will be fine. Won't we, Trisha?'

'I don't care either way,' said Trisha.

'No wild parties,' cautioned Sam.

'As if we would,' laughed Laura. 'When are you going?'

'Day after tomorrow.'

'I'll take you to the airport,' offered Laura.

'That's okay. We're going to drive.'

'To Spain?' said Trisha. 'It'll take you for ever.'

'That's what your dad wants. Who am I to argue?'

* * *

McKinley slotted the packs of money behind the door panels of the BMW. Sam and Terry stood at the back of the car, watching him.

'It's not illegal is it?' said Sam. 'Taking money out of the country? I went to Spain with the last lot in a briefcase.'

'This is two million quid, Sam. Customs would sit up and take notice if they spotted it. They'd be all over us like a rash. We'll go over in the car and fly back. McKinley can drive the BMW back, the drugs'll come in the vans.'

'It's got to be the most expensive BMW in the world,' said Sam as McKinley eased more packs of banknotes into the doors. She smiled slyly. 'I've just had a thought.'

Terry raised an eyebrow. 'What?'

'Let's just get in and drive. Take the money and run. Two million quid, we'd be set up for life.' Terry looked at her incredulously and Sam smiled. 'Joke,' she said.

Terry shook his head. 'You had me going there, Sam. You really had me going.' He looked at his Rolex. 'Come on, McKinley, get a move on. We've got to meet up with Fletcher and the boys at the ferry terminal.'

'Nearly done,' said McKinley.

Terry hugged Sam. 'You okay?' he asked.

Sam nodded. 'Butterflies, that's all.'

'You don't have to come. I can handle it.'

'Think I'd let you drive away with the money?' said Sam.

Terry looked hurt. 'What do you mean?'

Sam lightly slapped his cheek. 'Joke,' she said. 'No, I wouldn't miss this for the world.'

* * *

Frank Welch squinted through the viewfinder of his camera and clicked away from the driver's seat of his Rover. The motordrive whirred and he focused the long lens on the three white vans as they headed towards the ferry. He recognised the drivers. Roger Pike. Kim Fletcher. Steve Ryser. All of them on Terry Greene's payroll. And following them in his BMW, the man himself. Terry Greene. And with him in the back, his wife.

Welch knew that he couldn't follow Greene and his team on to the ferry. He hadn't brought his passport with him and Superintendent Edwards had his warrant card. All he could do was to photograph them and find out when they were due back.

He focused the long lens on McKinley and snapped several shots of him, then photographed the registration plate of the BMW.

As he took the camera away from his face, a large black and white photograph was held up against the driver's side window. Welch flinched, then stared in amazement at the photograph. It was of Roger Pike pushing a piece of wood under the rear tyre of Welch's Rover on the day he was on surveillance outside the offices of Greene's accountant. It was a good picture, clearly showing the look of delight on Pike's face and the nails studded in the slab of wood.

The picture was whipped away, revealing a large man in a dark overcoat standing next to the car. Welch wound down the window.

'You haven't a clue what they're up to, have you?' said the man.

'Who are you?' said Welch.

The man opened the door and climbed into the passenger seat. The Rover wasn't a small car, but the man's bulk made Welch feel suddenly claustrophobic.

'You're in the job?' asked Welch. The man had the confident air acquired by policemen and career criminals, a sense that they were better than the general population, a cut above the rest.

The man tossed an envelope into Welch's lap. Welch opened it gingerly. Inside were more surveillance photographs showing Welch on Greene's tail.

'Piss-poor surveillance, it has to be said,' the man sneered. 'Every time he needs some privacy, he sells you a dummy.'

'I'm on my own, you know,' protested Welch.

The man nodded at the white vans. 'Do you want to talk about this or not, soon to be former Detective Chief Inspector Welch?'

Welch took a pack of breath mints from his pocket and popped one into his mouth. He nodded. 'Okay. What have you got?'

The man took another photograph from his pocket and handed it to Welch. Welch looked at it and felt a surge of excitement. It was a black and white photograph, slightly grainy as if it had been blown up. Terry Greene shaking hands with a familiar face. Geoff Donovan, a high-profile North London gangster.

'The reason that Terry Greene is on his way to Spain with his missus and Andy McKinley and the rest of the seven dwarves is that they're putting together the mother of all heroin deals. Ten million quid's worth.'

Welch frowned. 'How do you know?'

'I read tea leaves. How the hell do you think? I've a man on the inside.'

'So why don't you take this to the Drugs Squad yourself? It'd be a feather in your cap.'

'I'm starting to wonder how you made chief inspector.'

Welch's frown deepened, until realisation dawned and a knowing smile spread across his face. 'You're on his payroll,' he said. 'He's got his claws into you and you want out.'

The man stared at Welch, his eyes hardening. 'Some things are better left unsaid.'

'I get rid of Greene, and you're off the hook,' said Welch triumphantly.

'Maybe I'm talking to the wrong cop,' said the man. He held out his hand for the photographs but Welch moved them out of his reach.

'No way,' said Welch.

'Okay, then. But we handle this my way or not at all.'

Welch nodded slowly. 'Okay.'

'First thing, you keep well away from Greene and his associates. You carry on the way you're going, you'll spook him. Agreed?'

'Agreed,' said Welch.

'You wait for my say-so, then you can come down on him like the proverbial.'

Welch looked down at the photograph of Greene and Donovan. If he could catch two of London's biggest villains red-handed, he'd be able to write his own ticket. 'Who are you?' he asked.

The man patted Welch on the shoulder with a shovel-sized hand. 'You can call me Blackie,' he said.

* * *

Superintendent Edwards dipped his digestive biscuit into his cup of tea as he studied the overtime sheets in front of him. The door to his office burst open and Edwards jumped. His biscuit broke into two and the wet half disappeared into his cup.

Frank Welch stood in the doorway, his cheeks flushed and his eyes wide like a child desperate to open his Christmas presents. Behind him was Edwards' secretary. 'I'm sorry, sir,' she said, 'I told him you were busy.'

Edwards waved her away and pushed his cup and saucer to the side. 'Exactly what part of suspension don't you understand, Frank?' he said.

Welch closed the door and walked up to the superintendent's desk. 'The part where Terry Greene puts together a ten-million-pound heroin deal,' he said. He dropped a stack of photographs on to the desk.

'Holiday snaps, Frank?'

Edwards looked through the surveillance photographs. Pictures of the BMW and the three vans driving on to the ferry.

'There's two million pounds hidden in the panels of the BMW. Greene's using it to fund a heroin deal in Spain. Street value of ten million. He's planning to drive it back into the UK through France.'

Edwards looked up, frowning. 'Says who?'

'I've a man on the inside,' said Welch.

Edwards flicked through the photographs. He raised his eyebrows as he got to the picture of Greene and Donovan. 'Geoff Donovan, gangster of this parish?'

Welch nodded eagerly. 'That's right. Greene's fixed up to sell the heroin to him.'

Edwards flicked through to the next photograph. It was of Pike sabotaging Welch's tyre on surveillance. The superintendent frowned at the picture. Welch saw what he was looking at and scooped all the photographs off the desk.

'You're on suspension, Frank.'

'So get me unsuspended.' He waved the photographs in the air. 'This is major, but without me it'll turn to shit.'

Superintendent Edwards thought about it, then reached for his phone. 'Let me make a call,' he said.

Welch beamed triumphantly.

* * *

McKinley drove the BMW down the driveway to Micky Fox's villa. Terry nodded appreciatively. 'Nice place,' he said. 'I could go for a gaff like this. How about it, Sam? Fancy moving to Marbella? We'd certainly be among friends.'

'Until they get extradited,' said Sam. She got out of the BMW and walked towards the front door, where Fox was waiting for her with outstretched arms.

'Sam, you're becoming a regular here,' he boomed and gave her a bone-crushing hug.

'Looking that way, Micky,' she gasped.

Fox released her and went over to shake hands with Terry. 'You're putting on weight, my son,' he said, patting Terry's stomach.

'What can I say? It's Sam's cooking,' said Terry, putting an arm around Fox and walking into the villa with him. McKinley and Sam followed.

'You'll like Oskar,' said Fox. 'He's an all-right geezer for a Russian.'

Oskar, large bearlike man with a grey ponytail, was standing over a barbecue at the poolside, stabbing chunks of steak with a large fork. He had stripped to the waist, showing a scarred chest and an old bullet wound in his flabby stomach. He was sweating profusely and he wiped his arm across his forehead as Terry and Fox walked out on to the terrace.

Two young Spanish boys were swimming in the pool, and another was lying naked on a lounger.

'Bit bohemian this, Micky,' said Terry.

Fox laughed and slapped him on the back. 'Oskar, this is Terry!' he called.

'You have my money?' Oskar shouted.

'Doesn't believe in small talk, does he?' Terry said to Fox. He gestured with his chin at Oskar. 'When do we get the gear?' he shouted.

'When I get the money!' shouted Oskar.

'This is like a fucking pantomime,' Terry muttered.

'Oh no it isn't,' said Fox, and he burst out laughing.

'Carry on like this and you'll be in the pool with your fancy boys,' said Terry.

'That's the plan,' said Fox.

Oskar walked over, the fork in his hand, and shook hands with Terry. 'You like steak?' he asked.

'Love it,' said Terry.

'We are barbecuing,' said Oskar.

'Yeah, do you want to stay for a bite?' asked Fox.

Terry nodded over at Sam, who was standing on the terrace with McKinley, shading her eyes against the bright Mediterranean sun. 'Thanks, Micky, but I'm going to take Sam out for dinner.'

'Good idea,' said Fox. 'Where are the vans?'

'They've gone straight to the garage. You can get the compartments welded tonight?'

'Sure.'

'What about my money?' asked Oscar.

'McKinley'll get it for you now,' said Terry. He pointed at the barbecue, which was smoking furiously. 'I think your steak's burning.'

'I like it burnt,' said Oskar. He grinned, showing a mouthful of blackened teeth.

* * *

A waitress with jet-black hair and a swimsuit model's figure opened a bottle of Dom Perignon and filled two fluted glasses. Terry waited until the waitress had walked away before raising his glass to Sam.

'To us, yeah?' he said.

Sam smiled and they clinked glasses. The restaurant was on the side of a hill with breathtaking views of the sea. The tables were covered with crisp white cloths and each had a silver candelabra and a rose in a crystal vase. Sam looked around, soaking up the atmosphere. Most of the tables were occupied by couples, and there was a lot of whispering and hand-holding. 'It's beautiful,' she said.

'Yeah, Micky says the food's good, too.'

Sam sipped her champagne. 'Nice to be away from the kids for a while.'

'They're hardly kids any more,' said Terry. 'Laura and Jamie have flown the coop, and Trisha'll be off to university soon.'

Sam sighed. 'Where'd the years go, Terry?'

'Hey, don't sound so despondent, we had our good times.'

Sam smiled. 'Yeah, we had our moments, didn't we?'

A waiter arrived at the table with their food. Sam had ordered sole, and Terry had lamb chops.

'So when are you going to retire, Terry?' asked Sam.

'I'm too young to retire,' said Terry, cutting into one of his chops. 'I've a few years to go before I get my bus pass.'

Sam put down her knife and fork.

Terry could see that she was building up for an argument, so he put up his hands to quieten her. 'The rough stuff, that's over,' he said quickly. 'Whiter than white, I promise.'

'How white?' said Sam. 'What about the clubs, for instance?'

Terry winced. 'The clubs are a problem. Kay's sold me his share.'

'What?'

'He wanted out. I got it for a song.'

Sam looked at him suspiciously.

'Come on, Sam, try your fish,' cajoled Terry.

'Last I heard, George Kay wanted to buy *you* out.'

'People change.'

Sam looked at him suspiciously. 'Do they now?'

* * *

Laura knocked on the door to Trisha's bedroom. 'Yeah?' called Trisha.

Laura pushed open the door. 'Cocoa?'

'Yeah, thanks,' said Trisha. She was lying face down on her bed in T-shirt and jeans and leafing through a plastic folder.

Laura was holding two mugs of steaming cocoa. She put one down on the floor next to Trisha and sat down on the bed next to her. She reached out to touch the folder. 'What's this?' She opened it. It was full of newspaper clippings. All of them about their father.

'What does it look like?' said Trisha, rolling over and staring up at the ceiling.

'You kept all these?'

'It doesn't mean anything,' said Trisha. She looked at her sister, and brushed Laura's hair away from her eyes. 'Have you been crying?'

'A bit.'

'Because of Jonathon, yeah?'

Laura sighed. 'This thing about him going to Canada just doesn't make any sense,' she said. 'He's never talked about Toronto before. I think Dad's scared him off.'

Trisha took the file and flicked through it. 'When did you first know what Dad did for a living?' she asked.

Laura shrugged. 'God, I don't know. There were always some pretty strange people around the house. And Dad was always coming and going at all hours.'

'Mum never said, did she?'

'She was probably in denial,' said Laura. 'I didn't know about the drugs, not until the tabloids turned him over. That was a bit of shock. Jonathon hit the roof.' She took a sip of her cocoa. 'Wasn't all he hit,' she added quietly.

'He hit you?' asked Trisha. 'Jonathon hit you?'

Laura didn't say anything but she pulled a face.

'He did, didn't he? Bastard.' Trisha's jaw dropped. 'That's why you were in hospital, wasn't it? That bastard hit you. God. Dad should have killed him.'

'Trisha!'

'I hope Dad did run him out of town. He could have killed you, Laura.'

'It wasn't that bad, Trish. It was the glass coffee table that did the damage.'

'I'd never let a man hit me. Ever.'

'That's easy to say,' said Laura. She smiled at a photograph of her father on the front page of the *Evening Standard* along with the headline 'LONDON'S TOP DRUGS BARON?' 'It's funny,' she said, 'Jonathon was born with a silver spoon, pretty much. Public school, Oxford. Straight into the City. But he's got a real hard side to him.' She tapped the cutting from the *Standard*. 'Dad, after all he's been through, after all this, he's still a softie really. Never laid a finger on any of us.'

'He shouted and stamped his feet a bit,' laughed Trisha.

'Yeah, but it's not like we didn't give him reason to,' said Laura.

They smiled at each other. 'He's okay, I guess,' said Trisha.

'Yeah, he loves Mum to bits.'

'He walked out on her,' said Trisha, defensive again.

'She threw him out,' said Laura. 'Doesn't mean they don't love each other.'

'You think?'

Laura ruffled her sister's hair. 'Drink your cocoa.'

* * *

Sam and Terry walked hand in hand through the square, the moon above almost full. It was a warm night and Terry had slung his jacket over his shoulder. The air was heavy with the smell of oranges from the orchards at the edge of the village.

Terry raised Sam's hand to his lips and kissed it softly. 'Are you okay?' he asked.

Sam nodded. 'Thank you,' she said.

'For what?'

'For the meal. For bringing me along.'

Two teenagers walked past them, arm in arm. She had long blonde hair and was laughing and resting her head on her boyfriend's shoulder. He had black curly hair and tight jeans and stroked her arm as they walked. Sam smiled at the two lovers. The girl couldn't have been much older than Trisha. She snuggled against Terry.

'It's almost like it used to be, isn't it?' she said. 'Dinner, champagne, a moonlit walk . . .'

'. . . and bed?' Terry continued for her.

She pinched him and laughed. 'You've a one-track mind, Terry Greene.' Ahead of them was a pretty stone-built church with a square bell tower. 'Look at that,' said Sam. 'It must be hundreds of years of old. Do you want to go inside?'

'In a church?' said Terry, pretending to be shocked. 'Now who's got a one-track mind?'

'I meant have a look around,' said Sam, 'and you know I did.'

Terry grinned. 'Yeah, come on.'

They walked into the church. It was cool and peaceful, with high vaulted ceilings and pink-painted walls. The lines of oak pews were worn shiny smooth from generations of worshippers. They walked hand in hand towards the altar.

Sam looked across at Terry. He was smiling and his eyes glinted as he looked at her.

'I was just thinking, it's like our wedding,' said Sam.

Terry nodded. 'That's what I was thinking, too. Takes you back, doesn't it?'

'We had poached salmon, didn't we? Salmon in a watercress sauce.'

Terry frowned. 'What made you say that?'

Sam sighed. 'It was something Grace said. Last time I saw her.'

Terry put his arm around her. 'I miss her,' he said.

'Yeah. Me too,' said Sam. She gave his arm a small squeeze. 'I want to light a candle.'

Terry took his arm away and she went over to a side table where more than two dozen small candles flickered in front of a painting of the Virgin Mary. She took a fresh candle, lit it, and then stood with her eyes closed for almost a full minute while Terry watched.

She opened her eyes and smiled.

'So what did you wish for?' asked Terry.

'That's birthday candles. You don't ask for wishes in a church. You ask for forgiveness.' She looked at him steadily. 'Anything you want to confess?'

Terry grinned. 'Not without my brief present.'

Sam smiled thinly and nodded to herself. She walked over to the front pew and sat down. Terry sat next to her.

'Are you being honest with me, Terry?' asked Sam.

'About what?'

Sam shook her head sadly. 'That's the wrong answer,' she said. 'You're either being honest or you're not. It's like being pregnant. No half measures.'

'Always with the trick questions,' said Terry.

'Always with the evasive answers,' said Sam.

Terry looked at her seriously. 'I'm being up front, love,' he said. 'A new leaf. A new life.'

Sam looked at him, wondering if he was telling the truth. She stared into his blue eyes for so long that she started to feel dizzy

'You know I killed Snow, don't you?' he said eventually, his voice dull and flat.

At first Sam couldn't believe what he'd said. She frowned, going through the words, making certain that she hadn't misunderstood.

Terry continued to stare at her. 'And you know about Alicia.'

Sam's eyes hardened. She felt a cold chill run down her spine. It wasn't fear. Or horror. It was anger. A cold fury that she had to fight to keep under control.

'She didn't mean anything,' said Terry. 'She didn't then and she doesn't now. I'm not even sure that the kid's mine.'

'It's got your eyes,' said Sam. She lowered her voice to a whisper. 'You shouldn't have lied,' she said. 'If you'd told me the truth, maybe . . .' She couldn't bring herself to finish the sentence.

Terry tried to take her hand but Sam pulled it away. She didn't want him touching her.

'It was self defence,' said Terry earnestly.

'Of course it was,' said Sam, her voice dripping with sarcasm. 'And Morrison? That was self defence, too?'

'He tried to kill me, Sam.'

'Who? Snow or Morrison?'

'Give me a break, will you, Sam? I'm trying to be honest with you here.'

'Trying? It's an effort, is it?'

Terry growled and sat facing forward. They sat in silence. There was a noise behind them and Sam turned to see an old woman kneeling at the back of the church, her face lined like old parchment, her head covered in a black scarf. 'He was on my back for weeks,' said Terry quietly. 'He'd found out about the kid and said he wanted money. Said if I didn't pay up he'd tell you about Alicia and the baby. Maybe even go to the papers. Kept going on about me stealing his wife from him and that I owed him. It was bollocks, she was going to leave him anyway but he wouldn't listen. Said if I gave him ten grand he'd disappear.'

'And you believed him?'

'I figured it was worth a try. I didn't want you hurt, Sam. Honest to God I didn't.'

'Oh, this was all for me, was it? Why do I find that hard to believe?'

'This is God's truth, Sam.'

'You took a gun with you, though. Didn't you?'

'That's what I'm saying, I didn't. I took the money and that was it. I went there to pay him off. Okay, I was going to get heavy and tell him that it was a one-off payment, that if I ever heard from him again his life wouldn't be worth living, but no way was I carrying a shooter.'

Terry sighed and ran his hands through his hair. He leant

forward, his fingers interlinked, almost as if he was praying.

'I took him the ten grand, but he said it wasn't enough,' whispered Terry. 'He was as high as a kite. God knows what he was on. He pulled a gun and started waving it around. I grabbed for it. It went off.'

'You shot him?'

'It went off, Sam. We were both holding it. It all happened really quickly, but I think his finger was on the trigger.'

'You think?'

'It's a blur, Sam. I'm not going to lie to you. Anyway, he dropped the gun and went running through the house like a headless chicken. I don't think he was too badly hurt.'

'He was shot.'

'It was a twenty-two. Small calibre. There wasn't that much blood.'

'Oh, that's all right, then.'

Terry put a hand on Sam's knee but she pushed it away. 'Sam . . .' he protested.

'He was shot twice, Terry,' she said coldly.

'He went running up stairs, banging off the walls, like he didn't know what he was doing. I went after him. To see what sort of state he was in. He got to a bedroom and started rifling through drawers, looking for something. Then he passed out. Slumped on the floor. I walked up to him, thought maybe he was dead. He wasn't. He was still breathing. So I went to call an ambulance.'

'Very public spirited of you,' said Sam.

'Sam, I'm trying to tell you what happened.'

'Are you, Terry?' snapped Sam. 'Are you? Or are you trying to make yourself out to be the Good Samaritan here?'

'I was leaving, Sam. I was on my way out. I was going to call an ambulance, cross my heart.'

'So what happened?'

'He had another gun. He came around as I walked away. Grabbed another gun from somewhere and let me have it. Damn near blew my head off.' He held up his right hand, thumb and first finger an inch apart. 'He missed me by this much, Sam. This much.' He rested his elbows on his knees as he leaned forward. 'I still had his gun in my hand. I shot him. It was instinctive, Sam, I didn't think about it, didn't even know what I was doing. He shot at me, I turned and shot him.'

'In the head?'

'I wasn't aiming, Sam. I wasn't trying to kill him. I just wanted him to stop shooting at me. You've got to believe me, it was self defence.'

Terry sat back in the pew and waited for Sam to speak. The old woman at the back of the church grunted as she stood up. She crossed herself and left.

'Why are you telling me this now, Terry?'

'Thought I'd clear the air. Turn over a new leaf and that. Start as we mean to go on.'

He sat up straight and looked Sam in the eye. 'I've changed, Sam. Cross my heart.'

He reached across to hold her hand. Sam let him and they sat together, staring at the altar, hand in hand.

★ ★ ★

Terry crawled into the van and inspected the compartment that the mechanics had built into the base of the vehicle. It was about three feet wide, five feet long and three inches deep. He nodded appreciatively. 'Tidy work, Micky,' he said.

Micky Fox was standing at the back of the van, holding a bottle of San Miguel. 'Yeah, they're good lads. Used to shoe horses at the bullfighting stadium.'

Terry crawled out of the van. He'd already checked the other two white vans, and Oskar was supervising Fletcher, Ryser and Pike as they filled the compartments with plastic-wrapped packages. The heroin. Sam was watching, and McKinley stood next to her, his arms behind him like an undertaker at a funeral.

'You're sure about this, Terry?' asked Fox. 'You're just going to drive them through Customs?'

'*I'm* not, Micky. Sam and I are flying back this afternoon. Kim and the boys'll drive the vans back.'

'They've got more balls than me, I can tell you.'

'Nah, it's going to be a piece of cake,' said Terry. 'They'll fill up the vans with cheap booze in Calais then drive over on the ferry. Customs won't give them a second look. They'll be one of thousands of day-trippers carrying booze. If they do get stopped, worst that'll happen is that we'll get done for the booze. They won't be looking for gear.'

Fox looked over at Sam and she smiled and shrugged. 'My husband assures me that he knows what he's doing,' she said.

* * *

Sam and Terry got back to Heathrow early in the evening. McKinley had driven them to the airport in Malaga in the BMW before heading off on the long drive back to London. They walked through the terminal and queued for a black cab.

'Are you nervous?' Sam asked, as they settled into the back of the taxi.

'It'll be fine,' said Terry. 'They've done the booze runs a thousand times and the vans have never been searched.'

'My heart won't stop pounding,' said Sam. 'It's like everyone's looking at me and they know what I've done. I almost died when the immigration officer checked my passport.'

Terry took her hand. 'It'll soon be over. Then it's straight and narrow.'

'I hope so, Terry.'

When the taxi dropped them outside the house, Terry put his arms around Sam and gave her a hug. 'Can I borrow the Saab?' he said, nibbling her ear.

Sam pushed him away. 'Terry, we've only just got back.'

'It's business, love.'

'Trisha and Laura will want to see you.'

'I know, but I've got something to take care of first.'

'What?'

'Business.'

'What sort of business, Terry?'

'Best you don't know, love.'

'I thought we were partners in crime?'

Terry laughed. He let go of her and held out his hand. 'Come on, give me the keys and stop messing about.'

Sam sighed in exasperation, then handed over her car keys. Terry kissed her on the cheek and went to the Saab.

Sam let herself into the house. 'It's me,' she called.

'We're in the kitchen!' shouted Laura.

Trisha and Laura were eating pasta at the kitchen table. 'How was the second honeymoon?' asked Laura.

Sam smiled. 'Bit quieter than the first,' she said, putting her bag down.

'Where's Dad?' asked Trisha.

'He's got work to do.'

Trisha pulled a face.

'Any of that pasta going spare?' asked Sam.

'Sure,' said Laura. She got up and busied herself at the cooker.

Sam sat down and took a drink from Trisha's glass of milk. 'How'd you feel about moving to Spain?' she asked.

'What?' said Trisha, putting down her fork.

Laura turned around, a look of astonishment on her face. 'Mum?'

'I was just thinking, that's all.'

'I thought you hated Spain,' said Laura.

'Not the place. Just the fact that we always meet up with your dad's friends when we're over there, and they're . . . an acquired taste.'

'That's putting it mildly,' said Laura. She heaped pasta on to a plate and poured on tomato and mushroom sauce.

'But I was thinking it'd make a change. Get away from the cold and the rain.'

'What about school?' asked Trisha.

'There are schools in Spain. English schools.'

Laura put the plate of pasta down on the table and gave Sam a fork. 'How long have you been planning this?' she asked.

'I've not been planning anything,' said Sam. 'I'm just thinking, that's all. There's nothing really holding us here, is there? Not now that Grace has gone.'

'And Jonathon's out of the picture, is that what you mean? I'm on my own so I should move to Spain, is that it?'

Sam reached over and patted Laura's hand. 'I just thought we could all do with some time in the sun, that's all. Don't read anything in to it.'

'Is he going, is that it?' sneered Trisha. 'Dad's running away to the Costa del Crime and we've got to go with him.' She banged her fork on the table. 'Jesus Christ.'

'I meant you and Laura and me,' said Sam patiently. 'A new start.'

'Without Dad?' asked Trisha. She frowned and leaned forward. 'Are you leaving him, Mum?'

Sam shook her head. 'You two can be a real pain at times. I was just asking if you fancied spending some time in the sun, that's all. Forget I asked.'

'I wouldn't mind,' said Laura. 'Lie on the beach, get a tan. Yeah, I could go for that.'

Trisha nodded. 'Yeah, me too.'

'What about Jamie?' asked Laura.

'I'll talk to him. He's got his degree to finish but he can come and spend holidays with us.'

'You sure about this, Mum?' asked Trisha.

Sam nodded. 'Oh yes,' she said. 'Quite sure.'

* * *

Frank Welch opened his eyes and reached out for the ringing phone. 'It's me,' said a voice.

'Who?' asked Welch sleepily.

'Will you get a grip, Raquel.' It was Blackie.

Welch sat up in bed and squinted at his watch. 'It's four o'clock in the morning.'

'Well, fuck you very much,' said Blackie. 'If you don't want the bust, I'll give it to someone else.'

'No!' said Welch quickly. 'It's okay. I'm here. What's happened?'

Blackie didn't say anything for a couple of seconds, and Welch thought that the connection had been cut, but then Blackie cleared his throat. 'The vans have arrived back in the UK. Thought you should know.'

'What about Greene?'

'They got back yesterday. Both of them. Flew into Heathrow.'

'Why the hell didn't you tell me they were coming?' asked Welch.

'Because I don't want you spooking them,' said Blackie patiently. 'They've got several vans and my snout doesn't know which one the heroin's in. But he does know where they're divvying the gear up the day after tomorrow.'

'Where?' said Welch, his heart pounding. He reached over to pick up a pen from the bedside table.

'My snout's not going to tell me until he's sure,' said Blackie. 'When he calls me, I'll call you. Until then, keep your head down.'

The line went dead. Welch sat where he was, cradling the phone. One more day and he'd have Terry Greene. And Samantha. The anticipation was almost unbearable.

* * *

Terry was pacing up and down in the sitting room when his mobile phone rang. It was McKinley. 'Bloody hell, McKinley, I was starting to think you'd got lost,' said Terry.

Sam walked in from the kitchen, taking off a pair of oven gloves. Terry gave her a thumbs-up.

'We're all here, Terry,' said McKinley.

'Got through Customs okay?'

'Didn't give us a second look.' Terry beamed and gave Sam another thumbs-up.

'Andy, you're a star. Where are you now?'

'The factory.'

'Magic. Make sure the gizmo's working. I'll call Donovan and fix up the meet. You stay right there.'

Terry cut the connection. He went over to Sam, picked her up off the ground and whirled her around. 'It worked, love. We're home and dry.'

'We're home and dry when we've been paid for the gear,' said Sam. 'Come on, put me down.'

'Spoilsport,' said Terry, putting her down. He kissed her and she slipped her arms around his neck. 'Bedroom,' he said, pushing her towards the door.

'What is it with you and money?' she teased. 'Whenever you get any, you get randy.'

'Best aphrodisiac there is,' said Terry. He kissed her again, hard on the lips.

Eventually Sam pushed him away. 'You're counting your chickens,' she said. 'Let's wait until we've got the money, yeah?'

Terry grinned and nodded. 'Yeah, you're right. We'll celebrate later. Let me call Donovan.'

Sam nodded. 'I'll get ready.'

Terry phoned Geoff Donovan and told him that they were ready for the exchange, then locked up the house and went out to the car where Sam was waiting for him. It was a cold day and she'd put on a long black coat and gloves. Terry climbed into the front seat.

'I don't even get to drive my own car now,' said Sam, getting into the passenger seat.

'Sam, after today you can have a dozen Saabs,' laughed Terry.

* * *

Frank Welch looked around the assembled officers with a smug feeling of satisfaction. There were more than forty men and women in the room, more than half of them armed.

On the wall behind him were surveillance photographs of Terry and Samantha Greene and their henchmen, and Geoff Donovan and his team.

Superintendent Edwards stood at the side of the room, his arms crossed. He looked at his watch. Welch smiled at the superintendent and nodded confidently. Welch was holding his mobile phone. He'd had it on charge all morning and had a spare battery in his pocket. Blackie had said he'd call as soon as he knew where Donovan was picking up the drugs.

Edwards had suggested that they keep Donovan under surveillance but Welch had persuaded him that he had to be given a free rein. If Donovan got wind that he was being watched, the whole operation would be blown. Edwards had pressed Welch on the identity of his informant but Welch had held firm. Blackie was his source and he wanted it to stay that way. The arrest and conviction of Terry Greene and Geoff Donovan was his ticket to the top and he wasn't going to throw it away. He popped a couple of breath mints into his mouth.

* * *

Terry parked the Saab around the back of a warehouse close to the disused factory where the exchange was due to take place. 'No point in drawing attention to ourselves,' he said to Sam as they got out of the car. He put his arm around her as they walked towards McKinley, who was waiting for them at the shutter door. 'You sure you want to be here?' Terry asked.

'Bit late to ask me now,' said Sam, turning up the collar of her coat.

'McKinley could drive you home.'

'Nothing's going to go wrong, is it?' asked Sam.

''Course not,' said Terry, giving her shoulder a squeeze.

'Then I want to be with you,' she said.

'You've changed,' said Terry, with a smile.

'You changed me.'

McKinley ushered them into the disused factory. The three white vans were lined up at the far end of the building, the rear doors open. There were stacks of beer and lager in front of the vans. The BMW had been parked at the other end of the factory, pointing towards the exit. 'Donovan's not arrived yet,' said McKinley.

'He'll be here,' said Terry. 'You stay by the door, keep an eye out for him.'

Fletcher, Pike and Ryser were sitting around a table playing cards. They'd opened a case of lager and there were several cans on the table. 'Don't get up, lads!' Terry shouted over at them.

Sam noticed a metal arch that had been erected near the door. 'What's this, Terry?' she asked.

'Metal detector,' he said. 'Same as they use at airports.'

Sam frowned. 'Why's it here?'

'Donovan's an old mate, but that doesn't mean I trust him,' said Terry.

* * *

Frank Welch jumped as his mobile rang. 'Yeah?' he said, putting the phone to his ear.

'You got a pen?' It was Blackie.

'Yeah, I've got a pen. Have you got the address?'

'Why the fuck do you think I'm calling?'

The detectives and armed police in the room tensed as Welch scribbled down an address in his notebook and cut the connection.

Welch looked across at Superintendent Edwards. 'It's on.' He strode over to a large-scale map of London. 'They're here,' he said, tapping the map.

Edwards walked over to the map and looked at where Welch was pointing. 'With the heroin?' he asked.

Welch nodded enthusiastically. 'Terry Greene's waiting to hand the gear over. His whole team's there and Donovan's on the way.'

Edwards patted Welch on the shoulder. 'Good job, Frank. Well done.'

'Right!' shouted Welch, pointing at the door. 'Let's get to it.'

* * *

McKinley popped his head around the shutter door and whistled to attract Terry's attention. Terry looked across at McKinley, who gave him a thumbs-up. From outside came the sound of car doors opening and closing.

'Okay, lads, showtime!' Terry called over to Fletcher and his team. They put down their cards and hurried over to join him. Terry winked at Sam. 'Soon be over, love.'

Sam smiled and looked at her watch.

McKinley walked into the factory with a broad-shouldered man in a black leather jacket. Behind them were four large men carrying bulging holdalls.

The man with McKinley nodded at Terry. 'How's it going, Terry?'

'Getting better by the minute, Geoff.'

Geoff Donovan was a shade under six feet with close-cropped hair and designer stubble. He noticed the metal detector and frowned. 'What the hell's this?'

Terry smiled amiably. 'I didn't want any nasty surprises,' he said. 'You don't mind, do you?'

Donovan's dark brown eyes hardened fractionally and his smile tightened. 'How's about you and your boys skip through first, yeah?'

Terry shrugged. 'Sure.' He waved at Fletcher and his team and gestured at the metal detector. They went through one by one. McKinley went through last. The detector beeped and Donovan and his men tensed.

McKinley frowned and went through the pockets of his jacket. He pulled a face and shook his head, bemused. Then he put his hand in his trouser pocket and took out a handful of change. He grinned apologetically. 'I was playing a fruit machine last night,' he said. 'My luck was in.' He put the coins on a table and went through the detector again. This time it remained silent.

'Satisfied?' Terry asked Donovan.

Donovan smiled and motioned for Terry and Sam to go through the detector. Sam sighed. She took her mobile phone out of her bag along with her keys and put them on the table before walking through the detector. Terry followed.

'Okay?' he asked Donovan.

Donovan grinned. 'I feel so much happier now.' He reached inside his leather jacket. ''Course, this is where I pull out a shooter and take the money and the drugs.' He looked over at his four companions. 'Right, guys?'

Terry stiffened and Fletcher and his team looked around anxiously.

Donovan grinned and took his hand out. Empty. He made it into a gun and mimed shooting Terry. 'Gotcha!' he laughed.

Fletcher and his team laughed nervously. Donovan guffawed and gestured for the four bag-carriers to walk through the detector. Donovan was the last through. He grinned, walked over to Terry and hugged him.

Terry turned to Sam. 'Sam, this is Geoff Donovan, the meanest son-of-a-bitch north of the river.'

Donovan smiled and held out his hand. Sam shook it. His huge hand engulfed hers but he had a gentle grip. 'Second meanest,' he said. 'You haven't met the missus. But don't tell her I said that. Pleased to meet you, Sam.' He looked around the factory. 'So where's the gear, then?'

'In the vans,' said Terry.

'Let's get this over with, then,' said Donovan. 'We've all got homes to go to, haven't we?'

* * *

The Rover screeched around the corner, its front bumper only inches away from the police van in front of them.

'Take it easy,' said Welch. 'We want to get there in one piece.' He put two breath mints into his mouth.

'Sorry, guv,' said DS Clarke, dropping down a gear. Welch had a street directory in his lap and he was glancing at it as the Rover sped through the streets. They were ten minutes at most away from the location that Blackie had given him.

DI Simpson was sitting in the back of the car, drumming his fingers nervously against the door.

Behind the Rover was a blue van belonging to SO19, the Metropolitan Police's armed response unit, and behind that were a further six cars full of detectives and Drugs Squad officers and two more vans of uniformed officers. Bringing up the rear were two dog units. Welch had requested a helicopter, but Superintendent Edwards had said he didn't have the budget. It didn't matter. Welch reckoned he had all the manpower he needed to bring in Terry Greene.

Welch's heart was pounding in anticipation of putting Terry Greene back behind bars, where he belonged. And all the credit would go to Welch. There was no way Blackie would want to admit his involvement, not if he'd been on Greene's payroll. All the glory would go to Welch, and he was determined to take full advantage of it.

He couldn't wait to see the look on Greene's face when Welch snapped the handcuffs on him. Geoff Donovan, too. And then there'd be Samantha Greene. Welch smiled to himself. That was what he was most looking forward to. Looking into the eyes of Samantha Greene and telling her that she was under arrest. The anticipation was almost painful, and Welch could feel the start of an erection. His face flushed with embarrassment and he opened his legs and adjusted his trousers. He realised that Clarke was looking across at him, a look of puzzlement on his face. Welch snorted and pointed ahead. 'I didn't say slow to a crawl,' he snapped.

* * *

Fletcher put a block of notes into the automatic money-counter, and it whirred through them. Pike wrote down the number on the digital read-out and Ryser stacked the notes into one of several suitcases. Sam and Terry watched. 'I didn't realise ten million pounds took up such a lot of space,' she said.

Terry put his arm around her. 'It's going to set us up for life, love,' he said. 'For life.'

Sam nodded. 'It better had, Terry, because I'm not going through this again.'

McKinley was leaning against the BMW, his legs crossed at the ankles, watching Donovan's four heavies unpack the heroin from the vans.

Terry gave her shoulder a squeeze. 'You get a kick out of it, though, don't you? Come on, admit it.'

'I don't know if kick is the right word,' she said. 'More like scared to death.'

'Nah, it makes you feel alive. Really alive. It's like after Vesuvius erupted.'

Sam frowned. 'What are you talking about?'

'Vesuvius. The volcano. After it erupted, the fields around were covered with people making love.'

'It always comes down to sex with you, sooner or later, doesn't it?'

Terry grinned. 'It's taking risks. It makes you want to celebrate being alive.'

Sam shook her head and raised a warning finger. 'If this is a roundabout way of saying you want a quickie, you can forget it.'

Terry laughed. 'Maybe later?'

Sam laughed along with him. 'Maybe.'

Donovan had taken one of the plastic-wrapped packages from each of the vans and put them on the table where Terry's crew had been playing cards. He tore a hole in each of the packages and checked samples of the heroin with a testing kit.

'You're getting suspicious in your old age, Geoff,' Terry called over to him.

'Just making sure there's no problems down the line,' said Donovan.

Sam looked at her watch.

'Don't worry, love,' said Terry. 'Won't be long now.'

* * *

Clarke pulled up next to the SO19 van. Armed police were piling out and checking their weapons, and two uniformed officers were studying the factory building through binoculars.

The windows on the ground floor were boarded up and there was a 'For Sale' sign above the delivery entrance. 'We could get a floor plan from the estate agents,' said the chief inspector in charge of the armed police squad, a tall, gangly man with a shock of ginger hair. He hadn't bothered to introduce himself by name and Welch had the impression the man resented not being allowed to lead the operation. Welch had been insistent, however: it was his operation. His glory. The armed police were just the hired help.

Welch shook his head. 'No time,' he said. 'We're going in as soon as the Land Rover gets here.'

'There's no rush,' said the chief inspector, adjusting his bullet-proof vest. 'They're not going anywhere.'

Welch's nostrils flared. 'This is my operation. I decide when we're going in.'

The chief inspector narrowed his eyes but didn't say anything. He nodded once and went over to talk to his men, running his hand through his ginger hair.

'Okay, guv?' asked DI Simpson, handing him an opened pack of chewing gum.

Welch shook his head. He was still sucking his breath mints. 'Where's the Land Rover?'

Simpson gestured towards the main road. 'It's on its way.'

'Soon as it gets here, we go in. Crash through the door and we all pile in.'

'Bloody hell, guv. If they start shooting it'll be a bloodbath.'

Welch winked. 'Don't tell anyone, Doug, but my man says they're not armed. It's a gun-free zone in there.'

* * *

Sweat was pouring down the man's spine and he desperately wanted to scratch his back, but he knew that to do so would risk giving away his position. He cradled his gun in his arms as he crouched behind the stack of oil barrels, but kept his finger well away from the trigger. His instructions had been clear. He was to watch and wait until the building was stormed. Only then was he to go into action. Until then his orders were to watch. And wait.

The targets didn't appear to be armed. They'd all walked through a metal detector, but that didn't mean there couldn't be weapons hidden near by. He recognised most of the men there. Terry Greene. Andy McKinley. Geoff Donovan. And the woman. Samantha Greene. He'd spent the morning studying photographs while he was being briefed. It was imperative that there were no mistakes. His balls would be on the line if anything went wrong.

He was wearing a black woollen ski mask with holes for his eyes and mouth, and black overalls. Black was the best colour to wear. It inspired fear. People were more inclined to obey orders from a man in a black uniform. The Nazis knew that. So did the SAS. It inspired fear and obedience. So did the mask. The mask was soaked in sweat and the wool made his skin itch. He wanted to look at his wristwatch, but he knew he had to keep all movement to a minimum. He strained to hear what they were saying.

The one called Donovan held up a small test tube and peered at its contents. He nodded. 'Looking good, Terry,' he shouted.

Terry Greene was watching his men counting the money. 'Be easier to suck it and see, Geoff,' he said.

Donovan pulled a face. 'Never touch the stuff,' he said. 'Mug's game.'

The man rolled his shoulders inside his overalls. The tension was tightening his muscles and he forced himself to relax. He'd have to move soon and he'd have to move quickly.

* * *

Welch grinned as the Land Rover arrived with four uniformed officers. An extra-large metal bumper had been welded to the front to act as a battering ram, and the windows had been reinforced with wire mesh. The driver was wearing a protective helmet and a bullet-proof vest. The three officers with him climbed out.

Welch waved at the factory. 'Right, let's do it,' he said. The SO19 chief inspector led his men towards the factory, fanning out as they approached the entrance. As they got to within fifty feet of the building, the Land Rover surged forward, heading for the metal-shuttered delivery entrance. Two uniformed officers followed with large Alsatians straining at their leashes.

Welch started walking, flanked by Simpson and Clarke. The rest of the team spread out, walking purposefully but making sure that they didn't get ahead of Welch. Behind them, the Drugs Squad and the uniformed officers followed.

The Land Rover slammed into the metal shutters and crashed through. The armed officers broke into a run and poured through the opening, shouting staccato commands for everyone inside to lie down and offer no resistance.

Welch felt the adrenalin pump through his system and he broke into a trot. Simpson and Clarke jogged after him and within seconds everyone was running towards the factory, whooping and cheering like a group of football supporters on the rampage.

They ran into the factory, their shouts echoing off the walls. The armed officers were standing around the Land Rover, guns pointing down at the ground. Welch frowned. He whirled around, looking for Terry Greene. His heart pounded as he realised that apart from the police, the factory was empty. Totally empty. There was nowhere in the factory for them to be hiding.

The SO19 Chief Inspector came over and glared contemptuously at Welch. 'Great tip, Raquel.'

'There must be some mistake,' said Welch. There was a burst of laughter from the armed police and several of them looked over in Welch's direction.

'Dead fucking right there's a mistake. And it's standing in front of me. You're going to have some heavy questions to answer back at the station.'

'They must have gone. They were here and they left. We were late.'

The chief inspector shook his head. 'Look around. This place has been empty for years. Face it, Raquel. You were given a bum steer.'

Simpson's mobile phone rang and he walked away to answer it. The chief inspector went back to his men.

Welch put his hands in his coat pockets and walked to the middle of the factory. The chief inspector was right. Terry Greene hadn't been anywhere near the factory. No one had. One of the Alsatians was cocking its leg against the wall of the factory.

There was more laughter from the armed police as they headed back to their van.

Simpson came over, holding out his mobile phone. 'Guv, it's the super. Wants to know how we got on.'

Welch shook his head. He was going to need time to get his story straight before he spoke to Superintendent Edwards. He had a lot of explaining to do, but for the life of him he couldn't work out where it had all gone wrong.

* * *

Geoff Donovan tested the third batch of heroin as Terry stood watching over his shoulder. Donovan nodded. 'This is bloody good stuff, Terry,' he said.

'Told you,' said Terry, patting Geoff on the back. 'They know their heroin, the Russians.'

'You going to be bringing any more over? This is ten times better than the shit we've been getting though the fucking Turks.'

Terry grinned. He lowered his head and put his mouth close to Donovan's ear. 'Could well be, Geoff, but for fuck's sake don't tell Sam.' Terry straightened up and looked over at McKinley, who was supervising the counting of the money. 'How's it going, lads?'

Fletcher put the last block of notes in the automatic counter and watched as they whirred through the machine. Ryser wrote down the number and handed the final total to McKinley. 'It's short,' said McKinley.

Donovan frowned. 'Say what?' He put down his test tube and stood up.

'It's twenty quid light,' said McKinley. He held up the notebook. 'Have a look for yourself.'

Donovan took out his wallet and handed Terry a twenty-pound note. 'Can't be bothered with a recount,' he said. 'Life's too fucking short.'

'Pleasure doing business with you, Geoff,' said Terry,

pocketing the note. The two men shook hands, then hugged and clapped each other on the back.

Sam was pacing up and down by the BMW, and Terry went over and gave her a hug. 'It's all done, love. Let's go home.'

Donovan shouted over to his three heavies and told them to put the packages of heroin into the holdalls. Fletcher, Ryser and Pike started to pick up the suitcases.

'Andy, open up the boot, yeah?'

McKinley nodded and walked over to the BMW.

Suddenly there was the thunderous roar of a shotgun and everyone flinched. Four men in ski masks burst in through the doorway. Three of them were holding handguns, the fourth had a sawn-off shotgun. Another masked man appeared from behind a stack of old oil barrels at the far end of the factory, holding an assault rifle.

'What the fuck's this?' shouted Donovan.

The men ran over to Fletcher and the team, waving their weapons and screaming. 'Drop the cases! Get on the floor now!' shouted the man with the shotgun.

Two more men in ski masks appeared at the back of the factory. They ran over to Donovan and his crew, waving handguns and shouting. Donovan's men stopped putting the heroin in the holdalls and raised their hands in surrender. One of the masked men picked up one of the holdalls. 'Don't you fucking dare!' yelled Donovan. The other masked man smashed his gun against the side of Donovan's head and he fell against the side of a van, blood pouring from his scalp. The man who'd hit him began kicking him hard in the stomach, grunting with each blow.

Fletcher, Ryser and Pike lay face down on the floor, their arms outstretched. Two of the masked men picked up the suitcases.

'That's my fucking money!' shouted Terry.

'Terry, no,' cried Sam, grabbing at his arm. She pulled him back. 'Leave it,' she shouted. 'Let them have what they want.'

A heavily built man in a dark blue ski mask and a camouflage jacket stepped in front of Terry and pointed a large handgun at his face. 'Do as she says,' he said.

Terry snarled at the masked man. 'Do you know who I am?' he shouted.

'I don't give a fuck who you are,' said the man.

'I'll get you. I'll track you down, and when I find you, you are fucking dead. Dead!'

The man in the blue ski mask took a step towards Terry, cocking the automatic with his gloved thumb.

'Terry, watch it,' shouted McKinley. He ran over from the BMW and stood in front of Terry.

Terry pushed him to the side. 'I can handle this, Andy. It's not the first time I've looked at a gun.'

Donovan staggered to his feet, propping himself up against the van. Two of his crew went to help him.

Terry pointed at the man in the blue mask. 'You're not gonna get away with this. On my fucking life I'll seal your fate.'

The man stepped forward and kicked Terry in the stomach with a booted foot. Terry fell backwards and banged into Sam, gasping in pain. He hit the ground and Sam screamed.

McKinley roared and charged at the man.

'Andy, no!' screamed Sam.

The man fired, once, and McKinley pitched forward, his hand clutching at his chest.

* * *

Terry stared in disbelief as McKinley slumped to the ground. 'Andy,' he gasped. McKinley's feet twitched and then went still. 'Andy!' screamed Terry. 'For fuck's sake, no!'

The shotgun blasted again, scattering pigeons in the roof overhead. Flakes of rust sprinkled down like dirty snow. Terry tried to get to his feet, but a bolt of pain shot through his stomach where he'd been kicked.

Donovan was hustled towards the exit by his three heavies, all of them bent double. One of the men with the holdalls let loose a volley of shots, and bullets thwacked into the wall above Donovan's head.

'Terry, come on, get out of here!' shouted Donovan. 'They'll fucking kill us all.'

Terry continued to stare at McKinley's prostate body, unable to believe what he'd seen.

Sam rushed over to McKinley and knelt down next to him. 'Andy!' she cried. She reached her hand into his jacket. 'Oh God, Andy, no!' She pulled out her hand and held it up. It glistened redly. Sam turned to look at Terry, tears in her eyes. 'Terry . . .' she said.

'Sam, get away from him,' Terry shouted. The man in the blue ski mask turned his gun towards Sam but her attention was focused on Terry. 'This is all your fault, Terry,' hissed Sam. 'This is all down to you.'

Terry pushed himself up to his knees, ignoring the pain in his stomach. 'Sam, get out! Run!'

There was a faraway look in Sam's eyes as if she wasn't listening. She turned slowly to look at the man in the blue ski mask.

'You've killed him!' she moaned. 'You've fucking killed him!'

'Sam, no!' Terry screamed.

Donovan and his crew ran out of the factory, cursing and swearing. Bullets thudded into the wall near the entrance.

Terry's ears were ringing from the noise of the gunshots and the air was thick with the acrid smell of cordite.

Sam slowly got to her feet. The man in the blue ski mask kept the gun levelled at her chest as he stared at her with unblinking eyes. Even from where he was kneeling, Terry could see the man's finger tightening on the trigger and the look of determination in his eyes. Terry knew without a shadow of a doubt that the man was prepared to shoot Sam.

'Leave it, Sam!' Terry shouted. 'Leave it!'

Sam took a step towards the man in the blue ski mask, tottering like a sleepwalker. Her hands were outstretched, her fingers curved like talons. McKinley's blood dripped from her right hand. The man took a step back, the gun pointing at her chest. Sam kept on walking. 'You bastard!' she hissed.

'Sam!' screamed Terry, holding a hand to his stomach as he struggled to get up off his knees. 'Sam! No!'

'Get back!' shouted the man in the blue ski mask.

'I'll fucking kill you!' Sam screamed, and she rushed towards him, her hands grabbing for his masked face.

'Sam!' yelled Terry.

Sam grabbed the man's throat. The gun went off and Terry flinched. Sam stiffened and her head went back.

'No!' Terry screamed. 'No!'

Sam slowly slumped down against her assailant, her hands clawing down his chest. She dropped down on to her knees and then fell sideways. She twisted as she fell, and Terry saw a patch of glistening blood on the front of her coat.

The man in the blue ski mask moved back, staring down at Sam's body. He looked at his gun, then back at Sam.

Terry stared at the man in horror. 'What have you done?' he screamed. 'What the fuck have you done!'

* * *

Kim Fletcher got to his feet. The masked men were all staring at Sam, who lay unmoving on the concrete floor. There was an eerie silence, as if everyone was holding their breath, waiting to see what would happen next.

Pike looked up at Fletcher, who motioned for him to stand up. Terry was bent double, holding his stomach with both hands. He was in shock, his mouth moving soundlessly.

The man who'd shot Sam slowly raised his gun and pointed it at Terry.

'Terry!' Fletcher yelled. 'Watch out!'

Terry looked up and saw the man in the blue ski mask

taking aim. He staggered to the left just as the man fired, and the bullet went wide, smacking into a steel pillar.

From outside, Fletcher heard car doors slam and the roar of a high-powered engine as Donovan and his crew sped away.

Ryser was getting to his feet. The masked man with the shotgun whirled around and fired, narrowly missing Pike. Bits of shot peppered Fletcher's jacket but he wasn't hurt.

'Come on!' Fletcher roared, and charged towards Terry, who had stopped moving and was cursing at the gunman. Ryser followed.

There was another deafening shotgun blast, but Fletcher didn't look around. His eyes were fixed on Terry.

The man in the blue ski mask whirled around in a crouch, both hands on his gun, and fired two shots at Fletcher. The shots went wide and Fletcher grabbed Terry by the coat and hustled him towards the BMW. Ryser helped support Terry, who kept muttering his wife's name.

The gunman fired again, and the offside rear window of the BMW exploded in a shower of glass.

'Terry, come on!' yelled Pike. 'We've got to get out of here.'

Fletcher threw himself into the driver's seat and started the engine and Pike grabbed the rear door, throwing Terry into the back as a bullet embedded itself in the front wing. 'Come on, come on!' yelled Fletcher.

Ryser pulled open the front passenger door, and had barely dropped down into the seat before Fletcher stamped on the accelerator and the BMW leapt forward.

As Ryser slammed the door shout, Fletcher powered the BMW towards the man in the blue ski mask. The man let off a volley of shots and then dived out of the way as the BMW surged through the doorway. Fletcher caught a glimpse of the bodies of McKinley and Sam lying on the floor like broken dolls, and then they were gone.

Terry peered out of the window but Pike pulled him back. 'Keep your head down, boss!' Pike shouted. The BMW roared down the road, away from the factory. The slipstream from the broken window ripped through the car and tugged at their hair.

'Jesus Christ!' said Fletcher, flooring the accelerator. 'I thought we were fucking dead there.'

'Sam . . .' whispered Terry.

'Who were they, Terry? asked Pike.

'Got to be the fucking Kosovans,' said Fletcher.

'Bastards,' hissed Pike.

Terry looked out of the rear window. 'Sam . . .' he repeated.

Fletcher looked anxiously over his shoulder and exchanged a worried look with Pike.

'There was nothing you could do, boss,' said Pike.

Terry didn't appear to hear him. 'Sam . . .' he muttered, his voice little more than a hoarse whisper.

* * *

The man with the shotgun went over to the entrance and looked out, then turned and waved. 'They've gone!' he shouted.

The man in the blue ski mask tucked his handgun into the belt of his trousers. He walked slowly over to where Sam and McKinley were lying and pulled off his blue ski mask.

He prodded Sam's arm with his foot. 'It's okay,' he said.

Sam opened her eyes and rolled over. 'God, Zoran, that was terrifying.'

'You were perfect,' said Zoran Poskovic. He held out his hand and pulled her up. 'What an actress!'

'I was scared to death.'

Poskovic picked her up and gave her a bone-crushing bearhug, squeezing the air from her chest.

McKinley sat up and opened his jacket. He examined the fake bloodstain on his shirt and grinned up at Sam. Sam smiled back. He stood up and they embraced.

'You're a star, Andy,' she said.

Poskovic shouted to his men to collect the drugs and take them out to their car.

'You're going to have to be careful, Zoran,' said Sam. 'Terry's not stupid, he'll put two and two together and he's going to be after your blood.'

'He'll be too busy running from Donovan,' said Poskovic. He gestured at the suitcases. 'Unless you're planning to give him back his money.'

'That's the last thing on my mind,' laughed Sam. 'Can your guys give Andy and me a hand with the suitcases? And there's something in the boot of the Saab I need.'

* * *

Terry stared out of the back window. 'Are they following us, boss?' asked Fletcher from the driving seat. He changed up a gear and pushed the accelerator to the floor.

Terry shook his head. 'No,' he said.

'Thank fuck for that,' said Ryser. 'They were well tooled up.'

'Yeah, they were, weren't they?' said Terry, a far-off look in his eyes.

'We were lucky,' said Pike. 'Bloody lucky. They missed me by inches.'

'Yeah,' said Terry. 'But they did miss you, didn't they? No one got hit.'

'They shot out the window of the motor,' said Ryser as he checked the rear-view mirror.

'Yeah, but no one got hurt,' said Terry. 'Except for Sam and McKinley.' He frowned. Then he shook his head. 'Something's not right,' he said. 'Stop the car.'

'What?' said Fletcher, twisting around in his seat.

'Stop the fucking car!' shouted Terry.

Fletcher brought the BMW to a stop in a screech of brakes. 'What's wrong, boss?' asked Pike.

Terry rubbed his chin. 'I don't know,' he said. He frowned as he thought back to what had happened in the factory. The sawn-off shotgun. The handguns. The threats. McKinley's rush towards the masked men. The gunshot. Sam's reaction. The blood on her hand. The look on Sam's face, and then her rush towards the killer. Sam being shot and falling to the floor.

'They only shot McKinley and Sam,' said Terry, 'but neither of them was armed. None of us was. They must have seen that we weren't shooting back . . .' He shook his head. 'This doesn't make any sense.'

'Boss, they could have killed us,' said Ryser.

'I don't think so,' said Terry. He tapped Fletcher on the shoulder. 'Back to the factory, Kim.'

'I'm not sure that's a good idea, boss,' said Fletcher.

'Do as you're fucking told!' shouted Terry.

Fletcher's cheeks flushed and he did a hurried three-point turn and headed back to the factory. Terry stared out of the window, his face a blank mask.

'Are you sure about this, boss?' asked Pike. 'They might still be there.'

Terry gave Pike a cold stare and Pike looked away quickly.

Ryser pulled up in front of the factory. 'You lot stay here,' said Terry, opening the door of the BMW.

'We should come with you, boss,' said Fletcher. 'They might still be inside.'

Terry shook his head. 'There's no need,' he said.

Terry walked slowly back into the factory. It was deserted. He walked over to where Sam and McKinley had been shot. There was no blood on the concrete floor, but there were indentations in the dust where they had been lying. Terry smiled and shook his head slowly. 'Oh, Sam,' he whispered to himself. Then he saw the television set on a table. As he walked closer he saw that it was a combined television and video player and that there was a videocassette in the slot with 'Play me' written on the side.

Terry ran a hand through his hair and looked up at the roof

of the factory, where several pigeons were sitting in the rafters, cooing softly. 'Sam, Sam, Sam,' he whispered. He pushed the cassette into the slot and pressed the 'play' button.

The screen flickered, and then she was there, smiling at the camera. Full make-up, a soft blue shirt, a thin gold chain with a small crucifix. 'Hello, Terry, how's your luck?' she said.

She paused, and Terry folded his arms, still shaking his head.

'I know you're probably not a happy bunny at the moment,' she continued, 'but believe me, you'll see the funny side in a month or two.'

She paused again, as if giving Terry time to react. Terry just smiled and carried on shaking his head in wonder.

'Twenty-some years a wife and mother, you owe me, Terry Greene. I deserve a holiday in the sun, so that's where I'm going, with Trisha and Laura. I'm not hiding, I know you'll be able to find me, but if you do turn up on my doorstep, it had better be with a smile on your face and a bunch of flowers in your hand. I've got all the evidence I need to see you go inside for a long time, and it's all tucked up in a safe deposit box, so be nice, yeah?'

She looked into the camera and smiled a little sadly.

'You shouldn't have lied to me, Terry. Don't do it again, yeah?'

The screen flickered and went black. Terry stared at the television for several seconds, then he began to laugh. He threw back his head and laughed long and hard, and the pigeons above his head scattered and flew around in flurry of wings.

* * *

The taxi pulled up in front of a large villa perched on the top of a hill overlooking the sea. Blackie got out and stretched. He patted the roof of the taxi. 'Wait,' he said.

The driver nodded eagerly and smiled, revealing that his two front teeth were missing.

Blackie went over to the massive wrought-iron gates. They weren't locked and he walked through and along the driveway. He went around the side of the villa, keeping close to the wall. He could hear splashing, and laughing.

As he turned the corner, he stopped dead as he was confronted by a large man. A large man who was smiling, with an amused look in his eyes. 'Chief Superintendent Blackstock,' said McKinley. 'As I live and breathe.'

'Where is she?' asked Blackie.

McKinley gestured with his chin. 'Poolside,' he said.

Blackie nodded and headed towards the swimming pool. McKinley followed.

Sam was sitting by the side of the pool, reading a newspaper. On a table next to her was a bottle of champagne in an ice bucket. Laura was lying on a sun lounger, and Trisha was swimming in the pool. Sam saw Blackie and she stood up and waved. She popped the cork out of the champagne bottle and poured three glasses. She handed one to Blackie and one to McKinley, then raised her own glass to the detective. 'Couldn't have done it without you, Blackie,' she said. 'Thanks.'

They clinked glasses, then McKinley toasted them both.

Blackie sipped his champagne and looked across at the villa. 'Nice place,' he said. 'I hope you haven't spent it all.'

Sam grinned and nodded at a briefcase by the side of her chair. Blackie picked it up and swung it on to the table, then clicked open the locks. It was full of cash. Fifty-pound notes. 'These better not be moody notes, Sam,' he said.

'You know me better than that, Blackie,' said Sam. She nodded at the money. 'And they say crime doesn't pay.'

'I don't think they do, actually. Not any more.' Blackie shut the briefcase and drained his champagne glass. 'You heard from Terry?' he asked.

Sam shook her head. 'How is he?'

'Lying low,' said Blackie. 'Geoff Donovan's after his blood.'

'Terry can take care of himself,' said Sam. 'He's a big boy.'

Blackie picked up the briefcase and left. Sam and McKinley watched him go.

'The best police that money can buy,' said McKinley. 'That's what they used to say about the Met.'

'Yeah, but it can't buy you happiness, can it, Andy?'

McKinley looked at her, concerned. 'You okay, Mrs Greene?'

Sam sipped her champagne. 'Yeah, I guess so. We'll see how it works out, yeah?'

'He never stopped loving you, you know that.'

'Yeah. I know.' She reached over and clinked glasses with him. 'To crime, hey?'

McKinley grinned. 'Yeah. To crime.'